LIVING PRISON

Slocum could not prevent himself from being fascinated by the size of the thing, and intrigued by how it worked, as machine, as community, as threat, as instrument of travel, as creature—for he also saw it as something alive. The *Smuggler's Bible* insisted all human organizations were alive, over a certain threshold of size. It made sense that something as big and unitary as this vessel should follow the same rules of existence.

So he stepped carefully as he watched the officer disappear, as the gangway was raised again. Walked precisely over the cracked cobbles while his eyes traveled up the hull, two decks to the main working level, then up white-painted accommodation levels, one, two, three more decks, where a figure rendered small by distance leaned against the rail, looking down at the wharf. Dark, was his first impression; slight, wearing some kind of cloaky garment and a long white scarf that snapped in the wind; long hair that snapped also, fragile, he—

He tripped over a rusted cable that lay coiled like a dead boa in his path. Managed not to fall, hopping sideways without dignity to keep his balance, even saved his coffee without scalding himself too badly.

When he looked up again, the woman had gone.

BOOKS BY GEORGE FOY

Contraband
The Shift
The Memory of Fire
The Last Harbor
Asia Rip
Coaster
Challenge

THE LAST HARBOR

A NOVEL

GEORGE FOY

BANTAM BOOKS

THE LAST HARBOR

A Bantam Book

PUBLISHING HISTORY

Bantam trade paperback edition / July 2001
Bantam mass market edition / March 2002

ISBN 0-553-57884-7

Published simultaneously in the United States and Canada

Bantam Books are published by Bantam Books, a division of Random
House, Inc. Its trademark, consisting of the words "Bantam Books"
and the portrayal of a rooster, is Registered in U.S. Patent and Trademark Office and in other countries. Marca Registrada. Bantam Books,
1540 Broadway, New York, New York 10036.

PRINTED IN THE UNITED STATES OF AMERICA

OPM   10   9   8   7   6   5   4   3   2   1

In memory of my father, former commissaire de bord on SS Normandie, *who loved the great ships.*

ACKNOWLEDGMENTS

My heartfelt thanks to Jon Matson; the Writers' Room; Pat LoBrutto; and Elizabeth, Emilie, and Alexandre Foy, who all helped me during the course of writing this book.

THE LAST
HARBOR

ONE

SLOCUM STARED AT HIS diesel engine.

It lay cold and inert in the cave of his engine room. The glow of the engine-room light evoked a smug shine from the arcs of small drives: the alternator, the fuel pump. It left shadow behind the metal casings that protected the cylinders, and beside them, like succubi nestling closer to protect the addiction they themselves had both crafted and subverted, the injectors and pipes that fed his pistons the oil without which they could not fire.

Slocum picked up a wrench and gave a quarter-turn to the banjo nut clamping the fuel pipe to the top of his Number One fuel injector. Today the engine reminded him of some brute and overwhelmingly stubborn animal that had decided to lie down and that no amount of kicking or pulling or even whipping could persuade to move. On other days it had reminded him, respectively, of a prehistoric beast; of a coded relic from a murderous civilization; of an instrument of sexual torture from an inquisition no one remembered. Always such images were dark and ugly. Always they drew on a rage that built up in him in inverse ratio to his ability to fix the engine. The best he ever got, after cleaning fuel lines, reaming the filter, disassembling the part of the injector he could get to and steaming that out, was a half hour of smooth running. Then the injector would seize up, the flow of fuel would dwindle by half, the engine would run rough. Eventually it would stop dead.

Slocum wormed his torso out of the engine hatch. The rage was still dark in him. He threw his wrench at the deck so hard it bounced. He glanced at the clock on the forward bulkhead. It read 08:48. The Mechanic was almost two hours late. Slocum felt like picking up the wrench and throwing it down harder; so hard it made a hole in the deck, rocketed into the bilge below, and stabbed through the fiberglass skin of his hull, letting in the harbor water to fill his boat. The water would be cold and laden with poisonous chemicals and it would sink everything he had left at this point but at least it would flow, move, create change. It did not matter to Slocum in this second if the change was good or bad. What maddened him was the feeling of being stuck, unable to go forward or backward.

He climbed the four steps to the sloop's cockpit and peered up and down the length of Coggeshall Wharf to where, in the fog that lay thick on this harbor before noon, the dock's structure got confused with the buildings of Town.

No sign of the Mechanic or his brilliantly lit truck. It did not surprise him. The Mechanic had shown up only once, the very first time, ten days after Slocum had first e-mailed him. He had told Slocum what was wrong with the injector and vowed to return the following week with the spare part he needed. He did not show up that week, or the next, or in the weeks after that. Since his first visit Slocum had e-mailed and telephoned almost daily and never succeeded in talking to the Mechanic again; only to digital mailboxes that took his messages and made machine promises in return. On the two occasions Slocum got a message back, and a response to his reply, the Mechanic had set up a time for his next visit, and then failed to turn up or even explain his absence.

He was the only mechanic in Town or in the surrounding area who condescended to service the small marine diesels, made by the MarDyne Corporation, of the type that powered Slocum's sloop.

The harbor wind was damp and cold on Slocum's shoulders. He went below again. He picked up a box of rusted parts the Mechanic had left on his first visit. They were not MarDyne parts but bits of injectors of different makes. The idea had been that Slocum would save the Mechanic time by trying each and every part that might possibly fit his injector, in case it came close, in which case the Mechanic might lathe away the differences. In this fashion they could bypass the bottleneck of ordering spares from MarDyne, which took a year to fill orders and then often as not would send the wrong part.

Slocum had tried every part in the box, twice. None came close. Today, he had gotten out the three parts that were least different, in case the Mechanic could see there an opportunity to retool the metal, to make one of them do the job. He stowed the box in the tool locker under the forward port settee.

Slocum switched off the engine-room light, replaced the movable companionway that led over the engine's hatch to the cockpit, added a couple of briquettes to the coal stove on the forward saloon bulkhead. Despite the control of his housekeeping actions, the anger was still great in him. It was not a good anger, the kind that tightened the focus of problems and also steamed up pressure inside until you were forced to derail from the steel tracks of what you were locked into and plow off in a different and unexpected direction. No, it was the worst kind, the blocked kind, that condensed and lived off the fat of everything that had gone wrong and finally grew so bitter that it must end up corroding the vessel that contained it. Slocum picked a battered coffeepot off the stove and poured the grounds into his waste bucket. He opened the box of Antioquia coffee he had bought from a smuggler in the Sunset Tap, spooned out a heap, set the percolator on a burner, and lit the flame. As he did so he heard a thump from forward. Because the sloop was small he saw the agent of that sound almost as soon as he heard it. A creature that looked at first like a ridge of bone and scars bound together by fur and a startling, malevolent golden stare ambled from the forward cabin, where it had been snoozing in the V-berth, and aimed its gauntness toward the companionway leading outside. Seen close-up it resolved into something feline, a cat by any other name, an animal changed by habits of aggression. This cat, to judge by its wounds, had been involved in every scrap and civil war on the stretch of coast between Bangor and Biloxi; after which it must have started a few extra brawls just to keep its paw in. It had lost its left eye and one incisor and part of its tail. Both ears were so tattered they resembled pennants left up in the rigging of a ghost ship abandoned centuries ago. A long scar on which no fur grew disfigured its left hindquarter, and its right forepaw had stiffened in healing from a break so that it had to jump a little on the left to keep its balance. Slocum, whenever he saw the cat, was struck by the sense that this animal always carried, in metaphor if not in fact, a swordbelt and a rusted cutlass and a brace of black-powder pistols with which to board ships that took its fancy.

"Hello, Ralfie," Slocum said. The animal, without looking at him, uttered the long "raaaalf" which—together with its habit of throwing up every couple of days on any surface that looked clean—had earned it its name. The cat took the steps with a disjointed movement that, in its co-opting of different motions to produce forward vector, achieved an empirical grace. Its footsteps pitted forward on the deck overhead. Slocum, muttering "shitgoddamn," hastily followed the cat's path underneath the deck, down the saloon's length, past the head, into the forward cabin. He reached up to shut the forward hatch, which was propped on its own screwhook to let in air.

He was too late. With a cavernous groan the discharge pipe from the processing plant cleared its throat and hawked out several hundred gallons of washdown water that had accumulated in a holding tank from the night shift. The pipe opened onto the harbor ten feet forward of Slocum's sloop, but the convection of its length often swirled the sludge in such a way as to spray the bow, or fire onto Slocum's deck a rope of hake intestine or a scrod head, which Ralfie would promptly snag.

Sighing, Slocum sponged up the slop that had sprayed through the hatch. He fetched the washdown bucket and a mop from the lazarette. He filled the bucket with shore-water and oil soap and cleaned the deck, wondering ritu-ally and for perhaps the eightieth time why he put up with the drawbacks of this berth, knowing at the same time the reason: because it was protected by a row of dolphins from the wake of the ferries, because it was next to the dock se-curity booth and thus sheltered from more human danger, because it lay in a nook of wharf that deflected the prevail-ing wind. Ralfie limped back with mackerel backbone, growling to warn Slocum off its booty. "Don't you dare take that below," Slocum told it. Seagulls screamed, danced, followed the fish plant's garbage as it drifted with the tide. There were a lot of seagulls; this was the last processor left in the harbor to feed their lust for offal.

When he had finished washing down the deck he straightened on his mop. He checked the mooring lines automatically, then looked to port, across the harbor. Though most of the Town was veiled, the fog lay less thickly on the water, and Slocum could dimly make out the cross-stitching of masts and rigging and power-generating windmills on the harbor's other side where almost two thousand people lived on boats not unlike this one, rafted and docked together by a cat's cradle of lines and tackle among the remains of the Whaling City Marina; tied more, or so it seemed to Slocum, by the desperation of shared fantasies that sustained them in that environment. For around them lay only dying saltmarsh and a ruin of condos that had gone bankrupt with the marina, victims of unsuspected pollution and serial crashes among the machines that ordered the world's twenty-four-hour financial markets.

Slocum looked long at Whaling City. The sight, as he had known it would, did something to his anger. It did not diminish it at all, in fact it added to the piss-off. But it also took the edge away by injecting a dose of confusion, with the vapor of messages lost, poorly understood, or never sent; gross particles of his life whose removal now loomed larger for him than their erstwhile presence. Finally it altered the anger's chemistry to a structure less heavy. It became, ultimately, more damaging; but in its changed nature it was something from which he could turn away, for now, with only moderate difficulty.

He breathed down to the very sump of his lungs, feeling the fog and the stink of fish and the bad algae and tar of Coggeshall Wharf grind down the mucus of his nasal passages. As he stowed the bucket and mop in the lazarette he thought that this compartment was getting as untidy and out of control as his personal history. The space was filled almost to the top with mooring lines, an emergency tiller, bumpers, a small outboard motor, fiberglass wax, linseed oil for the teak, and cleaning brushes, all falling out of boxes and racks meant to contain them. It came to him then that if he abandoned the discipline of keeping his sloop neat and ready for sea—and never mind how unlikely departure was, given the dysfunction of his diesel—then he

might well lose the only constant in the time/space of his
. current life and the only thing that held him together now.

He remembered the *Smuggler's Bible*. It was a popular
book in Whaling City and he had not read it for a long
time as a result. It contained an appendix about the importance of boat maintenance. He could not remember the
exact words so he went below and searched the over-
crowded bookshelf atop the port settee until he found
the paperback. The chapter was titled "Appendix to
Navigation Religion" and began:

> *The art and practice of ritually and rigorously keeping
> track of your position in space and time is the clearest and
> most karmic aspect of smuggling philosophy. But it's also
> vital to remember it is only part of the life-philosophy that
> includes navigating your environment and grokking all the
> creatures and forces within it. Obviously, the craft that is
> your vehicle for navigation—from the fastest digitally
> camouflaged jet running hot software into the eurozone, to
> the slowest cruising ketch ambling, lazy as any tourist
> bathtub, with its guts full of Blue Mountain ganj' into
> Florida waters—is also the grooviest expression of that
> navigation. It follows that, to hold tight in the groove of
> that philosophy, you have to devote a significant percentage
> of your day to making sure all systems that keep your craft
> afloat and moving, viable and hidden in its surroundings,
> are in outtasight working order.*

Slocum returned to the cockpit and bent over the
lazarette. The spare mooring lines, he noticed, were over-
flowing the milk crate he kept them in, and one of their
uncoiled ends had slipped through the opening that let the
exhaust pipe out of the engine compartment. Under that
opening lay a space where the propeller shaft shone naked
between the aft engine-room bulkhead and the stuffing

box it passed through on its way outside the hull. If too much of the line came adrift while under way, it could get wound up in the spinning shaft, which would roll it until the coils jammed between the stern gland and the V of bilge, stopping the engine and probably bending the shaft. If that happened in a storm—or in some other emergency situation where he had to use the engine, such as when trying to get out of the way of a large ship at sea—it could imperil his sloop, and his life.

The *Smuggler's Bible* was right. Slocum heaved the milk crate out of the lazarette, dumped all the lines into the cockpit, uncoiled and recoiled every one until they all lay prettily tied at his feet. But seeing the lines nestled like eggs in the crate did not help much. It did not give him the feeling of satisfaction—of a small victory wrested from the weight of defeats that pressed on him from all sides—that such tasks often imparted. He did not continue tidying the lazarette, though the compartment still needed washing and rearranging. Instead, he stowed the milk crate, locked the compartment hatch, and went below, into the main cabin. Ralfie had gnawed the mackerel spine and left it on the little hooked rug next to the saloon table.

I have to get out of here, Slocum thought. He threw the fishbone in the slops bucket and wiped down the rug. He opened the hidden compartment behind his bookcase and took his Universal Credit Card from the shelf he hid the ship's papers on. He took his reefer jacket from the hanging locker opposite the head. He checked to make sure the forward hatch was locked and the seacocks—the valves that let salt water for washing and engine cooling through the inviolable hymen of his hull—were all shut. He hesitated as he passed the navigation table, with the small lights and dials of the ECM-pak that hooked up to Wildnets and marine radio and other channels of communication riding sideways or above or under the regular networks of communication stitching the outside world together like a universe of electron spiderwebs. It was nowhere near as powerful as the old lust that tied him in to these outside webs as tightly as a caught fly. Still, the temptation to turn on the ECM and put out a thin probe of data communication—nothing much, just a search through a Wildnet, a pirate channel; splice on to an Internet thoroughfare, see if the Mechanic was online, only the Mechanic—it was awfully hard to resist.

Slocum grunted as if he had absorbed a small blow. He pulled the jacket tighter around himself and jammed a watch cap on his head. He went out into the fog, slotted the washboards into place, closed and locked the hatch. Then, after checking the mooring lines one final time, he climbed the rusted ladder that led to Coggeshall Wharf.

TWO

SLOCUM WALKED HARD, PAST the security trailer where MacTavish the guard sat, baleful in the milky lighting, down the line of warehouses. They were four stories high and hundreds of yards long and built of brick, or gray granite. The buildings originally were erected to house textile mills to take advantage of fulling water from the Aquidnet River, and of cheap Portuguese labor that first came in on sail-powered whaling ships. Then, when cheaper textiles from the south and east bankrupted the mills, some were abandoned and some converted into discount clothing dealers and a number were taken over by fish dealers, who served the scores of draggers once based in this town. When the fishing died, the Flash workshops and software studios moved in, selling Internet services, electronic daytrading, online games, Web genetics.

Since the Infocrashes the warehouses had stood largely empty again, their windows covered with plywood on which teenagers scrawled verse of boredom and frustration. Now weeds grew on the disused railroad line that ran along their sides, and fences walled off the hazardous-waste sites where the mills had dumped their poisons.

Slocum followed the tracks, hunched against the wind that blew this chill mist off the saltmarsh to the south. He turned left down an alley, warily skirting a lean-to in which dark figures festooned with wires and the burned-out husks of cellphones and Walkmen and 3-D headsets huddled around a chemical fire. He heard something behind him, or thought he did. When he turned back to check, the teedees were still in their lean-to and he was alone.

The alley ended at a Town fishing dock that was squeezed between the marine portion of a large theme park and the hurricane barrier. The hurricane barrier was a metal door about seventy feet deep by two hundred across, which slid on underwater tracks built across the harbor bottom to shut off the port from the vast saltmarshes and the ship channel to the sea. The climate had been changing slowly over the years, and hurricanes had increased in size to the point where the average strength of the storms had gone up a notch, as these things were measured, to level 3. And they no longer were spawned only from July to October but spun up the coast, like drugged dancers, all the year long.

Today the barrier was open, the vast gate retreated, slotted deeply into gears and workings hidden under hillocks in parks on either side of the harbor mouth. Waves built up along the channel lapped through the sable shadows of the gate, and the tide swirled like green serpents through the confines of the lock. A ferry came through, on its way to wherever ferries went, and its wake cracked and slapped against the riprap. Slocum climbed the hillock and looked to the south, over the ship channel down which the ferry passed. This was something he did almost every morning, to encourage himself, planning in his mind how he would one day motor the sloop through the barrier, and the outer harbor, and into the winding, shifting channels that led through the marsh and islands to the ocean.

He turned away quickly, because instead of offering the

hope of escape and new horizons, all the channel reminded him of today was how impossible it would be to leave the harbor without an engine. The prevailing wind was southerly here, and the channel so long and twisted that you could not, even with the best seamanship, negotiate it under sail alone. That was a problem the old whalers did not have to face, because the marshes and barrier islands had only built up since the last whaler had been mothballed in the theme park. The changes in the coast happened as a result of the same climatic shift that sharpened hurricanes in the Sargasso Sea and wore away beaches on other parts of the coast. It was the sand from those beaches that washed up here, by some dynamic of tide and wind and deep geology.

Slocum turned and strode down the hill, letting the slope accelerate his steps till he was almost running. He avoided looking across the harbor to the marina. He did not want to look toward the head of the harbor, though the mist mostly hid the hills inland and those structures of architecture and life he avoided in that direction. Was his current life built entirely on avoidance? he wondered; and did not care to pursue that thought either. Yet it was clear to him that under the pressure of this day's frustration he was going to have to come up with goals and motivations of more substance than the whims and boat maintenance typical of his days so far.

He trudged head-down between the rotting warehouses and the great and complex slum of rusting fishing trawlers rafted against the hurricane-barrier wharf; angling northwest through streets made darker by the contrast between their poor frame houses and the lights that glowed and jizzed behind the high wall of the theme-park-cum-historical-area. A form of motivation was suggested here—something that, if it was not a replacement for diesels and a plan of voyage, was still better than aimless promenade. It could have come from the direction of the street he was now walking down, or from the cracked asphalt and litter, the sideways chitter of rats marking this part of town. Or it could have been the usual reason coming into play, seeping up unbeknownst to him as he focused on his anger and the courses he could never plot or take. It guided his footsteps right, into the Grid, where none of the streetlights worked and the potholes were so big they revealed underneath them large stretches of cobblestones on which the cars rolled now by choice. Here the Cape Verdeans lived three to a room in Victorian boardinghouses that looked like death ships, their paint flaking like reflections of sea, their porch bows sagging as they crested waves of abandoned appliances, their clotheslines like brightly patched rigging, their sails of laundry bellying full of the dark wind. Slocum dodged escaping children and pursuing aunts and dogs and a lost tour bus. Between the Lisboa Bar and the E-Z Kredit Laundorama, a plate-glass window with a purple neon sign advertised:

MADAME LING
PSYCHIC ADVISOR
CONSULTANT TO
THE
STARS
Marital Problems a Specialty

and Slocum went inside.

Madame Ling was a woman in late middle age who wore layers of fake-silk shawls and beads and scarves and makeup to disguise the fact that she was not Asiatic in any way, as she would have preferred, but a Brazilian from Pare Province. She sat in her window, illuminated by the purple neon, framed by silk screens with Cantonese characters. She had been told they meant Prosperity, Happiness, Longevity. She read tarot for the lost or curious, while mothers and children used her laundromat next door, and men walked through the back door of the Lisboa into her kitchen and chose girls to take upstairs. More often, though, the men hung around, drinking wine and eating for a nominal sum the generous Portygee stews Madame Ling kept simmering on the range. In any well-run whorehouse such hanging around would never have been permitted, but the girls were lazy and Madame Ling erratic in her discipline. Also the cops and the Sagres gangbangers had gotten less greedy since the fat pickings of the theme park came to Town, and that eased the financial pressure on the brothel. Now she frowned as she saw Slocum, and gestured toward a couch beside the reading area. She was reading the tarot for a young Azorean woman who, to judge by the few words of English they used, had four kids and whose husband was sleeping with the wife of a former fisherman. The fisherman, who was known to be violent, hung out at the Lisboa.

Slocum picked up a copy of the weekly *Shine*. It featured on its front page a paparazzo shot of the boyfriend of soap star Amy Duggan slipping furtively out of a 3-D virtual-sex parlor in North Beach. Beside it ran an exclusive report on a cliff-top mansion in Kauai built by Wycliffe Sloane. The mansion was ringed with an electronic field that would immobilize anyone who touched it. Sloane was one of the ten richest men in the world and *Shine* said he was the Number One target of international hostage takers. He also, once, had been Slocum's boss, although at so many removes that Slocum had seen him in the flesh only a couple of times, at big company dedications, and never to talk to.

Madame Ling gave the Azorean woman a short reading and advised her to take her husband away for a dirty weekend. She relied on the ex-fishermen of the Lisboa for in-house security that the Sagres could not or would not provide; she was going to minimize trouble as far as she could.

The woman and her baby both left in tears. Madame Ling said, "Slocum, you want girls or drink or coffee? Because da girls all gone down to the Sunset for customers, and da coffee is not hot."

"Did Luisa go?" Slocum asked.

"Luisa gone too. You interested?" she continued, frowning. "I thought she turn you off."

"She doesn't turn me off."

"You have not taken her upstairs for months now. Months and months, *Madre de diosh,* it is not good for a man, you are not old."

Madame Ling had eyes like the tributaries of the Amazon River where they came down from the Andes, muddy and slow but full of hidden fish whose appetite and shape you could only guess at. She fetched him a cup of cold coffee. She insisted that he pay and charged it on his UCC. He finished the brew quickly but Madame Ling must have been feeling guilty about the coffee because she offered to read his tarot for free. Slocum shook his head but she ignored him, arranging the greasy cards in the serendipitous patterns she favored, two lozenges this time, completing them toward the point where they almost touched. Her words, fattened by a Portuguese accent, ran practiced and smooth. "The Moon, reversed decision, you had come to a choice about something, something is very strong in you, perhaps you will take Chevette for the night, yes?" She winked so hard that a small flake of makeup broke off her crow's feet and returned to powder on the floor. Both the wink and the words were casual and it was clear she was running through a patter she did not pay attention to herself. "The Hierophant, financial security—good. So you can afford to pay. And now—" She flipped the last card and laid it with care so that it formed the link between the two lozenges. Then gasped, as if the act had completed a circuit of energy that physically shocked her. "Wheel of Fortune, reversed," she whispered, and glanced at him to watch his reaction. "A danger, Slocum—a person maybe, anyways a big force of complete darkness—it will come out of the west and destroy you."

"Unless I sleep with Luisa?" Slocum said, getting to his feet.

"Woman is strong," Madame Ling said, nodding. "She can affect how dese forces act together, not directly but she can change your force just enough to change da direction, you know?" She laid a bony hand on Slocum's arm. "You do not believe me."

"You give me the Wheel of Fortune reversed every time," Slocum said. "You pretend you're shocked, every time. You've been doing it for seven or eight months—since I've known you. But the danger never comes."

"Maybe Luisa already save you ass," Madame Ling replied huffily, riffling her cards and flipping them with the speed of a croupier into one pile. "Maybe da danger builds and builds. Go," she added, "go to da Sunset Tap, I got no time for waterfront bums, you give me da blood-presh. Go." With an abrupt gesture she clicked off the purple neon, and the brothel parlor returned to a gloom into which the Chinese prints and lanterns sank like foundering boats.

———

THE SUNSET TAP LAY two streets away at the top of the grid of mean streets separating the two secure areas in Town—the Moby Dick Theme Park and Casino area to the south, and the Federal area, which included county courts and online-bank offices, and a few fancy and well-guarded apartment buildings for lawyers and online bankers, to the north. The base of the grid was Highway 18, which directly linked the theme park with the main highway that crossed the head of the harbor. The Sunset Tap was a bar across from the disused train station. It took up the corner of a building that had once been a Five &

Dime. You entered it from the corner, passing Freitas, the bouncer, who sat on a stool by the door and challenged all male customers to punch him in the stomach, to see if you could make him fall. No one ever could.

After Freitas you walked along the right wall, between the counter and a row of booths lit by glass bricks. All the woodwork in the bar was cheap laminated material, painted black, now peeling away from itself. The floor was black lino, also peeling, though what was underneath, as in the streets outside, was a stronger frame, of oak and maple hardwood in this case, gone dark with glue and filth.

At the far end of the Sunset Tap was a space crowded with tables and booths somewhat isolated from the first half by the counter on one side and a booth and coat rack on the other. This part of the bar was hung with old life-rings and lobster-pot buoys and high-flyer flags from the boats that used to go codfishing and swordfishing and trawling for flounder hake redfish haddock and all the other forgotten bounty of the continental shelf. A mannequin's torso stood inexplicably in one corner. Racks of black light made all the clients in the business half of the Tap look several days dead. The biggest table this morning was taken up by Madame Ling's girls, who were talking about how cops had found the body of a murdered prostitute from a big town up-coast to the southwest. "It's the same one," said May, "you don't get guys picking up girls at rest stops and leaving them on like the highway exactly three days later like everywhere."

"With their throats cut," Shaneeqwa, May's friend, pointed out, sucking on her Kent.

"With her throat cut," May repeated, nodding, happy with violence.

"Yeah, but," said Danielle, who always prefaced her sentences with "yeah, but." "Yeah, but you got these sickos in almost every city now, they got a new one every week in *Shine*."

"Not with the highway," Luisa said quietly. "Not with the throat."

Luisa was small and dark and young; nineteen, Slocum thought, twenty at the most. She sat in her chair as if the chair had more power than she, thin white arms folded across her belly. She wore a shift that was too thin for the temperature and humidity, and a cranberry-colored cardigan pulled so tight at the waist it almost went around twice. Her eyes were as big and black as an oil spill. When she saw Slocum the skin around them crinkled, and she looked away. As Slocum's eyes adjusted he made out the room's other occupants. Lopes sat in the corner under the TV talking to himself. Cakes read the paper at the table beside him; she and Lopes tended to hang out together, because they were both boat people. They both liked looking at Madame Ling's girls, though that was as far as they ever got, for different reasons.

Slocum thought about ordering a beer, measuring that idea, as people did, against the various forces at play inside his head. He had been through several cycles of frustration and hope and disappointment this morning, and fatigue from having to cope with the ups and downs was starting to build. So perhaps he could use a coffee. Madame Ling's brew had been so cold that he had taken only a couple of sips.

Then again his frustration from the Mechanic—though it had settled into lower gear, more suited to distance and less obtrusive on the minute-to-minute—was still stuck at cruising speed. And that irritant had been refined by the thought he'd entertained earlier, that he was plotting the courses of his life on a chart whose only landmarks and beacons were negative—reefs and maelstroms, areas that he could not approach without risking grave damage. This, he had always suspected, was a poor way to live. "A danger," Madame Ling had said, "a big force of complete darkness."

Could she have been referring to this chart made of nothing but menaces to navigation?

Only the warmth of beer or something stronger could make a mark against the chill growing like a glacier in that part of his mind. He turned to the bar and stood there till Obrigado, the bartender, had ignored him long enough to make a point. His point was that Slocum was nobody and nothing and he, Obrigado, was chief Khan of this realm and a leading citizen of this town with many more important matters to take care of and he would serve this nonentity, Slocum, whenever he damn well got around to it.

"A beer," Slocum said, when Obrigado came over. Obrigado pulled him a draft with practiced gestures that did not require him to look at glass or tap or Slocum. Slocum slid his cashcard through the reader. The Whip was also here, he saw, half hidden behind the coat rack. This was a surprise because the Whip's wife threw a fit whenever he came to the Sunset Tap even after work hours. It was rare to see the Whip in here during the day. He had a jambook computer open in front of him with the antenna flipped open and a 3-D mask—a "face-sucker"—lowered over his eyes. So perhaps he was working in the Sunset Tap; maybe that was how he had justified it to his wife.

The images in the Whip's face-sucker changed so rapidly that the colors, playing across his features, looked like light from an old-fashioned movie projector beamed onto his face.

The beer tasted good. It went into the chambers where Slocum was too full of cold feelings to move well, or stop and relax, and it warmed those feelings, eased their belts a little. Slocum looked through the glass bricks at the deserted station; seen through the thick glass it was wavy and indistinct, like a dream building. He felt a brief but powerful desire for images that were sharp and precise and colorful and under his control, like the images the Whip was looking at now. The memory of those images increased the cold feelings, maybe even doubled them. He thought of the people huddled in the lean-to, bundled in ancient video. He gritted his teeth and took another swallow and watched Lopes and Cakes in the corner. When Cakes saw him looking she threw her black hair behind her shoulder blades, which meant she was irritated. She hunched over the table, eyes sunk in shadow. Her chin, which was delicate, jutted in Slocum's direction.

Abruptly she got to her feet, shrugged her motocross jacket tighter around her shoulders, and stomped past him, out of the bar.

Slocum shrugged inside, because Cakes was mad at him half the time for no reason he could figure out. She lived at the shallower end of Coggeshall on a former offshore racing boat that always had mechanical troubles, and he figured maybe those problems were getting to her as they were getting to him. Shaneeqwa had gone on to a famous assassin that *Shine* journalists often wrote about. "They say he could be a Hollywood actor, the kind like Ethan Hawke they always play Anglos. They call him the Gatsby Killer." May thought he sounded cute. Luisa crinkled her eyes at Slocum again, which canceled out the bad karma Cakes had laid on him going out. She did not come over to see him though. That was OK with Slocum, who did not have the energy to parse the conflicting currents of emotion Luisa always evoked in him close-up. He took two solid swigs of his beer and for two or three minutes thought of nothing much, which in itself was a good way of thinking this morning—or not-thinking, though that in itself was a kind of thought, like an engine running in neutral at a stoplight.

An off-duty cop named Leaky Louie punched Freitas in the gut on his way out. "Pussy!" Freitas called, after he had caught his breath. "Wimp! Come back soon."

Someone right behind Slocum said, *"O grande nave."*

Slocum sighed. He did not have to glance at the mirror behind the bar to see who was talking. The voice was raspy and low and conspiratorial. Every phrase ended in a cough, and then a quick suck as Lopes put the cigarette to his mouth. Slocum closed his eyes and finished his beer. He turned to face Lopes and raised his chin at him as if in agreement, though Lopes had spoken in Portuguese, and Slocum did not understand that language.

"*O immenso nave.* You gonna to have to learn some *lingua,* Slocum, you stay on Coggeshall."

Lopes also lived on Coggeshall, at a fish dock at the shallow end, on a sterndragger even more beat up and eroded than the other former fishing vessels in the harbor. It was so battered and full of leaks that people said he had shored I-beams between the keel and the bottom to keep it from settling into the mud.

"I don't plan to stay on Coggeshall," Slocum grunted. He thought of ordering a second beer but Lopes might interpret that as an invitation to keep talking. Lopes could be good company, when he'd had just the right amount of booze, neither too much nor too little. This morning Lopes had not had enough. He was a short, beefy man with a huge Arab nose and graying hair that fell over his shoulders like volcanic rain. He had a habit of glancing up at you when he said something, then lowering his eyes, as if to avoid watching his barbs sink in. When he'd had lots of booze he would sing and gossip and make people laugh.

Not enough booze, though, and all the Arab fatalism of Andalusia would spout out of him, bull's blood seeping from a badly sealed gourd, and he took much joy in bad news.

"The ship," Lopes explained. "The big ship."

Slocum stared at his empty glass. Lopes glanced at him, and looked down again. "What are you talking about?" Slocum said.

"A big ship is coming. You will see."

"To the Town?"

"To the Town."

Slocum decided to leave. Lopes in his fatalistic mood would tell any story provided only that it was black and depressing and full of doom.

"There was a guy in Ohio, long ago," Shaneeqwa said. "He would cut up boys he had tricked upstairs, for sex. He put their different parts in Tupperware containers in the refrigerator."

"Shut up," another girl said. "Look, you got Luisa upset."

The door slammed. When Slocum looked, Luisa was gone. Every girl he had slept with, Slocum thought, or tried to sleep with at least, had left within five minutes of his coming in. "She too sensitive," Shaneeqwa said. "That's ancient history."

"There hasn't been a ship in this harbor in fifteen years," Slocum said. "Not a big ship."

"Who told you that?" Quick, suspicious. Lopes looked behind him as if the source of false news, the contradictor of stories, was in this bar even now, waiting to fuck up his plot.

"MacTavish told me. But everyone knows. Since the fishing ended, there's nothing here anymore for a big ship to take. And nobody can afford what it might bring in. Even the ferries," Slocum added, "they don't bring anything in or out. No one even knows why they keep running."

Lopes looked up at Slocum's eyes. "You gonna have to move you sailboat." He looked down quickly. "It's a big ship all right, big as any that ever come here. Belongs to the Syndicate," he added.

"The Syndicate," he repeated, when Slocum did not respond. "You probably don't believe the Syndicate exist, Slocum. Richest, most powerful people in the world, but you don't believe it, Slocum. You don't believe in nothin'."

Slocum looked at Lopes now. He could feel the anger

flare in him like a fire that had suddenly found a new, dry patch of tinder. He knew from his reaction that he agreed with Lopes: He did not believe in much. It was one of the things Amy accused him of, at the end. The fact that it was mostly true made it a powerful accusation.

"What do you mean, I have to move my boat?" he asked finally, in a voice that was as even and cool as lakewater at dawn.

Lopes grinned. His teeth were the same color as his skin.

"Coggeshall Wharf," he said. "It's the only deepwater dock left in Town. And you on the deepest part of it. But you don't believe in the Syndicate," he continued, throwing up his hands as if in defeat. "You don't believe in the big ship. You don't believe in nothin'." He coughed and ash fell from his cigarette onto his sweatshirt. He turned away and walked back to the corner, shaking his head.

"Full of shit."

Slocum's head jerked up. Obrigado was looking at Lopes's back.

"Full of shit," the bartender repeated. He turned away and continued wiping glasses. Slocum swiped his card again for a tip and left the Sunset Tap, turning right to cross North Sixth Street, toward the waterfront.

THREE

WHEN HE GOT BACK to the sloop it was half tide. He had to use care in climbing down the last few rungs of the ladder; they spent a quarter of the day underwater and were thick with semirotted codium and Irish moss.

He warmed the percolator and poured a cup of coffee. He wanted only one, enough to clear away most of the beer fumes but not enough to wake him completely. He had enjoyed the two minutes of no-thought that came to him like a windfall in the Sunset Tap and he thought that maybe the residual beer fumes with just a shot of caffeine might allow that effect to occur again. But even as he leaned against the chart table and drank the coffee he found his thoughts shifting restlessly in response to random perceptions. The settee over the locker that held his engine-room tools. Ralfie, fast asleep on a blanket on the settee; which brought the usual questions associated with Ralfie, such as where had he last puked? And where had he come from when he showed up in Slocum's cockpit, curled under the dodger on a coil of line, with two fresh wounds leaking blood on the deck?

The ancient leather-bound ledger he had found in the

Spouter Bookshop before it went out of business. The book was empty, its pages blank. But Slocum, who had bought from the Spouter a half-hundredweight of magazines even older than the ledger, was starting to glue into the book's thick vellum images from those magazines that meshed with the stories he used to tell his daughter. And that was an area he really did not want to enter.

The *Smuggler's Bible*. He finished the coffee in one swallow and changed into his County Diesel jumpsuit. He climbed back to the cockpit and unlocked the lazarette. He spent much of the afternoon removing from the locker the cleaning products and brushes and sponges and a spare dinghy anchor and two handpumps and the emergency tiller and cans of paint and linseed oil. He recalled seeing a bunch of old milk crates along the railroad tracks and he scavenged up and down the line until he found them not far from the camp used by victims of teledysfunction. As he was repacking the gear in the crates he looked aft. His sloop, tied as it was to Coggeshall Wharf, which followed the trend of harbor north and south, also pointed along that azimuth, with the bow aimed hopeful southward toward the hurricane barrier and the sea much farther beyond.

Looking aft usually brought him a view up-harbor of the wharf's shallow end, with Lopes's ancient dragger moored, together with a couple dozen other fishing vessels, to a pair of ancient, anchored barges; then, through a thickening of vapor, the bridge across Fish Island; and, at the top of the harbor and in the distance, the highway bridge leaping the narrows and eroding into gray.

By noon, however, the mist tended to burn off. Now Slocum clearly saw the upper river—the last houses of Town proper, the giant white dome of the Bayview Mall. Beyond them lay a scratching of evergreens, then hardwoods; and a tower five hundred feet high, dominating the gentle hillsides to the northwest.

Arcadia was the official name of the tower. It looked like a purplish wedge of steel, sharp end up, on which four big and four little glass doughnuts had been spiked; smallest on top, biggest on the bottom. The doughnuts contained offices, thousands of them. The steel spike held elevators and maintenance conduits and, at the bottom, a lofty purple-draped auditorium that seated five thousand. It was supposed to resemble a pine tree, and among the kinder nicknames it had earned in the Town was the Christmas Tree. It was also known as the Spike, Lawn Dart, the Hypodermic, and X Marks the Spot, for the big illuminated X on its second-largest doughnut that was the logo of X-Corp Multimedia, the company it housed.

Slocum lowered his eyes immediately. This made him think, by association, of Lopes. It wasn't so much that he did not wish to see the tower. Though he had known that structure as intimately as any other in his life, it was so big and strange, so unmeasured in the effects it created in the lives of humans, that it did not affect him much, just glimpsing it in this way.

No, what he did not want to look at was the hills surrounding, the glimpse of a sea inlet to the left, and the roofs of houses so large they could clearly be distinguished from such a distance, disturbing the hegemony of trees.

Slocum fixed himself another pot of coffee. He went to find more milk crates. He worked harder than ever, cleaning out the spilled oil and paint that had accumulated against the lazarette's forward bulkhead, but he seemed to have lost the edge of beer, and he never located again the indefinable knack for not-thinking he had caught hold of, then let go, at the Sunset Tap. Even as he scrubbed and rinsed, stacked and stowed, coiled and tied, images came back to him. He would concentrate on scraping off one particularly bad patch of antifouling paint and an image would flicker and short out for a few seconds—then, as soon as he rested, it came back, or else another one returned that had been triggered by the first. Finally, because it was so tiring to fight them in this way, he let the images come without struggling. Squatting in the gloomy confines of his aft compartment, neatly tying away the last milk crates of gear, he let the images resolve themselves into a story. Then or later he was never sure the story had ever really happened in that way, but he was pretty certain all the elements had occurred on their own at roughly the same period in his life. And the story was simple, the way daily life could be simple when observed in a certain light. He worked in the second doughnut from the top, which was pretty high up, both in space and in the troposphere of X-Corp Multimedia. He had arranged, the previous autumn, a big contract with a Web-serf complex in Kano. The quality was assured by a young data navigator named Ibrahim Wolof and the pitch that came out of Kano that particular afternoon was prompting ecstatic e-mails up and down Arcadia. Milton Verve mentioned it to Razia Luzzato. There was a rumor that Wycliffe Sloane had seen the rushes. Slocum was pleased with the work, and instead of doing a power rocketball match with Lazarus Motieff or Ziam Bargh or Jack Fulsome or some of his other usual partners, he chose to go home.

Home then was a house in Bayview. Bayview was "A Secure X-Corp Community"—or so said the sign at the entrance guardpost. In fact it was a town entirely owned and operated by X-Corp Multimedia, with its own cops, schools, fire department, and bylaws. It occupied both banks of an inlet of the sea called the Acushnet River, just to the west of Town. Slocum's house was big, and the architect had designed it to mesh with the lax syncretism in vogue at the time, like most of the other houses in Bayview. It had medieval turrets and a huge sloping glass wall and a triumphal arch for an entrance and a Chateaux de la Loire mansard. It also sported a Grecian arbor and Moorish windows and a swimming pool decorated like a

Roman pleasure parlor. Slocum was still feeling good as he left his car in the garage and followed the walkway past the pool to the Tuscan kitchen that overlooked a pocket vineyard and Amy's herb garden out back. The sense he'd had lately—that his life was running away with him, that he was cut off from anything real, that he was suffocating in a cottony substance and maybe he wasn't even alive sometimes—was gone or at least pruned way back.

He had not seen Stacey Quinn, with whom he'd been sleeping, to the occasional annoyance of them both, in a month.

Today, with the Kano results, he felt he could climb all the way to the top at X-Corp Multimedia and buy out other multinationals and restructure the world the way he, Slocum, wanted to remake it. This, he sensed, might well put paid to his stubborn and inexplicable sense of disconnection.

He remembered searching for Amy or Bird and not finding them in their rooms or in the gym or the video den. He paged their cellphones and their portable headsets; there was no response. Suddenly he imagined it as it must have happened—the lean, rat-faced men in dark clothes and wetsuits and waterproofed automatics, snaking by night past the security cameras, the neoprene shielding them from heat sensors. Bird's terror—the fury Amy would use to mask her own.

Finally Amy had clicked back—they were walking up from the beach club, she told him, and never understood why he laughed and laughed to hear her, so casual and even loud; and Slocum walked out to meet them in what he remembered as one of the rare clear days and the westering sun lathering up the landscape in orange. Bird was maybe twelve. When she saw her father she broke loose from Amy, ran to him, and hugged him around the chest as tightly and unashamedly as she used to hug him around the knees when she was three. It seemed odd that now he could not remember exactly what was wrong—a disappointment at school probably, a clique that had snubbed her—the Bayview Middle School was as stratified socially as X-Corp Multimedia, which supported it and gave it life. But Bird was sad and by the grace of coincidence her sorrow had destroyed the strange distance she had been acquiring with puberty, and on the same day (he thought) as the good news from Kano had swept his own dissatisfaction out of his head.

Amy was generous about this stuff and happy to see them close like that and they had all gone home and ordered in some QuikViet and they drank one of the special bottles made from the grapes out back, the Chateau Slocum Grand Cru, as Amy called it. Even Bird drank half a glass, watered down. And then, sitting on the couch by the kitchen hearth, they strapped on their half-suckers and watched *Pain in the Afternoon,* which was Amy's favorite interactive. All three of them talked to the actors, dealt with some of the problems, which at that point in time probably involved Jeff's leaving and Larissa's illegitimate baby and the arrest of Lance for info-smuggling in Tadjikistan. And it had all been fine and no-stress and Bird snuggled next to him and held his hand in hers and they had moved in tandem to the rhythms of the Flash.

The latter part of this memory, Slocum was fairly sure, was not the same evening, but what the hell: In his memory, after Bird fell asleep, he and Amy went to their bedroom and watched more adult interactives. He told her about Kano and she was happy for him and they made love with the people of different dramas walking around in 3-D colors before their eyes. And that had also been fine, and if in fact it was the same day it would have made that day about perfect.

Still, what he remembered most of all at this point was the tightness with which Bird had hugged him on the Country Club hill, the feel of Bird's hand dry and trusting

in his. That, and Amy's smile, which was not an uncompli-
cated smile because even then the issues between them
were big and growing and Bird was inextricably part of
them—yet he remembered the mercy in her face at that
point. It had seemed part and parcel of the rare orange
sunset, and at the same time greater, wrapped in a chain reaction: All the warmth in him bounced as if by a laser
beam off the woman in front of him who reflected it in
part from the trainee woman who hugged him generously
around the waist; and so on.

Slocum had almost finished with the lazarette. He
stowed the dinghy outboard, piled a few odds and ends in
the last milk crate, and left it unlashed. He climbed out,
groaning from the stiffness in his back. In the cabin he
changed into street clothes, then locked up and climbed
back to Coggeshall Wharf.

The fog was darkening toward evening. He had spent almost the whole afternoon bent into the stern compartment. He set off in the opposite direction from the
hurricane barrier, toward the revolving bridge that cut
across the harbor just north of Coggeshall Wharf. This
time he moved with no sense of meandering or question;
the string of images that trundled through his head as he
worked in the lazarette had triggered a direction in him
much greater than the vector this morning that brought
him to Madame Ling's and the Sunset Tap. It was nothing
big, it was like an itch in your sock; but like an itch you
could not ignore it. He crossed half the bridge. The evening breeze ran threads of mist through his hair, and he
dug his hands deeper in his pockets for warmth. The revolving section of the bridge leaped half the harbor,
nestling its west end on the mainland to cross to an island
in the middle that was home to some old radio towers and
abandoned tugboats and of course dead fishing boats. The
second, fixed, sector took off from the island and landed

on the eastern side, just north of the old Whaling City Marina.

From halfway over that second span you got probably the best overall view you could achieve of the marina. Slocum leaned on the railing, which was of iron, badly pitted with rust. He watched night settle over the deep fretwork of masts and rigging and Bimini tops and battery windmills and antennas and laundry lines and canopies and swordfishing pulpits. He stared at the outline of rotting storage sheds and the abandoned condos behind. He looked hard for one boat in particular, but even with a concentration of vision and the great drive in him to catch a glimpse of this boat it was impossible to tell for sure, at this range, which was which, so thickly were the hulls packed together. He watched the lights spring into life, one by one, kerosene lamps and Christmas strings and Japanese lanterns and spreader lamps. Soon, as the detail of boats and masts faded into the advancing dark, the whole complex looked like a firefly colony that rose and fell, almost imperceptibly out of phase, in the harbor chop. The sounds that reached him, loud enough to make it against the trend of the southerly wind, included recorded music, a wailing child, a roaring outboard, the whir of windmills, the creaking of dock gear, the frapping of halyards on aluminum spars, the screams of kids playing, a shouted warning. They were dim against the wind, confused as a lost transmission, or the sounds of a city of ghosts long drowned in an unspecified section of sea. Eventually Slocum straightened, shrugged his jacket tighter around him, and trudged slowly back across the bridge to Town.

FOUR

THE CHURCH WAS DOWN the road from where they used to live in Bayview. He entered it with a stranger, someone he had met in a different country; Slocum was on his way back. What he wanted most of all right now, for he was very tired and sleepy from travel, was to go home—to fall like an earth-returning arrow into the warm bull's-eye of Amy's breasts; to hold Bird and breathe in the child smell of her: fresh pastry and peaches and the ink of spelling primers all mixed together. But some odd attraction drove him on. It was like the memory of another dream, a dream about this church containing a secret he needed, obliging him to follow this stranger across the cool flagstones of the vestry. Their steps boomed. He was so tired now he could barely move. Boom, boom. His fatigue grew, and the booms were louder now as well. The contradiction between their volume and the quiet of the church forced him, reluctantly, awake.

It was· dark. The security lights reached even this far down the wharf, shooting arrowheads of orange light through the portholes to reflect on random surfaces in his cabin. The loud sounds, in his waking world, came from above. Someone banging on the sloop's main hatch. Slocum flipped on his reading lamp. The clock on the forward bulkhead read 06:04. He slid out of his bunk, dislodging Ralfie, who yowled. He stepped into the County Diesel jumpsuit and zipped it up.

"Who is it?"

"Security."

The night guard's voice was rough and deep. Slocum pulled out the balks of wood that kept his hatch jammed shut. MacTavish slammed the hatch open and removed the washboards, dropping them carelessly in the cockpit. A disturbed seagull croaked in protest. MacTavish's greatcoat filled the hatchway as he came down. He smelled of wet wool, cheeseburgers, whiskey. His face was rectangular and full of ridges and planes and faults like a glacial landscape. His eyes burned. Everything he did was large and full of friction. Stooped against the low deckhead, he examined the cabin, an infantryman's sweep that took in terrain, enfilades, opportunities for ambush. When the scan was finished he looked at Slocum, who was sitting on the settee, staring wistfully at the roiled blankets of his bunk.

"You're gonna have to move your boat," MacTavish announced.

Ralfie was crouched on the deck now, gagging. Slocum switched his gaze to the cat. He hoped it would not puke on the hooked rug again. It took a few minutes for the guard's words to make their way through the sense of time-and-space-distorted that came from being woken up in mid-dream. When Slocum finally registered the words he looked up.

"Move? What are you talking about?"

MacTavish grunted. He took off his greatcoat and slid himself carefully to the opposite end of the settee, watching Slocum across the varnished cherrywood of the saloon table.

Slocum sighed. "I suppose you want coffee."

"It's awful early," the guard agreed.

Slocum got the percolator ready and lit the stove. He opened the icebox and took out milk. He was low on ice. Coggeshall Wharf had shore power—outlets that hooked up to the boat's 110-volt system—but the sloop had no refrigeration unit and for coolant Slocum relied on giant blocks of ice that he bought from Coast Seafood. Coast was the last fish processor still working in the harbor. They owned the warehouse above Slocum on the wharf and their facilities extended a quarter-mile to the south. The ice-plant was at the processor's other end, just before the theme park. Fetching ice was probably Slocum's most onerous chore in connection with living here. Sometimes he could get bags of ice cubes from Obrigado, or from Cakes (when she was talking to him); Cakes had a reefer unit. But cubes did not keep the way fifty-pound blocks did.

MacTavish sighed when Slocum handed him the mug. It was a large, misshapen, fired-clay mug thrown to resemble a spouting sperm whale. The handle was the tail, flipped upward. It had been fashioned by someone in the clay workshop in Whaling City Marina, and though not very stable it held heat well. MacTavish had been a master sergeant in a Scottish infantry regiment that took in no recruits under six-foot-two and he had seen action in the Antarctica troubles, the Caucasus Water Wars, and the Kashmir crisis. He kept his hands folded around the mug the way infantrymen did, simply enjoying the heat and the feeling of hot coffee to drink and the idea of having a little more time to drink it in.

He flipped out a pack of cigarettes and glanced at Slocum, who shook his head. MacTavish sighed, turned the pack over once, and said, "There's a ship coming in, Slocum. A big ship."

"No way." Slocum stared at the guard. His thoughts were moving as fast as they could against the current of drowsiness. He remembered what Lopes had told him at the Sunset Tap; but what Lopes said specifically and what one heard at the Sunset Tap in general was so unreliable, so often false, that he had put it out of his mind.

It occurred to him that the guard might have heard the same rumor, that it might yet be untrue. But for MacTavish to actually do his job of managing the wharf because of a mere rumor from the Sunset Tap would be unlike him. MacTavish rarely lifted a finger, even when he was cut-and-dried supposed to, if such an action would not procure him whiskey or cigarettes or a copy of the black-magic magazines he read without respite.

"You'll have to move north, I reckon. To one of the barges." MacTavish took another sip of coffee and watched him carefully through the steam.

"No way," Slocum repeated, with less conviction. "I don't believe there is a ship."

Then Slocum realized it did not matter if this ship was rumor or truth, because even a rumor could have solid consequences; more dangerously, it could be the expression of another reality that existed for reasons he knew nothing of. The guiding reality here was this: Someone, for one reason or another, wanted Slocum to move his boat.

"I signed a contract," he continued. His voice was low from sleep and strain. "It's a Town contract, it's signed by da Silva." Da Silva was Town counsel. "It says, I get this slip—*this* one," he pointed out the portholes, "for one year."

"They can cancel it. The contract."

"Only if I don't pay."

"Aye," MacTavish said, and flipped his cigarette pack once more. Slocum got the illusion, all of a sudden, that MacTavish was his father and he, Slocum, was ten years old. Again he experienced that feeling of sick powerlessness as the old man explained to him how he must do some chore like chopping firewood or mowing the lawn that he wished with all his heart to avoid. Something he dreaded. Though his father had been easy on him most of the time.

Slocum shook his head. MacTavish's words had suddenly made him feel vulnerable, rejected, like a traveler stopped at the border of a country in which he sought refuge, to be told he was not welcome there. It struck him that he finally felt at home on Coggeshall Wharf. It had become for him a place of refuge—more, it was a safe harbor after his chosen sanctuary had turned into a zone where all the solid foundation-beams of himself had proved rotten, and sagging, and not where he thought they were anyway.

He did not want to move off the wharf. It would be awkward and difficult to shift a sloop with an engine that could cut out at any movement. The barges were not the wharf, they were exposed to the southwest and open to the wake of white ferries. He wondered whether to reveal to MacTavish his ace in the hole. It would make more sense to keep that in reserve; MacTavish was not the one he had to convince. Still, the Town would have this information anyway, it was hardly secret. And he found he desperately wanted to convince the guard, because it might make him feel better now. It might lessen this nagging doubt that came out of the fact that his sloop and himself could soon be cast adrift, quite literally, once more.

"I paid," Slocum said. "I paid a whole year in advance. I have the paper receipt."

MacTavish shook his head.

"Ye don't understand," he replied. "Yon ship's too big. This is the only place in the harbor it can safely tie up."

"There's the dolphins." Slocum jerked his chin away from the wharf, to port.

"They're no set up for a big ship. They'd only have a wee platform for the gangway."

"That's not my problem," Slocum said. He glared at MacTavish. He knew the way his eyes looked and how his voice sounded right now because he recognized the way he was acting; it was the armor he used to put on when he negotiated deals in the second doughnut of Arcadia Tower. It was a blank, aggressive, don't-give-anything-away kind of carapace. It was hard and strong and impervious to entreaty. It surprised Slocum that his armor could slot into place so fast and automatically almost a year after he had left Arcadia. MacTavish stared back at him for a full minute. Then he smiled. The smile was wide, too wide for anything that had been said until then.

"Och," the guard said. "Nothin's forever, eh, Slocum? Nothin's forever. Perhaps," he added cryptically, "the pictures will tell us. Eh?" He pulled a silver object from his greatcoat pocket. It was a small digital camera of brushed aluminum. He pointed it at Slocum and pushed the shutter button. The flash spawned novas in Slocum's vision; by the time his eyes cleared, MacTavish had slipped the camera back into his pocket.

Almost instinctively, Slocum opened his mouth to object. At X-Corp Multimedia they were trained to be fierce about copyright pirating and unauthorized use of images. But he was no longer at X-Corp, and MacTavish was not a copyright pirate. MacTavish, in fact, was simply very weird, and Slocum was still sleepy, and all in all he could make a sound case for not saying anything. And finally this was what he did—merely watched as the guard finished his coffee and stood up and climbed the companionway. The boat lurched slightly as he transferred his weight to the wharf ladder. Slocum thought that MacTavish repeated the words "the pictures will tell us" as he climbed the rungs to the wharf, but against the slap of waves and the wisp of a growing breeze he could not be certain it did not come from the echo those words had set off in his own head.

THE CLOCK NOW READ 06:22. MacTavish's words, echoed or real, were already receding into the feel of early morning, of broken threads of sleep, of interrupted dreams.

But their implication and the effects of that implication were solid as concrete and as heavy. They lay all about what Slocum thought and how he thought it as he sought to regain control of this jumpstarted dawn. He used the head. Because the showerstall overlapped the space the toilet occupied, he stowed the toilet paper and a navigation manual that he read on the john before starting the water heater and the electric pump and taking a shower. Afterward he dressed in his khakis and sweater and fed Ralfie. He made himself an omelet, sniffing carefully to make sure the eggs were OK, adding dried chives and hot chili powder as Amy used to do. It was Amy who had taught him how to cook. He wondered if, in some part of her mind, she had always been preparing him to live alone—and discounted that thought as too distant from hard perception to waste time on. What lay close to perception, though, was the possibility that he might really have to move his sloop. He was impressed by the power of the opposing conviction in him. He had a right to be here, he would not move, he had nowhere to go from Coggeshall Wharf until he left for good, in the direction he wanted, down the marsh channel and out to sea.

Slocum cleaned up. Sleep and the intervening time had sanded the edges of the rage that was so strong in him yesterday. The anger was still around, though softer, more attenuated in form, as if the harbor might have moved overnight inside his brain as it had outside the sloop's hull, changing the contours of the dawn, stretching the solid till it appeared formless, and vice versa. When he had finished cleaning up the galley and the saloon and making up his bunk, he put on his workboots. He knew already where he was going but because it was too early and he did not want to wake up the anger fully, he avoided dwelling on it for now. Instead he looked at the maintenance section of the *Smuggler's Bible* and made a partial list of some other areas that needed attention. He should check the sacrificial anode—the tear-shaped hunk of zinc, bolted and glued to the outside skin of his boat, that was wired to the rudderpost. It served as a ground for the electrical charges inside and outside the hull, which meant that it would be first to electrolyze in reaction to those fields. But so many of the power cables under this old harbor were corroded and shorting that there was always a lot of juice in the water and the zincs had to be changed frequently. For if they wore out, other parts of his boat would start to ground out and decay instead: the rudderpost or the propeller or the engine itself.

Also, the electricity-control panel needed some switches replaced, and he had to put a red lens in the light over the chart table. With a red lens he could use it for after-dark navigation without destroying his night vision, once he got his diesel fixed and the sloop got under way.

Slocum put down his pen. He searched in the hidden compartment till he found the chip he wanted. It was a visiting chip, with the Mechanic's name, Flash address, and physical location printed on top. Once slotted in the ECM, it would play a ten-minute video clip of the Mechanic successfully overhauling an expensive marine diesel. It was much too early for the cannery discharge but he shut and dogged the forward hatch anyway. Ralfie was sitting on the lazarette hatch, watching the wharf for rats slinking home as darkness abandoned its positions. "Yo, Ralfie boy," Slocum whispered, and the cat ignored him pointedly, with the arrogance all cats took on after a good breakfast.

As SLOCUM WALKED OUT the main gate of Coggeshall Wharf, MacTavish leaned out of the security trailer. He held the digital camera's memory spindle in one hand. He waved it at Slocum.

"We'll see noo," MacTavish muttered darkly. "We'll see." His eyes in their caves seemed baleful and unfriendly as he watched Slocum pass.

Slocum walked north up Front Street. He got the same feeling he'd had earlier, on the railroad tracks: that someone was following him. Maybe MacTavish was coming after him for some reason. He turned, but the street was deserted. He passed fastfood restaurants that sold nutrition rich in fat and salt to the low-income people who lived here and to the slightly higher-income people who took the wrong ramp off the spin of highway leading from the Interstate to the Moby Dick Theme Park. He passed Flash parlors, arcades that rented 3-D interactive games. He looked away as he went by. He passed corner stores and garages and boarding-houses and regular three-story frame houses painted, like the houses in the Grid, in colors of the Algarve and Andalusia. After a while the colors changed a bit to reflect the hotter colors of Bahia, Maputo, Cape Verde. Some houses stood with roofs open to the fog and blackened bones compound against the sky. Lots that normally might be called vacant were full of weeds, locust trees, abandoned cars, raccoon jungles. Thin men fed fires in trash barrels. The Interstate loomed and roared overhead. The entrance ramp was blocked with giant concrete pots; only the theme-park by-pass conducted traffic from the highway to the Town, and that did not go to the Town itself, but only to the toll booths at the park's entrance. Above the vacant lots and the smoke and the fog, the corrupt glow of Bayview Mall now occupied half the horizon line. A video billboard on the mall approach showed a clip from *Real Life,* an X-Corp in-teractive drama Slocum had worked on once. In the video, Larissa Love, madly firing machine guns, drove an armored car through a fort filled with slavering dark-hued terrorists. REAL LIFE—LIVE IT! the sign urged.

In an alley beyond the highway, a bearded white man danced spasmodically. He wore a 3-D headset and a loose tunic. Under the tunic, most likely, he carried a jag—an apparatus including belt-computer, micropumps, and IV manifolds that injected a precisely metered dose of various fast-acting stimulants and depressants in step to a program of video and sound playing on the headset. Slocum moved to the other side of Front from the jagger, and walked faster. Railroad tracks surfaced, like history itself showing through the makeup of Flash-era life in the roadway's center. They were the other end of the line that ran parallel to the warehouses by the lower harbor. Now Slocum discerned, between a condemned housing estate and a chop shop, just south of the first parking lots of the mall, a swath of security lights and razor-wire fencing in the midst of which vinyl-sided warehouses were ranged in some kind of order. The gap next to the chop shop was closed with barbed wire and the same sort of concrete pots that protected the Interstate. An access road meandered through a short stretch of carefully preserved wetland; the upper harbor river lay just to the east. The road led to a tall gate of razor-wire, a chain-link fence, and a guardhouse much bigger than the one watching over Coggeshall Wharf. A sign beside the gate read:

THE MAINTENANCE
AND ENGINEERING ZONE
@BAYVIEW MALL INC.
★★★
NO TRESPASSING
appointments only
THIS MEANS YOU!

A retractable steel barrier poked out of the concrete in front of the movable gate. The barrier was locked in up position, its steel fangs bared to traffic. The guardhouse beside it had smoked glass, loudspeakers, searchlights, antennas, infrared scanners, and video cameras. As Slocum approached, the cameras zoomed in on his form and a spotlight shone in his eyes. When he got within ten feet a voice blasted from the speakers.

"Stop right there, pal! Can't you read?"

"I can read," Slocum said. "I already read it."

"Speak up!"

Slocum shaded his eyes with one hand, trying to see through the glare of light and the smoke of windows.

"I came—"

"Speak up!" the speakers said. "The pickups aren't ...

"Aren't picking you up," the voice continued after a slight pause. "I mean, that's what pickups are supposed to do, isn't it?"

"What do you want me to do?" Slocum asked, more loudly. "I came—"

"I mean," the speaker voice interrupted, "I *don't* mean pickups. I mean, not the truck pickups. I *meant,* the mikes. We have microphones that pick you up. Not literally."

Slocum was at first confused, even a little frightened by the lights and noise of the security booth. Now he felt irritation popping up like sweat from the effort he had to put into this exchange. He started to move forward and the speakers barked immediately: *"Stop right there, pal!"*

"I'm here to see the Mechanic. The diesel mechanic, in Shed—" He looked at the visiting chip.

"No one gets in without an appointment. Read the sign!"

"In Shed 4-G," Slocum continued stubbornly. "If you—"

"We have no appointment listed at this time. At this time," the loudspeaker repeated, as if to reassure itself.

"I would like to speak with him. I would like to use your intercom—"

"Speak up!"

"The intercom—"

"Out of the question."

"What's out of the question?"

"Talk louder!" the voice said. "I was going to say, the pickups are not functioning appropriately, they could be out of date, or unserviceable because of the humidity, but."

Slocum shut his eyes. The glare hurt them. He resisted an urge to put his hands against his ears to dull the ache caused by high speaker volume.

"Anyway you might have got the wrong signal."

"Got the wrong signal about what?" Slocum asked in his normal voice; a voice, he was beginning to think, that sounded tired and dispirited and weak—even a little old, compared to the armored version he had used with MacTavish. He opened his eyes again, away from the glare, toward the sign.

"Pickup, pickup," the speakers yelled crossly. "Look! I don't mean *pick* you *up,* not literally, or even figuratively, the other sense—though you might think so the way people just assume we're here to arrest them. But we're not going to lift you physically, are we? No way."

Slocum noticed, as he looked at the sign, that under the staring orange someone had neatly scratched a pair of symbols: a vertical line with three short hashmarks drawn horizontally across it, like a fishbone.

An inverted arc, like the top limb of the sun, sheltering a single point.

Slocum looked at the symbols for a few seconds. Then he lifted his eyes to the left, over the gleaming razor wire, toward a loading bay that read 3A. Behind the warehouse that sheltered dock 3A, presumably, lay another warehouse where the Mechanic worked and where his answering machine lay on what Slocum imagined was a greasy shelf, storing messages from Slocum and other unhappy clients owning small, dysfunctional marine diesels up and down the coast.

Finally, Slocum turned and walked back the way he had come. As he walked, the speakers dwindled in volume behind him, but slowly, as if the Zone guard were boosting the volume to compensate for the increasing distance between them.

"Oh no, pal, oh no! You think you can just show up and go as you please, and our pickups won't pick you up? Huh? Not literally, as I said.

"And I don't mean the other thing. Like, at a singles bar. I mean ..."

The wind rustled through the cattails of the bruised wetlands.

"... leave?" the speakers asked.

FIVE

IT WAS STILL EARLY morning but Slocum felt as if the day already had overflexed and eroded him. As he turned the corner on County Street, a gleaming eighteen-wheeler, the kind with yellow lights all over the cab and neon under the chassis and lights in rows winking down the trailer and Christmas lights outlining the bumper and foglamps and wrecking lights on top of the usual turn signals and double headlights—all lit, all staining the fog with their colors—came barreling down the hard roadway so fast that Slocum had to leap sideways to avoid being mowed down. Triple airhorns blasted. There was a marked absence of airbrakes hissing. Slocum stood on the curb, heart pounding, watching the huge truck, the words COUNTY DIESEL stenciled on its side, disappear into the mist. It was galling, he thought, to be almost killed by a truck from an outfit that could repair his engine in an afternoon if it wanted. But County Diesel worked only on big accounts, large engines, the kind the Mechanic only wished he could work on; machines with thousands of horse-power. County mechanics went up and down the coast in trucks like that to service power plants and mall generators and giant tankers. As a result, since the last big trawlers had gone to scrap, they never worked in Town anymore, even though their base, their workshop, was in the Zone.

Once back in the Town proper, Slocum looked for a telephone booth; you could still find one in really poor areas, neighbs so abandoned people could not even afford cellphones. He himself did not carry a cell; he had canceled the family account, to Bird's limitless disgust, when he got involved with the ICE. He had done it partly to make a statement his family would notice, and partly because that was the ethos of the place he was involved with; at that point, he had wanted to adapt to the marina, even to the way he communicated. Cellphones were Outside, they were part of the mechanism that the big companies, the Orgs, used to control your time, through a system of false appointments and unnecessary scheduling and constant Flash—the relentless panoply of video events that induced the need to seek out more such events, to the exclusion of getting together and creating something like the Whaling City Marina, and the Independent Credit Entity it sheltered.

This did not, Slocum reflected, prevent members of that community from gossiping over the Wildnets, or lining up five at a time and at all hours at the ancient phone booth near the shower buildings. And plenty of them, those that could afford it, used cellphones, no matter what the *Smuggler's Bible* said.

He could use the Whip's cell, Slocum thought. It would do no good, but he would call the Mechanic, while he was in the neighborhood. Maybe if the Mechanic heard him leave a message saying he was right around the corner, he would pick up the phone and agree to see him. The Whip lived not far from here, up a slight hill to the west, in a neighborhood that was no longer in the Town's jurisdiction but lay within the limits of Bayview. Though not in the closed area, it benefited from the subsidized school system in Bayview and thus was popular among the lower dough-nuts in Arcadia. As he got there the mist lifted in a way that had become rare for the Town since the climate changed. Slocum could see all the way to the hurricane barrier. It was open. He always checked; if some mean weather he had not heard about came charging up the coast, the closing of the barrier would be his final warning.

His sloop was hidden from view behind the old Bone Cement warehouse and the fish-processing plant. The life-sized fiberglass sperm whale at the center of the Moby Dick Theme Park flashed in the rare sun, surfacing, spouting, diving, its twin flukes upended in a welter of chlorinated foam.

The Whip's house was the third in a row of ranches. A Winnebago was perched on blocks outside the kitchen door. Slocum knocked on the trailer's aluminum door but no one answered. The Whip kept his imaging hardware in the Winnebago. The Whip's car was in the driveway, so after a moment's hesitation Slocum knocked on the kitchen door.

The Whip's wife let him in. She wore running tights and a T-shirt three sizes too small. She was very pretty. Her hair was made up in a style pioneered by Amy Duggan, on *Pain in the Afternoon*—long henna-dyed ringlets on one side and cut very short on the other. Slocum knew Dolores had never missed an episode of *Pain;* even when she was in labor with Howard Jr. she had watched the interactive over a headset. Dolores opened the door wider but said nothing when Slocum wished her good morning. The main room was half kitchen, half living room, separated by an island with a sink and cabinets on which high school hockey calendars hung thickly. The Whip sat at the kitchen table, surrounded by a yard sale of coffee cups, coffeecakes, muffins, butter, milk, and other appurtenances of breakfast. Sloughed-off hockey sticks, gum wrappers, 3-D spindles with names like *Planet Blast!* and *Zephyro,* and body sensors for spindle games betrayed like the aura of a ghost the semi-solid absence of an adolescent boy.

The Whip's face was fleshy and mobile around a thick nose and lips. He tended to check his gut automatically, pulling the flab there with broad fingers. The Whip that morning was in what had come to be called 4-D: While he tapped at the keys of a belt-top jambook computer that interacted through wireless links with the various Nets, the Whip watched the images surfacing in response to his commands on a 3-D backscreen that fitted like a visor over the top half of his face. Meanwhile, he kept track of a gossip show on a digital-TV screen that took up an area as long as the couch on the living room's opposite wall.

When he spotted Slocum through the lower, clear portion of his visor, he pushed it halfway up and hooked the belt-top shut but did not sever his link with the Nets. Slocum realized he was staring at the belt-top and the digital monitor, and forced himself to turn away. The Whip got up and gripped both of Slocum's biceps in greeting. Then he checked to see what Dolores was doing. "I suppose you want coffee," Dolores said, reminding Slocum, uncomfortably, of his own words when MacTavish showed up earlier on his sloop.

She poured him a cup in an X-Corp mug. Slocum had met the Whip in Arcadia Tower, where he did contract maintenance as part of a team checking that the switches and routers and servers on which Net communication depended were functioning properly. Slocum, who was always running late for important meetings and frankly did not have time for chitchat with maintenance men, barely talked to him in Arcadia. Then he fetched up on Coggeshall Wharf and ran into the Whip at the Sunset Tap. The sight of a vaguely familiar face amid the confusion and panic of what had happened to him pulled at the filings of Slocum's heart like a magnet.

Slocum asked if he could use the cellphone. Dolores

objected. "I was going to call Veronique," she said. The Whip countered, "Ah come on, if he just needs to check something, it'll only take a minute." Dolores said, "*How*-ard," and he shrugged.

Slocum dialed the Mechanic's number. The line was busy. He felt a sudden bubble in his chest. The Whip cut him a piece of coffeecake laden with pecans and frosted sugar. Slocum remembered how Bird, when served coffeecake like this, would always cut a wedge from the section of cake that had the most icing.

He did not touch the cake. Dolores changed channels on the monitor. An announcer with a mustache like a British colonel barked hysterically about Amy Duggan, who was rumored to be two-timing her husband Mahal Schrenk, who also acted on *Pain in the Afternoon,* with Vincenzo Stronzo, a nineteen-year-old actor from *Real Life.* Dolores picked up the cellphone but her number was busy and reluctantly she put it down. Slocum claimed it once more. He felt a curious kinship with Dolores; they both were focused on an archaic line of communication and the relationships it created, all of which might be silly or useless but that for now consumed all their attention. The digital backdrops shuffled dramatically behind him. The anchor somberly announced that another serial killer was in action, targeting people in 3-D television, people in showbiz, men and women famous from the Flash—he spoke the word "Flash" as a century ago a Catholic might have said "the Pope."

"The Gatsby Killer," the announcer continued. "Police suspect he may be a failed actor, because of his WASP good looks." A police hologram revolved slowly behind the anchor. The face was square, well balanced. The eyes were extraordinarily blue, the hair so blond it was almost white. The cops could be right, Slocum thought. The killer was handsome and utterly forgettable, like a thousand actors and actresses on the Flash, which favored some lost ideal of Saxon bloodline. This was probably in reaction to a population that was growing steadily more mixed, the whites turning darker and the darks lighter, which, Slocum believed, both genetically and culturally was a good thing.

Slocum possessed an authentic Anglo name from New England, but he was an eighth black and an eighth Oneida on his mother's side. And his skin, though light in hue, had a shadow to it, as if history had stood in the way of the sun.

"He uses his private-school contacts to locate hits," the announcer said excitedly. "He blends into his surroundings, he is a master of disguise." Slocum remembered Shaneeqwa, and her attempt to scare Luisa with such tales. It was accepted that at least a dozen serial killers were active in America at this point, and one of them was picking up hookers and murdering them up and down this very coastline. But murdered hookers did not rate the same kind of coverage as a threat to a Flash star.

Slocum tried the Mechanic's number once more. This time, it rang. Dolores stared at the handset. Slocum's heart rate quickened. A click sounded. The voice that followed was the Mechanic's, but it was recorded and Slocum had heard the words so often he could repeat them by heart. "Hi, I'm either online or working in the shop right now, but leave a message or e-mail me at 2dogsdiesel@bayviewonline.net and I'll get right back to you. Have a nice day."

Slocum clicked off the cellphone. He handed it to Dolores, who spun on one heel and walked out of the kitchen.

The Whip watched her go. "Don't worry about it," he told Slocum, "she doesn't mean anything." He took the face-sucker off his head and fitted it over Slocum's.

Slocum ripped it, far too quickly and violently for the circumstances, off his face. The Whip stared.

"I'm sorry," Slocum mumbled.

The Whip went pale. "Oh jeez I forgot—Slocum, I'm

sorry. I mean, I should be the one to apologize—" He pulled at his stomach flab with his right hand, grasped Slocum's right biceps with his left.

"It's fine," Slocum told him.

"It's just the marsh, babe. I told you about the marsh, I think I got a line into it and I wanted you to see. It's cool as hell."

"I know," Slocum said, "It's OK, I just can't. You know."

The two men stared at each other for a moment. Slocum got the sense he sometimes got, that time did not exist, that random events kept happening because of momentum, like rocks tumbling down a mountain long after a climber higher up had dislodged them. Yet in all that momentum he, Slocum, was not moving anymore.

The announcer said, "The killer wears chinos, button-down Oxfords, tassel loafers. He leaves cheap hardcover printouts of *The Great Gatsby* on or near his victims. Police says his hit list may include targets as famous and wealthy as Amy Duggan, Wycliffe Sloane, and William H. Gates IV."

Slocum left.

He took Water Street, parallel to Front Street, on his way back. Part of the motivation was a desire for variety. Most of it, he knew, had to do with avoiding the concentration of Flash parlors on Upper Front. Though he had ripped off the headset quickly, the brief glimpse of movement, real and dense—no, more real, and denser than normal life—had bothered him more than he wanted to think about. Perhaps it was because Slocum believed he had outflanked the problem that he was so utterly surprised when, after walking around a truck unloading beer beside a Cape Verdean bar, he found himself face to face with a parlor.

It was a low-rent place, a former movie theater whose name, The Metropole, still hung in dead plaster letters over the marquee, with a newer vinyl suffix reading 4TH DIMENSION. The canopy was decorated profusely with ranks of

multicolored video displays showing a sample of the dramas a client could rent inside. That was standard for such
arcades. In his first, shocked vision of the place, Slocum
nonetheless recognized some of the Flash classics: *Lizarda,*
in which Mahal Schrenk was turned into a reptile, which
paradoxically gave him both tremendous sexual appeal to
women and mystical powers in the Flashmarkets; *The Shift,*
where the hero went back in virtual time to solve an 1850s
murder and found the killer pursuing him in the present.
The street panels did not boast the Malaysian joysticks and
feedback gloves some of the fancier parlors offered. For
there were upscale Flash parlors as well as cheaper ones, in
places like Kensington, Greenwich, and Juan les Pins; parlors with attached restaurants serving five different varieties
of truffle.

But this old theater looked dingy and unclean, with the
carnie lights flashing under the canopy and around the entrance and the neon announcing ENTER THE 4TH DIMEN-
SION. A listless ticket taker read *Shine* inside his bulletproof
booth, and the inevitable knot of teedees, their own receivers hung dead around their necks, clustered at the
biggest and most colorful panels like moths around the
brightest candle.

It was seedy and depressing, it was the opposite of the
glitz and uncommon drama that was the come-on of 3-D
videos. It stopped Slocum as dead as if he had run into a
glass wall. His breath came short, sweat cracked into his
armpits and ran down his back. The surprise, he supposed
vaguely, meant that the defenses he habitually maintained
against the cheap lure of the Flash were down, his psychic
defenders like cops eating doughnuts in some twenty-four-
hour diner of the mind; and all the pent-up images, the remembered arcs of bliss, came shooting like a wayward
galaxy through the gap thus abandoned. These memories
were deep, he perceived them with his body the way he

remembered other vital events in his life, like Bird's birth, or his first real kiss.

Desperately Slocum tried to remember the first girl he had kissed, and could not. His hands tautened as if they could grip a joystick, his neck muscles tensed, ready to take flight, or dive off a cliff, or spacewalk or follow an undiscovered fish at four thousand feet under the Pacific. Ah, for a moment he wanted it most desperately, he wanted the face-sucker in front of his eyes, and the instant choice of sweet worlds it offered. He wished to sit at the controls of *Wanderbird* again and try to make it back to human civilization from the alternative universe behind the violet phase of Cygnus X-6. As commander of the *Wanderbird,* he had found planets back there so lovely that the sight of some of their flowers had made people cry, or so they said in the Flashblurbs for that game.

The thing was, he believed it. Because he had been on those planets and, in the course of examining them in the spaceship's lab with the chief scientist, had helped craft those flowers. The chief scientist's name was Breena Jakes, and through the constant interactive stochastics that Desai-X-Corp produced he had helped craft her too; the *Wanderbird* menu took your profile and adapted details to your tastes both conscious and veiled. He had been half in love with Breena Jakes, he even suspected he ended up loving her more than Amy, though Breena existed only when he put on a headset, and Amy, most of the time, was more present than that.

More than Breena, though—more than that glow of 3-D infatuation—he remembered the rush of great space, and oceanic loneliness, and numbing speed, because the velocity of light was not a limitation in the Flash and *Wanderbird* moved fast. He had never, in all the years of playing, sorted out the clues that would allow him to win, and the *Wanderbird* to return to her home sun, and in many

ways it was because he did not want to. He got what he
needed from being lost in a beautiful ship in a search that
had no finish and always brought new perspectives on con-
ceptual beauty and physical danger.

Slocum shut his eyes. He told himself to resume walking, past the parlor. He found he could not move. This was
because both sides of him aimed to go simultaneously in
different directions. The half that needed to evade the
Flash told him to walk around the Metropole, and the half
that sought the ease of 3-D ordered him to move toward it.
Closing his eyes of course approximated what 3-D did
best, by breaking apart the workaday world of streets and
teedees and creating a dark space, a neutral stage for drama,
where he could invent whatever spatial and temporal coor-
dinates he chose. He had been adept at making that switch
and he supposed that part of his brain was still good at it
because once he closed his eyes the effect was instantaneous. Against the miniworld of his eyelids he saw varied
images, bits of other three-dimensional dramas he had
flashed on or that Bird or Amy were fans of. *Rikka's
Messengers* had been Bird's favorite and he had gone into
that drama with her quite often. In fact both he and Amy
had roles assigned to them in *Rikka*. Slocum was Roger,
the klutzy father who stayed home and beat his brains figuring out where his daughter had gone; and Amy was the
mother, Anita, a witch who in the normal course of events
had trained Rikka to be a witch as well and now could not
accept that Rikka had proved more adept at concocting
potions than she. Rikka one day had gotten on the bus and
disappeared to have adventures in—well, anywhere Bird
fancied; the point of the game was partly for her parents to
figure out where she was and try to bring her home, and
partly for Rikka to save the world's endangered animals
from the evil warlock Sikpru, who had stolen their genetic
codes and wanted to kill all living animals in order to craft
a perfect monopoly.

They had played the interactive game for hours, after dinner, on weekends, over the last two years before everything changed. They had played it so much, and talked enough about it when not playing, that it seemed to Slocum that their family lived in *Rikka* more than in the house they slept in and the community in which they shopped and where they went out quite often for dinner. Their last vacation together had been to a *Rikka* theme park. He wondered vaguely where he got time for *Wanderbird,* or *Pain in the Afternoon,* which he sometimes visited when he had been working hard and felt he should be with Amy more. Of course he could join her from the office, but *Pain* had been full of beautiful people and places and the suggestive effect of all that sometimes had welcome physical consequences for both of them. How long could you watch two lovely actors eating conch fritters and drinking rice wine under palm trees in Lombok and then taking off their sarongs and slipping into the warm sea and you right with them, watching this happen as if their eyes were yours and their hands your hands, before you needed to feel with your body what they felt with theirs? Before things changed, he and Amy had made love often as they watched their actors make love in *Pain,* and it had not been separate and yet it had been separate to the point where he had felt like he was making love with his wife and he was also making love with the actors in *Pain.* Of course this 3-D intimacy had killed the one element Amy and he had that was fully theirs and no one else's—

Slocum opened his eyes. He had noticed, even in his old life, how the quick switches, the change in crystal memories, that you honed on the Flash as you opted for different scenes or games, worked the other way as well. Admiration could swing to contempt in a microsecond, pleasure into discomfort, lust into repulsion. It had happened just now, so fast he could not recall how it came about.

Slocum started to move. He walked past the Metropole.

The lights reflected cyan, magenta on the thin features of teedees, on his own hands as he strode and swung his arms. He did not dwell on the images flashing outside the theater, nor did he need to stare in the opposite direction. His loneliness, and the pain that came from wanting to see Bird in any given hour and not being able to, had alchemized, like one of Rikka's most powerful potions, into an absolute disgust. Now every color and movement of the Flash in 3-D or flat video seemed to him a poison so foul it could kill just by brushing against your arm. He sweated more copiously. His throat contracted, he felt an urge to vomit; but he did not need to step into the road to avoid the Flash, his new contempt had power enough to move him right past the theater and through the crowd of teedees who parted silently then regrouped in his wake, insubstantial and delicate as the moths they still reminded him of around the video panels. That feeling of strength—or, if not strength, a revulsion whose force passed for power—did not last long. A dam formed farther down his stomach, which had filled with acid from the sough of his dislikes and needs. Kneeling in the gutter, he threw up coffee; and the hues of his vomit, reflecting brown and yellow and a little blue from the Metropole flashing up the street, were like a mockery of the bright colors he found in interactive drama.

———

MACTAVISH SPOTTED SLOCUM WHEN he entered the security gate and emerged from his trailer to greet him. As always, his size and darkness seemed to take away units of wattage from the spotlights, and he resembled a great black condor, unwrapping its wings in anticipation of dinner. He held something in his fist, and as Slocum approached he unpalmed it, like a magician, flipped the plastic square so that it was face-up in his hand: an instant print from a digital camera. It was the shot he had taken of Slocum in his cabin earlier that morning.

But MacTavish had done something to it. The blue of the cabin's fiberglass had spread like a stain over Slocum's chest. His hand had turned into a vermilion splotch in the shape of an eagle, and his face was chained by a violet vine to the engine-room hatch. Slocum knew MacTavish copied the computer file that held the print, then drew the free-association runes of his overheated obsessions on the spindle with a magnet.

"Here," MacTavish growled. "Here's your future. Don't say I didna warn ye." He marched back into the booth.

Slocum's first impulse was to drop the picture in the nearest puddle, but it would not do to piss off MacTavish. Anyway the guard often concocted such pictures, claiming he could predict the future with them; it seemed to do no one any harm. He slipped the print into his hip pocket.

Back on the sloop he relit the ship's stove and put on a sweater for good measure. His stomach felt better. He poured a bowl of cereal and forced himself to eat it though it tasted like cardboard and the milk was starting to sour.

After that he changed into his jumpsuit and took the Project from the bookshelf where he stowed it. He laid it on the broad table of his navigation station and switched on the chart light.

The Project was what he called the ancient ledger in which he was pasting old-fashioned prints and other hard-copy illustrations for Bird. Slocum turned the pages slowly, following the stories he had told his daughter long ago, when she was too young for interactive. They were the stories on which he had based the outline for *Rikka*. But *Rikka* had been storyboarded by professional screenwriters and had very little in common with the tales he had told Bird when she was three or four and he was trying to get her to sleep. In fact he only half remembered the stories, and wondered how much was real memory and how much he was making up as he went along to fill in the gaps. He wasn't sure—he wasn't sure how effective any of this would be, with his painstaking script snaking between the glued oblongs of filigree, the ancient black-and-white artwork that only approximated what he had put down in words. He wasn't sure Bird would retain any affection for the saga of Claire, the original Rikka, and her troupe of dysfunctional raccoons. But Slocum did know that he loved the feel and smell of the book's thick paper, regardless of how much Bird might or might not appreciate it; he, Slocum, liked to open the ledger and work on this story.

The cereal did not bother his stomach. It did not cheer him up either. Slocum felt that if he had to paint a picture of his physical and mental state right now it would look like the aftermath of a battle. One of those all-out battles from the last century where tens of thousands of soldiers were slaughtered and nothing was left afterward but churned mud and puddles of blood and splinters of bone and, here and there, the burned skeleton of a tree.

Slocum took out one of his last bottles of the de Lauzère cognac that X-Corp gave its managers at holiday time. He filled a glass a third of the way. He cut out a print of a magnificent bearded man pointing another man, whose clothes were tattered, down a tortuous and perilous-looking canyon. THE VALE OF PERFIDY, the caption read. He pasted that by his account of the start of a journey that Claire and her dog Nidd had undertaken in the very first story he had made up for Bird.

A ferry passed close by, and its wake broke against the pilings and rocked the sloop even in the sheltered pocket of wharf where it lay. The fog lost color and light. The security lights switched on. The brandy warmed Slocum's gut and made the rest of him relax somewhat as well. He switched on the ECM-pak; it was a smuggler's device, a bundle of different wireless links with a jamming function

and a program for Wildnets thrown in. He did not need all
the spectra and channels the ECM provided, but the sloop
had belonged to a smuggler of rare tropical stimulants and
the pak was included in the purchase price. So was a spe-
cialized navigational hard drive Slocum had only the
vaguest idea how to use.

He switched to AM and tuned to the Town station.
WFDO broadcast in Portuguese. As far as Slocum could
determine it had only one DJ, a man with a deep and rough
but somehow soothing voice who played requests all night
for the unhappy wives of the Town. Slocum had never
heard on this station anything but Lisbon ballads, *fados,* full
of plaintive Arab grace notes and the soft slippery slush of
Portuguese. One problem with the ECM was that no matter what other frequency you chose, it was programmed to
turn on the marine radio frequency, the VHF, as well. Thus,
though the general run of transmissions was *fado,* and the
occasional soft announcement or ad for a supermarket that
sold *bacalhao* and *linguica,* occasionally a faraway voice
would break in from a ship or more often a tugboat invisible over the horizon, beyond the gray and twisting saltmarsh, over the lip of ocean.

He poured himself another shot of cognac. The sloop
creaked as it rubbed against the wharf's pilings. The halyards rang.

As Slocum focused the front of his mind on picking
pictures and pasting them and savoring the depth of
brandy, in the back of his brain he sensed a kind of balance
establish itself—as if, in retrospect, the colors of his vomit
had been a gift, had somehow neutralized the brash hues of
the Flash in the Metropole 4th Dimension. As if the effort
he had made in trying to find and nail down the Mechanic
in the Zone in some way started to compensate for the
hours of waiting on his sloop for the man to show up.

As if the Project he worked on, through the value of
the processing he added in his mind, could somehow make

up for the fact that he so rarely saw his daughter. Though
he was losing touch with her with every hour and day that
went by.

Though he missed her.

"All ships," said a voice on the VHF. "This is *Stella
Maris,* two barges in tow, entering ship channel outbound
past Brenton Reef, over."

"E uma coisa mas bonita pelas muhleres de Pappy's Bakery
em Fairev," said the announcer on WFDO. *"Eu os amo todas."*

Ralfie galumphed down the companionway. He crunched
cat food and settled on the bunk. Slocum poured himself
more cognac. He checked his mooring lines. He sat down
at the chart table and worked on the Project again. The radio played ballads called *Fado da pouca sorte* and *Rosa da
Noite.* It was well after 1 A.M. when he turned in.

SIX

SLOCUM WOKE UP COMPLETELY.

It was as if he had stepped from one state to the other, as clearly as changing airplanes. One second he was asleep and the next he was as awake as if he'd been up for hours with coffee and everything. He knew something had woken him but had no idea what.

He lay in his bunk, listening.

The security lights irradiated the wharf above him. Otherwise it was dark. No sounds besides the slurp of water, the frap of a halyard, a far-off car engine. Ralfie snored regularly against his ankles.

And a rumble started. It began slow and low and quickly grew loud and deep. It sounded like something the size of a house, made of brick and steel, turning over and over in an underwater hopper maybe ten meters away. There were clanks and catches of metal included in the general fracas and they seemed to touch the sloop under the waterline and shake it ever so slightly.

As suddenly as it had started, the rumble tapered off and died.

In the silence it left came a rush of water like a toilet flushing in the next room.

Slocum lay still for a few seconds. Now that he had to think, he noticed the unpurged tiredness and the brandy thick in his brain passages. The strangeness of that noise, and its volume, scared him a little. His mind turned up useless descriptions like earthquake and monster and destruction to explain the unfamiliarity. He had to introduce a small cop of reason to bring that traffic into line.

Finally he got up. Ralfie pawed at enemies in his sleep. Slocum peered out the porthole that gave him a view to the east, of the harbor and the ICE—or, most often, what he knew was the harbor, with all its views veiled by an invading mist.

Darkness only. A thick and textured darkness that Slocum assumed, because it was the assumption to make, was the deeply woven obscurity that came when night and thick fog were braided together. Cups and shoehorns of light bounced off the wavelets of the wharf, reflecting a higher light the source of which was hidden from him by the porthole's narrow diameter.

Slocum threw on his jumpsuit, unblocked the hatch, and stepped into the cockpit, holding on to boom and cleated mainsheet for stability.

To starboard: the greased black pilings of the wharf, and the deeper blackness of the rats' domain between pilings and the walls of the fish-processing plant higher up.

To port and well forward lay a tugboat. It rocked slightly in the stretch of water between the sloop and the row of dolphins separating and protecting him from the harbor proper. It was a harbor tug, not from here—the last of the Town tugs had left when the Arctic grounds went the way of the local fisheries. The freighters that brought frozen fish from the north had stopped coming shortly thereafter, and then the tugboats that served them left too. This tug was neat and fat in the way of all harbor tugs. It showed on its stumpy mast two vertical white lights, indicating the vessel was actively engaged in either pushing another vessel or towing it alongside or towing it astern with a total tow-length of less than 200 meters; but Slocum saw no barge or other vessel in all the utter darkness to his left.

Though that darkness seemed to take off from the water in a manner very sudden and specific from how night and water usually behaved.

Slocum looked farther to the left, and up.

Thick darkness climbing the wall of night, utter and black. Yet set in the middle of this stretch of it was a bright yellow circle about the size of a dinner plate. And another.

And then an unending row of bright yellow circles, higher than that, and above them, a line of square windows, and then three more.

A sort of ledge, in which lights were set at intervals, jutted horizontally over the windows.

At that point fog started to veil the details of this apparition. Perhaps because of the contrast fog afforded, Slocum could make out a top deck that was not quite as dark as the rest of this obscurity. The windows at this level were not yellow or bright, but dim and tinged with green. They seemed to Slocum as high as the clouds or higher; yet something rose even higher than that, a single white light shining vertically over Slocum's head. It tore the windblown fog in strips, and through those strips Slocum occasionally spotted a couple of stars. So that he got an impression, which was of course false but which nonetheless stayed with him, that this light was so high it was tearing constellations right out of the sky, bringing them down through the hole in the night, and flying their sheen like a banner.

"A ship," Slocum whispered.

His whisper was not a statement but a hypothesis suggested by incidental data—the shape of portholes, the partial code of what could be, should be, a steaming light.

But words were powerful things. Maybe it was only

because Slocum's night vision, with a suddenness that might also have been borrowed from his days on the Flash, had switched on; at any rate, as soon as he said "ship," Slocum began noticing other details. Well forward of him a column of water two feet in diameter gushed into the harbor, and accounted for the flushing sound he had heard earlier. A low barge was moored at the southern tip of Coggeshall Wharf. The single red light it showed, Slocum knew, meant it was a fuel barge. On the other end of the horizon offered him by fog and perspective, the darkness seemed to chop off in a shallow vertical arc behind which a couple of security lights from the upper wharf were visible, as well as a distant traffic signal.

Above the fourth line of portholes, a median line separated the vast expanse of dark hull from an expanse higher up. When Slocum's eyes traveled along that horizon forward in relation to his sloop, he saw a couple of tiny human figures moving and ducking along what was most likely the rail of the ship's foredeck.

The tug shuddered. A scribble of white appeared under its counter, where the propeller was, and it moved forward, perhaps in response to an unspoken prompt, a radio signal. The rumbling started again, gently at first, then growing in volume so that the air seemed to come in waves modulated by whatever caused that noise. In the water between Slocum's sloop and the huge vessel, the heads and shoulders of writhing silver-white water-giants appeared as the ship's own propellers juddered grudgingly into reverse.

Slocum's mouth hung open. The ship—for it definitely was a ship, he had accepted that some instants ago—was so big that at this moment and point in the night he could not conceive of anything larger. From his perspective it filled the harbor and two-thirds of the sky and he would never get over that first impression, and the almost superstitious awe he felt on first seeing it. Even the whirlpools and rips created by it in the water were so big that they would have swallowed a good-sized sloop. They spoke of propellers twenty or thirty feet in diameter thrashing with the power of a hundred locomotives; and in a process parallel to what the ship was doing to his wharf, they made Slocum feel like all the space inside him was being taken up by awe, and disrupting the normal control lines of his body, and he was going to piss himself where he stood from the effects of that trauma.

And then the wash from the propellers hit Slocum's sloop. It was bounced brutally against the pilings of Coggeshall Wharf, pushed forward against its springs and sternlines. The fiberglass groaned; the pilings sagged and moaned. The glass was strong, the docklines were nylon and resilient, the bumpers on the sloop's side were thick and well tethered. But only sixty or seventy feet separated the sloop from the enormous side of the ship beside it. For a panicked moment Slocum imagined that now he would pay the price of having refused to move his boat when MacTavish asked him to. The captain of that giant ship was simply going to moor in his space regardless. All fifty thousand tons or whatever of it—Slocum had no calculus for measuring an object that took up all dimensions before him—would ease slowly against Coggeshall Wharf and flatten his little sloop into shards no thicker than a matchbook and no one on the ship would even notice the impact.

Slocum's awe swelled into a dread almost superstitious in its fatalism. He saw the little boat's remains dragged down, one-dimensional, by the half ton of lead in its keel. He saw himself and Ralfie bleeding and flat as church plates as they slid into the cold water. Then logic stepped in and he told himself that the skipper and crew of the tug could see him and would not let that happen. Or at least, they would not let that happen on purpose.

The other side of the ship must be resting against the line of dolphins, and that, as he had suggested to MacTavish, was where the great ship would dock. Turning toward the wharf now, searching for witnesses, he noticed one man, then two, standing thirty feet down the wharf from him by the rusted bollards against which the bigger trawlers used to moor. A tall figure in a military cloak smoked a cigarette and gazed up at the maneuvering. These last details did not ease Slocum's panic or reduce the dread in him, because they meant the black ship was planning to tie mooring lines to his, to Slocum's, berth, bringing him more deeply into the web of forces and resistance that the captain had to deal with in docking. After all, though he might not wish to harm Slocum's craft, it would take only the slightest miscalculation of tide or wind or engine or winch for one end of the ship to drift too far from the dolphins. An error of only a few degrees, a single hawser snapped or inexpertly attached, would allow that monstrous hull slowly, ever so slowly, to drift unleashed across the space between the dolphins and the wharf and crush Slocum's boat. The ship must have a draft of forty feet, its keel lying only a meter or two higher than the bottom at low tide; its mast touched the clouds. It was probably full of bunker tanks and cargo holds into any of which you could fit eight of his own tiny craft. Slocum thought of rushing below and picking up the cat in one hand and the Project in the other. He would climb up to the wharf and start running inland, as far as he could, until the fact of his inefficiency and lack of ability to cope with waterfront forces would fade and thin and finally achieve unimportance.

He did not move. He was unsure if it was dread or panic or uncertainty or even a weird kind of confidence that stopped him. And now the tug was butting its buffalo-beard against the ship's side, and water exploded from under its stern. It was pushing away from Coggeshall Wharf, away from the sloop. Slocum felt a surge of warmth, of pathetic gratitude for that little harbor tug straining its guts out to keep his sloop safe.

From out of the darkness forward, then aft of the sloop, heaving lines were thrown. The eyes of hawsers as thick as a weight-lifter's arm smashed into the black water. Men in dark jackets appeared on the wharf up and down from where Slocum was moored, looping the hawsers' eyes over long-disused bollards. Winches hummed overhead. They must have been dragging hawsers on the ship's other side because the space between the little sloop and the great metal wall started to expand, slowly, like some fine, incremental equation.

"Hey, Slocum."

He started. A shape stood at the top of the ladder. It was too small to be MacTavish, and anyway the voice had been higher than his, and female. She had a thin face, dark hair, hands jammed in the filthy motocross jacket that Slocum had only once seen her take off.

"Cakes. Come down."

She made no move, just stood staring at the wall of ship that loomed over them both. The water gentled slowly. The winches continued to hum. The tug hooted, and Slocum jumped and felt embarrassed. Eventually he climbed the ladder and stood beside Cakes. The hawsers leading from ship to wharf were tautening now. The ship itself seemed to have stopped moving, though it was difficult to tell for sure, so thoroughly had distance been changed by the ship's domination of the waters between the invisible dolphins and the quay. Once, when the fog thinned, he caught a glimpse of a single funnel imprinted against the stars, generating a strong fan of smoke that was only slowly absorbed into the Milky Way.

"Shitgoddamn," Cakes said. "I can't believe it. I heard about it in the Tap but—"

"Shitgoddamn," Slocum agreed.

"How big you reckon that is?"

"I have no idea."

"Gotta have diesels big as a mountain."

Cakes also was obsessed with engines. She owned a clapped-out offshore-circuit racing monohull. It, too, was a former contraband runner, with two 500-horsepower gasoline engines. One of them worked OK and the other was permanently broken. There were more gasoline mechanics around than diesel engineers but no one seemed able to fix her engine so it would stay fixed. Part of the problem might have been that Cakes always ended up sleeping with the mechanics in an effort to ensure top-notch service for not much money and eventually, Cakes being Cakes, the engineering problem got tangled up with emotional issues and then Cakes was alone again and her engine still wasn't running right. At times like these Cakes realized she hated men and then she tried to sleep with one of the girls from Madame Ling's or any other female who showed up. No one knew for sure if Cakes really hated men or liked women and it didn't seem to matter, because what was clear about Cakes was that she was more interested in marine engines than sex or people. This was a characteristic for which in the last few weeks Slocum had come to have increasing sympathy.

A tall figure marched down the dock. It lurched over Cakes and Slocum. The visor of its hat dipped. There was a smell of whiskey, of cheeseburgers, the glint of eyes in a cavern of sockets. Cakes said, "Shitgoddamn," again.

"I told ye, Slocum," MacTavish announced balefully, "I even scryed the photo for ye. But would ye listen? Noooo. And noo look at yer wee boat." His arm flung out, taking in all of Coggeshall Wharf, the ship, the hawsers, the puny-ness of the sloop. "Noo look at it!"

A beep sounded. MacTavish, who held a tiny radio hidden in one large palm, put it to his ear, and straightened to attention. He swiveled and marched down the quay. His greatcoat flapped. Lights shone in the abandoned cement warehouse, just up-harbor from the processing plant. A couple of cars stood parked by one of the loading docks.

"You wanna coffee?" Slocum asked Cakes after Mac-Tavish had gone. "Or cognac?" He had slept with Cakes a couple of times soon after he got to Coggeshall Wharf, in the days when she thought he knew something about engines. He thought it would be nice to sleep with her again. They wouldn't have to make love, he thought, assuming that was an option—just hold each other in the deep V of his forward berth. Just warm each other's body and listen to the waves slap up the waterline. It would feel good to have someone to hold with a ship as big as that looming only a few meters away across the slip. It would be nice to hug someone in the aftermath of panic and the backcurrent of cognac; to kiss someone and not have to explain how emotions got tangled on the wharf.

Cakes looked at him for a few seconds. Everything he wanted to do with her and to her and all the reasons why she would and would not passed between them in that time. She said, "Thanks anyway, Slocum." To explain what had already been communicated, she added, "I might have company on the boat. Shaneeqwa," she added unnecessarily, and Slocum knew she wasn't really expecting Shaneeqwa, or no more than usual, it was just a fantasy that came in handy for situations such as these.

She shrugged deeper into her motocross jacket and left. A light wind off the harbor took the wing of her hair and threw it behind her. The same wind was wrapping around Slocum's jumpsuit and sending patrols down the cuffs and neck, and he was trembling slightly from the cold that rode the wind northeast. He stole another look at the ship—hell, with something that big, it was more like the look was all around him and he was just letting it into his eyes a little more. A square door opened far up the hull, letting out a wash of light, a snatch of music, an impression of warmth.

Slocum went below. The brass clock read 03:52. He got into his bunk. After only a few minutes he got out again. The thought of that monster in the same berth was too much for him to lie still. He peered out the porthole. The ship appeared closer but when he poked his head out the hatch, he realized that was due to the difference in perspective and it was where it had been all along. The docking crew had disappeared and the tug had moored farther south and put a line ashore. Thick hawsers led from wharf to ship's fairleads in a smooth arc interrupted by the vertical saucers of ratcatchers. A truck with a winged serpent painted on its side moved slowly along the abandoned warehouse and stopped at the base of a gangway. The gangway led from the concrete plug of pier joining wharf to dolphins, to the door in the ship's side. A small guardhouse had already been set up at the gangway's base. A deckhand on watch there said something to the driver, and laughed.

Slocum drank more brandy from the bottle and turned in once more. Ralfie snored. Slocum lay with his eyes open, watching the reflection of light off water dance through the portholes and across the deckhead above him. He knew he was tired because his thoughts were not holding form for long, and even the nameless dread that had stayed with him, if only in miniaturized shape, ever since he first saw the ship, was melting and breaking apart as he thought of other things: ratcatchers, Cakes; propellers, MacTavish. Walls that reached the stars; winged serpents. Eventually the dread stopped, changed gears, shifted into reverse. It moved back into the awe he had felt the first time he saw the ship. (Slocum rolled over and his eyes closed.) It warmed him as Cakes would not. It became a feeling almost of joy, the kind of excitement he'd had as a kid when he saw a piece of machinery so big and complex that he had no idea what it was, but which he liked anyway because it spoke of factors in the world that were greater and more powerful than his parents or school. He couldn't remember now what those things he'd seen had been—combine harvesters? jumbo jets? giant cranes? Objects that could change other objects in ways he might never predict, nor could his mother or father or the principal or anyone else.

SEVEN

COFFEE. ON A MORNING like this it was not a pleasure. It was not a ritual of the preparation of stimulants that imparted structure to the no-man's-land between dreams and consciousness. Nor was it a kind of liquid appreciation of the aesthetics of cargo and distance; of beans ripening on volcanic slopes in lands where people carried machetes and talked of passion as if it were a favorite cousin.

Slocum had drunk coffee from all of these perspectives; he knew what he was talking about.

What coffee was on a morning like this was a necessity of life. No, on a morning like this coffee *was* life. It was the key that unlocked the drivetrain that allowed you to move; it was a black alchemy that produced an elixir making more bearable the coming pain of the day.

Slocum sniffed at the steam rising from the percolator. Even the steam changed his perspective a little bit. If every morning, he reflected, was a balance between the flight into entropy and an iron chain of action, on a day like today only coffee made such balance possible. He poured the brew and took a gulp. Without java, he thought cheerfully, he would fall apart or implode. The different atoms and particles of his psyche would veer down into a killing density or scatter up like motes in the wind, leaving only an impression of matter, a remembered laughter, a fleeting sense that something had been here briefly and then had gone forever.

Slocum took another gulp. He closed his eyes tightly and opened them again. Despite the joe, moving would still be very difficult. Part of it, he figured, was simply not getting enough sleep, and part of it was the brandy; he must have drunk three or four cupfuls of the stuff before he turned in for good last night. A lot of it was the accumulated frustration of yesterday and the hangover from almost getting drawn into the Flash and the strain of pulling himself out of it.

That had been touch-and-go, and close escapes left scars.

And a lot of it was that goddamn ship.

Slocum got off his settee and stared out the porthole. Yesterday the view from this porthole had been a round sample of harbor: the water of his slip, the dolphins, the port's main channel, sometimes a white ferryboat. Because of the fog he could almost imagine that the sea lay beyond, for usually the harbor just got eaten away by the poor visibility until you had no horizon except the water.

But now what he saw was the greasy water and then a brief visible pantyline of bottom paint with a hieroglyph marking the ship's waterline and then the solid black wall of hull rising forever. In the light of morning the hull did not seem as solid and of a piece; he could make out welds, and curling trails of rust where the paint had flaked. But the immensity of something that entirely filled his porthole and the length of Coggeshall Wharf and then some still produced a bug of either excitement or dread, and that fluttered in him, despite the fresh coffee, much as it had before he had gone to sleep.

Slocum found the aspirin bottle and swallowed three

tablets. He had forgotten to replace his milk so he drank the brew black. It did not matter; he preferred it that way today, there would be less to buffer its impact. He slipped on his jumpsuit and workboots, opened the hatch, and climbed into the cockpit.

Well, maybe it did not take up half the sky, Slocum thought. The light of day brought a bow and stern into focus, and you could see it had a beginning and an end, even if the stern started so far aft of him, at the very beginning of the dolphins that protected Coggeshall Wharf, and the bow extended well beyond the down-harbor end of the wharf. Daylight too revealed intimate details of the vessel's structure, and like a woman who relied on the holism of makeup and fashion and hair to wreak her illusion upon the world, the ship did not seem quite so formidable when you could see the details: the rust he had noticed earlier, and a five-o'clock shadow of weed at the waterline, and the ropes fastening tarps to lifeboats, and a goosenecked vent twisted askew, and dozens of awkward companionways and ladders linking the accommodation decks, and the life rafts on the second highest deck, and gray streaks where the teak rail had weathered, and the way diesel smoke, way high up—maybe a hundred twenty feet above him—had smudged the funnel's trailing edge.

A helicopter shelter, just behind the funnel, had clearly been tacked on as an afterthought.

Slocum sipped his coffee. His neck hurt from gazing at the top decks. The ship was still very goddamn big. Its hawsers were multicolored and thicker than his mast and they hung like fallen trees across the berth, only a few feet over the water at the perigee. Because his mast rose forty feet over the hawsers at their lowest, he realized now he could not move out from under them. Which meant that he was trapped in his berth until the ship left; or unless he could persuade the captain to let go his mooring lines one at a time and let him out.

It was not an issue, Slocum told himself. The ship would leave long before he got his engine working. But the idea of being pinned in his berth by the hawsers doubled the feeling he'd had yesterday of being trapped by his sick diesel, by his inability to cure it. *He could not move.* That MacTavish had offered him the opportunity only twisted the feeling in him, made it dirty and his fault—so uncoupling its power.

Slocum sipped his coffee. It did not make him feel good or even excited to look at the huge ship anymore. He did not care if it belonged to the Syndicate or some other rich men's organization. The shape and distribution of the portholes clearly showed it was a passenger ship, built for transporting not cargo but a relatively small number of people, in luxury and at speed for as long and far as they cared to travel. He did not care to answer the questions the ship posed, like where had it come from? What was it doing here? When would it leave and where would it go and what did it look like inside?

So he stared up and to the right, at the Coast processing plant, and thought about getting ice. Looked down the wharf. A County Diesel truck was pulled up on the thin jetty that ran out to the dolphins. He looked automatically across the harbor, aft of the ship, but of course he could not see anything because of the ship's size; he could not see the Whaling City Marina.

And so the ship taught Slocum something. Because before it arrived he had thought he was cut off from the marina. He thought the fog and half mile of water that divided the two sides of the harbor were a barrier that completely separated him from Bird and Amy and the life they'd had before and all its histories. Now he realized that what separated you could also be seen as a link, if it was strong enough and old enough and if what came after separated you more. What had been a *half mile* now became "only" a half mile; a distance he could swim across, if he owned a wetsuit. Now even that half mile was taken from him. Slocum had always lived in or near small cities and he knew by instinct how relative distance was. A neighborhood was defined by the people you knew and how often you saw them and talked to them. If an easy bus line connected similar streets you could count people two miles away as being in your neighborhood, whereas the next street over, fifty yards distant, might be another town, off-limits because of a railroad bridge or a gang turf war or a simple difference in the quality of delicatessens.

What had happened here was the destruction of visual closeness and the sense that, even if he could not make them out individually, Slocum might discern his wife and child through the neighborhood they lived in. If something bad happened—a fire, the effects of a storm—he might notice immediately and go over. Without such proximity he was that much more a stranger, reduced to hearing what happened by rumor or by radio, like the rest of the world. Now that he could not see them, his only means of contact, in his mind at least, was to go there physically, which was no picnic. It involved either walking as he had the night before last, across the bridge, or the faster but more tiresome way: launching the dinghy, fitting its outboard, and motoring around the ship and across the open harbor.

It was like half of him being cut off from the other half, Slocum thought.

He climbed the ladder to the wharf. He had to step carefully to keep his coffee from spilling. He stared up at the ship with mixed resentment and determination. He was not going to let this thing get the better of him. He would keep the berth; and he would have his morning coffee amid the burn of fog and in a place from which he could see the marina.

Slocum walked down the length of the wharf. On the up-harbor end, around the concrete spur, more trucks had clustered. One of them was the County Diesel rig, one of the big ones, like the truck that had almost killed him yesterday. A panel truck from Vieira's Bakery stood behind it, with a van from a florist in the Bayview Mall, and another van marked with the name of a ship's supply firm down-coast. A couple of cars, bright new models, were grouped by the old Bone Cement warehouse, which paralleled this part of the wharf. The plywood had been taken off the windows next to what used to be the office doors. A man in officer's uniform came out of the warehouse and walked fast toward the jetty. A couple of men wearing identical jeans, denim shirts, and deck shoes laughed at something he said. The gangway had been raised so it hung ten feet off the jetty to prevent entry, like a lifted drawbridge; now it was lowered. The officer walked up the gangway, which was long enough to reach from the jetty, up the cruiser stern, and eighty feet along the ship's side to the doors, three decks and perhaps fifty feet up. Slocum made sure he did not slow, let alone stop, as he watched. He was not going to give this overbearing presence the satisfaction of obvious interest. Yet he could not prevent himself from being fascinated by the size of this thing, and intrigued by how it worked, as machine, as community, as threat, as instrument of travel, as creature—for he also saw it as something alive. The *Smuggler's Bible* insisted all human organizations were alive, over a certain threshold of size. It made sense that something as big and unitary as this vessel should follow the same rules of existence.

So he stepped carefully as he watched the officer disappear, as the gangway was raised again. Walked precisely over the cracked cobbles while his eyes traveled up the hull, two decks to the main working level, then up white-painted accommodation levels, one, two, three more decks, where a figure rendered small by distance leaned against the rail, looking down at the wharf. Dark, was his first impression; slight, wearing some kind of cloaky garment and a long white scarf that snapped in the wind; long hair that snapped also, fragile, he—

He tripped over a rusted cable that lay coiled like a dead boa in his path. Managed not to fall, hopping sideways without dignity to keep his balance, even saved his coffee without scalding himself too badly.

When he looked up again, the woman had gone.

He was sure it had been a woman, though he had no idea why. Her slight build, the long hair, cloak, scarf—all could have characterized a thin man, perhaps a man in poor health. Maybe the slight curve of her to windward where the breeze pressed close to her body had fostered his impression? He had a feeling she was drinking coffee as she looked over the Town; her arms rested in front of her as he would have done in holding a coffee mug on the teak rail. Surely a passenger, he thought. No steward would wear such clothes, not on the levels with big windows and views, where the dining salons and libraries must be situated. He did not know how he knew that the ship carried dining salons and libraries.

His earlier conviction that this was a passenger ship was reinforced, because it had so many accommodation decks, because it lacked the gantries and large cargo areas of a freighter, and bore no pipes or derricks as a tanker or a drilling ship would do.

Slocum skirted the jetty, continuing toward the end of the wharf. Cakes's circuit racer lay on the side of the breakwater marking the limits of the refurbished part of Coggeshall, surrounded by the plastic sausage-links of anti-pollution devices to keep gasoline from leaking into the harbor when she tested her engines. Which was a joke; the harbor was already thoroughly polluted by aniline dyes from the mills and PCBs from a plant upriver that made electronic components. The federal government had tried to clean it in the years when they had the money to undertake such a massive task, and had given up. A little gasoline probably would do no extra harm, were Cakes in an engine-testing mode; but for now the *Miss Slew IV* was battened down and silent.

Slocum continued on to the last slip on the wharf. It consisted of a couple of anchored barges, connected to the wharf by a gangway that sagged in every dimension. The barges should have been condemned long ago and at any rate should not have been part of Coggeshall, which had been renovated and made secure to accommodate a new industrial zone. The industrial park never happened; the Mall Zone in Bayview had sucked off all available investment. In any event, old Barboza, on the council, had insisted on keeping a fishing dock in the new and improved Coggeshall Wharf. Now the barges were clotted up with trawlers whose owners had defaulted on mortgages when the fishing went south. The banks had no use for draggers either so they just lay there, abandoned for the most part, silting up with weed and rust and cormorant shit. All except for the dragger Lopes had taken over. Above the waterline at least, Lopes's boat looked pretty good. He had windowboxes with geraniums growing out of them on the rail beside the wheelhouse. Slocum took even more care crossing the expanse of scabbed decks, corroded rigging, and abandoned gear till he got to the very end of the barges. There he stepped across the boats tied to each other at the end, getting as far out in the harbor as he could, beyond the ship, almost beyond the dolphins, sitting on the dogged-down hatch of a sterndragger called *Nostra Senhora de Santa Maria,* looking east.

Seagulls planed in a moderate wind, darting quick glances below, anticipating sludge. Down-harbor a squat black-hulled dragger with a whaleback bow sidled against the southwest wind to the processor wharf. Slocum did not have to see its name to recognize it. The boat was called *Valkyrie* and belonged to Lars Larsen. It was the only fishing vessel still working out of the harbor, and it was coming in to the Coast plant. Coast still bought the old Norwegian's fish, though no one knew why—they made their money not from fresh fish but from frozen blocks of seafood brought by truck from working seaports to the south.

Slocum looked at other things as he sat and sipped his coffee but always his eyes returned to the marina across the water. He thought, as he watched it, that the place looked the same as the first time he'd seen it. That lack of change always felt odd because much else had changed in his life, and in relation to the Whaling City Marina and the credit entity that was its core. But there it lay, starfiltered by mist, the tangle of rigging and masts, docklines and pilings, and the warped facades of the condo development behind, with the fuzz of sickened saltmarsh extending from it on both sides like the claws of a yellow-green crab. Behind the marina rose a jagged hairline of third-growth pitch pine and then the tower of an old-fashioned town hall and rooftops of suburbs farther south. He remembered seeing it like this across the harbor when he used to drive into Town looking for god knew what. Just restless, he thought, searching for a perspective different from the gleam of Arcadia and the expensive toys Bayview could offer.

He had not found it in the Town. One day he decided to look at the harbor from the other side. It was tourism, sheer tourism. There had been some goal to his drive: a park at the southern end of the eastern arm of the harbor, now surrounded by marsh. Someone told him the salt-marsh had been invaded by a weed growing wild from its origins as a bioengineered form of organic circuitry. Hackers were hiking the marsh, searching for clumps of the weed so they could build their own organic-memory tower. He had gotten lost as soon as he left the highway, and in trying to find his way back had wound up following a poorly maintained service road that ended at the gates of the condo community.

He had been about to make a U-turn when something caught his attention—was it the sign reading THE CONDOS AND MARINA AT WHALING CITY COVE, over which someone had painted INDEPENDENT CREDIT ENTITY—WELCOME TO THE FREE WORLD? Or had it been the bizarre aspect of those once-demure streets, now lined with misshapen cars and guerrilla gardens in which tomato plants powered like alien life? Or the sight of children left to run wild amid the love-apples and jalopies and rhythm from an electric bass sounding somewhere in the depths of that complex?

He did not remember now. Whatever it was, it had triggered his curiosity. He drove his car down the main causeway, slowly, wary of potholes and kids. Grownups watched him carefully. His car was a gleaming current-year fuel-cell sports model with one of those long pseudo-English hoods and chromed baffles. What he had paid for it would have covered the down payment on half of this complex when it was new. The causeway ended in a ragged village green where marina and condos touched. The docks in front and an office building on one side, boatyard sheds and a travel-lift on the other, compressed the rest of the space as in a sandwich. The filling was made of half-repaired boats, a couple of porches converted into cafés, unattended street booths, a station-wagon-cum-pancake-vendor, a rotted gazebo defended by slouching teenagers, and kites—kites everywhere; he learned later that this was unusual. It was Kite Day, and a lot of people joined the competition for best kite in a variety of categories (prettiest, most agile; ugliest, most destructive).

What had interested Slocum most of all was the density of people. He saw people in Arcadia, but they were separated by cubicles, linked electronically. They met in the flesh in knots of three or five at a time, as if obeying some law that prohibited public gatherings, though no such rule was on the books. In the residential sections of Bayview people moved by automobile. Outside the family circle they grouped only rarely, in chichi seafood or Tibetan restaurants that held twenty-five at most. Or they went to cocktail parties of fifteen people or fewer, where three-quarters of the guests immediately went online in any case. Only the children met regularly in large groups, in classes that (so Bayview laws demanded) could not exceed twenty students and were notable for their audiovisual aids, the Flash learning, the travels each child could take with a three-dimensional mask.

There had to be sixty or seventy people in this fake New England village square. It almost made him laugh out loud for a moment because the developers of the condominium complex so clearly had wanted to build a nostalgic forum out of thin air and all-weather plywood; and they must have failed, else why had they gone bankrupt? But the people here were squatters—had to be, feckless interlopers on abandoned property, no landlord would put up with what they had done. They had moved in and created, rent-free, exactly what the designers imagined happening for profit and according to their own tight rules.

Of course the place was a mess; the grass on the "green" knee-high, the fronts of well-built houses stove in or roughly extended to form workshops and bars. Paint flaked everywhere and the cars had holed mufflers that exploded like cherrybombs and smoked like fumaroles.

Yet people were doing things, and doing them together, even if a lot of the activity was maybe less productive than a businessman would have liked—too many people in bars, for example, or playing cards or gossiping or rebuilding boats or jalopies that should have been junked fifteen years earlier, or selling food out of kiosks that the Bayview Board of Health would have instantly burned.

Slocum parked his car and locked it. Immediately every boy in the square walked over to gawk at its exhausts and touch its chrome. He walked into a snackbar and drank a coffee that wasn't bad and ate a Portuguese muffin with beach-plum jam that was really good. People noticed him but didn't make it too obvious. It was cool outside; a woodstove crackled in one corner. Slocum found that simply leaning on the counter and watching people move around and call to one another made him feel less restless, as if something were happening here that could take him out of himself for a while. Could curb his impatience, and the feeling he'd been having more and more frequently of late, that he had missed a vital appointment, but had no clue as to where, or when, or with whom. The short-order cook chatted with him—he assumed Slocum was a volunteer for the ICE, which Slocum figured was the Independent Credit Entity listed at the entrance, and what the hell was that exactly? Some form of community organization, a relic from the drug populism of the last century? He finished his muffin and ran into trouble because the snackbar credit reader only accepted something called an ICE card. Which was how Slocum had gotten pulled into the whole thing, if you wanted to get technical about it. To pay for his food he had to register at the ICE office and arrange for a very expensive credit transfer from Outside to their boutique bank. The office was across the green, which was where he met Dark Denny, and how he got interested in the theory of Whaling City. And of course Dark Denny was curious about him, before he got interested in Amy; and everything had followed from that encounter.

Still, looking at the ICE now from this dilapidated dock, what he remembered most strongly from those early days was not the complicated stuff of involvement and excitement and deep structural change in his life. What he remembered was the coffee, and the taste of beach-plum jam, and looking at a bunch of people he did not know who argued with or ignored one another or did all the things humans did, half a hundred of them encompassed in the single frame of a snackbar's plate-glass window.

EIGHT

ON HIS WAY BACK Slocum examined the top decks of
the ship but saw no sign of the woman he had noticed earlier. A helicopter had appeared, moved out of its shed; a
mechanic checked its vital parts.

Slocum spotted the note as soon as he got back to the
sloop. It was jammed between the removable binnacle
cover and the flange of his compass housing. He knew instinctively what it was. In any event, no one else around
here left him notes. No one else had news for him, good
or bad.

Mr. Slocum. The replacement part for your
YQM20 Injector needle valve seating is available.
Its serial # is 1840059-QMD-M. Unfortunately
MarDyne no longer ships parts to retail distributors
or mechanics. It only ships to big outfits like
County. But as we know they don't repair small
engines. I will do a Netsearch and scout around.

No signature. Slocum crumpled the note in his fist and
tossed it into the harbor. A seagull dove, then dropped the

paper, shrieking angrily. Curiously, Slocum felt almost nothing. It was as if his attempt to find the Mechanic yesterday had not only filled the specific receptors demanding action for his boat and diesel and therefore from the Mechanic, but had temporarily satisfied the centers in him requiring forward motion of any kind.

Also, watching the ICE had brought up issues beside which even his engine and its problems no longer loomed large. The engine would get fixed someday. It would just take a little more time. Of course it had already taken too long, but that was the way boats and engines worked. Or so Slocum told himself, watching the crumpled paper jitter slowly up-harbor, driven by the wind.

After that, Slocum went to work, focusing on maintenance, which was not forward motion but felt more circular, like the gyre that kept a helicopter in place. He removed faulty switches from the electronics panel and noted their serial numbers. He figured switches were common enough that he would not have the same trouble with these as he'd had with the injector. He fired up the ECM-pak and Web-searched "marine supplies" and found an outfit called DownCoast Chandleries that stocked switches. He ordered a dozen, and a four-inch teardrop zinc as well, so he'd be ready when he found time for that repair.

Then he borrowed MacTavish's dolly and walked out of the secure area and down the tracks to the southern end of Coast Seafood. He charged two fifty-pound blocks of ice on his UCC and trundled them back, wrestling the dolly around junk and ruts and over sleepers to the wharf. When he got to his berth he broke out a sailbag and a line and lowered the blocks one at a time into the cockpit. From there he manhandled them down the steps into the cabin and through the hatch of his icebox.

He was hungry now. He toasted two slices of stale bread and ate one with jam only. Then he washed his hands and opened the Project once more.

He reflected that maybe if he did not fight the separation he might cope with it better. If he dwelled on their separate lives even a little, by taking up again this story that was destined to cross the harbor, to be given to Bird, to be harbored and cherished on the boat she lived on that was not this boat, then perhaps it would reinforce the strengths he knew lay at the heart of this situation. Because a proximity still existed, and never mind the ship or the visual context. Affection still bound them, no matter what guilt or anger had built up in the meantime.

He cut out more images. A dog that was nothing like Nidd, the dog in his story, but that might serve for one of Nidd's friends. A lithograph of a countryside with fine moving clouds would illustrate a tale in which Claire met a living wind that took the form of clouds when it wanted to speak to humans, and disappeared as breeze when it didn't. He had told that one to Bird when she was three. Somehow looking at the ICE for so long made it much easier to remember that time. They had lain side by side in her bed and as he told the story she dropped off to sleep. The feeling he'd had on nights like those, listening to his daughter breathe softly at his side, he knew was as close as he ever needed to get to utter peace, to contentment.

He found a pseudo-medieval etching that even included a dragon, in a tapestry in one corner of the dungeon keep; that was a triumph of sorts. He cut out a streetlamp, another dog, a window. He read through his notes, rumpling the papers in his haste. He glued three images in the right order for a story he had not yet transcribed. Moving faster and faster, he glued in a windmill that had no place in any of the stories. He stopped, aghast, staring one by one at the pages he had just finished. The clouds image was in the wrong sequence. The rest of the pictures were not really right for the tales they were meant to illustrate. They would all have to be cut out and glued elsewhere or replaced. He slammed the ledger shut, so hard that bits of flaking ancient paper were shot sideways by compressed air. Then he opened the book again, reluctant to let pages joined by glue and rage stick together, and left it to dry.

He removed his jumpsuit. He put on a clean pair of denim pants and a shirt and a commando sweater. The clothes he had worn yesterday and this morning were not dirty but he wanted fresh clothes now. From this impulsion he knew exactly what it was he was going to do that he did not want to form into words. So he did not form the words but instead brushed his hair and put on his reefer jacket and went up to the cockpit. He moved with confidence and strength. He felt as if he had stored up thoughts and desires about the direction he was going in and had sat on them for days without letting them travel anywhere. Now they had built up to the point where, with a click that was almost audible to him, they simply moved off toward the place they had to go, and all he had to do was come along for the ride. The lack of choice robbed these actions of a lot of their angst; or perhaps it was that he was moving fast enough that he did not have time to worry. What would probably happen in a few minutes was dramatic enough that it would change the givens he had to worry about anyway, making reflection, at this point, quite useless.

In the backstage of his brain he sensed that the force of this impulsion gave the lie to his earlier belief, that seeking out the Mechanic had freed him of momentum to move; surely this blind quest for action and change in him was merely the acting out of this force on a different plane? And so Slocum realized, in a bent sort of way, that what he was doing now was not only the result of his swelling feeling of separation from his family, but also a reaction to a sense of paralysis that took up more and more of the landscape of his life in this harbor. He climbed into the lazarette, unlashed the outboard he had so carefully stowed yesterday, and heaved it onto the deck.

He untied the canvas belts that kept the dinghy secured to the cabin roof and half lifted, half dragged it to the port quarter. It was a small boat, made of fiberglass with thwarts at the stern and midships. The glass was stained by harbor tar and worn away at the oarlocks and some of the inner lining was cracked, but the hull was still watertight. He lowered it gently into the water and climbed in. Then he lifted down the outboard and clamped it to the transom, lowering its propeller into the water and locking the engine in vertical position. He checked the fuel tank; it was half full. He unscrewed the vent on the tank cap and checked the ignition lead was on tight. He opened the fuel-feeder valve, opened the choke, gave it a third throttle, wound the starter cord around the wheel, braced himself against the stern thwart, and yanked the cord.

The engine howled. It vented a beachball-sized puff of violet smoke and began shoving the dinghy, tethered by its painter, into the side of Slocum's sloop. He leaped up, untied the line, and almost fell overboard as the boat took off under him. He pushed the tiller to starboard. The skiff scraped along the sloop's side, then reared away, toward the high black wall of the ship. Slocum fell backward into the bilge. Sitting up, he grabbed the outboard's tiller and adjusted course, moving to the center of the waterway separating wharf from ship. When he was back on track he scrambled onto the midships thwart and looked forward, his cheeks pink, hoping no one had seen that maneuver.

Even at five knots the dinghy took a long time to cruise the length of the great hull. Ducking as he passed under the lowest hawsers, Slocum peered at the curtained portholes, the water-discharge pipes that filed by overhead and to his left. When he got to the bow he cut in so close that the numerals indicating the ship's draft were as tall as he was against the red bottompaint. The prow overhead looked like a mountain about to topple over on him in all its hundred feet of curved steel. Slocum had visited cities to the south and this reminded him of the buildings he had seen there and how they blocked off the air, invaded sections of sky in a way that not even Arcadia Tower, for all its height and fantasy, was capable of. He wondered to whom the ship really belonged. It had no name or home port painted on bow or stern, which was unusual. It apparently carried no group of passengers, though this in itself meant nothing, since it might be between cruises. It also showed none of the swimming-pool parasols, the windscreens of shuffleboard areas, the huge orange brand names and floodlights that characterized ships hauling people for pleasure. And yet it was too vast to belong to an individual.

Slocum wondered if Lopes, for once, had known what he was talking about when he said it belonged to the Syndicate. If so, was the woman Slocum had seen a member of that group? He did not think so, somehow. She had seemed too young—more, she had seemed frail, in both bones and attitude, in a way no member of the board could afford to appear.

Then he was in the harbor chop and the dinghy was pounding eastward. The direction he had to look in drove the ship from his field of sight, as the task of keeping the boat on course while steering into bigger waves drove idle guesses from his mind. The mist was about average and the marina just visible beyond the scrim of humidity ahead. A foghorn sounded and a ferry detached itself from the Steamship Authority dock and picked up speed heading down the harbor. Slocum slowed further and steered northward, parallel to the channel, to give the ferry plenty of maneuvering room. He watched it slide by, rust painting brown ropes down its white sides, gray radar scanning, crewmen stowing line. The ferries were the biggest craft that regularly used the Town harbor but this one looked small compared to the ship. Its wake, though, was big enough to swamp the tiny dinghy and Slocum had to slow down even more and nurse his craft over the four-foot swells of black-green water. Even so, a gallon of harbor slopped over the side.

It began to rain, so lightly that it was hard to distinguish raindrops from the scud of seawater as the dinghy breasted the waves.

Ten minutes later he was entering the embrace of the bridge on one side, and the arm of marsh with its sponge of cattails and moss on the other, that protected the little marina. Shortly thereafter he reduced speed to a walking pace and entered the main channel of the ICE.

The main channel had nothing to do with the marina as it was originally conceived. A normal marina had neat rows of parallel docks with rafts attached at right angles against which client craft moored as primly as girls at a school dance. A normal marina catered to people with disposable income. It could afford to maintain pilings capped with white lead, and shaded lights every eight feet, and coiled water hoses and power lines and crew-cut dockboys in golf shirts and deck shoes.

But this marina had died and gone to financial hell and a few boats had stayed on in Hades. As word spread of free dockage, craft from up and down this section of coast had shown up to grab their twenty or thirty feet of pier. These were not pleasure palaces, the owners of which would never place their expensive toys in the risky legal territory of squatting. They were vessels, usually shabby, belonging to people who had cut their losses and decided to live on the water, often because they were in trouble of one kind or another and preferred real estate that disappeared easily. And more boats came; it seemed that every marginal maritime type on this stretch of shoreline heard of the marina within six months of Whaling City's bankruptcy. When they ran out of dock they started to raft together. As moorings were free to begin with, it was hard to deny access to latecomers on the basis of any right other than, perhaps, seniority. Anyway, seniority got its due, since the longer you'd been there, the closer you were to fresh water and power and shore. Pretty soon dozens, then a hundred, then two hundred boats were clumped into great concatenations of hull and line that extended from the docks like branches from a spruce. By this time the pilings were starting to rot and the docklights were burning out and rafts were coming adrift. Two years after the first squatters showed up, the Town harbormaster condemned the marina as unsafe, and it was true that if a hurricane hit head-on it would have turned the whole shooting match into kindling and driven it onto the marsh. But the Town was unwilling to allocate funds to arrest everyone and impound and store their boats as the law required. And soon enough people began to get together on their own to discuss sharing heavier moorings, or access to fresh water, or building a system of rafts that might survive a storm. Some of the pilings were repaired, and new chain was purchased to link the rafts to anchors or solid ground.

Despite these improvements, it was still an incredible maze of crossed anchorlines, tangled rigging, and mismatched bows, sterns, masts, cabins, docklines, clotheslines, antennas, radar, and windmills that Slocum edged his dinghy into that afternoon. It felt to him then as it felt to him always, like crawling through underbrush in the deep woods. Only this underbrush was of oaken bowsprits and stainless-steel cable, of nylon sails and caulking compound, of manila vines sheltered by the limbs of booms. Instead of pine and grass and moss what you smelled in this forest was tar and paint and the sharpness of fiberglass wax. There were bad odors too, stuff that was the underside of living on the water: fetid holding tanks, charred barbecue grills, rotting barnacles, spilled diesel, the gas of a sickened marsh. But all in all Slocum liked this forest, mostly because it was inhabited by people the way a forest was lived in by animals. Two men whom Slocum recognized, and a woman he did not, argued and drank on a converted lifeboat. Over a horizon of wooden sloops he saw De Vere, the metal-sculptor, winch welding equipment into the cockpit of his patrol boat. An ex-cop named Wayne grilled pork chops on the stern of a one-ton racer. A woman sang invisible and off-key from the galley of her ancient Hatteras. Someone said, "Hey, Slocum," in a surprised but friendly tone, and Slocum turned around and missed whoever it was because he was already past the boat the voice had come from. Among the details, kids screamed, appeared, vanished. You could track their urgent games by the orange of life jackets, which were as ubiquitous here as diapers. The rain put a sheen on marine aluminum, cut silver geometries on the thick black water.

At the pink cabin cruiser he turned starboard, into a narrow canal consisting mostly of sailboats. Perhaps three-quarters of them were wooden and old-fashioned and their bowsprits and dolphin-strikers made navigation even harder, and he slowed down as far as his engine would go, the carburetor gasping for air, remembering how hard it had been to steer the sloop down these channels. Merely the memory of it shrank his scrotum, and his heart beat faster, though the dinghy was maneuverable enough to thread its way easily around the flags and sticks of this maritime slalom. Finally he turned left at the J-boat, noticing with sadness that the yacht's varnish was badly peeled and the wood underneath had tanned to a dark gray.

Six boats down from the varnished sloop lay Dark Denny's catamaran.

Slocum cut the engine. As it died he gave the hot metal a pat. The outboard was the reverse of his diesel; it was tiny and always started right up and kept running until he chose to shut it off. It needed no spare parts. Slocum sometimes fantasized that the engines of his life ran in a closed system and the sole reason the outboard worked was that the diesel did not. If that was true, he wondered why he had not yet enjoyed such correspondences, such benefits of balance, in his personal life—then the dinghy was next to Denny's boat and he had no more time for fantasy. He steered his little boat into the cramped water-alley between the catamaran and the Tahiti ketch she was moored beside to port, and came to rest in a cradle of snublines and bumpers and springs, and ropes holding sunken buckets of beer or kids' crab pots. He tried to keep the skiff from scraping the sides of the two larger craft. He still had a fair amount of way on and the gunwale ran a short scar down Denny's gray paint. Slocum grabbed the standing rigging, stopped the skiff, fumbled for the bowline. His heart was banging harder. He felt a little bit like he had when he was about to throw up outside the Metropole 4th Dimension. A baby wailed, a couple of boats up-channel.

Movement happened in the cockpit above him. No transition: Suddenly Amy was there, as she had not been there a second before; staring down from the catamaran, the long auburn hair hiding half her face as it habitually did, her head cocked a little to the left. It was how she held herself when shocked, and coming to grips with a situation that she already knew would require too much precious energy to sort out.

"Slocum," she breathed.

"Hi," he said. It was a stupid thing to say. Amy was always impatient with what she called "froth"—ritual forms of address, unmeant invitations, pressures of contact no one believed in.

She brushed back her hair. Slocum wiped drizzle off his face, and looked toward the bow of Dark Denny's cat. It was in its usual lousy state, deck covered with cormorant shit, water barrels and propane tanks lashed here and there, the nylon halyards green with mold. He wondered vaguely—as he always did when contemplating Denny's boat—why someone so convinced of Hawkley's inevitability should ignore the *Smuggler's Bible*'s precepts in other matters. But Slocum did not really notice the details. He was avoiding looking at Amy so she would not read from his expression how weird he felt. Seeing his wife like this filled him with so much tension that everything around him seemed to react, the way a broken power line would turn railings into humming snakes that could explode bushes a hundred yards away. The sky, he felt, moved in and out; the black water of the marina pulsed with overload.

"Bird's not here," Amy said, "anyway."

"I just," Slocum said.

Amy turned aside. Slocum looked back at her. Amy's nose was slightly curved, her neck was long, her eyes dark. Her lips were set in the neutral, straight position they assumed when she had all her positions locked down tight. She wore her glasses—she must have been reading when she heard him. The harbor still keened and the sky still pulsed but Bird was not here and Slocum knew that nothing between them was going to change, on this day at least.

"Where is she?"

"Where do you think? It's a school day."

"I thought she came home for lunch."

"There's a cafeteria now. She hasn't come home for lunch in three months."

Slocum thought about this. Once he would have known about every play date, every quarter-hour alteration in bedtime, every minute variation in his daughter's schedule.

"I didn't know," he said. Amy frowned: more froth.

Dark Denny's face appeared in the hatchway. It was a pleasant face, at least Slocum had always thought so; long, with lines that smiled easily and worried a lot. He had eyes of a cowlike gentleness that were almost the same color as Amy's.

"Oh, hi, Slocum," he said. He glanced at Amy. "I'll leave you two alone."

"We don't need time alone," Amy said quickly. Denny nodded, and retreated down the hatch anyway. He was learning, Slocum thought. Only a month ago Denny would have wanted them all to sit down and have a coffee and talk things out. Amy was wearing a light sweater that was Denny's and too big for her. Now she pulled it up to cover her neck.

"I just," Slocum said, and stopped again.

"It does no good to 'just,' " Amy told him. "It does no good to treat this off-the-cuff, Slocum. You feel unhappy, you get into your boat and drag your unhappiness over here. Well it's not fair to us, it's not fair to Bird, I'm glad she's not here."

"I have a right to see her."

"That's not the point." Amy looked straight at him now. Her mouth was even flatter, so neutral it could have split an oak. Her eyes had gone ocher as they did when she was angry, or about to come. She crossed her arms under her breasts and shrugged her shoulders and Slocum recognized what her body was saying: It was still chilly. "Bird doesn't want to see you right now. You're too much for her to deal with. She's had too many other things changing in her life."

Slocum looked aft and noticed Bird's pink bike lashed to the stern rail, next to the grill. It still had the Barbie streamers he had put on for her last birthday.

He looked farther aft, into the tapestry of marina rigging, at the shuttle of fog weaving grayness in and out like a loom. It would do no good to argue with Amy. Slocum had bargained down Web art directors and cyberserf agents the world over, using the logic of commerce like a scalpel, cutting tough deals against people who palavered for a living. But when it came to arguing with Amy he always felt as if the logical propositions he relied on turned to jelly and he was lost and fumbling and ineffective in his discourse. It never stopped him from trying; it simply made failure predictable. So he said, "You know, you caused this particular change. I mean, not being able to see her," and she shot back, "Yeah, but who brought us here? Who turned our world on its head? Maybe we were blind, Slocum, maybe we were stupid, I see that now, you know I do; but things were safe and easy until you changed everything."

"I wasn't trying to—"

"You never tried to." She looked at the harbor. "I'm trying to make the best of a lifestyle you forced me to choose. And so is Bird. But she just cannot deal with your unhappiness right now."

"I'm not trying to make her unhappy." He was looking at the harbor too. The debate was losing steam. It always happened this way—Amy crushed his arguments, then they both lost interest. In Bayview they would be standing in the kitchen at this stage, staring at the pocket vineyard. He had grown to hate grapes by association.

"I'm trying to protect you, too," Amy said more softly. "You're too damaged now, you don't know what you're doing, it confuses us too much."

"Amy—"

"Maybe in a couple months. Maybe at Christmas. You know?" She still wasn't looking at him. "Just leave us alone for a while. We'll all know better how to handle this."

"But I want to see her."

He said it despite himself. Both Amy and he knew the discussion was over but this came from somewhere deeper than the dynamics of debate. It was an expression of pure need, of the sense of great wrongness that engendered that need. Amy glanced at him, and for a second her mouth changed shape, and her hand went to her throat. For an instant Slocum thought that maybe, maybe something had altered shape, maybe Amy's resolve or anger or both had weakened since he had last argued with her, so that the power and rightness of his desire to see his daughter could slip through her defenses and turn other locks; which in turn would slide back bolts. Maybe then the high force of all that attracted them to one another as a family would click back in, and what was wrong and unnatural, like not seeing Bird, would vanish; and what was right would be allowed to achieve its just value, like a capsized sailboat coming back to even keel.

She turned her head, crossed her arms tighter. Another ferry passed down the middle channel, heading north this time, toward the Authority dock.

The ferry's wake reached the marina. Slocum watched the familiar chain reaction. The outer phalanxes of boats lifted and swayed. As the waves got closer, the nearby masts and superstructures began to lift and roll while the boats that had lifted earlier rolled the other way and settled down. Denny had been one of the pioneers of Whaling City and the wake took a while to reach his craft. When it did, all around them the boats rose, pulled to one side then the other, rubbed and stretched their lines and creaked piteously. The baby stopped crying. Bilge pumps started up, water splashed. Then, not so suddenly, the boats stopped moving and everything was as it had been before. Amy said, "You should go now," and he nodded and untied the line he had looped over the cleat and began pushing his dinghy out of the crack between the two boats.

Amy called, "Wait a second."

He looked up. His heart was pounding again. She climbed down the hatch, then reappeared with a sheaf of papers.

"I've been meaning to send this on, it was forwarded from Bayview. I'm sorry."

He nodded again. He took the mail, half of which was paper and half the nubs of minispindles that you read by slotting them into your computer. His impulse was to throw it all over the side—none of the bills and relationships of his old life had much relevance anymore—but it would be a gesture that she would have contempt for and rightly so. He wedged it in the belt of his pants and refastened the reefer jacket. He shoved the dinghy clear and pointed the bow down the narrow canyon of boats, toward the first bend in the channel, toward the harbor.

NINE

A LONG WAY AWAY, somebody called for help.

He called on a circuit shared by ancient servers and cables and node links. His voice was patched through pirate transmitters, mobile phones, and multiple relays bought in chunks from satellite wholesalers who, for a big enough cut, would not check too closely into some of the parties involved.

He called on a Wildnet named Staring November 933.7, though the name didn't matter, it would be changed within a week, ten days at most—as would the radio frequencies, the Web addresses, the transmission times, the FTPs and coding, the whole system of illegal routing and patching that allowed communication to happen, unmonitored and thus illegal, on the dark side of the worldnet.

The transmission faded. The voice link was poor but Slocum had heard something in the man's tone that spoke of desperation, of a threat real and great. "Get us out of here," he had said in accented English. "They have stopped Jeanne's group and [undecipherable] pinned down and Ensevli is burning."

The voice link faded. Slocum touched the keys of the

jambook computer that was the heart of the ECM-pak. The ECM's guts fitted into an aluminum suitcase that was meant to be as portable as a simple laptop. The smuggler who owned the sloop before Slocum had screwed the top of the suitcase to the ceiling over the chart table. By unlocking the clasps, the monitor swung open in front of the operator as he sat at the navigation station. The keyboard was wireless and thin and could be placed anywhere.

Slocum hit "back" to return to Staring November's flight page. The radio frequency on which the call for help had gone out was the third of seven on this Wildnet. It was listed only as "emergency callup," with the nearest URL in Sierra Leone. This meant nothing, since a Wildnet link could literally circle the world twice, hitting a dozen different countries and twenty different PCs as it was patched from link to link. It was one of the reasons Wildnets were hard to track.

Slocum chose another callup Web address. This link was fast and First World and had no voice component. A graphic surged across the ECM's small screen. It showed a fantastic jet aircraft from whose cockpit cartoon bubbles appeared that contained the messages being sent. *No drops on Rita next week,* one bubble, labeled Soupy, said, then vanished with the noise of a wave collapsing. *Rita's ready,* another bubble, called Ferret, answered.

Soupy reappeared. *Victor's late,* he commented, *we'll have to wait for the next window.* Pop went Soupy, for good this time, followed an instant later by Ferret.

It was smugglers' traffic, Slocum figured. Much of what Slocum had seen on Staring November had to do with contraband. It was usually boring, vague references to times and places and schedules, but occasionally something more urgent would crop up: an arrest, or a change in the patrol routes of military satellites or surveillance planes that shook the whole system by which stimulants or pirated spindles or rocket-propelled grenade launchers were skipped from one part of the planet to another. Sometimes there would be a reference to a specific geography: temperatures twenty below zero, an airstrip built of mangrove logs, heavy wind from typhoons. That was what Slocum listened for. In the absence of movement from his own boat he could at least vicariously enjoy the travels of other people, in aircraft and cars with hidden compartments and boats like Cakes's that tore the ocean the way a bandsaw ripped laminate.

This afternoon the smuggling traffic held little of interest to Slocum. He had switched on the ECM when he got back to give him something to do so he would not have to think about Amy or what she had said or that glimpse of Dark Denny or just the feeling of being back in the ICE. He knew damn well he was avoiding the issues all this raised and that it was unhealthy to do so. But the grace period that started in the Sunset Tap was over; the tiny psychic respite that his brain, through some transient twist in chemistry, had wangled itself was played out. Now it felt as if, on the mountain of frustration and imbalance built up within him over the last few weeks, the visit to the ICE had constructed another, equally bitter mountain. And he was just not big enough or tall enough and his stomach and brain did not have room to take in all this misery or process it right now.

What he really wanted to do was escape into somebody else's world, to a place, like the transmissions of smugglers, where the givens were dramatic and lethal enough to force close attention, even from those who only eavesdropped. But the Metropole had done a number on him—even as he cruised Wild, the memory of his revulsion was coming back, fully as strong as his need for relief. And that was good because it meant he now felt no more than a passing lust for the quick shots of Flash that the Wildnets threw at you.

Here, for example, the jet that carried Soupy and Ferret

began to turn and bank and zoom through cumuli and over jungles thick with ruined temples. Then it rocketed through a hole in the cloud cover into the dank indigo of space, and vanished north of Orion's Belt. He felt only a brief pang when it happened and even that was partly because of the resemblance to *Wanderbird* and how she had started her journeys. It would have been different, no doubt, if instead of watching the screen he were watching this through a virtual-reality headset, but he was not.

Slocum flipped through all seven channels of Staring November, looking for the purple icon of voice link. In the twenty minutes he had been cruising Wild only that call for help had engaged him, had pulled his attention the way he wished to be pulled. Only that tiny opening into a world where something so fierce and deadly was occurring seemed to match the enormity of loss he felt once again inside him; only escape might mask the prospect of that loss growing until it took him over and killed all tendency toward movement. And he got lucky, if you could call it that; he had almost given up when something scratched in his earphones and the violet icon glowed.

A word, indecipherable against the background of static, was repeated twice. Then, in the same accented English, a phrase in clear: "... hundred civilians or more. And also the sick ... the tunnels, and the Apaches are coming in ... the Apaches. Oh, the fire."

Static again.

"... out for nine—"

Static came back. This time it was even and unchanging and it continued until the ECM automatically broke the link.

Slocum's breath was coming fast. He was not thinking about Amy or Bird or Dark Denny. He was imagining a tunnel full of women and kids and old people. He saw helicopters sending in their wire-guided rockets that pumped flammable chemicals and shrapnel into confined spaces. He was imagining the loss of blood and the loss of emotion in the split second between fire and darkness. He clicked back and forth across the seven channels.

On channel 6 a different matrix appeared on the monitor, with a pink window in the middle against which short sentences scrolled almost continuously:

PLIVDA. DO YOU THINK HE OPERATES IN THE TWIN CITIES
DONKEY. HE MIGHT HE'S ALL OVER
ROL99. DO YOU KNOW HE CAN DISGUISE AS ANY RACE EVEN
MINNESOTAN?
BET-E. HAVE YOU CHECKED OUT THE NEW GATSBYKILLER
WEBSITE?
DESTRIKTO. PLIVDA, DO YOU LIVE IN ST PAUL
DONKEY. OLE BLUE EYES IS BACK
ROL99. LOL, DONK

Slocum noticed for the first time, on top of his window, the words gatsbykillrchat@talksites.com blinking in lime-colored font. The scrolling continued, relentless.

PLIVDA. DESTRIKTO, WHO WANTS TO KNOW
DONKEY. TRUE FACT
BET-E. GATSBYKILLRFANS.COM

The sloop rolled to starboard, and did not roll back. Slocum had lived long enough on a boat to know what that meant. A roll back and forth was a normal event caused by wake from ferries or chop kicked up by an easterly wind. A one-way roll meant that someone had stepped off the ladder and onto his boat. The sloop leaned more to that side and still did not roll back; a second visitor had come aboard.

Slocum took off his headphones. He felt an irrational rage against whoever had set up the Gatsby Killer chatroom. He knew Wildnets were simply ad hoc groupings of individual computers set up as servers, with short-term or fake licenses and pirate wireless to frustrate surveillance for as long as possible. He knew they ran on secondhand equipment and were notoriously prone to failure or weak signals. This allowed stronger, legal transmissions functioning via links on the same frequency—like talksites.com—to break in to Wildnet transmissions. The Sierra Leone patch he had heard, fraught with static, was a prime candidate for such intrusion.

It didn't matter. While Slocum was avoiding thinking about Amy it meant he could not blame her for the back-logged emotion in him. But, because humans were trained in cause-and-effect, he needed to blame someone for the blockage. He could not blame the diesel or the Mechanic for this one. He could, however, blame gatsbykillrchat@talksites.com for breaking in to a message as full of fear and need as any he had ever heard.

Slocum quit Staring November's temporary homepage and clicked off the modem and cellphone components. He left the receiver on, tuned to WFDO. The plaints of *fado* took up softly where the images and messages had left off, from the corners of the cabin where his speakers hid. *O namorados da cidade.* A container ship announced its ETA for a port a hundred miles away. Slocum got to his feet, feeling as if he had just taken an aborted trip on *Wanderbird,* or on some other sort of magical machine that you boarded by sitting at the nav station and that turned you into strongforce and shot you instantaneously to the Antarctic or Jaipur or the Cabrini Rings of Saturn and just as quickly—too quickly—returned you to where you were sitting. The feeling was about a fifth of the strength he used to get from the Flash but that was partly why he could allow himself this small travel via Wildnets. Anyway, this afternoon the Nets' deficiencies, like their attractions, were of tiny importance compared to what he really wanted to ignore. And now even the compulsion to evade had to defer to the immediate problem of finding out who stood on his deck.

Slocum slid back the hatch. A man stood against the fog. He wore a dark blue and quite fashionable monkeyjacket and a black tie and blue pants. A blue officer's cap was pinned neatly to his waist by one elbow. He had sunken eyes and a thin mustache and big nose and jaw that seemed to aim upward even when he was looking down the hatch at Slocum; a man in touch with vectors, a man in two worlds, Slocum thought; or someone who wanted to give that impression. Slocum recognized him vaguely. Shoulderboards with three bars denoted a rank that on airlines mean copilot and that probably meant the same thing on a ship. Slocum was sure he had seen him at the gangway of the huge vessel now looming like a mist-repressed psychosis over Slocum's right shoulder. The fog had thickened as it usually did toward evening. The ship's portholes burned in the false dusk.

Oddly, the woman behind was dressed similarly to the man. She had on the proto-uniform many women in Arcadia Tower wore to symbolize both their adherence to and defiance of a male business ethic that stole its symbols from dead armies. What this uniform did specifically was signal inclusion in a corps of females within the male culture, who used the tools and power forged by men at least in part to further the interests of their gender. Instead of rank boards, she sported on her shoulders two red stars fanciful enough to conjure images of an older Russian Empire.

She did not have the posture of a soldier. She stooped slightly, like a cautious marsh bird, peering well ahead of her flight path with popping eyes. Her hair was set in gel and savagely drawn back. Her eyebrows moved constantly. She had long fingers and a mole on her neck. Her lips were full and generous, though Slocum knew she was thin and tightly audited inside. Her name was Vera Consalves, and she was one of three selectpersons on the board that ran the Town. When she saw Slocum she stooped farther, ducking around the binnacle and the officer, to stand in front of the hatch.

"May we come aboard?" she asked, neatly poaching jargon privileges from the man beside her, as well as undermining what authority he might have arrogated by standing first in line.

Slocum said nothing. He stepped back into the cabin. He knew why they were here; there was only one reason both Vera and the ship's officer would bother visiting him. The knowledge did not improve his mood. But his father had always insisted that anyone who came to your door who was not an actual enemy should be welcomed, asked inside, offered coffee. Sometimes Slocum remembered his childhood as an endless succession of plumbers, gas inspectors, and mailmen, as well as the mothers of brides who came for business with his father, all sitting around the chromed kitchen table with cups of coffee they did not really want, confused to distraction by hospitality. When both visitors were standing on the cabin sole he motioned them to the settee and switched on the main saloon light. Belatedly, he dragged Ralfie off the settee cushion and checked quickly to make sure he had not thrown up on the upholstery or left a string of fish guts for the visitors to sit on. Ralfie, making hawking sounds, limped off to the forward cabin.

"This is Mr. Slocum," Vera told the officer, opening a jambook computer. The officer was looking at the nav station. He took in the ECM, glowing on standby, and the hard drive for the Virtual Navigator. "This is Matt Zurbruegge—he's first mate on the ship."

"Would you like coffee?" Slocum asked.

"No," Vera said. Slocum could tell the mate had been

about to say "yes." Now he looked at Vera for a hint of what to do.

"It's still pretty hot," Slocum said.

"We can't stay long." Vera touched a joystick on her laptop.

"I'd like some." The mate looked directly at Slocum for the first time. He had shiny dark-gray eyes, like semiprecious stones; the kind crows collected, Slocum thought. Vera sniffed and avoided looking at Slocum, and fiddled with her computer while Slocum warmed up the percolator. She waited till the pot was steaming before saying, "Mr. Slocum." She flipped her joystick for assistance. "You were officially notified two days ago by Mr. MacTavish, the wharf security manager, that you would have to move your vessel to make room for the ship. You did not do so."

Slocum poured coffee into a blue mug and placed it on the table in front of the mate.

"The ship, obviously, came in anyway, but you, uh, impeded the vessel's movement by not moving. We could have had you moved, of course—I'm not sure why MacTavish did not have you moved."

"MacTavish did not have me moved, Vera," Slocum said slowly, "because this is my slip."

"This is a Town slip." She spoke sharply. "This is Coggeshall Wharf, which is a designated redevelopment area. You only rent space."

"I rented it for a full year." Slocum refilled his mug. He poured smoothly and evenly. He kept his tone smooth as well. "I have a lease. It refers to this slip specifically. It does not give the Town the right to evict me except for nonpayment, or other nuisance clauses that do not apply here." He was talking like a Town lawyer, Slocum realized. He was, with some success, locking his emotions away in a strongbox so that outside the box he could fit together clear arguments to further his interests. For the second time in two days he was vaguely surprised by his ability to revert to a stage of life that, before and after he quit it, and even sometimes when he was in the middle, had felt like a foreign country to him.

The mate took a sip of his coffee. He raised his eyebrows. "This is good coffee," he said.

"There are practical considerations," the mate added. He spoke English with a clear diction that would be easy to understand over the radio and that sounded entirely school taught. Slocum wondered what his country of origin was. Like the ship's, his homeport was notable by its absence. "As you see," he continued, "we have had to rig spring lines fore and aft of your vessel. We tried to be careful but you never know what can happen." The mate opened his hands and closed them as if to describe all that could go wrong in the process of caring for a ship. Slocum wondered if this was some form of veiled threat and decided it was not. A lot could go wrong in docking, that was the truth of it. And the mate did not seem a man for whom subtlety was a big component of life.

Vera looked at the coffeepot. Slocum thought she probably wanted some, now that it was ready and sanctioned by the mate, but was too proud to contradict herself. Then she looked at the mate, clearly wanting him to finish so she could get on with the business of clobbering Slocum and his boat with official pronouncements. The mate sipped his coffee.

"There is a hurricane coming up the coast," he added.

"There is always a hurricane coming up the coast," Slocum said.

"True. But the computer model for this one runs it pretty close to this harbor."

"The models belong to Flash corporations," Slocum said. "Flash corporations have a vested interest in getting people worried. People who worry about hurricanes spend hours on Flash networks to see if the storm will hit them. They buy plywood and supplies and flashlights from advertisers. They watch Web footage of waves breaking docks, and the wind pulling off roofs, and traffic lights swinging in the wind. Ads for home insurance. Interviews with grannies in high-school emergency shelters."

"You think the model is wrong?" The mate sounded genuinely surprised.

"I think the predictions, shall we say, err on the side of prudence by a factor of about ten."

"If I remember right," Vera said brightly, watching her tiny screen, "you used to work for a Flash corporation. X-Corp Multimedia," she added, glancing at the mate for longer than seemed necessary.

"That's how I know these things," Slocum agreed equably. He remembered what Lopes had said in the Sunset Tap. "If I remember rightly," he added, then stopped. The fact that he wanted to throw Vera's words back at her was an indication that the airtight bulkheads keeping arguments separate from emotions were beginning to leak. But these bulkheads, he reminded himself, were partitions custom-built for Arcadia only. He had left Arcadia, and Bayview, so he could think and speak without reference to boxes like these. "If I remember rightly, Vera, you worked for X-Corp too. If you know what I mean."

She looked down at her computer and sighed, as if this task, already too menial for someone of her stature, was becoming even more of a chore. It was only a little sigh, though it could be interpreted in many ways. But it broke what discipline remained in Slocum's thought and discourse. The wash of mixed dialects, of emotion and argument and memory, swirled and blended into one great linguistic group of refusal. If he had been resolute not to move his boat before, Slocum felt he was a thousand times more determined now. Vera could threaten him with legal Armageddon, the mate could offer to let all umpteen thousand tons of his ship drift casually against the side of his sloop, he would not move. He would not move until he was ready to move, and leave Coggeshall Wharf under his own steam.

"You would only have to shift fifty meters," the mate added, gesturing vaguely to the east. The onyx eyes, which had been aimed at Slocum, flicked down at his coffee mug. It was empty. "If you know what I mean," he added, and almost smiled.

"You could come right back," Vera said, "soon as the ship leaves." She had been staring at his bookshelf. Now she looked at Slocum again. Her gaze seemed the product of great internal pressure. Slocum remembered Vera from X-Corp Christmas parties, to which all the selectpersons, as well as Representative Geary, usually came. She had always seemed poised and charming and without foundation; one of those people who talked a great deal and the more they talked the less, you realized, they were actually able to do.

Vera kept looking at him. Slocum thought now that there was foundation to her, and it was based on what the *Smuggler's Bible* talked about, which was how power was sucked up by large organizations that used people like Vera to do what they wanted. The book said this made those people twisted and unhappy because they had to accomplish unnatural acts for the "orgs" and in the end they never got back, in power or money or anything else, as much as they put in.

"I told MacTavish," Slocum said, "I'm telling you: This is my slip. I signed a lease with the Town. I will not move. And if you try to do something weird through the Town," he added carefully, "like change the status of the wharf, I think you might have problems with Barboza."

The mate looked at his mug again.

"Thanks for the coffee," he said.

"You want some more?" Slocum asked. He was feeling good; he was feeling almost entitled. Vera had tried to pull something on him. But he still had information about her and about the Town and information was power. He had used that power and Vera had listened.

Vera shut down her computer and slid out of the settee. The mate handed Slocum his mug. Slocum said, "Did that woman send you? The one on the ship, I mean." The mate replied, "I don't know what you are talking about," and followed Vera up the companionway—then stopped, abruptly, his head butting Vera's ass as she halted and leaned back into the cabin. Slocum waited for her to say something. She glanced at Slocum, then at his saloon: at the settee, at the forward cabin with the sheets rumpled and Ralfie sitting bunched in the middle of them, sniffing his own vomit; at the screen of the ECM jambook, glowing secretively to itself in the nav station.

Her eyes popped so hard it seemed they must have some material effect on the softer objects in his living quarters.

But Vera said nothing. She simply stopped looking, and turned, and climbed the rest of the companionway, into the cockpit. Because of the vagaries of tide the sloop was hanging away from the wharf, and she waited while the first officer trod on one of the sternlines, pulling the vessel tight onto the pilings, before stepping gingerly onto the ladder and climbing back to solid ground.

TEN

AFTER THEY HAD GONE, Slocum cleaned the coffee mugs and wiped the saloon table and swept the deck and then mopped it. Ralfie jumped off his bunk, yowled, limped up the companionway, and disappeared. Slocum mopped up Ralfie's puke, wiped the sheets, put them in the overfull laundry bag, and remade the bunk.

As he worked, the brief sentiment of power he had savored earlier disappeared. Slocum, ten months gone from Arcadia, realized he had forgotten one of the more basic rules: In situations where players in similar positions of power-scarcity shifted their positions in secret, one must never show what weapons one held until it was necessary.

He had hit Vera with what he knew about her political alliances and the alliance structure in Town Hall and now she knew what he hoarded in his arsenal of options and it had not bothered her. Slocum still thought she was the kind who talked as a substitute for real power; if she did not talk when she left, did that mean she had gained power over him? Worse, did it mean that she was used to power enough to remember the rules of using it as Slocum had not?

After Vera and the mate had disappeared he found they had kidnapped with them the rest of the sentiment Slocum had discovered when MacTavish visited him; that Coggeshall Wharf had, without his being aware, acquired the shine and soft corners of home.

Now Slocum felt the wharf was just another part of the world, a place where the fog leaked everywhere and steel rusted fast and everything tended away from softness and into jagged corners and sulfurous smells. Now it was just another place that he could, and must, leave behind.

His sloop, on the other hand, had taken up the slack. To Slocum his thirty-five-foot vessel had suddenly clothed itself with even more of the attributes of shelter. Notions of rest, womb, castle, den, warmth, sustenance, heartsease were shoved into an admittedly graceful construct of fiberglass and steel and wood—but a delicate web that could be sunk or crushed by any common or garden misstep of mooring, weather, or traffic. Such was the dark side of refuge. Still, he had felt that way about his sloop before; he felt three times more strongly about it now.

He did not believe the mate's warnings. The ship's officers had maneuvered competently around his boat in docking. Even a hurricane, roaring across an already sheltered basin, must be impotent against the web of ten-inch hawsers they had strung to hold the ship.

The danger would come if he changed berths. He would have to deal with rusted-out barges, unbroken ferry wake, the constant pressure of wind, unknown obstacles underwater where no one had dredged since the fishing died.

Maybe he should have explained all that to the mate. As a seaman, he would have understood.

Slocum stowed the cleaning equipment. He finished his coffee, looking around the saloon automatically. The invitation spindle Amy had passed on to him was loose on the bookshelf, where he had stashed it after coming back. The snailmail markings showed it came from Kumpunen's office; the delivery deadline was two days from now. He wedged it next to the tide chart.

Otherwise the cabin was clean and everything was stowed. It bore no traces of Vera Consalves or the man she had brought with her. It did not make sense to Slocum that someone like Vera, who dealt in unspoken arrangements centered around gew-gaws of authority, should sit in his cabin for fifteen minutes and not leave some trace to be scoured off with hot water, brushes, and abrasive detergent. But everything was as it had been before. *Fado* lilted from the speakers. Slocum glanced at the communications pak, thinking he should switch it off, punch the "power" button.

As soon as he looked at it a jolt of pure desire ran up his spine. It was not as strong as the attraction he had felt outside the Metropole but it was more specific. "Come to me," the ECM-pak seemed to whisper. "Borrow a headset, or buy one, the Flash parlors sell them even now. Turn to your Net station, log in to *Wanderbird;* in less than a minute you will be sitting in the bridge recliner and watching the crimson depths of a galaxy you have not yet visited, one on the other side of the Cygnus black hole. Gaze through the ports above and below, where the ship's titanium sails are set if the cosmic wind, of spacedust and gravity tides and solar particles, is in the ship's favor. Feel the gentle thrum of her motors and the occasional psychotic episode of her navigational computers, and the strong engine that backs them up as the ship dives over the event horizon, deeper and deeper into what may or may not come to pass. In some part of the ship, Breena will be running a bath of recycled water scented with Arcturan freeze flowers, for she always bathes before an experiment she thinks will go wrong, and the noose chains they sampled from a frozen river on their last planetary landing appear"—Slocum's fingers twisted with the need to curve around the ship's joystick.

Strong as that need was, however, his overall desire remained significantly less than the black and opposed surge he had felt after looking at the Metropole's panels.

The image he'd had of *Wanderbird* faded, mostly, from his mind. He thought it might be better not to provoke revulsion, as he had in front of the Metropole; rather, he must steer it somewhat, divert the energy of this addiction into an outlet similar yet different. In that way it might not dam up and accumulate power so quickly.

He could, for example, venture forth over the Wildnets again, though he probably had sampled too many of them earlier. It had been a long time since he got a flashback of desire the way he had just now, after sampling Staring November.

Usually he felt a little burned after surfing, so that he had to stay away from Wildnets for a day or two to let that vulnerability subside.

Or (Slocum thought) instead of the Nets he could Vox someone. He could Vox his father.

Slocum jerked forward, surprising himself by the abruptness of his action. He tapped out commands on the keyboard, calling up a no-frills Net portal from which you could not plug in to interactive 3-D video drama even if you wanted to. Breathed a little easier, from choosing that option.

Slocum's father had moved to the Southwest seven years ago, in part to alleviate his lung problems. His lungs had not improved much, and the area he moved to was inundated with other old people who had left their jobs and families in search of hot dry weather. Thus his business, which was shooting wedding photographs, dried up and atrophied with his lungs. Now he spent most of his time on the various Nets and Webs of the Flash, watching 3-D soaps, traveling from one three-dimensional tourist spot to the next, exchanging messages with others like himself.

When Slocum called up his online name, a little camera

icon on the upper right-hand corner of the screen informed him that Slocum senior was already online and within ten seconds his father himself responded. His voice, which had gotten as dry and cramped as his lungs over the years, rattled out of the saloon speakers; at the same time his words were translated and scrolled across the ECM's monitor accompanied by whatever image the elder Slocum was patching into at the time.

"I was thinking of you just yesterday," his father said, and a wide-angle shot of flat orange mesa, with a single ribbon of barbed-wire fence strung along a two-lane, flashed on the terminal.

"What were you thinking?"

"Oh, nothing much." A couple of coughs, dry and quick—his father would not even have noticed them. "You know, it was your mom's birthday last week."

Slocum said nothing. He had forgotten. His father would never hold that against him, which was a way of holding it against him anyway. "It always makes me remember." Don't do the pics thing, Dad, Slocum found himself thinking, don't—Knowing as he thought it his father would do it, he couldn't help himself, even now his cursor would be flicking faster than fingers through his archive of digital photos, selecting one of the hundreds labeled LILLIAN, with date and occasion, exposure time and F-stop attached.

The image came. Slocum's mother, maybe twenty years ago. Even then she had looked worn out.

"You didn't have to do that," Slocum said.

"Ah," his father replied. Surprise in his voice, some of it real. "I'm sorry." And the image switched quickly into another desert view. The phrase "She never was much of a fighter" printed itself across the screen of Slocum's mind; it was a kite-tail thought, made irrelevant by changes in image and conversation. "I thought of you anyway—wondered how you were doing."

"Yeah," Slocum said. "How are you doing, it's—"

"How're Amy and Bird?"

"Still the same, I guess."

Still the same, I guess, the ECM-pak scrolled out, the letters bright yellow against a dark-green background.

"You two still, what, separated?" The link was fiberoptic broadband, devoid of interference. Slocum could hear the care his father put into that sentence. A latticework of interest and careful neutrality that masked disapproval. His dad liked Amy. He had always thought Slocum lacked consistency. He believed Slocum had mishandled his marriage, and though he would never say so directly, this belief had always lain quite clearly in his choice of questions. Of course the ECM monitor formed only the words *what, separated?* without any of the lattice at all.

"Still separated," Slocum agreed.

"You don't sound good," his father said. "You sound bad."

"Well that could be," Slocum said. "I haven't seen Bird in two weeks." *I haven't seen Bird in two weeks,* the monitor repeated. Slocum turned away from the ECM.

"And Amy?"

"I saw her earlier today. I don't really want to talk about this."

"Okay," his father said. Slocum waited for the image shift. It came, quite shocking—a wedding in a canyon. People dressed as Apaches. On closer inspection some of them *were* Apaches. "It's better to talk about it, you know."

"I know."

"But if you don't want to—"

"I don't." The still would be 3-D on a correctly configured system; in the latter stages of his career Slocum's father had changed technologies to suit the times, providing three-point, three-dimensional video coverage of weddings that the bride and groom could later walk around, "in headsets and the comfort of your new home," as the brochure put it.

"It's just," Slocum continued after a second or two had passed, "Amy keeps telling me to wait. She says I'm too confused, too confused for both of them. I mean, what the hell is *that* supposed to mean?

"And now Bird doesn't want to see me anymore."

Slocum, turning around his cabin, glanced back at the screen without meaning to. The wedding shot had vanished. A picture of a coyote pelt nailed to a weathered door filled the background. Were there any clichés of the Southwest his father had not shot? Slocum wondered. But his father was as sappy as a trailerpark housewife and, either because of that or as a precondition, tended to prefer clichés. He shot them, one after the other, for clients. He sought them out in 3-D soaps like *Vanessa Grande, Thunder Beach, Pain in the Afternoon.* The last words Slocum had spoken scrolled up the screen and disappeared.

"They'll come back," his father said at last. "Just give 'em time. If you get back into a stable situation—get back like you were, they'll, uh, come back." He coughed again. "Maybe not to live with you, you know, but to live around you somehow. Especially Bird."

"I don't want a stable situation," Slocum replied. "Not like I had. I don't even think Amy wants it. It's been almost a year, Dad, and they're only getting farther—" Slocum stopped. He'd had no intention of talking about this when he had gone online to find his father. It did not make him feel good—it felt like he was halfway back into the mad welter of emotions he had plunged into beside Dark Denny's boat. He could not exit easily from that unhappiness—and yet, half in the Flash like this and half out of it, he could not fully explain or sample the situation either.

"They're stronger than us." Images shifted. A black-and-white mutt, head cocked; that one made Slocum smile. A huge woman dressed in nineteenth-century clothes, bearing shotguns. Ma Barker. "Stronger and tougher. Remember that."

"You were always good at useless information," Slocum told him.

His father laughed, and coughed again. This cough was longer, more strained. When he had finished he said, "I'm sorry about the shot of your mother. I wasn't trying—you know."

"I know," Slocum said.

"Talk to you," his father said.

"Talk to you," Slocum replied, and signed off the portal.

Slocum shut down the ECM-pak. In one corner of his mind he visualized his father in a yellow suit, tapping out the Web address for a personalized program that would feed him a diet of his favorite 3-D reruns until he went to sleep.

He put out food for Ralfie but the cat didn't appear at the sound of his dish clattering. The saloon felt both cramped and empty after having been crowded with Ralfie and the ECM transmission and his father's voice. Even Vera and the ship's officer had filled it with human presence in a way it had not been for weeks. The taste of emptiness—Slocum faced up to it—the taste of solitude—was not unusual. Slocum lived alone and he was usually honest enough with himself to live with the consequences. In this case the ache of loneliness that came back to him now had its good side, to the extent that it displaced the Flash lust, and the images of *Wanderbird*.

But Slocum was male, and reluctant to endure even such a providential discomfort if he did not absolutely have to.

Slocum used the head and collected his laundry bag. He put on his reefer jacket and workboots. He closed the head and galley seacocks, shut off shore power, locked the hatch, and made sure the docklines were secure. He climbed the ladder to Coggeshall Wharf and looked down at his boat, checking a final time. He looked up also, to where the huge ship lay humming, a flat city stretching from horizon to horizon of mist. The great hawsers curved solidly from the wharf's bollards. They approached the black water and came close as a metaphor to touching the complex reflection of the ship, then soared high, high up to vanish into the dozen fairleads of the real thing. The hawsers were so big, the ship seemed so immutable that they reinforced his earlier impression: These were immovable objects, like bridges or arcs cut out of black stone. They were tangible rebuttal of the mate's arguments; surely no storm, however strong, could shift such massive mooring systems.

The gangway was up. A deckhand dozed in the guardpost. No one was visible in the lit portholes and windows or on the decks on which lights shone to illuminate the way for late-night promenaders. The woman Slocum had seen earlier was absent. He wondered if he had imagined her, or made her up out of disparate elements—a steward with a scarf, perhaps. The chief officer had not known what Slocum was talking about when he mentioned her.

It was still drizzling. Slocum shouldered the laundry bag, turned his back to the harbor, and set off for Madame Ling's.

————

THE LAUNDROMAT WAS BUSY when Slocum got there, and the Lisboa next door was hopping too as mothers parked their kids next to the dryers and ventured into the bar looking grimly for husbands or fathers or, failing that, a glass of *vinho verde*. A television blared the canned laughter of a talkshow. The TV was old and 2-D, so half the forms were not visible and half the shapes too bright. Slocum ran his Universal Credit Card through the reader and selected two loads, soap, with bleach for the diesel stains. He was already turning to pick a machine that did not have too long a queue so he could punch the number in when a loud beep sounded from the digital reader.

Slocum turned back. The screen read:

WE'RE SORRY MR. SLOCUM
THIS CARD HAS BEEN CANCELED
WE CANNOT PROCESS THIS REQUEST
PLEASE CONTACT YOUR CREDIT INSTITUTION'S WEBSITE

A stylized face with a downturned smile flashed across
the screen, which then flipped back to introductory mode:

HI!
WELCOME TO MADAME LING'S E-Z KREDIT LAUNDERAMA
&
FIRSTATLANTIC CREDIT SERVICES
PLEASE SWIPE YOUR UCC CARD HERE

The intro mode included a face that smiled:

☺

Slocum swiped his card again. The beep sounded once
more. The characters on the "we're sorry" screen were
puce and angry. A couple of women turned and looked at
him when they heard the beep. People in this Town where
jobs were fastfood and tenuous and poverty a fact of life
should have been familiar with this kind of event, but even
so they stared at him. An overweight Brazilian woman
clicked her tongue, whether in sympathy or disapproval,
Slocum could not tell.

Slocum put the card in his pocket, dragged his bag over
by the window, and looked out at the yellow reflection
from the Lisboa sign and the purple neon of Madame
Ling's fortune-telling shop being melted by rain over the
plate glass. He told himself it had to be a mistake, that his
card could not really be canceled; but the feeling of panic
that appeared out of nowhere when he saw that screen just
kept swelling. Along with the panic came a tripling of the

sense of being alone and without comfort and it was not just a mood anymore, not just an emotional reaction to Amy. There was some logic now in this state of mind because the UCC was in many ways what made you a person in normal society.

The card was what you got when you were eighteen that allowed you to go into the world on your own as full man and proud and no longer bowlined to apron strings. It included your driver's license and social security and voter's registration and the username for your principal online service provider. Although it didn't take much to get your card canceled—a stubborn overdraft would do it, or simply declaring it lost or stolen—people tended to be awful careful about not letting that happen because once your UCC did not work you were effectively paralyzed. You could not draw cashcards or buy broccoli, drive legally or purchase gas or go to the 3-Ds. If you lived in an apartment building and worked in a job tower as most did, you couldn't get to your own flat or show up at work without going through an incredible rigmarole of interviews and digital fingerprinting and laser scanning of the iris.

Slocum's face stared back at him in the yellow, blue, and black reflections of the street. It was a long face, with an extended nose and chin and a mouth that couldn't decide which way to turn and ended up compromising, changing its mind, half smiling then turning down a third of the way across its length. His hair hung over his forehead like black and untended ivy, changing the angle of neon, deepening the shadows under the eyes, nose, lips.

His face looked old, Slocum thought. It looked like his father's—it looked like he was ill, or dying. He wondered if his father was dying. He couldn't remember if the old man's bouts of coughing had been worse than the last time they had Voxed. Slocum turned back to observe the laundromat, the ever-moving kids in cheap aniline colors, the efficient brown hands of their mothers sorting and folding.

One of the mothers had absentmindedly placed her infant on his laundry bag to change its diaper. The TV now showed a weather show, the half-assed colors of 2-D transferring satellite images of a hurricane rolling the edge of Florida into a tumbleweed of acid greens and yellows.

He was perfectly aware of volume in this place—the 2/2 beat of the machines, the blast of vents, the squawk of telenoise, the background of Portuguese, the cries of children—but all of it seemed muted compared to the sharp single note that had come from the UCC reader.

Slocum pushed both his hands into the flesh of his face and kneaded it. It was ridiculous how bad this made him feel. It was, he figured, a hangover from his old self, his pre-ICE self. Though he had put almost all his cash into a trust account for Bird when he left Arcadia, he had plenty of credit left in his current account—at least enough for another sixteen months, the way he was going. And he was better equipped to deal with this kind of crisis than he had been a year ago because the whole point of the ICE had been to set up a local economy that had nothing to do with the international credit matrix everyone else belonged to and depended on.

That was how he got involved in the first place. When Dark Denny and Zoe Chase and Feingold had set up the Independent Credit Entity in the disused condo office, the idea was at first simply to provide cheaper services for the twelve dozen boat families that lived year-round in their aquatic squat. The ICE set up a line of credit—with FirstAtlantic, as it happened—for big Outside purchases but otherwise the theory was that people in the ICE community would barter with one another as far as they could for what they needed. Of course everybody kept his UCC, that was understood, this was no monastery situation; but when word got around and suddenly there were more than two hundred boats docked in the marina, a lot of different goods and services started moving through and the barter net worked well. Stuff the Whaling City people did not have often could be swapped for with a couple of similar ICEs, one inland, one well to the north. When Slocum went into the ICE office on his first visit and mentioned what he did, they had welcomed him enthusiastically, because Slocum knew a lot about Web production and they were starting to run most of their barters with other ICEs over the Wildnets.

Of course what it came down to on a day-to-day basis was other forms of cards—ICE chips with a fixed amount of barter credit that you could trade back and forth. And there was plenty of stuff you still needed the UCC for. Even the *Smuggler's Bible* set a target of only thirty-seven percent; maybe two-fifths of your living necessities should be bought and sold within the community, or the external community of similar nodes, for a measure of control over your own life to be wrested back from Outside.

Getting even that far had been hard. Slocum attended too many meetings where the *echt*-Hawkleyites and the compromisers had almost come to blows, sometimes over broad lines of ICE theory but more often over picayune issues such as whether to broker diesel fuel, what to do with recycling, or what color to paint the travel-lift.

But it was enough for Slocum. He had felt good, for a while at least, to be less dependent on a structure of corporations like the one he had worked for, lived with, lived for in Bayview; more reliant on people whose faces and prejudices he knew and could take into account. He recalled how those whose UCCs had been vaporized were able to fall back on ICE chips to make ends meet. At least, they were able to sell objects they made or services they could render and thus avoid the iron choice they would have had to make on the Outside—to sign up for work with the state, which had no work, or go out on the unforgiving streets. Slocum had hired a number of the vaporized; offhand, he could recall babysitters for Bird and a couple of men who cleaned weeds off the bottom of his sloop. The sitter had been a flake but the divers had done a good job.

Slocum picked up his laundry bag again. It felt heavier than before. A dark patch marked where the baby had rested. He still had a few ICE chips hidden in the compartment behind his bookshelf; enough to buy bread and beer and other daily essentials available in the ICE. Yet with all these reassurances he felt, if anything, worse than when the credit screen first beeped at him.

It was all coming together, Slocum thought—the absence of Bird, and Amy's continued distance, and the diesel problems and Vera and how sick he was of living alone. That was when he understood that a big chunk of his depression also had to do with the plan that had been in the back of his mind all along. It was an assumption based on proximity and habit, because this was what he always did on laundry days—but now he could not eat at Madame Ling's.

Because the fortune-teller was Portuguese, by culture if not by birth; and while the Portygees in Town were often kind and would help you out in a serious situation, the rest of the time they demanded credit up front for just about everything.

Madame Ling was no exception. Slocum bent the UCC savagely between two fingers. To think of Madame Ling's kitchen, and the big pot of stew that would be simmering on the stove in there, made his saliva flow.

He decided to go in anyway. He was starving. He could not remember when he had last eaten a real meal. Cakes would be there, and maybe the Whip. He could cadge a piece of muffin. He could talk to somebody. Hunger, and the awareness of it, kept his thoughts short. God did he want that stew!

Slocum stood up and heaved the bag to his shoulder. He went out the door, navigated around the Sagres gangboys clotting at the entrance to the Lisboa. He rang the bell of Madame Ling's.

It took a while for someone to answer. He peered between the purple branches and leaves of Madame Ling's neon, through the plate glass of her fortune-teller's window. Her table was empty, the *tarecchi* neatly stacked on a vinyl doily. The only noise came from the Lisboa. So did the smells, of beer and wine, of smoke and piss. Even the TV was dark; such was the scale of Madame Ling's thrift, it extended to switching off sets that were intended for twenty-four use at immeasurable wattage. Slocum worried that, for the first time he could remember, Madame Ling might have opted not to serve dinner in her kitchen.

He experienced the feeling—by now he was almost used to it—that he was being watched. He figured it was, once again, a false impression, and glanced only casually behind him.

This time, he was right. A Sagres leaning in a doorway across the street stared at him, spat messily, and stared again. The graffiti over his head looked familiar: a three-quarter square with a stem, this one holding another square with a dot inside.

A couple more gangboys strolled over, swaggering as Sagres did. They all looked at him and laughed.

A door inside Madame Ling's opened. A rectangle of light poured onto the linoleum. A man, thin and stooped, entered the parlor. When he unlocked the front door Slocum recognized Lopes. The alarm rang, and shut off. Lopes grunted when he recognized Slocum and led the way through the parlor.

Sound grew in Slocum's ears. Voices raised in conversation. A radio. And now a smell of garlic and cabbage and sausage, mixed with cigarettes and wine, blossomed amid the whorehouse odors of wall-to-wall and disinfectant and condom latex. The stew smell grew stronger in Slocum's olfactory centers. When he entered the kitchen it felt like breaking out of the clouds into a tropical climate of light, noise, and chatter.

There were at least ten people in the little kitchen. Slocum checked them over like a specialist of the little con casing a crowd of rubes. The hunger was so strong in him now that it directly connected his brain stem with his motivational centers. All he could move toward was scoring a plate of the boiled dinner cooking on Madame Ling's range, and the hell with what he had to do to get it.

He worked his way around the edges of a big table. Cakes was sprawled in an armchair with Dinette on her lap, talking to a woman with red hair and the giggles. Lopes went straight over to another ex-fisherman, a graying, elkhound-featured Norwegian named Swear. "Yer full of shit about the stock assessments," the Norwegian told him. He was fairly drunk.

"If you had time to think," Lopes answered, "ya'd realize how the stock assessments are lies to keep the Archer-Daniels trawlers doing stock assessments." He hit the wall with one fist. A scale model of the Tagus Bridge fell off a shelf and was neatly fielded by the giggling redhead. Slocum saw the little jambook computer open and glowing and its antenna pointing toward the nearest satellite before he spotted the Whip, talking quietly to Madame Ling. She nodded at Slocum and pointed to the credit scanner on the breadbox. Slocum hesitated, then slid his card through. Maybe, he thought, it had been a problem with the laundromat's scanner, or a temporary glitch in the connection. At the same time he knew from experience that this type of problem at this stage in his life had snuck through a hole in the universe that was too narrow to allow for happy coincidence. That was his theory anyway, and it seemed backed up and consolidated at every turn by incidents like Amy and his struggle with the diesel and the imbroglio with the ship. And every validation augmented his theory and of course the sense of cosmic injustice that went with it and the perverse feeling of importance that went along with *that*. So he was almost glad, in a fatalistic kind of way, to hear that insistent beep and watch the letters change to puce.

"You card no good, Slocum," Madame Ling pointed out, frowning.

Slocum shrugged.

"You can't have no dinner, no wine wit'out dat card."

"I'll put it on mine," the Whip offered. His smile as he did so was a little strained and Slocum knew from this that Dolores would find out and not be happy. The Whip would never admit that Dolores was a constraint in his life; it was one of the things people liked about him. He had a wife who would drive anyone out of his mind with her endless demands that he stay home and do absolutely nothing except events that included 3-D soaps and her friends, who also watched the same roster of stories. The Whip did not stay home; he got out as often as he could without pissing Dolores off to the breaking point. Still, while he was out he never once had been known to complain about her or her demands. His friends in Town called him the Whip, as in "pussy-whipped," but they were also protective of him for the very reason implied in their choice of epithet. Slocum shook his head, thinking he would not be the one to get his friend into further trouble. The redheaded woman glanced at Slocum.

"Your card is maxed?" she asked. All at once her giggles dissolved. Her mouth sagged and her lips swelled and tears ran down the channels of her cheeks. Slocum stared at her. Cakes got up, dislodging Dinette, who fell on her ass with a thump on the floor, then yawned like a cat and lit a cigarette. Cakes put an arm around the redhead's shoulders. The Norwegian called, "Now yuh stop dat yuh!"

Smoothly—as smoothly as a Sagres might flick out a switchblade—Cakes flipped out her own UCC, one-handed, and swiped it through the scanner; then tapped out her cypher, and the code for dinner. She glanced at

Slocum, mouthed "you owe me one" in his direction, and
turned back to the redhead.

The volume around the room picked up. Lopes and the
Norwegian were in full cry, but their argument had
skipped. "You tink da feds help us out, boy are yuh wrong,"
the Norwegian said. He had lit a pipe and was having trouble smoking and drinking at the same time. "Dey bought us
out so dey could get rid of us." Two of the girls entered
with a young man in a sports jacket and argued at and above
and around him to Madame Ling. Slocum wondered where
Luisa was. On one level he was glad she was not here, but
the thought of her deep brown eyes made him sad all of a
sudden. Another contradiction he would set aside in favor
of the urgency of chow. Madame Ling got up, like a dirigi-
ble casting off landlines, scattering the girls. At the stove she
stirred the great casserole with a spoon that read CASCAIS.
The girls sat down next to Dinette and looked through a
magazine called *3-D Video Starz*. Slocum's stomach was actively hurting and he welcomed the hurt because it was
sharp and it made everything else recede further still.
Madame Ling started humming and then as she stirred she
began to sing. It was *A Moda das Tranças Pretas,* a *fado* from
the right bank of the Tagus.

> *Como era linda com seu ar namoradeiro*
> *té lhe chamavam "menina das tranças pretas,"*
> *Pelo Chiado passeava o dia inteiro*
> *Apregoando raminhos de violetas*

Her voice was harsh and her notes fell and rose even
against each other. They quavered and broke on both ends.
E pouco a pouco todas deixaram crescê-lo. Dinette joined in all
at once. Her voice was sweet as a choirboy's. Madame Ling
glowered and sang louder. Suddenly she stopped and
shrieked "*Madre de diosh,* eat!" with such authority that

everyone quit what they were doing and dragged chairs over to the table.

Dinette served. It was her punishment, meted out by Madame Ling.

The stew was everything Madame Ling was not, or maybe it was everything Madame Ling wished she was and could only try to be in her cooking. It was hot and open to different interpretations. It was generous with the smoky *linguica* and with potatoes, carrots, cabbage, garlic, thyme, salt, and red wine. It was flexible; it allowed room for excursions into pure broth, a kind of subocean of salt and herb and mustard; or forays into the realm of marinated pork, the race memories of salted meat and explorers, the underground Aztec dreams of spuds.

Slocum ate two bowls and Madame Ling's glower got worse. She sent Dinette up with the next man to sway in from the Lisboa. The carrot top was giggling again, grabbing Cakes's arm to hold herself upright against the humor. The Norwegian looked even more like an elkhound. Slocum concentrated on eating—his stomach was full but he did not want to stop, because he had a feeling that all the issues his hunger had preempted would then flood back and swamp him. He drank wine, but not too much, for the same reason. The third helping of stew tasted a little different; less salty, slightly sweeter with carrots, pasty from dissolved potatoes. Slocum had noticed that Madame Ling's stews tended to change over time as well as space, bringing out tastes, densities, and olfactory positions one might not have suspected of them at first. The same was true of her dinner parties, and now Slocum began to wonder, Might there be a connection? Could the forces of heat and convection, of varying salinity and well and flow, of stir and scoop create a dynamic that entered the bowls, the spoons, the gullets, and stomachs of the diners and somehow cause a similar and quantitative change?

Slocum took a third Portuguese muffin, buttered it, and

sopped up the last of his broth. Scraps of conversation floated to the top of the party like bits of turnip. "Give him a blow job," Dinette's friend said, "but what, you think that's, like, a tip?" The Whip said urgently, "... for a way to find out if all the different connections are really working together or if the marsh is just like Wildnets, like a lot of little gardens." "We'll go for a spin," Cakes said, "you ever gone down the channel at eighty-seven knots?" "Look at dat fuckin' ship," the Norwegian was grunting. He had bought a bottle of port from Madame Ling's commissary and was sitting morosely on Shaneeqwa's knees. Slocum leaned forward, the better to hear what Swear had to say. "How can yuh look at dat ship and not tell me dey run tings around here. X-Corp Holdings and Rio Sur, dat owns most of Synodyne. And Synodyne," he ended triumphantly, "owns fifty-one percent of da joint venture that owns da draggers."

"If that ship belongs to X-Corp," Lopes said suspiciously, "why is it here? They already got a tower here."

"Dey got diesel problems," Swear said.

"How you know that?" Lopes was still suspicious.

"Larsen told me," Swear countered. "He knows all about dat ship."

"Larsen, Larsen," Lopes said, closing his eyes in disgust. "Everybody thinks what Larsen says is like from god or somet'ing."

"If god existed," the Whip began; "but he is like certainty; we all want certainty but we know it can't exist." A prostitute whose name Slocum did not know, who had been lying low in case Madame Ling needed another scapegoat, said, "Oh you and your there's-no-god-bla-bla talk again, why'nt you fuck yourself *carajo.*"

The talk decreased in volume. Slocum could not tell if that was because of what the hooker had said or if it was a coincidence. Or maybe his earlier insight had been correct, and one of the convection cells in conversation had collapsed at the same time as a current dense with sausage burst out of the cabbage layer trapping it inside the boiled dinner. He wanted to help the Whip here; the Whip was looking down at his computer, muttering, "I got a right to say what I'm thinking." His fingers touched the 3-D mask softly, lustfully. Slocum asked Swear, "How did he know it belongs to X-Corp, or the other company—Rio Sur?"

Swear gazed at him blearily. He'd had a lot of port, was having trouble focusing, and his pipe was out. He took the pipe out of his mouth and stared at it in resentment. He lifted the bottle and took a slug. He looked up at the Tagus Bridge, and swayed. He was seated on a kitchen chair but he swayed anyway. "I *hate* dat fucking bridge," Swear said.

"Larsen told him," Lopes told Slocum.

"Larsen told me," Swear agreed. "He has contacts."

"Fuck Larsen," Lopes said.

Someone nudged Slocum's elbow. He looked around. It was Luisa, not looking at him—her hair pulled up, the long floury neck exposed. She continued to not-look at him, she walked around the table and sat next to Dinette, who had just come back down; she wanted Slocum to notice she was not looking at him. Madame Ling dropped anchor beside Slocum's other elbow. "You take her upstairs," she whispered hoarsely, lifting her chin toward Luisa. She had drunk enough wine that she was no longer eyeing everybody's plate to check if they were taking more than their share. "That girl needs some joy, ma' frien'."

Slocum looked at her carefully. Madame Ling's makeup had been chipping for some time. Whole Antarctic glaciers of rouge base had calved and floated off in the greenhouse effect of her cooking. "I don't think I'm the one who can cheer her up," Slocum said; though he had tried to once. And Madame Ling nodded, confirming what had gone unspoken between them, that she knew absolutely everything that went on upstairs. "She can help you, with you little problem." Slocum had imbibed enough *vinho verde* that he did not want to let that one go, nor let that image of himself—wounded, needy—take on more life around here than it had already. "It's just a bad time," he muttered, "a bad time for me"; and Madame Ling, who had heard thousands of such excuses, gripped his elbow harder. "I know you card no good, Slocum," she said. "But see, you help Luisa, she help you, get you out of your little troubles, big troubles too.

"Ah, go on, I run you a tab for tonight," she continued, holding right hand to left breast dramatically. "You problems, dey give me da blood-presh."

Slocum wasn't certain if she really meant for him to sleep with Luisa, or if she had forgotten about Cakes and simply meant a tab for dinner, and the wine included with it. Anyway she had moved on, unlocking a cabinet and taking out two more bottles of wine. And the brothel's bush telegraph sent this news up and down the firetrap and from girl to girl along the corridors of the old rooming house: Madame Ling was in an expansive mode, and they had twenty minutes' worth of unbilled wine and other indulgences to exploit. Girls drifted down like dandelion chaff, in bathrobes of varying quality.

"Lookit those Lisboa boys," Shaneeqwa said. "Like them leaf-cutter ants, cuttin' out their frustration and draggin' it over heah."

"Like we don't have enough, like, tension," May agreed.

Dinette began singing again: *"Passaram dias e as meninas do Chiado."*

Slocum made his way to where the Whip talked into his headset. His expression—he resembled a runover skunk—made it plain to whom he was talking. He hit a key and pushed the set to the back of his scalp.

"She doesn't mean to," he told Slocum. "She told me this morning she liked you, you should come over more often."

Slocum hesitated. When he moved to the ICE he had told himself he was shifting to a life where all the little tricks of accumulating knowledge about people and power

over them, all the convenient lies and omissions by which
you hung on to such power, would no longer be a part of
his life. He had tried hard to live like that; he had noticed
pretty soon that the ICE was no more free of lies and
power plays than Arcadia. He too had failed ultimately.
Which did not mean that he should not keep trying.

"Next time, I'll come at a better hour," he told the
Whip, who nodded, pleased; and just that stupid little mis-
truth and the effect it had warmed Slocum's stomach in
those few places the stew had not gotten to yet. Dinette was
singing *Fado do Campo Grande* and the avian purity of her
voice pulled Slocum up and up as if he could fly and she
had shown him a crack through the clouds that oppressed
their planet. He took a sip of wine and it added warmth.
They were all friends of his, he thought: the Whip and
Madame Ling, Cakes who had bought him dinner and the
lugubrious Swear, May and Dinette who sang for him and
Lopes, and Luisa who still held his attention by avoiding it;
Shaneeqwa who told the truth and even the redheaded girl
now giggling again as Cakes led her back from the bathroom. They were friends and they accepted him and on a
planet where such friends existed, even broken diesels and
absent daughters must later revert to the lines of rightness
that ruled their orb, must come around to working again.

Slocum liked that feeling so much that he decided to
leave. He was standing near the door anyway, he would
back out discreetly. Fish and guests smell after three hours,
his mother used to tell him when he was young. He found
out much later that she had exaggerated, the saying usually
went "after three days"; but the principle of it was in-
grained in him. Too much presence drowned friendship in
a lake of ennui. You remained friends by making yourself
scarce. You held on to feelings like this by not pushing them
farther than they could go. And so he slipped out the parlor
door. The only one who noticed him leave was Luisa. She
looked at him directly, for the first time, as he eased the

door shut. In the light of the tarot parlor he saw himself in Madame Ling's mirrors and laughed. He was all purple, purple and black, a different man, a ghost of carnival. As he followed himself along the contiguous mirrors, another purple being drifted up behind him. He recognized Luisa in the glass at the same time as he turned to face the reality of her: small-boned, heart-faced, her thin hands clutching his upper arm. A faint tang, of cloves and coffee.

"Slocum," she whispered. "You heard what the old bitch said."

"I heard," he agreed, standing straighter in the purple. Her face under neon looked thinner and more haunted than usual, like a killing of violets, like the wives of dead knights he included in the stories he told Bird.

"Then come," she said, not-looking at him once more. "Try again with me." She put a hand hesitantly between his legs and he started violently. "Sorry," she whispered. "I'm sorry."

He said, "I'm sorry too"; because apart from the flinch there was no reaction there, none at all.

He put a hand on one of hers.

"I just don't think it would be any different," he said.

"I can make it different—" but her heart wasn't in it. She discouraged easily, he remembered. It was no wonder, she had gone through ten foster homes in three years. She repeated, "I can make it different, Slocum." It was words only, the training starting at last to stick.

"It doesn't feel different," he said, "in here," and touched his chest. He lifted her hand gently out of his trousers and let it fall. "Why should it?" He picked up his laundry bag and opened and closed the outer door as fast as he could. The alarm bell rang briefly. As he closed the door he did not look, yet he sensed that Luisa still stood in the shadows as he had left her, hands at her sides, her features racked by purple.

ELEVEN

SLOCUM'S GOOD MOOD HAD started to evaporate when Luisa came out with him. It was almost gone three minutes after he shut the door to Madame Ling's. Despite his new and food-induced strength, the laundry bag seemed heavier than ever. As he gazed regretfully through the steamed windows of the Lisboa Bar, he again noticed the garish television, and remembered what in the shock of his canceled UCC he had not absorbed before: that green-yellow tumbleweed swirling its way up the coast.

The hurricane.

The TV was now tuned to *Pain in the Afternoon*. The Portuguese stared at it obsessively. Slocum shouldered his bag and trudged off, into the driving rain. He sensed that someone had detached himself from the Lisboa crowd and was following him. But the stew still sloshed warm and rich inside, and in the illusion of power this imparted he knew for certain that his follower was an illusion. Or maybe just the Sagres gangbanger giving him the eye. Just as he knew how many hurricanes were cooked up in the stretch of Atlantic to the west of Gabon and kicked farther west by the Trades. With the ocean in these latitudes warm all year, they came peeling off the equator like so many bowling balls rolled back for another round, racked up to strike or spare off the continent's flank.

Most of them wobbled off into the gutter of the Atlantic. It was true what he had told Zurbruegge. A few of them—maybe one every five or six weeks—reached far enough up the coast for the Flash news departments to see an opportunity to boost their ratings and thus advertising revenues. A multiplier effect devolved, as he had also told the mate, from the Cassandra forecasts: sales of batteries, candles, gasoline, backup spindles, and gaffer's tape zoomed up. The weather typically turned hotter and muggier, and was cleaned up by the storm's outriders in two days of showers.

The first mate had not been lying, either. There was a hurricane; the tumbleweed Slocum had seen on the TV was tighter and more defined than most, and that was all. Tightness and definition meant the same thing in hurricanes as in people, or cancer: The enemy would be fiercer and more deadly. But a storm's severity had nothing to do with its vector, Slocum knew.

He turned once to check the street behind him. All that moved was a streetlight, hung over a crossroads, red and bobbing in the driven wind. A couple of teedees tended a garbage-can fire. A tour bus leaving the Moby Dick Theme Park raised pink water like a curtain. He thought of Luisa, purple and haunted as he had left her in the tarot parlor. But the ache she brought was an old ache and though it did not hurt less, it was familiar enough that he did not have to think about it much anymore.

When he got to Coggeshall Wharf, Slocum was no longer feeling warm with friendship and stew, but he was not feeling so bad either. The rain was hard enough that, perversely, it felt good to slog through its fresh and liquid touch. With good *linguica* and *vinho verde* inside him Slocum felt that there were bad things out there, sure enough; but they were within his powers to tackle. At the entrance to the wharf the red brake lights of a truck shone beside the greenish glow of MacTavish's trailer. As Slocum approached he made out the same serpent-and-staff motif he had seen on another truck two nights ago, right after the big ship docked. The words were stenciled in red block characters across the two rear doors: EMERGENCY BLOOD DE-LIVERY. An interior light shone on hefty metal racks with three Styrofoam boxes that read BIOHAZARD and URGENT—KEEP REFRIGERATED. On a stickum label underneath:

Type O+
★★★triple tested★★★

O positive. It was Slocum's blood type. He knew that from his physical. X-Corp required blood tests twice yearly as a condition of employment. A salvo of gust-whipped rain fired down on warehouse and truck and cobbles. Amid the greater noise and the increased chill of the rain Slocum had a quick fantasy, that the truck was delivering blood for him—that somehow, in the course of the last ten months, he had been hemorrhaging vital fluids, slowly but chronically, and not even noticed. Someone had been watching, however—perhaps the same person who followed him was keeping track of his red-blood-cell level and platelet count and had ordered the truck to come in and make up the deficiency. He had heard somewhere that passenger ships this big usually were equipped with a complete sick bay. Given the urgency and number of various blood-borne viruses showing up out of the world's hell-holes and getting spread by the jet migrants, they likely needed a dozen gallons on hand to ensure their passengers' safety.

Slocum shook his head. He trudged around the truck. MacTavish stood at the driver's window, checking off items against a clipboard. Rainwater dripped off the peak of his military cap and onto the list but MacTavish paid it no mind; his training had taught him that natural elements were something you suited up for and thereafter ignored. He was recounting some long Caledonian story to the driver, who was being polite. When he saw Slocum, MacTavish did not interrupt his flow but raised his hand to hold him till the tale was finished.

Finally MacTavish reached the punchline. The driver moved off in relief. The guard motioned Slocum toward his booth and in that deluge Slocum did not have the option to argue, for MacTavish would not have heard him. So he followed. There was little point in antagonizing a man as big as MacTavish, especially when he functioned as unofficial dockmaster. With two men crowded inside, the little office was excessively warm, and steam began rising from Slocum's soaked reefer jacket. MacTavish shoved aside a stack of magazines: *Warlock Weekly; Morgan le Fay; The Aleister Crowley Journal No. CXXV.* He picked up a walkie-talkie, announced, "He's here," and put it down almost guiltily.

"Who was that?" Slocum asked.

MacTavish did not answer. A wireless jambook lay on the small desk. It was hooked up to a half-sucker, the military version of what the Whip had used: a virtual-reality headset that allowed you to watch three-dimensional programming on the top half and keep an eye on what was happening around your physical person through the clear bottom portion. In MacTavish's regiment it was likely used to display maps and orders and realtime video surveillance of enemy forces from drones or satellites, so that even the lowliest infantryman had a general-staff perspective on the confusion of battle. This was something the highbrow commentaries had called "democratization of war" when it was introduced, conveniently ignoring the fact that the

infantryman had to follow the same stupid orders from
misguided generals as soldiers had had to put up with since
generals were invented.

On Civvy Street, a half-sucker paired with a jambook
meant no one ever had to live without Flash programming
if he did not want to, except, and only except, for the in-
convenient hiatus of sleep. Even walking and driving,
which previously had required turning off Flash monitors
so that you could safely navigate the concrete world, were
now relegated to the status of activities that could be carried out while multitasking—following the other, more
important, 3-D events broadcast to the upper portion of
your screen.

Slocum had once owned a half-sucker. Hell, he once
owned a half dozen of them. He had worn the gizmo in
his office, in the bedroom, while driving his car. He had
worn it taking a crap, going to sleep, and while making
love with Amy, in the days when they were still capable of
fucking. No—that was one half truth he had promised
himself not to fudge: when *he* was still capable of fucking.
He had thrown out the headset the day he moved out of
Bayview, and now he wondered why, because looking at
the sleek matte green of the jambook and the contoured
and half-silvered screen of the Flash goggles, he experienced an almost pure surge of desire for this device. This
was not a big and all-encompassing passion such as he had
felt in front of the Metropole, but a specific longing, narrow yet total in its brief spectrum, like a child's lust for a
toy—exactly like a child desiring a model locomotive or
a piece of candy. He could ask MacTavish to borrow it, or
rent it. He had a legitimate reason now, since he needed to
find and fix whatever glitch had happened to his UCC
card. The only way you could do that was by gaining access to FirstAtlantic's online offices, and that meant going
through the Net and its menu of 3-D selections.

"D'ye want some whiskey?"

Slocum dragged his gaze away from the headset. The guard had hung up his slicker and was opening the bottle. The peaty smell of Islay filled the booth. Slocum nodded, then changed his mind.

"No." He shook his head. "Who was that?" he asked again. "Someone's waiting for me?"

The guard poured a tooth glass full of liquor over his brown teeth. He groaned and closed his eyes. Behind his head, instaprints of the wharf's denizens were pasted across the fake laminate. Cakes, Lopes, Slocum. Drivers, messengers, cops, Town employees. There was a shot of Matt Zurbruegge, the mate, and crewmen in ship uniforms. All the pictures had been electromagnetically addled, codes for cyan and magenta triggered when they should have been shut off and vice versa so that wrong colors distorted the subjects' features. The distortions looked like faucets, like giraffes or hanger steaks or bottles of laundry detergent. Slocum asked, "Is it the guy from the ship? I already talked to the guy from the ship."

Through the trailer's streaming window Slocum saw that a squad of deckhands, led by an officer who looked like the first mate, had come down the ship's gangplank. They were unloading the Styrofoam boxes from the truck and carrying them back up. They were being very careful; three deckhands shared one box and a fourth shepherded them up the gangway calling hazards. Presumably the gangplank was rainslick and slippery. The men looked like some medieval morality illustration of the rewards due sinners: ants with pale faces clambering up the side of a black mountain to the portals of a demiurge. By the guard post, the officer and a deckhand chatted with the truckdriver.

The officer turned and walked toward MacTavish's trailer. Slocum said "Ah shit, MacTavish," and opened the door.

"Don't leave," the guard warned.

"I already talked to him."

"Hear what he has to say. Look, I poured ye a glass of whiskey."

"I told you, I already talked to him. And I don't want your whiskey."

"Ye shouldnae cut yourself off, Slocum," MacTavish said seriously. "Ye saw what your picture said. A vulture cloud forming about your chakra of balance; the only defense to that is openness, like, a broad-seeking search for all solutions on the off-chance that one might save your arse." Slocum had left the booth before MacTavish finished his fortune-telling spiel. He thought it was odd that Madame Ling, who was paid to tell fortunes, instead dispensed cheap counseling and rarely predicted anything if she could help it. Whereas MacTavish, a Scot who was as stingy as the cliché, never did anything else, and for free at that. Then he stopped woolgathering about MacTavish and Madame Ling because Matt Zurbruegge was heading across the wharf to cut him off, and Slocum's personal thermostat dropped another notch from its plateau of stew-warmth.

The mate stopped in the middle of a puddle, but he was wearing seaboots so it was all the same to him.

"Mr. Slocum."

Slocum stopped. He too was in the middle of a puddle but his workboots were half-soaked so it did not matter to him either.

"Someone on the ship would like to meet with you."

As well as his fancy seaboots the mate wore efficient navy-style oilskins that surely kept him fine and dry inside. In fact, everything about the ship that Slocum had seen so far seemed efficient and well funded and, above all, on a grand scale. Slocum found, as a result of this, that he believed what he'd heard at Madame Ling's—that the ship was an X-Corp property. X-Corp Multimedia was only one small part of the total X-Corp group. X-Corp

Holdings' profits were larger than the GDP of most of the planet's sovereign states; and with all that cash they were not shy about spending money on equipment. The VR headsets he had owned, Slocum recalled with a recurring spasm of lust, had been bought for him by the company, and they were top of the line; lovely, fast, and seamless in motion. Of course a company that lavishly equipped and compensated its officers expected those officers to be instantly available "if something came up." Amy and Bird had gotten used to the rasp of Slocum's jambook alarm summoning him to go online or even return to Arcadia at three A.M. to deal with a production glitch in Bangalore or Kuala Lumpur. They had adapted to fit the closed lifestyle of Bayview, where his colleagues were so saturated by X-Corp's schedule and X-Corp's problems that it was all, in the end, they knew how to talk about. Amy and Bird had worked at it, and found friends and common cause with other Multimedia families. And all that was "super" and "fabulous" (Org epithets they ended up using) because X-Corp, like similar giant organizations, was imbued with the self-fulfilling prophecy of P.R. "If you believe it, everyone will believe it; if you say it is good it will be good." All of it brilliant and magic until someone, for reasons surely pathological and antisocial, suffered a change of perspective. And then it was like all tightly imbricated and circular systems—you could not have doubts about a portion without doubting the whole; like the childhood game of rectangular, stacked-up blocks, you could not adapt or fit it any other way. If you pulled one piece out of the whole intricate construct, the whole castle came down around your ears.

If you did that—if you committed the unspeakable doubt—then everything after was chaos, black change, exile, and loneliness.

And Slocum said to the mate, and his voice was low and vicious, "You seem to think I have some kind of connection to you and your ship. You seem to think I have some issue to discuss with you. That there is even room for discussion, some little thing we have in common. Well there is not." He swallowed rain the wrong way and coughed. "I don't give a good goddamn about your ship or its problems or you. Now I would appreciate it if you left me the fuck alone."

"You asked *me* a question," the mate said.

"I did not," Slocum said, and moved off.

"About the woman," the mate said. "The woman on the ship."

Slocum stopped.

"And you said?" he prompted.

The mate did not smile. Slocum thought he was making an effort to refrain from smiling.

"Her name is Melisande Yonge," the mate said with exaggerated politeness, "and she would like to speak with you."

"I don't know her," Slocum said stubbornly, though his brain was working against him, creating a thumbnail image of the woman he'd seen on the lifeboat deck, arms wedged on the rail, holding a cup of coffee. He was positive, now, she'd had a cup of coffee warming in her hands. "I have no business with her."

"She asked me to ask you. As one neighbor to another, is what she said."

Now Slocum smiled. "Neighbor" was a term that was popular in Bayview. It emphasized in-group versus out-group, X-Corp people and their hard work and all the perks it had earned them over the less talented, less committed, less protected people living beyond the security gates.

He wanted to accept. Stubbornness and his usual, boring rage pulled him in another direction. Yet Slocum knew well that he still entertained a small curiosity about the woman. And he had a much larger interest in seeing what was happening inside the ship.

It was more than just a mariner's interest in an enormous and unusual craft—and Slocum, to his surprise and almost against his will, had become a mariner of sorts by dint of learning the little chores that kept a boat afloat and safe; he was interested in seeing such a massive version of his own vessel, seeing whether the same valves and laws that applied to his sloop applied to the ship also.

Still, the main drive of his curiosity was more elemental, and it had to do with the ship's very scale, and the relationship of that scale to his life. He wanted to understand what cousinhood it might share with all the other huge forces that had moved his life and changed it and made it work in different ways, or not work at all. Seen from that angle, his interest was simple: Something black, huge, and unfamiliar had materialized alongside his sloop, which was what his life was contained in right now. And it was a force that was kin to another huge dynamic that had been in his life but was not any longer. He wished to see how that new force flexed and changed and stayed the same; how it ticked.

"As one neighbor to another," Slocum repeated, and licked rain off his lips. "Who is Melisande Young?"

"Yonge." He pronounced it like *thong*. "With an *e*."

"Yonge."

"You have no obligation." The mate half turned away, a carnie playing the hard sell.

"You're right about that," Slocum agreed, and looked at the ship again. It had engine problems, he remembered; Larsen had said its diesel was malfunctioning. That this floating mountain might share a problem with his sailboat made him feel tickly inside. It also, very slightly, diminished the ship in his vision, as if he had come close to a king on his throne, and heard him fart. "You're goddamn right," Slocum repeated. He did not nod or say yes or anything else to indicate acceptance. He began walking in the direction of the gangway.

But for all his awareness of interest in—and consciousness of—scale, Slocum was not prepared for just how big the ship really was when you got right up close to it. He had been only as near as the base of the concrete spur, which still left an angle of water between the ship and himself. Walking along it now, the ship's stern and the black wall of its side just seemed to grow and never stop growing until, when he stood at the base of the gangway, they took over the perceived world. And that effect continued as Slocum climbed the gangway, walking carefully on wooden slats, holding tight to the aluminum rail because he did not like heights. The wind shook the ramp as he walked. The water below was a void of velvet into which the reflection of lights stitched points of color few and far between. On the slip's other side his sloop shrank from the size of a real boat to something different, something small and changed by its smallness, and finally into a 1:500 mockup of something real.

Meanwhile the monster came to life: the rumble of a giant generator, the beastly rush of three dozen vents. The great warts and wrinkles of its metal skin. Portholes the size of his hatch. After climbing maybe four stories, he and the mate reached the steel doors thrown open fore and aft halfway up the ship's side. He walked out of the chill and wind and rain into light, and a room so big it could have held two of Slocum's sloop; into a scent of wood wax and salt and flowers and the steam of restaurants and laundries: like a seaside country club, with a faint back-odor of diesel fuel and tallow. Fluted glass columns, lit from within, flanked a polished mahogany counter to the left. A brass plaque read PURSER, but this was actually a security office, for men wearing commando sweaters and pistol belts sat behind the counter, and behind them stretched a continuum of video screens showing vistas of deck, gangway, corridor. Walkie-talkies crackled on a recharge rack. A cardboard sign on a stand pointed aft down another corridor: COUNTY DIESEL → ENGINE ROOM THIS WAY.

The walls of this room were paneled in cherrywood. The light fixtures were fluted like the columns, or else bent into intricate vines, orchids, and other organic shapes. A bronze woman bearing a bronze vase from which more orchids exploded formed the finial to a broad spiral staircase also paneled in fruitwoods. Slocum did not stare but it took real effort.

The mate tapped Slocum's name into a terminal on the purser's counter and asked him to scan his thumb across a digital reader. An electric motor whined as the gangplank was raised. Zurbruegge, nodding to the security men, led Slocum leftward, down a corridor carpeted in red and paneled in mahogany and lined with doors and rails of teak. Signs read SATELLITE RELAY, TELECONFERENCING, H DECK. A small elevator hummed them upward, past G, F (breakout sessions), E, D (restaurant), C (Oceanus Lounge), and stopped at B deck.

B deck was not cherrywood. B deck was a mahogany-paneled indoor passageway overlooking the orange lifeboats and their davits and greased cables and electric motors. A porthole with curtains open showed a U-shaped cabin. It contained a credenza and two beds, blue blankets bearing a stylized seahorse motif, neatly turned down; a vase full of fresh roses. The mate led him outside, over a high coaming on which Slocum tripped, into a strange wind, a meanness of wind this high up. Salt-stained windows, and behind lay a library: green carpet, glass-fronted shelves containing hard-copy books, brass reading lamps like the opened bulbs of tulips, a walnut desk with inkwell and cream blotter and cream stationery on which, even through the window, Slocum could distinguish the seahorse symbol and a name—but he could not read the name at this range. Then they were past. They went through a couple more thick wooden doors to a third that Matt opened, gesturing so that Slocum would not trip over the lintel again. A corridor with painted steel walls and a sign reading STATEROOM 2-B and an unmarked door that the mate opened without knocking.

"Wait here," the mate said, "she'll be along." He hesitated and looked around the cabin as if checking that there was nothing Slocum could steal. He left, finally, shutting the door behind him.

It was a large stateroom, though not as big as the cabin Slocum had seen earlier, and it was a mess. Multicolored dresses, scarves, and brassieres covered a double bed. Through an open closet door women's shoes spilled out like the tongue of a multicolored avalanche. A fire of birch logs blazed in a tiny hearth; kindling, soot, and pokers lay like forest wrack before the chain-link screen.

This cabin was decorated much as the purser's lounge had been, with fluted glass and polished mahogany paneling and fixtures like stylized steel plants and green carpets woven through with the seahorse design. But the impression of luxury was subverted by untidiness and the sheer amount of extra objects scattered about. An armchair was piled high with magazines. A powerful telescope pointing upward led the eye to a skylight, while the scarves and a pair of flowered panties that festooned its knobs and traverses brought the eye down once more. The remains of a meal littered a dinner cart. Against one wall stood the largest single object in the cabin, including the bed: a giant aquarium, filled with trees of seaweed, multihued sand, a castle of deep blue glass, and the flicker, pause, and renewed flicker of sea life.

Slocum walked to the fire. Though small, it threw plenty of warmth if you put your buttocks right up to the screen. He watched the aquarium, trying to identify the fish. Some were obvious: a sea robin sidling up to a rock; the goateed chins and shawl fins of a couple of rare scrod;

the dark preserves of a conger eel in a hole in the biggest rock; the carpetlike flapping of small skate. Crabs made tout gestures across the sand. A bluefish charged drifts of minnows, slalomed around the castle's towers. Slocum abandoned the fire's warmth to peer at the castle from close range. It was all of indigo crystal and lit gently from within, like the column lights in this room and elsewhere on the ship. It had as many towers as an organ had pipes, a number of them fluted and flowerlike, so it was clear that this aquarium was no later addition to the decor but had been part of the first concept. Doors opened across dozens of balconies, through which the smaller fry came in or out depending on the proximity of bluefish. Slocum was not sure if he saw one more movement in the glass than could be accounted for by the troop of life in the aquarium, or if his sixth sense, perhaps, was growing better at screening. The feeling of being watched rose greatly in his consciousness, well beyond the itch he'd felt in recent days. He turned, and did not see her at first—there were three doors to the room, and between the open closet and the telescope a portion of the room was in shadow. Then he did—the transition was a result of a perception shift, whereby what had seemed a static collection of shapes resorted in his mind, and clicked off the algorithms for human, standing.

She had thin shoulders covered by a scarlet dressing gown that fell to the floor in columns so that for a microsecond he had the impression the ship had been designed to suit her. Or maybe it was the other way around and, because the whole ship was designed like that, she had dressed to match.

A white silk scarf was wrapped around her neck, which seemed to bend as it rose to support the oval of her face. Her nose was very straight until the end, where it turned up. Her chin and cheekbones were not weak but they did not quite work together—though they looked as if they might, in a plane projected forward from her face, closer to where she was going. Her hair was caught up in back and draped around her features in frondlike whirls and curves. Thin, a little crooked in how she held herself against the door; those were all part of his collection of first impressions of Melisande Yonge. But the ones that hit him hardest, and stayed with him longest, were: She was pale, so pale her skin looked like ricepaper lit from within; and the combination of that pallor and her sudden appearance out of nowhere and the particular presence of her convinced him, for another microsecond, that he knew her; more specifically, that he had invented her. For she was Lanne, the pale and not entirely benevolent Countess of the Northern March, in the Claire stories that he used to tell Bird at bedtime. She even wore Turkish slippers, of the sort Lanne might well wear, with golden filigree and toes turned up in a point, like her nose.

Then she moved, and of course she was not a figment of the ship's design, or of his daughter's bedtime fiction, but a strange woman in her late twenties who walked into the cabin and said his name without a question mark afterward.

He nodded. She gathered the columns of dressing gown around her. Her fingers were long and as white as the rest of her. Her hair was very black and glossy and her pallor made it blacker still. She opened her fingers, swept one hand around her, and said, "This is how I live. You'll have to excuse the mess. I clean up, but then I toss it around again." She did not sound apologetic; it was a statement of fact. She smiled and then her smile seemed to break, half her mouth going up and the other down, and she frowned.

"You *are* Mr. Slocum?"

Slocum realized he had been staring. His heart was beating too hard for this situation. But he had always liked the Countess Lanne, despite her occasional betrayals and her restricted fashion sense, and he could not get rid of the impression that he knew this woman because of the stories he had made up about her. Even her voice—soft, a little too high for her stature—was Lanne's. He cleared his throat and said, "You wanted to see me. I don't know why." She started to speak and he kept going, rudely, "I don't know what we have to say to each other."

She looked at him for a beat. The frown made short lines between her eyes.

"As neighbors. I told Matt—Mr. Zurbruegge—to say that."

"He said it," Slocum replied.

"Do you want a drink?" she asked.

His instinct was to refuse. You never accepted gifts from those you might have to bargain with, it gave your opponent an advantage. But his ass was warm from the fire and he had the feeling a drink would warm his insides the way the fire heated up his outside. Anyway, he wasn't going to bargain with this woman; he didn't have to bargain with anyone anymore, with the possible exception of Amy.

"OK," he said.

She opened a cabinet decorated with inlaid wooden jungles and took out two, then four bottles thickly cut in crystal. "Bourbon, absinthe, rum, champagne," she said. "I think there's port, also."

"Bourbon's fine."

"The port's quite old?"

"Bourbon."

She handed him a glass. A faint jingle, as of ice, seemed to accompany her movement. But she had not added ice. The glass was made of the same heavily leaded crystal. Like the castle, he realized. He noted with a certain amusement that she had poured him a lot of booze. Negotiating Tactic A-1, he thought; A for ancient, 1 for simplistic. He walked back to the fire and pressed his buttocks against the screen. She walked around the cabin, picking clothes off the deck and tossing them onto the bed. She moved impatiently, as if in a hurry to get somewhere. He heard the jingle again. Wind chimes, he guessed.

"Aren't you joining me?" he asked.

She snagged a riding coat that had to be cashmere by how it folded.

"I don't need one, right now." She tossed the coat on the bed, then threw her right hand to one side in a curious gesture, as if getting rid of more than the coat. "Do you know—did Matt tell you—why I wanted to see you?"

"Sure," Slocum replied. He took a sip of whiskey. He had been right; it switched on little lights in him all the way down his gullet and into his stomach, like lighting a runway for the takeoff of a plane of warmth.

"It's important," she continued. "For the safety of the ship. You know what I'm talking about—" She stopped and turned to face him directly. She was standing by the open closet now, and in the welter of shoes, in that avalanche of dozens, maybe close to a hundred pairs of different styles and colors, she stood barefoot. Her eyes were slightly slanted. The pupils were black-brown and very large, like those of a cat in the dark. Or like a jagger, he thought; like someone who injected jisi yomo and seven other drugs via a triage program, to kick her psyche in different directions in response to 3-D drama.

"You want me to move my boat."

"Matt—Mr. Zurbruegge—says he can't moor properly with you in the way."

"You seem pretty well moored to me."

She stared at him. Turned to glance at the porthole. Turned back. Until now she had not looked at him for more than a few seconds at a time, but now she was searching for information in his features, in the set of his mouth. He had the feeling that he had started existing for her more in the last few seconds than he had before, and it was a strange experience that he could not explain well.

She threw air away, with her left hand this time.

"I don't know the technical details." She was still looking at him. A good shot of arrogance lay in her stare, the confidence of a woman born to wealth and power and so used to the rarefied air of that plateau that she even breathed differently. Minor stuff, like dealing with logistics and people who worked for her, belonged to the lower regions—thick air, slow movements: the people of the plain. "But Matt says there's a hurricane coming and we would be safer moored right up against the wharf. You have to understand"—she glanced around the cabin, looked back at him—"this is where I live, right? If the ship is threatened, so am I."

Slocum took another sip of bourbon. His stomach warmed further. His ass was actually hot. He left the fire and walked to the porthole opposite the hearth and looked out. In front of him was the Town skyline, up to Johnnycake Hill and the Moby Dick Theme Park, and the elevated ramp to the highway. Below him, just over the lower rim of porthole, was the roof of the Bone Cement warehouse.

The steel depression in which the porthole was set smelled of tallow and salt. He stood on tiptoe, trying to find his sloop. He had to lean so far into the porthole that his cheek touched the glass before the tip of the sloop's mast came into view. He felt a surge of affection for his boat, so small and insignificant against the obscene scale of this interloper. He went back to the fire. Without looking at the woman he said, "What threatens you threatens me more."

"Then that makes us alike, doesn't it?"

He looked at her. She stood in the same cracked stance she had adopted earlier in the doorway, but leaned forward, as if in debate. And Slocum thought, he had been wrong. It was not arrogance—or rather, it included arrogance, but that was the smaller part of her manner. The way she stood did not denote an automatic authority, and the way she stood was less part of her than was that gesture of sweeping away. Impatience was more important, and bigger than impatience, he thought, was a demand for air; for a lack of impediments to vision, to oxygen, to travel. For an end to trammels and interruptions and the hemming in.

He breathed deeply. This cabin smelled like the rest of the ship with a hint of women's soaps added: lavender, hollyhock. The liner trembled a little as, eight or whatever decks down, another generator kicked in. Slocum felt as if a different generator had fired to life inside him as well, and all he said was, "We're not allies, if you want my berth."

"Why are you so stubborn?" she asked. She said this softly, without shifting her gaze or moving. The air between them was unclear. "Didn't Mr. Zurbruegge tell you we would pay expenses?"

"He told me."

"You know what he meant."

"I knew. Although 'expenses' was all he said."

"That's odd. Such—subtlety—it's not like Matt."

"I imagine there are ports where the 'expenses' are very high."

"There are ports like that."

"Do you live on this ship all the time?"

"I told you."

Still they stared at each other. The blacks and browns of her pupils did something odd: They appeared to move, lever apart, come together again as he looked. He broke his gaze first. He felt as if the strange air of the cabin could get him high. He sipped whiskey. The booze did not make him feel different. He walked over to the aquarium. He needed time to think. He did not trust this; he did not trust this. He had felt the same tightness of breath the first time he saw Amy and that had not lasted; hell, he had felt that way over Luisa, only not as strongly. With Luisa it had not thrummed in other parts of him the way it thrummed now. But never mind the strength, because none of this advanced one-sixteenth of an inch down the path of allowing his body to react to any woman the way it once had, and there was nothing different about his body now as far as he could tell. He sipped bourbon, only there was none left in the glass and that surprised him. The bluefish, attracted by the flash of outside crystal, approached the transparent wall. Slocum tapped the aquarium with his empty glass. The bluefish was gone—that was the only way to describe it—one instant it was there and the next it was not; just as this woman, reversing the effect, had not been there one second and the next had been present, when she first entered the cabin. It was that, Slocum realized, as much as anything, which reminded him of Lanne. She too had the ability to appear and disappear at whim. In Lanne's case it had been magic, but if you did not see the transition then other forms of similar motion were to all intents and purposes as miraculous.

"Don't," she said. "Please."

He turned from the aquarium.

"It frightens them?"

"Yes." She came closer. She was examining the glass box, checking for aeration, fungi, the presence or absence of fish. "To their ears, a tap is like a hand grenade going off."

"He doesn't like his home messed with," Slocum observed.

She smiled at that; one corner up, one down. He felt like he had won a prize in a street fair: Thereya go, the lady smiles, you gets yer pick of the enormous bear or the radio alarm clock.

"That's not his home," she said. "He likes the eelgrass in that corner, right? Maybe you can prove your point with that."

"All politics is local?" Slocum gestured at the aquarium with his glass.

"It has its villages, and towns."

"It has a castle," Slocum remarked, "that takes up maybe a quarter of it."

"Where the smallest fish live," she replied. "Look." Pointing at the minnows that, worried because the blue had just shot through their schools into a jungle of kelp, had shimmered off into twenty parts of the fortress: workshops, a corner keep, a cathedral, a monastery near the top.

"It's not exactly an open society," Slocum said, "if it has a castle like that."

When she looked at him again her eyes were not quite so dark. He added, coolly, "The castle changes things."

Three knocks on one of the inner doors. "Just a second," the woman said loudly. "I don't see how," she told Slocum. "You look at old towns, in Burgundy, the Lebanon, in Punjab, right? They all have their keep."

"This is more than a keep," Slocum said. "It's a safe place."

"And what's wrong with that?" she asked, and repeated, "What's wrong with that?"

"It changes things," he insisted.

The voice came from the closed door. "Melisande!"

"I'm coming, Shanti," she called. "How does it change things?"

"You don't think safety restricts you?" Slocum asked. "You don't think it cuts you off from all the messages? I mean, the world is full of messages, but if you live in something like that—"

"But it's not safe," she interrupted. She was almost whispering and she was bent toward him and sweeping her hand again as if to brush away the foolishness of his argument. From this distance he noticed that the scarf around her neck bulged slightly on the right side, over the valley between larynx and the tendons; something was concealed underneath, something mechanical, with machined angles; a wireless Vox link, perhaps. "Don't you understand how your allegory fails? How can it be safe, *when the real danger comes from within*?"

He was not interested in what she said anymore. He was watching her pupils narrow and expand and wondering if it was jisi and not really caring.

"This is the real danger," she continued. "What people

are always scared of in the end: That what terrifies them might already have gotten in."

The side door opened. A middle-aged, brown-skinned woman with short hair entered the cabin. She was dressed in a sari. She looked at Slocum and gave him a smile that was token, and a quick scan that was professional and hard. "We have seven minutes," she said, and began picking up shoes.

"I'm almost ready," Melisande said.

"I'd like to discuss this more," Slocum told her, and looked in the aquarium for the bluefish. "Maybe I'll come see you again."

"You can't," she said. "I mean, I can't." Both her hands scooped air now, and she grimaced. The frown lines were back. Slocum got the sense that she was used to this argument and only half listening to herself. It's how she keeps her portcullis locked, he thought.

"Security won't let me, there are too many—"

"Bluefish," he interrupted.

She shook her head, and did not smile.

"You can leave a message," she added. "If I can, if I'm not busy, if there are no—"

"No more talking." The woman, Shanti, appeared at Slocum's elbow. "I'm sorry." She took the glass out of his hand. The door through which Slocum had come opened. One of the security men peered in. When he saw Slocum he jerked his head sideways. Slocum noticed the jambook keyboard hung around Shanti's neck and at the guard's belt.

"Time to go," the security man said, not unpleasantly. "If you'll step this way—"

Slocum turned to look at Melisande again but already she was headed for the other door, following Shanti out. "I'll leave a message," he called.

She half turned but did not look at him this time, just kept going, barefoot, out the door, which closed solidly behind her.

TWELVE

THE TWO DECKHANDS who escorted Slocum back
down the layered decks and through the purser's area continued walking him all the way down the gangplank, across
the spur to where the trucks parked, and on to the warehouse. It seemed that this was the beginning and end of
the ship's territory within the already defined boundaries
of the Coggeshall Wharf Maritime Development Zone.

It was still raining hard. The fragments of light from the
ship, from MacTavish's trailer, from the refurbished section
of the former cement warehouse, pooled together on the
cold cobbles of the wharf. The refrigerator truck was gone.

Slocum walked toward his sloop. It looked dark and tiny,
like something abandoned and eventually forgotten in the
shadow of pilings; something the wharf's marine life, the
barnacles and mutated mussels, the codium weed and bor-
ers, would glom on to, creep over, and eventually drag into
the rotten depths.

His pace slowed. The idea of marine life reminded him
of the aquarium in Melisande Yonge's cabin, and the shining indigo palace where juvenile bass took refuge. After the
soft comfort of that cabin, the prospect of another evening

in the saloon of his boat felt inexpressibly grim. He had dried a little in the proximity of that hearth. Now he was as damp as if he had never gone aboard the ship, and although he could change in his boat, and light the little coal stove, it would take an hour to draw out the chill. Even if he changed clothes, they would be clammy from the humidity that was a fact of life aboard a small boat.

Slocum turned back toward the security gate. Mac-Tavish wore his half-mask and was bent over something on his desk and, unless he had the gate's videocam playing thumbnail on his visor, did not see him leave. Slocum turned left down Front Street, toward the hurricane barrier. He had no goal in mind save to avoid going home. He pulled the collar of his reefer jacket over his neck and dug his hands deep into the pockets. He needed to work off the odd excitement that had started up in him from the first couple of seconds when he saw Melisande Yonge standing in the cabin door, when he built up that first picture of her in his head. It had felt, then, the way your hand felt when it was near a short circuit, a place conducting electricity where no current normally should run. Dangerously near, of course, but still mostly isolated so that your hand got warm and the rest of you tingled with the physical knowledge that nearby was a force that could give all the molecules in your body a major shove, or even reshuffle them, or fry them outright if you got much closer.

He tried to remember her now. He could think of details—the cracked smile that didn't seem to know where to go—the V shape of her face, the pool of eyes, the tired stance. Her throwaway gesture; remembering made the excitement tingle further. He had not looked at her long enough, in the aggregate, to glue all of it into coherence. The Countess Lanne, on the other hand, he recalled perfectly; and, as he tried to remember, it was she he began to see in Melisande's place. And then even Lanne's features seemed to fade with the effort of recall. They blurred and spread wetly, bright in color but without definition or immanence of shape, like the reflected streetlights winking green yellow red; red green; between the boarded-up warehouses of Front Street.

Because when you got shocked it was not the specs of wiring and voltage you remembered but the convulsion in sinew and bone that flipped you in the room and lived with you thereafter in affect. And if human perception was a process of arranging familiarity—so that attraction worked by a system of memories cobbled together each time into something new—then where that process brought him now was back to Amy and the first time he saw her in the PR doughnut; and when he had seen her by the foreign subsidiaries espresso machine, where they had first talked.

She was on the tail end of her marriage—she and Harry just back from a not-very-successful patchup trip to the Caribbean. He still cringed at how predictable his opening lines had been. You would think he had read enough scripts to rig a cuter meet. But you made do with the material you had, and his material was: He had gone to a theme party for the release of an X-Corp 3-D about a commando's romance with a local *métisse* in the third invasion of Haiti, and he'd saved a bottle cap from one of the Caribbean beers they served at the release. Said something about how she must miss the sun, and pressed it into Amy's hand like a code.

Corny, poorly art-directed—but it worked. She had drunk Legba beer when she was down there and the cap brought back, apparently, good memories. After a few months of banter she had started meeting him at places and times arranged so there would be no possibility of running into Harry, who worked in production and had odd hours.

Slocum's workboots were heavy enough that the slog back from Madame Ling's had not entirely soaked them.

Now, however, he felt rainwater mushing even in the arc of his toes and the cave of his instep. Might as well enjoy it, he thought vaguely, and stepped off what sidewalk Front Street retained and into a pothole two feet deep. Remembered the feeling of joy, as a kid, of doing that, out of range of his parents' remonstrance, Oh how could you, that was your last clean pair of pants and now I have to do another load of laundry; it still felt good, he thought. And he sloshed forward, licking rain off his lips. The feeling of being watched was with him again but it was almost a friendly feeling; he might miss it were it to vanish. In any case, it did not interfere with the sense memories of childhood, his and also Bird's. For he saw their child too in his mind's eye, in a yellow slicker and green boots molded to look like frogs, stamping temporary holes in black water, her gray eyes ashine, raindrops dripping off her long, curved nose. The waterfall of rain in his boots and the state of being watched were secondary input now, faded by the release of memory, the 3-D video of Amy playing in his cortex.

Though there were skips in that video, breakdowns in production. Slocum's and Amy's meeting, such as it was, had good values, and so did the months they courted. She eventually told Harry and they split up like lightning cracking apart a sick oak, which left Slocum struggling a little in the second growth of her guilt and emotions still coiled like vines around her throat and Harry's too. That spring had been full of crisp colors, tension, drive. (He aimed deliberately for other potholes, making swells of the filthy water. His boots were heavy with the rainwater they bucketed up at every step.)

And then Amy got pregnant. He could not understand what happened to the transition; after Bird was born it was as if the editor had thrown the fast-forward switch for twenty minutes and all good colors and tensions had speeded to a blur of shallow vidcolors and an indecipherable cackle of words spoken too fast and at too high a pitch. Bird a mewling newt, taking first steps, second grade, kootie-covered boys. Amy with long hair, Amy's head almost shaved, Amy with a bob. All of that was his life, their life, what they had to remember and value. All of it was nothing compared to what he remembered best, which was how they ended up in that starter palace in Bayview. He realized now that memories, such as when he met Bird by the golf course, stood out because they were breaks in the pattern. The pattern, overwhelmingly, had turned into an ideogram of a shared solitude. They had lived alone, all three of them hermits in the parallel and luxurious halls of that huge house. The feeling of missing Amy even as he made love to Breena or Larissa in 3-D; as Amy fucked Lance or Mahal; well, that had been strong. And yet it was also weak compared to the feeling he got sometimes of just being so god-damned lonely at breakfast or after dinner or in any of the routine gear changes of their daily lives when they were supposed to move and roll each other's connections if only in the most predictable ways. "Cold out"; "Car's in the shop"; "Gotta walk the dog"; "Can you pick up some milk"; "PTA meeting tonight." Bird had broken her ankle at lacrosse and because of that they had talked and acted again as a family for a week or so.... And though they'd never had a dog, they did say those kinds of things, but even then it felt that while those statements should have provided cues for stronger stuff—affection, anger, disagreement—in fact they had said exactly what they meant and nothing whatsoever had lain under their words.

Oh, and he had to pull back again, he was still exaggerating. There had been flashpoints of anger, of love expressed, of humor, even. Bayview was a company town and Amy kept working for the firm till Bird was born, and they had plenty to laugh about at X-Corp: jealousies, spats, the affairs of others. The corporate culture, as a matter of policy, forced them to communicate electronically, or in great human alliance with the nodes of people glued together against isolation in places like coffee machines and restrooms. They went to the X-Corp theme island for vacations with Jedd and Maya Motieff. They rode in submarines and saw sharks, fell off jet skis, laughed at their own clumsiness. Jedd was a monster of ego but he had a good irony to him that Slocum relied on at work; Maya's gentle wistfulness appealed to them both. Their kid and Bird got along well in the early ages. A real family, he and Amy and Bird. When they had only one 3-D workstation—before Bird got her own hookup—they were forced to interact and negotiate over what they watched and it had been fun to work out a barter situation between Bird's teenage 3-Ds and Amy's kitchen dramas and the space fiction he himself favored. Like Monopoly, Bird commented; they had elaborated a system of credits. (He had used that structure later, in the ICE.) But now that he thought about it, was it not fitting that those hooks and gearings between them that had flipped today into his memory circuits revolved to such an extent around the Flash? And was it also telling that they had wanted it this way—that no one forced them to jack in to *Wanderbird* or *Pain* or *Rikka*? They woke up in the morning thinking about the stronger colors and shapes and contrasts of the Flash, until what he had come to crave—or so he sometimes surmised—was a relief from richness; a smaller spectrum of dimensions; a respite from the intensity of Flash life, the lesser drama of family matters.

Slocum turned to face the way he had come. The wind blew from the south and facing north his eyes were sheltered. A car turned west down School Street, its headlights painting stripes across washed-out brick. Otherwise this area was empty of life.

He resumed walking. The park that culminated at the hurricane barrier lay ahead and to the left. In this dark, in this rain, he would see nothing and anyway his walk had become a promenade that was inside, not out. Turning west up Union Street brought him along the south side of the theme-park wall, high enough that the shine and tinkle of the Virtual Whaling Voyage splashed against his cheeks and ears. "Thar she blows and whitewaters too and sparm at that," a manly voice yelled faintly, and was answered by "ahoy," "avast there," and "shiver me timbers" from the teleprompted and enthusiastic crowd. The rain hesitated, then strengthened. The wind kept on as before and washed most of the sounds northward toward the Grid. The giant white flukes of the automated "sperm whale" smashed a boat and tossed life-sized matelots through the air like candlepins. Slocum felt not even a microjoule of sensation as he watched this ersatz mayhem, and this too was an avenue into his last couple of years at Bayview.

The rain seemed colder. It trickled down Slocum's neck and he found that the idea of his saloon and its tiny stove had shifted from a dank, lonely feeling to one of rest and relative warmth. He wanted to get home. He turned right down Purchase Street, which would bring him over the top of Johnnycake Hill to William Street; William led straight east to the wharf's southern end. From the top of the hill, had the lasers and neon of the theme park not shattered the night with glare, he could have seen over the park and warehouses to the harbor and Whaling City Marina. He resented that invasion, the way X-Corp's theme park and casino had taken over what nobody had a right to own or abrogate, the black night and the scatter of second-magnitude stars and the dim glow of home on the horizon. Slocum shielded his eyes with one hand, mostly because he did not want to see that idiotic surging whale, though he could see it clearly in his mind's eye since X-Corp employees got free access to the park (not the casino) and Bird had liked going there on weekends before she got more interested in the Flash and the affect channels she was not supposed to surf. Tonight he would not see

Coggeshall Wharf or the black shape of the ship he knew lay behind the glare.

The way that light pervaded everything, even through shading fingers, was amazing, like the supernatural blood that soaked the world in 3-D vampire dramas. It even seemed to come from behind him, where the theme park was not.

Slocum turned. Most of the light behind was reflections from the Moby Dick but a significant percentage came from a Town police car that moved stealthily in his tracks, at exactly his speed and fifteen feet away. Its revolving rooflights were on, and so were its headlights, searchlights, and foglamps, though none of them made much difference to the street, given the competition.

The cruiser braked to a halt as soon as he turned. The driver was invisible behind smoked windshield glass. The slap of wipers was just audible over the chorus of "Blow the Man Down" that accompanied the half-hour "departures" of the *Pequod*. Out of nowhere, for he had not smoked in fifteen years, Slocum yearned for a cigarette.

"Hold it right there, sir," the cruiser's loudspeaker crackled, though Slocum was not moving anymore. "Put your hands where we can see them, sir."

The loudspeaker reminded Slocum of the security gate at the Mechanic's Zone. Irritation squirted, as it always did at the thought of the Mechanic.

"Move to the hood of the vehicle, sir. Put your hands on the hood."

Slocum stood, motionless.

"*Put* your *hands* on the *hood, sir.*"

Slocum did as he was told. The doors on each side of the cruiser opened at the same time. Two shapes in slickers, hats, and dark gloves got out. The right hand of each rested on the butt of a holstered pistol. One cop stayed by the driver's door. The other moved behind Slocum, pushed him so that his face practically touched the streaming metal of the hood and the fifteen-inch-high L of POLICE. The cop frisked him quickly. He dragged Slocum's left hand back and ringed it with cold metal and then did the same to the right.

Slocum was too surprised to be angry. He thought of blurting, "Here what's this all about?" or "This is all a big mistake," or "Do you have any idea who I am?" or "I wanna talk to my lawyer," but all those responses were straight out of a thousand cheap screenplays and anyway his lawyer was Jedd Motieff. He was unsure, since he had left X-Corp, if Jedd was his lawyer anymore. To say Jedd had not approved of the move to the ICE would be like saying the Atlantic was a body of water: true, but not doing the reality justice. Anyway, as a vestigial growth from his old life, Slocum retained the rich, educated professional's trust in the civic virtues of law enforcement. He had done nothing wrong, he figured. It was like his UCC card: Everything would come right when the misunderstanding was straightened out.

The cop put a hand on the back of Slocum's skull and bent his neck to fit him into the cruiser. The door slammed. The driver turned and looked at him. Slocum wondered if these cops wore dark glasses because they had to work around the lights of the Moby Dick. The driver looked away almost immediately, but despite the shades Slocum recognized him.

"Leaky Louie," he said.

Louie looked straight ahead. The other cop got in, cursing as he shook his hat free of water. The rain played jazz snares on the roof. The cruiser's jambook was set to audio. It said, "Bravo Six, you got a ten-ninety-seven on Acushnet and Fifth." The screen showed a map of Town and a scroll of radio messages. Slocum did not recognize the cop who had cuffed him. Leaky Louie put the car in drive and they drove down William and turned left on South Second. The cop riding shotgun fiddled with the jambook till classical music came from the speakers in front and the scroll of cop events was replaced by videos of a conductor, an orchestra, and clips of alpine scenes from a music site. "Mahler," the right-hand cop said, more happily. *"Das Lied von der Erde."*

"Anybody wanna tell me what this is about?" Slocum asked.

No answer. He looked through the grille from the slick black back of one cop head to the slick black head of the other. Silently he went through the mantra he had recited earlier—wealthy (or formerly wealthy), educated, non-criminal: untouchable. He could feel the reaction to a tough negotiating stance start up again, the Teflon coating his voice and reactions.

"Let me ask you this. Did Vera tell you to lean on me?"

The police radio interrupted Mahler, asking for the whereabouts of Detective Slate.

The cop on the right said, with a show of indifference that might almost have been genuine, "Who?"

"You know: Vera Consalves. Her and Barboza and Amaral appoint Vane. Vane, the chief of police? The chief tells you what to do. The chief reports to Vera. You *do* know the chief?"

"Keep it up, pal," the cop on the right said. "Just keep it up. You know."

"Now why you think Vera wants to lean on you?" Leaky Louie asked. It was the first time he had spoken.

"Because Vera wants that ship." Slocum watched the back of Louie's head. "You know, the one that just came in? She figures it brings money to the Town. And the ship wants to be where my boat is."

"Your boat?" Louie said. He glanced at the other cop, who snickered dreadfully.

"Lemme get this straight," the other cop said. "That ship wants *your* dock? What is your boat—the fuckin' U.S.S. *Enterprise*?"

Louie giggled at that. They both found it funny for a while. Louie leaned over and opened a thermos and the smell of coffee filled Slocum with lust and smallness. Mahler's violins surged and ran out. Finally the right-hand cop said, "We always got special orders to clean up riffraff hanging around the theme park. Sagres. Teedees. Bums."

Slocum said nothing.

"People who hang at the Sunset Tap," the right-hand cop added.

Leaky Louie did not glance at his partner. Slocum, with the hard steel gaze of the Slocum who worked on the second doughnut from the top of Arcadia, gazed at their equal heads. Something was off here—not that Leaky Louie hung out at the Tap, but that he seemed embarrassed by it. Surely the other cop knew Louie hung there too? Or was Louie supposed to be a plant, keeping the Sunset Tap under some kind of surveillance (though everyone knew who he worked for), and he was embarrassed that his cover was blown? Or was his frequenting of the bar being used against him somehow by other cops?

Slocum shook his head. He was getting a headache. He said nothing at that point but he felt his anger starting. When Slocum was a teen he had lived in a village north of Town and the cops were the usual kind: the good guys who liked drama and guns and believed in public safety, and the bad kind who were short and had small dicks, and enjoyed pushing people around to compensate. After his mother died Slocum went through a wild time when he was dealing with the totality of absence as teenage boys usually did—by breaking things, punishing the material world, trying to push so hard that something would give either outside or in. His father, who was disoriented and no good at discipline and worked all hours—that was his way of coping—had been unable to provide the opposition the boy needed. That task had been happily taken on by Officers Tobey and Burke, who liked beating up boys.

Slocum could still see in his mind the handsome black features of Tobey and the blond hair and meaty hands of Officer Burke. They picked him up regularly and made sure he was arraigned for trespassing, breaking and entering, disturbing the peace, driving without a license, drunk and disorderly. Before he was booked they always made sure Slocum was hit in the soft places that would not develop a bruise—the stomach and kidneys and balls.

Slocum eventually grew out of his bad behavior, Tobey was promoted off the streets, and things settled down. When he finished grad school and got a job and dressed for promotion, Slocum began to realize that the things Tobey and Burke had done to him would never have happened had his family been making the money he was at X-Corp; would never, ever happen in Bayview, where your exact rank in the X-Corp hierarchy scrolled up on the Bayview cops' screen as the cruiser drove by your house. He never grew comfortable with such privilege but he learned to put it out of his mind and even relax a little in the security it provided his family.

Slocum shook his head again. Tonight he had time traveled—gone right through the Bayview lessons to twenty-odd years ago, and adopted like a pair of old jeans the bad attitude he'd had as a teenager. It was a mindset common enough in the ICE, where a large number of marginals had congregated—though the cops there usually left them alone. Maybe, Slocum thought, living in the ICE had made him regress.

But he was not in the ICE anymore, he was not a teenager anymore. He had been a top-tier executive for eight years and he knew what rights he had both as an individual and as a former X-Corp Multimedia officer. He would get what he deserved by virtue of his civic status; he would call Jedd Motieff, if need be, and make these cops sorry they had ever fucked with him.

It struck him, in the surge of rage and confidence that

came with this resolve, that he had changed, all unknowingly, since he'd left Arcadia. The aggressive senior VP who had gotten what he wanted by demanding it from the world over the last few years had turned passive and uncertain—a wimp. If he expected to get what he desired now, he would have to revert, to some extent, to what he had been before he joined the ICE.

It was a lesson that applied to other issues besides this bizarre encounter. Nevertheless this situation was what he had to resolve first, before he could apply its implications to other bottlenecks. Slocum shifted in his seat. His shoulder was growing cramped in this position.

Then he leaned forward and said, "I suppose you two clowns don't know this ship belongs to the X-Corp holding company. And X-Corp, of course, provides half the Town's tax base because of the theme park, because it fronted the Indians for the casino"—he grabbed a quick breath—"and also it funded the charter revision so Arcadia and Bayview could be split off from the Town so X-Corp wouldn't have to fund lots of expensive workfare programs, or clinics for teedees."

The right-hand cop turned to look at him.

"Fuckin' fascinating," he said. His expression had not changed.

Slocum sat back. The symphony was sloping off for a cigarette break. The radio squawked, "We got a report of Sagres ten-twenty-two on Wamsutta." Another voice said, "Bravo fourteen responding." The tires licked rain off the pavement. Slocum said, "I was on the community relations panel for a year at Arcadia. But you know all that," he added softly, "don't you, boys?"

"We know all that," the right-hand cop agreed, not looking at Louie or Slocum.

"Why don't you switch off that fairy music," Louie said, glancing at his partner.

"You gonna turn on yer fuckin' Portygee shit?" the right-hand cop complained.

But before Louie could change channels the other cop said, "There it is." Louie slowed the cruiser, hissed it to a stop beside a long black car that was parked, lights out, before the locked doors of a state mental-health office. The right-hand cop lowered his window and Slocum's at the same time.

Slocum stared at the limo. This is ridiculous, he thought. He had seen this so many times—hell, he had so often produced this kind of meet that he almost believed he knew what would happen when the limo's windows whispered open. A Yakusa kingpin would be sitting there, a toadlike Yokohaman who licked his lips repeatedly and had fingers missing. Or a lantern-jawed African in a double-breasted suit, one of the Nigerian mob that ran the container areas in the nearest working seaport to the east. He was so wrapped up in the 3-D–drama version of what he expected that when the limo's smoked glass finally did drop, he was taken aback for a second.

"Vera," he said, finally.

The deathglow of streetlights penetrated the limo's interior only partially but he recognized the gelled hair, the full lips—and deeper than that, the tension of control that betrayed itself in the twitching of her eyebrows, the force in her fingers as she thrust a folded document through her window toward his.

"Go on," she rasped as he looked at the paper. "Take it."

"He can't," the right-hand cop said. "He's cuffed."

"He's cuffed?" Vera asked, and looked almost uncertain for a second.

"I'll take it," the cop offered.

"It's got to be official," Vera said.

"What is it?" Slocum asked.

Vera's eyes were well hidden in shadow.

"A notice of eviction," she said. "You failed the credit-worthiness part of the Capital Development Zone bylaw."

"The what?" Slocum coughed. His throat was dry. He repeated his words.

"Your UCC was vaporized," Vera explained. As if tired of the effort and the rain, she thrust the document toward the right-hand cop, who took it. She leaned back in her seat. Her voice came fainter but still clear. "What that means is, you can't legally be party to a Town contract anymore."

"But that's got nothing to do with the wharf," Slocum protested. "That rule has to do with big stuff—waste-hauling bids, school construction—you *know* that, Vera."

She waved one hand. The long fingers moved like seaweed in a current.

"Of course, if you move your boat, I'm sure we can make an exception. You have two weeks," she added.

"Two weeks?" Slocum said, and the surprise in his tone was real. "You're giving me two weeks? How long is that ship gonna be here?"

"Two weeks," Vera repeated. "Check it out. It's in your contract, under 'cancel.' "

The limo's windows hissed shut. Its engine started and it moved rapidly into the rain-lashed night.

"My turn," Louie stated quietly, when the limo's lights had turned right on Elm toward the Federal Zone, and vanished. He reached for the terminal. Before he could change channels the audio squawked, "Bravo eight." Louie picked up a headset, put it on.

"Bravo eight."

"Ten-sixteen at eighty-six Lower Cannon."

"Bravo eight, ten-four," Louie said. "We gotta civil control, drop-off at Coggeshall, we're on our way."

The audio crackled. Louie turned off the Mahler but did not switch to WFDO. The cruiser made sounds like serpents, like belly-sliding dragons as it did a U-turn and

accelerated up South Second. Its gumball lights were on
again and they cut spoonfuls of vision from the dark street:
an arc of brick, a parked taxi, two faces staring out the
windows of a pizzeria. Louie performed a slick controlled
skid into William and stopped the car in the middle of a
puddle fifty feet from MacTavish's trailer.

The right-hand cop opened the door for Slocum. He
stuffed the document Vera had handed him inside Slocum's
soggy jacket. "You have been officially served with a notice
of eviction with Town police officers legal witness to serving of said notice."

He unlocked the handcuffs and said, "Stay away from
the theme park." Then he added, sarcastically, "Sir."

He got back in and the cruiser did a three-point turn
and sped northward up Front toward the head of the harbor. Slocum stood in the middle of the puddle, in the di-
minishing strobe of cop lights, staring after them, rubbing
his wrists where the cuffs had bitten.

THIRTEEN

THE SUNSET TAP WAS a late-night bar but it reopened at
6 A.M. and served Portuguese bread and blueberry muffins
and drew a breakfast crowd of sorts. Freitas was off duty in
the early morning, sleeping in his room at the Carvalho
Arms, cocooned in Mexican Percocets and Ben Gay fumes
and the roundhouse dreams of ex-fighters; as a result, the
morning clientele did not include the bruised-knuckle
types who either were friends of Freit or sought to hurt
him and this changed the mood. It was more of a normal
early-morning feel, Slocum thought, warming his hands
around a coffee mug. Then again, maybe not; in a country
that had grown generally to look more and more like
Bayview and its clean, bright, and pain-free public areas, he
supposed most breakfast joints did not feature a Budweiser-
and-blueberry-muffin special. Nor did the backbone of
their morning clientele consist of hookers and former fishing skippers and crewmen off midwater trawlers with all
the fashion statements that went along with it: watch caps;
rubber boots (the canvas lining showing); T-shirts that still
bore a backtaste of hake.

The TV showed news: aircrash in Dusseldorf, Milan

bourse gone offline, change in MC for the 3-D Emmys, four hundred dead in Malaysian riots, plus a feature on the secret flan recipes of the Nodista guerrillas making a last stand against central government forces in Colombia's Antioquia range.

Fado played from Obrigado's speakers. The only reason Slocum could warm his hands at coffee and pick at his muffin was that Obrigado loved *fado*. Early in his days at Coggeshall, before he got used to simply switching on WFDO, Slocum had bought a slew of *fado* spindles by masters of the art: Carlos do Carmo, Pedro Homem de Melo, Amalia Rodrigues, Joao Souza de Silva. This morning he had brought the lot to the Sunset Tap and opened a credit against what Obrigado thought they were worth, which was a third of their real value but Slocum did not care. This credit chopped at the central insecurity that having his UCC card suspended had fostered in the core of his social being. And it reaffirmed, a little, the bad-boy joy he had felt on that day when he went into the ICE offices and—breath held in surprise at his own temerity—signed up to run their online node market. It had been a feeling thrummed through with thrill and even paranoia. It was not sharp and jagged but he had sensed that maybe one day this feeling might turn out to be stronger and longer-lasting than what he got even on *Wanderbird*. And on any other morning, since he'd been on Coggeshall Wharf, he might have dipped his thoughts back into that affect the way Bird used to dip the tip of her tongue into the gap left by a baby tooth. Except this morning a bigger gap had appeared in his back-cast thoughts; and that came from the vacuum of unresolved issues stemming from his visit to the ship.

De Melo sang *Fado da Sevem:* "*Corre a sua sepultura, o seu corpo, aindo ve.*" It was the second *fado* spindle Slocum had bought. He stared at the last crumbs of his muffin and tried to hammer together connections between his sense that something big had happened to him on that ship last night, and the superficiality of his memories of it. The fruitwood paneling, the smell of rubber matting and salt, the green-shaded lights of the ship's library: These he remembered. And that aquarium with its crystal castle filled with fish from seas just outside the shipping channel, life gone exotic thanks partly to the efforts of the men sipping beer and mumbling through mouthfuls of muffin around him; that was clear also. But the woman at the center of it was like the digital haze they put around the key parts of sexy movies in Flash channels screened for "family" viewing. He remembered the face and neck and shoulders of Melisande Yonge, for example, in general terms only. It was very odd because he could remember Breena Jakes, who had ever and always existed in digital form, with a clarity that he knew in his gut was not just a function of the quality time he had spent with her. After his first log-on, Breena had been burned onto the whorls of his brain like a well-advertised brand; and she had been clearer to him after one "voyage," as they called these Flash episodes, than the delicate nose and freckles of Bird, his daughter. And he had thought then—

What he had thought then was blown into a thousand fragments by Shaneeqwa, who slammed her coffee in front of Slocum, slammed herself down in the zinc chair, leaned forward and said, "What the *fuck* you do to *Luisa* you piece of *shit*?"

Slocum stared at her. She had a big round face and slightly slanted eyes that now narrowed with fury.

"What about Luisa?" he asked, already feeling guilty because of how the question had been phrased. A whiff of his training came back then; he told himself that this was a negotiating ploy, he did not have to assume the guilt, could in fact turn it to his advantage. He sat forward, using aggression against aggression. "What are you talking about, Shaneeqwa, you just come in 'n say—"

Shaneeqwa was uninterested in the strategies of negotiation. She continued, "Cried her eyes out like a starving baby half the night cuzza you and I'm *fucked* if I can figger out how you did that."

Dark eyes, Slocum thought. He had seen Luisa's eyes full of tears before. A small area inside him that coincided with such color and memory grew moist in sympathy.

"She doesn't belong at Madame Ling's," Slocum said, and then wondered why he had said that. As soon as he uttered the words he knew they were true. Oddly, it was the first time he'd had this thought. But truth had no place or relevance in a negotiation, if that was what Shaneeqwa was starting here. He managed to corner the last muffin crumb, and bring it helpless to his lips.

"So what did you talk about?" Shaneeqwa chugged her coffee and belched. "In the parlor."

"She wanted to sleep with me."

"And you said no?" Shaneeqwa's eyes were green and deep and they narrowed further as Slocum nodded. "I don't believe you. I seen you look at that child before, you wanted to all right."

Slocum washed down the crumb with a slug of his coffee. It was cold. He thought of Bird's nose and freckles, which were all he could remember of her right now. He thought of bargaining ploys, decoy scenarios, the multiple half-truths of market tactics and copyright protection. In spite of what he had vowed last night, he had little energy left to deploy these tools now. He said, "Looking at her is all I can do."

"No credit." A statement.

It would be easy and true to agree. He picked that tool up, and put it down.

"It's not the money. We just don't—sleep well together."

Shaneeqwa blew all the air out of her lungs and said, "Oh, dick! Luisa doesn't want *dick*! You think she couldn't get dick if that was all she wanted? Better 'n you on your best day. She wanted dick, she could do what we all do, but Madame Ling just lets her do a john when she feels like it, which is maybe twice a month, tops, and take bleach-and-laundry duty rest of the time.

"What she wants," Shaneeqwa added, sitting back a little, "is some respect for herself. And for some crazy reason what you think of that poor kid is important to her. She half in love with your sorry ass, poor bitch. It's souring the brood," the hooker went on. "You got eight professional women gettin' all maternal over her, it's boring, it's pathetic, like something outta *Pain*."

She looked over at the TV. The aggression had leaked from her voice, as if whatever was playing on the news program had drawn the poison that caused her to engage Slocum.

"Respect," she repeated softly. "But you're so wrapped up in yourself, like a boa snake twisted over something big it ate, which is all your starchy problems—you can't help her out—you can't help anyone." Shaneeqwa swiveled her body toward the television, then glanced at him from that angle resentfully, as if he had interrupted her viewing.

"What is it about you, Slocum? You hurting?" She shook her head. "Shit, we all hurting. Don't you get that yet? It ain't the hurting, or who hurts more. It's trying to ease that hurt in other people; it's the net of tries and failings and being shined off—*that's* what you remember about yourself, at three A.M., when the bottle of pills is all full and waiting on the night table. That's what makes you hang on, sometimes."

Slocum wasn't listening to Shaneeqwa anymore. The announcer had changed, and so had the graphics—the anchor was talking about location shots for the next season of *Thunder Beach,* and how the shooting might be delayed by a storm rolling up the coast. A graphic of the southeast coast showed at the center of it the same tumbleweed Slocum had seen on TV in Madame Ling's laundromat.

Only the tumbleweed was even tighter and standing farther to the northeast and a little ways off the barrier islands on that section of shoreline. A knot of ex-dragger-fishermen drifted over, to stand under the ceiling-mounted monitor, jaws set in grim happiness because being grim was what being a fisherman, even an ex-fisherman, was all about, and anyway they no longer had boats in the water to get creamed by a hurricane. Or if they did, then the boats had been repossessed by the bank and it did not matter.

The graphics read CATEGORY 3, which was a higher category than had been assigned to the storm last night. "It's tracking along the route of slaughter," one of the Norwegians said. "Right up the ass of the channel," another agreed contentedly. No one else in the bar paid any attention, and the segment ran its allotted thirty-five seconds. Then it switched to coverage of Larissa Love, who had abandoned Clelia Skrawn dresses for the split-screen designer statements of the Milanese designer Francesco Cavagliere. Slocum kept watching the TV but he was not absorbing the news about Larissa Love's fashions. He had vid-flipped—done the instantaneous switch to a more powerful image—to a shrieking, internal view of a wind full of trees and car parts and torn marshgrass roughing up eight-foot waves even across the harbor, and crowding its strength on the hundred-foot-high wall of the ship. The thick hawsers strained, tearing out entire bollards or snapping them one by one, cutting crewmen in two as they broke; and the hull gently drifting away from the line of dolphins, leaning away from the awesome wind; the gap of roiled water between the ship and Slocum's sloop narrowing ever so gently from sixty feet to fifty-five, to thirty, to ten—and then nothing as the ship simply reduced to zero the piece of water where Slocum's life was moored.

"You're not listening, Slocum," Shaneeqwa said. "You put me in a box, like 'hooker with a heart of gold.' Like, that's such a stupid expression anyway, stupid and insulting, like most of us don't have hearts 'cause we sell pussy for a living. *Boo*shit.

"But I'm worried about business too, 'cuz not only she don't pull her weight, she bringing the rest of us down."

Slocum dragged his gaze back to Shaneeqwa. He had trouble remembering what she'd been talking about.

Shaneeqwa stood. Her eyes flicked at him contemptuously.

"What?" Slocum said. "I don't—"

"Shee-it," Shaneeqwa said. "I get more attention from a table." She stomped off to the other side of the bar to see if she could score a drink off the draggermen.

SLOCUM GOT BACK TO Coggeshall Wharf eight minutes after he had left the Sunset Tap. This was faster than he had ever walked it. His saloon was still warm from the dawn stoking of the coal stove. The coffeepot was warm also, but he did not pour coffee or even take off his jacket. He sat on the nav-station stool, breathing hard from walking so fast. He switched on the ECM-pak, flicked the keyboard impatiently, watching the indicator lights blink to life.

SURVEILLANCE SCAN
WILD ACCESS

Icons blinked. They represented Wildnet frequencies, scores of them assembled in files, most of them now out of date since they changed weekly and sometimes daily. But he had no need to consult Wildnet frequencies for what he had to do. He called up his legit Flash access "world" and felt fear, for a moment, that the cancellation of his card might already have eliminated his access account. But the world appeared—no doubt they billed him monthly, and the month was not up yet—and with no wasted movement Slocum maneuvered the joystick to the correct village in the appropriate country in the server's planetary program, and slotted straight on to a Flash weather channel.

This service, since it was still federally subsidized, contained a portal for users who did not own headsets, and Slocum felt only a minimum tug of lust as the brightly colored images—which would have been so much brighter and more tactile in 3-D—swirled into the small screen of the ECM.

The rest of the screen was visual noise: shifting opalescent bits of jumbled data that replaced textures Slocum would have seen on a headset.

"Steering currents," Slocum told the voice control, and "Hatteras," and the screen altered to show eight different levels of jetstream over a ten-thousand-square-mile area of the midcoast. The fingers of the hurricane were just starting to brush at the barrier islands on the screen's bottom; but while the top levels of the jetstream were angled more or less straight up the coast, the bottom four levels, which (according to the *Smuggler's Bible*) steered the storm, aimed 65 degrees true, or more easterly than northward.

"Bookmark, piloting," Slocum commanded. "Chart, Atlantic region." The screen flipped to a standard small-scale sailing chart. Slocum ran his cursor along the coast. Then he touched the little compass icon in the corner. It read out 58 degrees true; and Slocum leaned against the aft bulkhead and closed his eyes. He was a little amazed at how cold was the terror that had seized him when he caught the television weather report and saw, in his mind's eye only, what the storm might do to his stretch of water.

He had known how far away in probability this storm was. In the course of learning about his sloop and sailing from various people in the ICE who knew a lot about such matters he had learned how many variables were built in to forecasts, how unpredictable even these chronic anticyclones must be. Essentially, you could fine down a hurricane strike when the jetstreams were dead on and a

channel of high seawater temperature led in your direction
and the storm was less than four hundred miles away; all
other predictions included far too many variables and were
too loose. And that was before you factored in the eco-
nomics of Flash-casting. He had been aware of all that.

Slocum's breathing eased slowly. He reminded himself
that the apparently favorable steering currents needed to
change only a few degrees to revise the critical danger area.
He would have to keep an eye on them over the next few
days. But now that he knew what was what and he was out
of range of the Sunset Tap and its crew of Cassandras, the
threat of weather could recede to a secondary plane of
consciousness. He started to shut down the ECM, then
paused, noticing the menu for the navigation hard-drive
blinking in the corner of his screen. Because he felt high
from relief he flitted the cursor to that menu and clicked,
and then, for the hell of it, went down the index till a
name caught his eye: "Tuavoa Atoll."

What the hell. Clicked on that.

He was glad he was not wearing a headset. The module
barely whirred, then a colorful chart of an archipelago
filled the screen. He clicked the cursor on the island
marked "Tuavoa," and a quarter of his screen filled with
real-time video of a long harbor with warehouses down a
jetty of coral rocks. Cocoa palms moved in a soft wind. A
rusty coaster swung at anchor in the harbor.

If he were in Tuavoa, if he knew how to use this program, he could click on where he was and where he
wanted to go, and the program would build a 3-D model
that showed where his boat lay relative to local currents,
tides, weather, water temperature, marine life, political
conditions. It would even steer the boat, if he had an au-
topilot.

Slocum sighed, logged off the ECM, and locked it back
against the deckhead. His eye caught on the invitation

spindle from the Kumpunens still stuck behind the tide chart and he plucked it off and threw it into the trash bucket. The RSVP deadline had been yesterday, or maybe this evening? At any rate Slocum never had any intention of responding and he wondered why he had held on to the spindle at all. The sight of it evoked inchoate stories and forms; he had an idea only that they involved Bayview and the Flash; but finally they settled down, circling around the one item that made possible a Bayview style of life, namely the Universal Credit Card, and by extension the cancellation of his account.

He typed the Whip's Flash name, and a note asking the Whip to visit FirstAtlantic Bank and check his UCC records. Slocum knew the UCC codes by heart and put them at the end of the message, typing slowly and deliberately because the codes were all-important and because giving somebody your UCC cypher was the ultimate expression of trust: In some churches, UCC cyphers were exchanged with rings. He had never exchanged UCC codes with Amy.

Now he poured himself another coffee. He looked out the harbor-side portholes as he sipped, at the black wall of the ship; put his face close to the glass and stared upward. The upper decks were almost invisible from this perspective, since they receded with every level. He could not see the top deck at all because of the cut of hull and the armature of lifeboats, railings, and companionways below. One of the chopper's rotors, and the funnel's tip, were all that was visible from here.

He tried to imagine again the face of Melisande Yonge and got no further than he had earlier. He wondered if she ever came ashore, and what exactly her role was in X-Corp Multimedia that she should rate passenger status on such a ridiculously outmoded and expensive method of transport. Though the outmoded aspect of it was the point, Slocum

knew; the more costly and out of date, the more obscene
the luxuries, the more a corporation gained face. A couple
of multinationals even ran their own trains. He probably
would not see her again, Slocum thought, remembering
how adamant she had been that he respect security rules in
contacting her. That was a disengagement tactic if he had
ever heard one. And he felt sad because of that. And while
part of his sadness was drawn from a pool of absence—that
a woman who inspired such fast and strong attraction in
him should be subtracted from his life almost as soon as she
had entered it—most of it fed off an underground lake that
was the usual and ongoing withdrawal of Bird, and Amy,
and even the cotton coziness of his old, spurned life in
Bayview.

He wondered for a moment if all loss worked the way
some South American Indians thought it worked: Being
born was exactly the same process as drawing water from a
deep well in which all life was held, and dying was simply
dumping that water back into the well for others to draw
on after you. Did loss work that way also? Did the huge
awareness of solitude and ultimate loneliness exist by itself,
like a giant transmitter blasting sadness over all frequencies—
something you could tune down in the company of certain
people; lovers, daughters—but whose endless AM ululation
ultimately drenched the ether?

Slocum shook his head, then started as something thud-
ded behind him. He swiveled, heart slamming, and saw
Ralfie skylighted against the hatchway coaming, his one
eye glaring madly into the cabin's gloom, ear cocked,
tongue hanging through the gap in his teeth.

"Shit," Slocum breathed.

"Yow," Ralfie moaned. He hopped his disjointed way
down the ladder toward a dogfish cartilage that he had
ripped off from the outflow manna and dropped down the
hatch to startle Slocum. Slocum picked it up by thumb and
forefinger before the cat could get to it. Ralfie stood on

his hind legs, and fell down, since one of them did not work right. Then he stood again, more cautiously, and aimed a left hook at the slimy skeleton, yowling his rage at Slocum.

In that split second Slocum felt a jolt of admiration for the animal. Ralfie was half blind, crippled, and probably a nonagenarian in feline years, yet still he got what he needed and was prepared to duke it out to keep it. What that said about Slocum, by contrast, was enough to make Slocum feel absolutely exhausted. He walked the cartilage to the cat's bowl, tailed by Ralfie all the way. He dropped the fish in, then leaned heavily against the galley counter.

What had happened to all the tough thoughts he'd had last night? Slocum wondered. In the cop car with his hands cuffed behind his back he'd been full of piss and chemicals, changing the formula of his own character so he could take back some portion of the world and kick and bend and grind it down into a cousin of control.

One night of sleep and those thoughts had washed away like an ebb tide and all he had left was this pathetic loneliness; that and the self-pity which, he was beginning to suspect, was becoming the dominant color in the amateur watercolor of his life.

Ralfie broke the dogfish cartilage in two, and dragged the fleshier half into the forward cabin, to hunker under the V-berth overhang, growling. Slocum sighed, picked up the discarded portion, and dropped it in the slops bucket on top of the invitation spindle. Which reminded him of Bayview, and the Kumpenens, and what he'd been thinking about Jedd—

Slocum retrieved the spindle and wiped off the fish slime. He rebooted the ECM, slotted the spindle into the port, and waited for the virus scan to vet it. The usual noise appeared, and text for the handicapped. Then a vidclip of men and women in jewels and brilliant robes dancing atop the walls of a hugely fancy palace.

PARTY
BYZANTIUM: THE FALL
at "The Saltbox"
Otto and Sheila Kumpunen's
bring a costume!
bring your face-sucker!

The date, Slocum saw, was today. The suggested time
was 7 P.M.

He did not feel aggressive anymore. He did not feel like
he was set to take control and bend the granite parameters
of his life into something that made him happier. He felt
like what he was: a tired father who missed his daughter; a
failed lover who had driven away his wife and even managed to sadden a whore who looked to him only for com-
panionship.

Slocum hit a couple of keys, pulled out the spindle.
Automatically he checked his e-mail—the Whip had already checked his and answered the earlier message. He
would visit FirstAtlantic's virtual office, no problem, and
take all his money—smiley face, ☺, joke—when he found
time, probably toward the workday's end.

Slocum logged off once more. He opened the hanging
locker, which lay on the sloop's starboard side between the
galley and the forward cabin. Ralfie, seeing him approach,
yowled threateningly and pulled the rest of his fish deep
into shadow. The dress suit he wore to X-Corp functions
hung there, a little musty but still presentable. Slocum took
his monkeyjacket off its hanger and put it on.

Jedd Motieff would be at Kumpunen's party. Kumpunen
was co-chair of X-Corp Multimedia, and no one who
cared about his place in the X-Corp Multimedia pecking
order would deliberately turn this invite down. Of course
Jedd's brother was Lazarus Motieff, who had amassed a fortune of seven billion U.S. dollars as an infobroker and
memory margin specialist, and Jedd had earned money on

his brother's coattails, so he was more independent than most of his colleagues on the top doughnuts. Still, Jedd enjoyed the extra power that came with being chief counsel and VP-legal of X-Corp MM, and he would be careful not to needlessly jeopardize his position.

Slocum opened the door of the head and looked at himself in the mirror. It was odd how a suit could alter the idea you had of yourself. He still did not feel aggressive or even competent, but seeing his form clad in that black silk monkeyjacket made him appear a little less pathetic—made him look at least theoretically capable of grasping the strings he used to pull in his old life, and tweaking them a little; enough perhaps to make his current situation less grim.

He would see Bird on a regular basis. Jedd would tell him to ask for more—more custody, or split custody at least. But he would settle for seeing her twice a week, or maybe even once.

Slocum turned to the drawers under the V-berth. Ralfie spat at him. He ignored the cat and started pulling out clothes, looking in the lower layers for his dress shirt.

FOURTEEN

CAKES HAD A CAR. It was a monkeyshit-brown sedan from the days of prehistory when mileage and the cost of steel were not a big factor. It was huge, and flat and broad like the head of a cobra. Most of the paint had flaked off and much of the steel had rusted and gaping, rough-edged holes marred the doors and rocker panels and floor.

But it ran. It seemed that the more Cakes poured money into her boat and seduced engineers and ordered fantastically expensive parts for the 500-horsepower, nitro-glycerine-injected, twelve-cylinder freshwater-cooled quad-carbed monsters that powered the craft, the less those engines performed.

On the other hand, Cakes ignored her car completely. She never changed the oil or tuned it up. And it ran the way a Frisbee glided, perfectly and without fuss. The same logic applied here as affected his outboard, Slocum thought as he got behind the wheel and sank into the rotted foam of the bench seat: Plenty in one sector of machinery meant dearth in another. Partly because she cared so little about the car—partly because it gave her so little trouble—Cakes was pretty cool about lending it, though she wouldn't lend it to Lopes, who tended to get drunk and smash cars up. What other balances of dearth and plenty ruled Cakes's life, Slocum did not care to guess at. She had been unpacking a box of gleaming new cylinder rings in the racer's cabin when he sought her out. No mechanic was in sight. She didn't quibble as she handed Slocum the keys, but gave him a look that seemed to assess once more his engineering prowess and his sexual abilities, and dismiss them both.

The sedan's exhaust made a noise like chain lightning that echoed between the warehouses of Front Street. The feeling of being followed did not go away when he was in the car, but it was softer, more abstract. By far the stronger feeling was one of backward travel, because since he had sold his Raptor he had only twice sat behind the wheel of an automobile. What he remembered now was driving the Raptor, screaming around on his malcontent excursions to Town, before he discovered the ICE. He smoked past the Zone, past the giant neon horse and rider flashing in blue-red neon that for no good reason had been chosen as emblem of the Bayview Mall, to the highway.

The Mall was already in the new township of Bayview as redrawn by X-Corp with the help of Vera Consalves; he had to drive only one exit past the Mall on the highway to reach a dedicated off-ramp to the closed community. Tastefully aligned cedars masked Cyclone fencing behind which lay manicured woods, dells, and the lights of three-story McMansions twinkling in the firefly dusk. Relaxxotunes trilled from weatherproof grounds speakers. The gatehouse here was designed to resemble a seventeenth-century country manor in miniature, but the barriers, tank traps, and security cams were modern.

Both guards sortied when Cakes's car pulled up. One of them was young and Slocum did not recognize him. The other was Teixeira, who had been a guard since Slocum had moved to Bayview. His round face registered shock, then the warmth of recognition, and finally a backwash of doubt when he remembered that Slocum no longer lived there, nor worked for X-Corp even. He examined Cakes's sedan and squared his shoulders. The other guard had retreated into the guardhouse, as rules demanded for conditions of assault, within easy reach of both the alarm button and the twelve-gauge pump Slocum knew was kept there.

Slocum reached inside his monkeyjacket. Teixeira stiffened. Slocum said, "It's all right, Tex, I'm invited," and pulled out the invitation spindle. Teixeira said, "You're going to Kumpunens'," and grinned in relief as he handed the spindle over his shoulder to the young guard, who slotted it into the booth's terminal. Slocum realized how lucky he was that Tex was on duty; a guard who did not know him by sight would have asked for his vaporized UCC card. No one could enter the closed part of Bayview with a vaporized card. Slocum had not thought about it because he'd never had his card pulled before. Like most people, when he was not actively thinking about a problem, he tended to assume none of the parameters had changed.

The young guard handed back the spindle. Teixeira said, "You know you can't drive that in here, Mr. Slocum," and Slocum said, "I'll park it in the delivery lot and walk."

"You can't walk!" Teixeira exclaimed in horror.

"But I want to surprise Otto," Slocum said. He could feel his confidence starting to wane. So much of this was based on bluff, because his being here was so clearly a mistake; obviously Kumpunen's social aide had not done her job and wiped him off the corporate guest list when he quit.

———

TEX ENDED UP DRIVING him. The mansions increased in size and number of garages as they approached the Island. Teixeira asked about Amy and Bird as they rolled past his old road. The Island was the most exclusive sector of Bayview's closed community. Each of its properties included a deepwater dock, a beachhouse, and a helipad. Only executives from the top two doughnuts were considered for residence there, and while no guardhouse stood on the short causeway leading to the Island, the guards could tell from various Webcams who came in or out.

Kumpunen's mansion was not unlike Slocum's former house, only it was larger in all respects: longer pool, bigger vineyard, a giant ballroom overlooking the Acushnet River. Shift-shin music splattered in the forecourt: Koto, Moroccan drums were mixed with Pacific surf, eavesdropped pulsars, the mating song of frigate birds into some kind of whole. The Shift-shin clashed with Relaxxotunes from the grounds. Guests moved in monkeyjackets and paneled robes from cars whose purchase price would have kept Mauritania alive for a week. Slocum thanked Teixeira and handed his spindle to a tall man whose slightly cheaper monkeysuit and security jambook marked him as a butler. Then he was inside.

It was a great party; Slocum realized that immediately. Amy and he had thrown good parties, their bashes had a certain reputation and people came, even the Kumpunens came twice. But this party was better, if you judged it by the decorations and food and drink and costumes and beauty of the guests and volume of talk and quality of music and what other standards could you judge a party by anyway? Offline couples strolled and chatted along walkways obscured by clouds of holiday lights. The swimming pool, which was really two pools linked by a sort of tropical river overhung with palms, was covered with fleets of origami boats bearing lit candles. Many of the guests had gone all the way with their costumes, obviously aping the book of a new production, since Kumpunen never did anything without a sales component. The robes of the Byzantines were beautifully embroidered; some of them carried icons that looked real. Ottoman invaders wore scimitars engraved with suras from the Qu'ran. Perhaps half the guests had clearly decided that if the choice was either to spend thousands on costumes or to wear something half-assed, they would wear no costume at all. He saw Milton Verve from P.R. dressed as Mehmet II and Divina Petti-bone in development and Hans Bugliese from offshore productions dressed as bashi-bouzouks. Hans, who had worked with Slocum for years, was one of the men who nodded, through their surprise. One woman, Slocum noted with an inward smile, wore the silver robes and chain of office of the Countess Lanne, from the Claire stories, from *Rikka's Messengers*—not Persian, perhaps, but not so out of place either. Rounding a column, Slocum almost walked into a woman wearing a Byzantine tunic that was long and opalescent. She had pale skin and an air of sharp intelligence and her hands rose as if to protect her jugular when she saw Slocum.

Slocum stopped. He was about to say "Stacey," but the name got no farther than his throat. The woman watched him for a beat. She smiled in a way that skewered and in-cinerated all the nice ideas a smile usually associated itself with, till nothing was left but contempt, and a delight in revenge. Then she turned away.

Now Slocum said her name, but it made no sound on his lips; just as sleeping with Stacey Quinn Fulsome—wife of Jack Fulsome, mother of Ethan and Lara-Quinn—ultimately had not made much sound in his emotional soundtrack, or his personal life. Fulsome never found out, as far as he knew. And Amy had found out only because he had told her, one foolish day when he thought he could use infidelity as an ax to chop their way out of the cul-de-sac their marriage had ended in.

Slocum took a flute of peach champagne and drank it too quickly. He passed a sequence of flat videos showing a party in San Francisco; the Golden Gate shimmered through fog and enormous trees on a high balcony. Down another walkway he came to the mansion's centerpiece, an eighteenth-century Cape Cod saltbox that had been transported to this site and covered in a glass dome so Kumpunen's mansion could be built around the antique dwelling. This was Kumpunen's den and media "room," Slocum knew. It had cost several million to move, install, and fit out. The rough shingles and crooked eaves of the tiny house always seemed out of place in its enclosing bubble of polished glass where split-level dining room met loggia. Slocum finished his champagne and as the rest of the chilled bubbles poured down his gullet he felt poured full of a jealousy more poisonous than Stacey Quinn's expression.

These men and women were so *good* at this, he reflected. He had done very well at X-Corp but they had done better. They had played with the team and stayed the course while he had faltered, and eventually failed. They were supremely wealthy and confident in their wealth and the privileges that went with it. They were powerful, because they controlled the stories and rhythms to which 90 percent of people in America lived and drank, shat and wept, ate and worked. They put their mark on the world in a way Slocum had never been able to match, in a way he now could not even dream of emulating. Ziam Bargh over there, with his iconoclast's beard and shaded contacts, had invented the Flash neighborhoods in which people could meet, shop, or work online in the context of selected episodes of their favorite drama or comedy. When Ziam needed to travel, he boarded a personal twin-engine jet at Bayview Flying Club, told the pilot where to go, and, quite simply, went.

Will Pengilly, now telling a joke almost everyone in his group found hysterical, had taken over his job in production. Alexa Neumann, who was actually quite pretty, as headwriter for PITA could tell herself that she had single-handedly defined the tastes and buying habits of an entire generation—not only in America but across half the globe.

Slocum eyed the saltbox again. He wondered how he had ever thought he could leave X-Corp, leave Bayview, and survive on what leverage he might garner in the un-wired world. It was so clear, looking at these educated, witty, committed people, that the power they wielded was impossible to match. It was unassailable not only because it was concentrated in the hands of these men and women and others like them in the four big entertainment Orgs like X-Corp; it was overwhelming because their power grew in this society the way Korea Weed flourished in New England ponds, because it did not have to browbeat the market to accept its dominance. For the market wanted nothing better. People wanted—no, people *needed* the 3-D stories that Multimedia conceived, focus-grouped, pro-duced, spun off, marketed, advertised, game-showed, resold, presequeled, reran, and remade. People would scream and protest not if X-Corp increased its market share but only if it withheld its products.

His colleagues. Slocum thought of flinging his glass to the Tuscan tiles. Instead he placed it on a Louis XIII side-board. The Independent Credit Entity had regarded them with contempt, as vilest enemies, but what the hell did the ICE have to offer? A half-baked philosophy based on black markets and smuggling cooperatives. An idea of nodes, in-dependent communities of fewer than ten thousand peo-ple, kept small so they could not develop the pathologies of scale that ended up turning the whole shebang into a self-interested life form. A gaggle of misfits committed to fi-nancing themselves, bartering with each other for what they needed, and avoiding, somewhat hysterically, the domination of Orgs like X-Corp.

Slocum's eyes remained on the half-Cape. He knew

where Kumpunen was, he knew where Motieff would be. The party out here was fine but it was nothing to the party going on inside that ancient cottage, because what was happening in there took in the world, the past, the future, the solar system, the universe. The past especially, in all the mauve melodrama of history, for this particular shindig.

Whereas the ICE had offered nothing but rotted boats, condemned buildings, a bunch of losers who could not even agree among themselves. The first day Slocum started working for the marina—goosing Web values on their barter site—he had been conscious of two divergent philosophies competing in the ICE. One school of thought liked the node as it was, more or less: an ad hoc group that got together to sustain individuals in a specific situation through a food-buying cooperative, and a credit union to make boat, small-business, and start-up loans and issue a localized credit chip; also workshops—fourteen of them—that repaired bicycles or crafted Webware, dinghies, goat cheese, power-generating boat windmills, and beef-bone scrimshaw for the theme park. These, then, were the "retros."

The other side were known as Hawkleyites, though both factions espoused Hawkleyite philosophy in name. Dark Denny was a Hawkleyite. The Hawkleyites generally ignored the component of humor basic to Hawkleyism and took at face value the goal of creating a community in which 37 percent of all exchanges occurred either within the node or between different nodes and similar communities. Hawkleyism considered Orgs like X-Corp to be alien, and potentially lethal, life forms, but it allowed for coexistence with them for practical reasons and because Orgs could sometimes do useful things that nodes could not. However, Dark Denny and the Hawkleyites, in their oratory at least, aimed for a network of independent, interbartering nodes that would slowly displace slaves of the

Megorg with a population of node citizens who controlled the most vital elements in their lives, especially work and food and shelter.

The fault lines did not invariably surface, but they came out often enough, especially around the credit union, which covered all aspects of marina life—such as whether to set up a diesel co-op, how to regulate anchoring (whether to regulate anchoring), what to call the marina; all these problems ended up split along factionalist lines, with Dark Denny and Louanne Krantz on the Hawkleyite ramparts, and Feingold and Zoe Chase fighting them in high voices and sometimes screams and thrown chipboard on the second floor of the condo duplex that housed the ICE. Slocum ended up more often on the side of Feingold and Zoe but he could not for the life of him remember why he kept coming to the ICE after that initial pleasure in the swarming of people. The best he could do was re-call the feeling he'd had, oh, maybe a month into his work at the credit office, the first time he had seriously mar-shalled his thoughts about the ICE—that it was not so much what the Whaling City Marina gave as what it took away; that it lessened the feeling of exhaustion, of having to plot for every detail of advantage, of having to spend every second of every day on the Flash. And all he remem-bered now was more of the same feeling. That it had let his engines spin at a lower gear. It had loosened the cables in him that kept him wire-taut and in command. It provided a place where he could switch off X-Corp stories, X-Corp headsets, X-Corp cellphones. Occasionally, being in the ICE allowed him to laugh out loud; being there gave him something to do where it would not put his career and self-respect on the line if he maybe could not do it better than the next guy down the ladder. The ICE gave him a place to fuck off; to sip coffee or look at people and not feel vaguely guilty about it. Not that X-Corp people didn't relax or sip coffee or even fly to Tuscany in order to sample a lifestyle where they could savor the moment. But whenever X-Corp people relaxed it was on agenda and with goals of relaxation so defined that it all ended up leaving them just as tense as when they'd left, especially if they fell short of those goals.

When Slocum bought the sloop it afforded him a private spot within that refuge to drink coffee. Of course the boat came complete with a world of things to replace, maintain, oil, repair, ignore, worry about; but again, these were issues that concerned him alone, and no one else would give a damn if he did them or not. Amy and Bird thought he was nuts when he brought them to the ICE, but Bird had quickly been sucked into the games of hinted sex and power of a tribe of teenagers who lived on the same raft Slocum's boat was moored against. It turned out later that those kids surfed affect but Slocum was unaware of that. At the time, he was simply glad that Bird seemed happy on his boat.

Then Dark Denny—who liked to argue with Slocum about some of the broader aspects of Web theory—had shown up on the sloop one weekend when Amy and Bird were visiting. He left a copy of the *Smuggler's Bible* with Amy and she got interested in the philosophy of the place. And Slocum had been proud then—yes, he remembered a feeling of real satisfaction because the credit entity had reached a takeoff point. Sufficient boats had crowded into the marina that, without warning, enough was available Inside to keep people fed and busy and it seemed everyone was trading with everyone else on the barter site he had designed. Out of nowhere he'd had a sudden, hot conviction that this thing was *working* and part of the reason it had worked was because of him.

The weekend Dark Denny met Amy and Bird had been a good one—Slocum remembered that now. The sun was out most of the morning and Amy had made them breakfast and then stretched out in the cockpit. "I see why you like this," she had said to him, and all of a sudden the sun seemed warmer on his skin.

———————

SOMEONE JOSTLED HIM. SLOCUM glanced up, startled. He had gone so far back in memory that he was half surprised to see Kumpunen's split-level dining hall and a crowd of X-Corpers in Byzantine robes brushing past him on their way out of the half-Cape. "Fourteen lightyears past the red dwarf, you'd think Farley would know about the methane clouds," one of them said. They were younger X-Corpers with the same peacock chatter and assassins' reflexes they all adopted—that he had adopted when he "came aboard." And Slocum felt himself, almost saw himself, flip—sensed the catastrophic turnaround, like an aircraft carrier throwing its engines into full reverse, like a jumbo doing an Immelmann, the "vid-flip" people called it, the same near-instantaneous reversal in sensation he had experienced in front of the Metropole. Without hesitation the X-Corp humans now walking away from him took on all the black and evil sheen of Darknesse, the soulless bloodsuckers from the eighth system beyond the Cygnus X-6 black hole in *Wanderbird*.

These people were killers, he reminded himself, just as he had been a killer once. If you savagely penetrated people's lives for reasons of p–e ratio and margin, you committed murder from the point of view of a classic human sensibility. The contempt in the eyes of Stacey Quinn had been the perspective of a top assassin in an assassins' elite, looking at him as she looked at everyone else—as loser, as failure, as victim—because what she did every day was hire and fire, demote and promote, deceive and manipulate people like him with the swift brutality of a knife-fighter. Ninja tactics in the doughnuts. Though these people never wielded the dagger themselves, Slocum had the quick and utter conviction that he was in some danger here. He had better accomplish what he had come to do and get out fast.

Slocum listened for noise from his stomach, wondering if it would react to what he was about to do the way it had in front of the Flash theater. His guts gurgled a bit, as they would have on a barrel-rolling airplane, but stayed put for now. Slocum took a deep breath. He adjusted his stock, sucked in his gut, and walked into the half-Cape.

He spotted Jedd Motieff at once, though Jedd did not see him. The cottage was crowded but no one noticed him except one of the cyberbutlers, who wordlessly picked out a full head-sucker—a virtual reality viewing mask that fit entirely over the face—and handed it to Slocum, wires laid ceremonially across his left forearm.

Slocum stared at the headpiece. It was Malaysian, a Perhatian. Some hackers, the Whip included, preferred the Indian Lakshmi, but this was still one of the finest and most expensive sets credit could buy. Its armature was of rare junglewood polished so hard you could see the reflection of the few lights burning clearly; the screen was limpid and dark as spilled night.

Slocum waited once again for the allergic reaction to hit: the revulsion of an addict who had cleaned his system of a poison, when that poison was presented to him pure and ready for injection. It would be the same feeling he'd had at the Metropole or upon seeing MacTavish's half-sucker, only worse because this set was so much better and the Flash offered here so much more fine. *Byzantium: The Fall,* he knew, would be the pilot for an eight-part series, a spectacular in 3-D so perfect and expensively rendered it would be like time travel, only with touch optional and thus largely devoid of risk. It had taken Slocum months to realize that the reduction in the sickening cottony quality of his life—a reduction that had happened in the ICE— was a result of his spending less time on the Flash. For him to put on this face-sucker now would be to accept a return to that suffocating softness, in exchange for an hour of the most intense colors available to man, or woman.

Slocum also waited for the revulsion he was still feeling for his colleagues to add itself to the nausea of allergy. He waited, and nothing happened. The butler stood patiently, ready to lead him through the scanner. Slocum thought that maybe he had already chosen the path back to addiction by voluntarily entering an X-Corp scene. Or perhaps everything had gone so wrong at this point that Flash addiction, with all its dead-endedness, held little horror for him anymore. He had tried to go straight, as Hawkleyites put it, and what good had it done him? All the things he really wanted were further away from him than before. His diesel was still fucked, and he could not see his daughter.

Slocum took a deep breath. He walked through the scanner. The butler muttered, "Finally," and then, more loudly, asked if he wanted adjustments made to his physical image. Slocum grunted, "No," and fitted the headpiece to his face. The butler clipped on the ankle and wrist sensors, and led him all atremble to a seat at the bar.

FIFTEEN

THE COTTAGE HAD BEEN gutted inside—the only remaining internal structure was a single black shaft that included the control stack leading back through X-Corp fiberoptic to the massive servers containing memory banks for this and other fantasies. Around the walls stood cabins with padded bunks, and bars—literally, cushioned counters on which players who preferred standing, or sitting in *Wanderbird*-style pilot seats, could participate more actively in the drama. The outer walls were all thinscreen on which played a loop from *Wanderbird*—galaxies flashing by, restful, silent. All the bunks and most of the barstools were occupied by guests. And the reason no one saw Slocum was that they all had on face-suckers and were moving and jerking solely in response to the drama happening in so much greater reality in the 3-D world surrounding them.

And so Slocum, with a brief, strangled whisper of "Bird," to remind himself of why he was throwing away what he had struggled so hard to attain, let himself fall. Flash dramas always opened with soft scenes to let the player acclimatize—in this case, wheat fields in Anatolia, with a white horse in the middle and a voice prompt, a woman, asking, "Do you wish to enter now?"

"Yes," Slocum breathed.

"I'm sorry. I did not understand your response?"

"Yes," Slocum repeated more loudly.

"Thank you."

Anatolia wiped into a party.

The fact that it was a party was a coincidence; it had nothing to do with the party going on in the twenty-first century in a house on the island of Bayview. The woman's voice explained softly that this was the *salle d'honneur* of the Palace of Blachernae and the fleet of Russian Vikings had linked up with an army of Bulgars to cut off the Byzantine capital. She went on to say that the emperor's boyfriend, stepmother, and chamberlain had all taken Bulgar gold, and only the second chamberlain, the emperor's nephew, was resolved to hold the city. Slocum—so the woman informed him—had defaulted into a role as an Anatolian "Theme," or governor, with divided loyalties. The nephew wanted to strip the Anatolian aristocrats of their lucrative privileges. The Bulgars, on the other hand, did not believe in the latest dogma of Constantinople's patriarch—that the will of god manifested itself in the frames of the icons as well as in the icons themselves—which the Anatolians accepted. Slocum tried not to be annoyed that the program had chosen a role for him; what difference did it make, given what he had come here for? Meanwhile, plague had broken out and a blizzard was imminent and—Slocum told the woman to shut up and the voice went resentfully silent.

Slocum—the Anatolian Theme—"walked" around the party. That is, he made walking movements as he stood at the bar, and the sensors around his ankles relayed it to a navigator program, which changed the world around him to suit. He noticed, almost casually, that he adapted automatically to sensor walking, though it took neophytes weeks to make the transition from normal movement; because of this beginners were known as "flailers," from the way they jerked around online. He chose not to think about his ease of readaptation. There were data here worthy of greater notice. For example, the fact that "crispness," a term Flash producers used to denote the realism and detail of visual and aural channels, had gotten even better at X-Corp since he had left. The men's robes were woven with care, their beards and hair authentically sculpted. The tables were piled high with roasted lambs, gamebirds, and sweetmeats. Half-naked servants dipped goblets from great amphoras of wine. Musicians played lyres and bouzoukis in one corner. The guests chattered, or fought. In the corners naked limbs wrapped around each other: cocktails, Byzantium style. Jedd Motieff was talking to Daniel Tsoukkiane and a beautiful woman who Slocum guessed had been video-imported for the occasion.

Jedd and Tsoukkiane stopped talking as Slocum came into visual range. Jedd's face had been scanned with the same loving attention to detail as everything else here, but he had ratcheted off fifteen years in the scan imagery, the software automatically softening wrinkles and restoring hairline so that he looked ridiculously young. His voice was still mature though, and he hacked out, "What the fuck are *you* doing here?" with all the authority and power he had gathered around him in the last decade and a half. "There's no outside link to this story—you're *physically* in Bayview."

Tsoukkiane shook his head in wonder. Jedd finished his goblet, wiped his chin—a nice touch. He took Slocum by the arm and led him down the hall to a doorway hidden behind thick draperies, behind which two women kissed. Jedd ignored them. The door led to a cramped spiral stair-case built of cold stone. Jedd began climbing. The stairs were slippery with blood for several flights until they came to the body that had done all the bleeding: a palace eunuch, a powerful one by his jewelry. Slocum, though performing only a tenth of the actions necessary for climbing, was actually getting tired by the time the stairs ended. Jedd led him onto a narrow rampart and leaned over the battlements, far into an indigo night. Constantinople was spread out on either side, fraught with the buttery glow of a great city lit only by oil lamps, fires, and torches. A squad of hoplites stamped feet and jingled weapons standing guard around the next level of defenses, fifty feet below. Beneath them, the walls plunged another hundred feet to the top of cliffs, which fell two hundred feet more to black water.

In the middle of that water, war galleys fought off a swarm of drakkars. The spoons of catapults in their waists were filled with orange fire, which they lobbed at periodic intervals into the rigging of the Viking ships. As the fire flew it described lovely orange arcs against the night. One of the drakkars burst into flame. It was beginning to snow.

"What the fuck possessed you to show up here?" Jedd began.

"I was invited."

"Otto better update his guest list."

"I guess," Slocum agreed.

"You haven't answered my question."

"No." Slocum watched the galleys. The crewmen from the burning ship jumped screaming into flaming water. "I wanted to see you."

"I should feel flattered," Jedd said. "I should feel, like, friendship overcomes vicissitudes such as leaving X-Corp. Leaving your home. Leaving your community."

"Bayview wasn't a community," Slocum replied.

"I know that," Jedd said. "I'm not a fool. I sent you e-mails."

Jedd turned to face him. He had a pleasant, pudgy face—light blue eyes, a girlish mouth that pouted when he got mad. "You left," he said. "Left, left, left—get it? We weren't good enough for you, you and your fine idealism."

"I," Slocum began.

Jedd ignored him. "This Hawkleyite crap. Don't you think I'm aware of that? Pop philosophy for losers who can't hack it online. Loners. No-edgers." He grunted. "So you took your family to become what cliché—the rebel philosopher? the nautical hermit? Shit-ass little sailboat in a watery slum."

Slocum opened his mouth, shut it again. Behind Jedd, Greek fire rose and fell, dimmed now by sheets of snow. The horizontal surfaces of the ramparts grew silvery under a coating of flakes.

"And now you're back. I suppose you want a favor?"

Slocum watched his friend. It was odd, he thought. He felt like a Fernsehen cliché; all his seven personalities lined up, tranquil spectators on the machicolations. Slocum the loser, Slocum the hermit. Slocum the hapless father, the addict, the wheeler-dealer. Let's not forget Slocum the confused son, the failed adulterer, and the last Slocum, the one you had to leave undefined for Fernsehen therapy to have any point. All carried equal weight, sitting and watching Jedd at this turn of plot. It was exactly at this juncture, Fernsehen postulated, that a statement closest to the "truth" was most likely to come out.

"I'm losing Bird," he said. "Amy left, and took her. Now she doesn't want to see me."

Jedd peered at him through the snow. Slocum could tell he didn't want to talk about this because getting involved professionally would mean getting tied up personally and Jedd didn't want to do that. But he was a lawyer, a good one, and he could not help defining the problem, if only for himself.

"And you want custody?"

Slocum nodded. Jedd shook his head.

"You really are incredible," he said. "We had a rocketball

date, the day you left—did you think of e-mailing me back? After all this time." He shook his head again, and looked back over the Golden Horn.

"The Flash world changes fast," he continued, less aggressively now. "People live in stories they choose, and the force of a story is the relationships between the people in it. More options are available—as you know, you helped produce them. And what does all this mean?"

Slocum said nothing.

"It means the old forms of power are changing, Slocum. It means that the old male forte—of going out in the world, tearing down material structures and putting up new ones; killing and enslaving, if you want to be crude, this Byzantine–Bulgar shit, if you will—it's less and less valuable. What's valuable now is not what the male brain does best."

"I don't see," Slocum began, but Jedd cut him off with a wave.

"I'm trying to tell you something, if you'd only listen. Not that you ever asked my advice, did you? It didn't exactly reflect well on me to have my best pal walk into the co-chairman's office and dump a half pint of blood on him by way of quitting. But listen up, just this once. What's valuable," Jedd continued, "is what *women* do best—not a big difference physically, but a lot of cultural training, a slight advantage in language skills, the lactation thing. People skills, Slocum, human resources. Organizing service Nets, taking care of groups of people whose basic needs are assumed and who now think mostly in terms of rank, and duties and obligations—background, not foreground. Hidden stuff, informal power structures. Women have been building those skills for millennia. And what I'm saying is, this filters through the corporation, the body politic, all the way to family court." He turned again, shifting his robe—a wind was blowing now, snowflakes driven horizontally from the east.

"Forty-six percent of X-Corp's officers are women," Jedd continued. He almost said it to himself. "The core of *Byzantium* is not the Bulgars or the battles, but the intrigues, the eunuchs, the affairs, the emperor's stepmother. In family court, most of the judges are women."

Someone cried out, and was fiercely hushed on the battlement below.

"You dragged your family from a secure position, a safe community with the best Flash access in the world. You dragged 'em to a waterfront ghetto. You quit your job, lost your stock options, your wife left you. I mean, I would never represent you. But even if I did, do you have any idea of what your chances would be?"

He turned his face aside, keeping his eyes on Slocum, and spat deliberately over the ramparts. Shaped his mouth to answer his own question, presumably with "shit" or "nothing" or "goose eggs," then thought better of it.

"Jedd," Slocum began, but Motieff had one last point to make.

"What was our rocketball rank, the last time we played?"

Slocum stared at him. "Six, I think. I—"

"I'm down to five now. Real close to four."

"Better than Otto."

"That's right. And what that means is—"

But Slocum never found out what it meant. A half-dozen men surged over the ramparts at that point. Four of them—big, blond, computer-generated Viking types—wore the uniform of the Varangian Guard. A fifth, small and dark and weasely, also wore a Varangian uniform, but he was not computer generated, he was Clifton Gibbs, a second vice president of development. The sixth person was a woman. She wore a headdress in the form of a coiled adder and carried a dagger whose handle was also shaped like a snake. Her face was youthful and attractive. It took Slocum a couple of seconds to realize it was Arvina

Parredieu, the second headwriter for *Rikka* under Razia
Luzzato; a woman he had hired four years ago, when she
was forty-two. Arvina hissed something very negative in
Slocum's direction. The Varangians bore axes and shields
and they advanced immediately, professionally, on Slocum,
who flexed his calf muscles twice, hopped easily over the
parapet, and fell four hundred feet to his death.

He grinned as he fell. He enjoyed seeing the whole
scene Flash-frozen in the automatic reaction to what his
senses assumed must be suicide: the galleys grappling with
longships, the suspended arc of Greek fire, the orange water where the longship burned, the distant shore of Asia,
the sheer granite walls of the fortress. A peregrine falcon
circled in the scrim of snow. Then the blur of black cliffs
and the rocks below growing at a fantastic pace and his
own heart slamming and the automatic cringe at—

—at white flash, total blueness. An absence of agony.
The woman's voice came back, soothing, conversational.

"Fatal error. Reset?"

"No," Slocum said. "Pick up here."

Which left him on the rocks where he had "died," amid
the sough of sea. A tall cloaked figure stood on a black
flight of steps. The figure nodded once, as if expecting
him. Slocum nodded back, not caring what skein of plot
he was getting tangled up in, wishing only to find Jedd
again, to pick up their conversation, to finish saying some
of the things he'd wanted to say while Jedd laid into him.

The cloaked figure looked like Death. Was this part of
Byzantium, some surreal or ethnographic hook? He wondered, with professional curiosity, how it might fit in to the
story. The figure moved gravely, through a fold in the cliffs,
to a small door set in the cliff itself. It took out a key of
stone that glowed like rubies, and inserted it into a key-
hole. Turning the lock, it held the door open for Slocum.

He found himself in a cramped tunnel hewn out of
rock and lit with torches made of tarred rushes whose

smoke hid almost as much as their light revealed. It went on for a long time, becoming upward ramps, staircases. Then, the sound of bouzoukis, laughter, and a glow of light filtered through tapestry; and Slocum found himself in the central hall once more, watching the festivities from behind another wall hanging, still looking for Jedd Motieff.

Jedd was not there. It took Slocum a while to be certain. So many of the men resembled him: slick, artificially young, so confident, so polished in how they moved their 3-D likenesses, so fluent in the little codes that signaled who was desirable and powerful, and who was yesterday's flavor. Leaving space around those to whom one gave the benefit of the doubt in case he or she should suddenly attain a position of greater heft in the appropriately Byzantine hierarchy of X-Corp Multimedia. The women all seemed to look like Arvina, though here their daggers were hidden in the silk of their gowns.

The fold into revulsion was less abrupt than it had been earlier, when Slocum had watched these people shorn of online accoutrements. Perhaps it was because that feeling had never quite gone away, despite the power of Flash environments to disrupt and scatter previous thoughts. Or perhaps the casualness of his distaste had to do with the ambivalent emotions Jedd had raised in him—for Jedd had been a friend once, and now he had turned into a hostile, and that change had been complex, not a black-and-white affair.

Yet Slocum found his perception shifting to black-and-white anyway; back to the Gothic mood he was in before he had marched into Kumpunen's cottage. In that mood, the typecasting of Parredieu and Gibbs on the ramparts had been perfect, their murderous mindset lovingly painted in zeroes and ones into the lying, backstabbing record of the Imperial Court.

Slocum's heart was speeding again, his breathing shallow. It was no longer from the effects of his own "suicide," but from a bolus of rage as poisonous as hemlock in a pot of milk. He should flip off his mask now, he thought; re-enter the "real" world and leave Bayview before Kumpunen realized he was here. Bail out, before the cyberbutlers threw him out on his ass.

Still Slocum hesitated. He yearned to do something to mark his passing. He did not want to leave this environment that he had, in some ways, helped create, without making his presence felt one last time. He did not want his former colleagues to think he was so insignificant and dispensable that he could appear and disappear from their online world as silently and ripple-free as a needle dropped point-first into a lake.

Slocum emerged slowly from behind the drapery. At once he spotted a pair of Varangians moving through the crowd, peering intently at faces. He sidled along the wall, bumped into a portal, started to round it—and stopped.

The portal was in the form of a winged lion crouching over a ball. The ball was transparent, made of glass. A keyboard glowed within. Slocum touched the glass, and the ball parted in the middle. He tapped in to his service account, gave his password, and typed in the Whip's online address. A thumbnail of the Airstream moving down an endless highway appeared on the screen of the lion's eyes.

ROADNOMAD—SUP, BABE
WANDERER—NEED A FAVOR AGAIN
ROADNOMAD—I LOGGED ON TO YOUR BANK, YOUR ACCOUNT'S FROZEN

Slocum stared. A frozen account was not an overdraft. It signified some kind of legal foulup, usually from a divorce or a death or some other change in tax status. But he and Amy were not divorced, and, recent evidence to the contrary, he was not dead. Slocum shook his head and tapped in:

WANDERER—DIFFERENT. LOOKING FOR A VIRUS
ROADNOMAD—WHAT KIND? WHAT FOR? THE BANK?!
WANDERER—BAD PARTY. SOMETHING TO FUCK IT UP
ROADNOMAD—FLASH PARTY?
WANDERER—YES
ROADNOMAD—LOL
WANDERER—CAN YOU?
ROADNOMAD—WHAT ENCRYPTION?
WANDERER—XCORP
ROADNOMAD—HOW BAD?
WANDERER—SHAKE EM UP?

There was a pause in the reply. Finally the letters reeled across the lion's eyes.

ROADNOMAD—HOPING YOU'D SAY THAT. I'M SENDING THIS WILD, MIGHT TAKE A MINUTE

It took forty seconds. A whirring came from the lion. Its mouth opened to reveal a port, with the plastic snout of a memory spindle protruding.

ROADNOMAD—CALL UP THE SPINDLE, COPY IT TO THE PARTY APPLICATION. IT'LL GO THROUGH THE VIRUS SCREEN JUST FINE
WANDERER—OWE YOU TWO BEERS NOW
ROADNOMAD—A DEAL. TAKE THE SPINDLE HOME WITH YOU
WANDERER—THX
ROADNOMAD—WANDERER, BE *SURE* TO DEMASK AS SOON AS YOU HIT COPY

The Airstream vanished from the lion's eyes. A message burned inside the glass ball: "Venice's Council of Twelve will pay you 100,000 sesterces and send a fleet if you give them Thrace once you are crowned basileus. Answer Y/N." Slocum hit Cancel, reinserted the spindle, typed in "A-drive." He called up the applications menu.

"Entertainment/Reception/Byzantium" was listed three items from the end of a lengthy queue.

He glanced around him one last time. More guests were dancing; slaves were dragging away empty amphoras. Pengilly was still telling jokes and the laughter that greeted them was more raucous. Some of his audience were drunk enough to openly make fun of him. Slocum still saw these people as sickening and unnatural but he found he was reluctant to leave. He would have liked to stay and drink Morean wine and flirt with untrustworthy women. He would have liked to walk around Topkapi and see just how many levels deep the Webmasters had gone.

But the Varangians were closer than before. Slocum took a deep breath, and in one fast gesture clicked on the "copy" icon and flicked off his head-sucker.

The effect in the blue-dark confines of the half-Cape was instantaneous. People at the bars looked around in panic, or froze. A woman swayed, and fell off her stool. A man screamed, "Otter! Otter!" Slocum ripped off the Velcro that anchored his wrist and ankle sensors and walked toward the exit. Someone leaned over the railing of his bunk and threw up violently, splashing Slocum's trousers with vomit. Slocum tried not to imagine what was happening in *Byzantium*—the walls moving in and out, floor becoming ceiling, characters turning into sewage or three-headed deer-ticks, blood sucked from apparent flesh, noses burning—he did not want to think of it and yet he thought of it and moved faster through the increasing hysteria in the preserved cottage. Past Jedd, who was doubled over on the floor, possibly to quell the pain of stomach cramps. The cyberbutler tapped frantically on a keyboard in the central pillar. Then Slocum was out, striding through the Christmas lights, the hors d'oeuvres, the knots of people just starting to turn, bemused, toward the hubbub from the half-Cape. Over the loggia, the swimming pool, registering now the shapes of those little paper boats—they all resembled the ship, the high hull, the helicopter shack, he had no time for side impressions. Security butlers beginning to group on the porch and move inside. Slocum went through the front doors at a half run, past a knot of limo drivers illegally smoking, down the gravel driveway.

But he could not so easily leave behind what had happened. He had not seen the floors disappearing and the solid forms of Byzantium subtracting themselves, as he knew they likely had done while the Whip's virus did its work. He had only an intellectual image of what Jedd and the other X-ers in the half-Cape must have seen. But his stomach—his stomach, on some level, knew what had gone down. Because now it reacted as if the lawn itself were starting to wobble and fold, the careful landscaping on each side stretch itself into cups and smiles. His gut spasmed, and then very efficiently heaved everything it contained toward the body vertical. And Slocum barely had time to crash through some rhododendrons and kneel in the lee of a spruce before he vomited everything he had eaten at the party, and, it seemed to him, everything that had passed his lips since the last time he threw up. The fog reacted like ice against his suddenly sweating skin, and an invisible grounds speaker whispered "Thunder Road," played by a mariachi band, through the gray and regimented flower borders of another Bayview night.

SIXTEEN

IT TOOK SLOCUM AN hour to walk back to the security gate. He was both sweating and shivering because of throwing up when he set off—he got steadily colder and trembled harder as he progressed. It was cool and damp but Slocum knew that his vomiting and resultant physical condition had nothing to do with the climate. He was also starting to realize that it was not the idea of what the virus did that caused him to be sick like that. Rather, it was a reprise of the allergic reaction he had experienced in front of the Metropole, only delayed, and somewhat more violent.

Twice he had to jump into the bushes to avoid a Bayview police cruiser zooming, lights a-flash, in the direction of Kumpunens'. The now-familiar sense of being followed was oddly absent, displaced perhaps by a rational fear of being hunted for what he had done to Otto's party. He did not think they would understand at first what had occurred, and the Whip had used a Wildnet, so it would be impossible to trace exactly where the virus originated. But Jedd had a prosecutor's mind and he eventually would correlate that conversation in *Byzantium* with what happened only minutes later. There might not be enough evidence for normal cops, although what Slocum did definitely came under the purview of the new Federal Online Felonies Act, and maybe even the Anti-Gang and Terrorist Environment (digital) statutes.

In Bayview, though, the cops worked for X-Corp, and X-Corp's say-so would be more than good enough for them to bust Slocum on suspicion.

So he watched for cruisers and stayed close to the border of trees along the parkway. The idea of being hunted made him feel low, but nowhere near as low as his disappointment in himself. How could he have opted to don a full mask so easily, Slocum wondered, when only two nights ago he had felt such hatred for MacTavish's half-sucker? And how could it be that, after eighteen months of going cold turkey off the Flash, he had waltzed into *Byzantium* and all its glitz and daggers without a break in virtual stride? Cold branches brushed Slocum and pine-smelling water sprayed his forehead as he walked, and his shoes were soaked with dew. He was shaking harder than before, yet these sensations felt distant and gray, as if they were happening to another person. Only now that it was back, as strong and insubstantial as ever, could Slocum realize how far he had pulled away from the cotton feeling that had invaded him on little cat feet in his preceding life. Only now could he see how the sloop, and her list of problems and maintenance chores, and the routine he had evolved in the wet, algae-stinking environment of Coggeshall Wharf— even the confusion and increasing sadness in the marina— had started to drag him out of that Flash-induced anomie, that increasing desensitization of everything, that ascendant don't-give-a-shit-ism; striking clearer and clearer I-beams of solidity and light across the trashed construction site of his life.

Only now that he had sold it downriver in one instant of self-betrayal could he appreciate both the magnitude of the mistake he had just made and the power of an environment that had slipped under his defenses so easily. This had been very different from, and much stronger than, the Metropole. It had pulled a switch whose power he had almost forgotten; flipped him straight back into the addiction that had anesthetized his life and changed it by the very act of fighting it. How, Slocum wondered, could he fight something so strong a second time? He had looked at the X-Corp drones and realized their power and danger to those who set themselves apart; but for some reason, in the controls and buffers of a true Flash environment, he had given in without a second thought to the very process that made his erstwhile co-workers so powerful and dangerous.

The thing was—Slocum's fists tightened as he trudged—he had lived in Bayview. He had been one of the few in this community who was aware, and everything about Bayview should have warned him away from Kumpunen's half-Cape. He remembered sitting next to Kumpunen's pool, at one of Otto's new-season bashes, agonizing for Jedd's benefit about whether his growing sense of disconnection was not neural—was not, in one word, Tele-DysFunction. Jedd reassured him, and when he visited medics approved by X-Corp's health plan they practically laughed him out of the teedee clinic. After that, when his sensation level lowered, like most people he simply cranked up the input. For example, when sleeping with each other was no longer enough, he and Amy started making love with face-suckers on, watching Amy Duggan and Mahal Schrenk do the same in an Aspen chalet on the adult version of *Pain*. It had felt good that first time, exciting and jagged both. But after the third time it wasn't as hot and soon it was just something to do as other sensations dulled. And while he did not understand it then, the great sadness—the abyssal loneliness—that he felt after fucking both Amys in *Pain* had seemed deserved somehow, as if it completed an equation whose factors he could only guess at before. So that pretty soon he came to prefer doing it to himself, and he knew Amy preferred it too. He first slept with Stacey Quinn a month after he surprised Amy climaxing alone under her 3-D mask in the screening den.

And after that came the bodysuit. Jedd Motieff had demo'd it one evening in his own den; in his house, down the lane Slocum had just crossed, after a round of rocketball. The suit looked like a scuba drysuit larded with multicolored wires. Jedd said it was wired in to the story you were inhabiting. It was full of tiny micropumps and 7-millimeter bladders that would swell instantaneously in specific places according to a triage program such as jaggers used. The program worked off the drama, causing you to experience physically against your skin and muscles what the actors in the drama felt.

He could make love to Breena Jakes now, had been Slocum's first thought when he saw the suit. He could make love with her all the way. Even as he thought this he felt dejected, because he already had the feeling that he did not really want to make love all the way with Breena Jakes. He wanted to make love the way he used to with Amy Snow, his wife in reality and in the flesh. But he ordered a bodysuit and used it every day for a week and it made him feel good in that extra-sharp and speed-y way you felt good in 3-D.

The suit was not enough, of course. It was pretty good for what it was, yet it remained a digital machine, neatly divisible between its algorithms and micropumps. It could not possibly do what it advertised, which was replace analog sensation. A few weeks after he stopped using it, Amy, prompted by an article she had read on *Online Shine* about Amy Duggan's paramour, set up an "interlude," as *Shine* termed it; she cued up an episode of *Wanderbird* where, in orbit around a planet that was all sea, they had to live in a weightless sphere full of long jellyfish that felt like silk and communicated only via oral sex. But for all Amy tried and

Breena tried and shit, even the jellyfish tried, he could not
come close to an erection.

That was not why he had started leaving Bayview—
flooring the Raptor down this very drive to the highway,
to the ICE; in fact, Slocum had made that first voyage at
least two weeks before the jellyfish episode. What set him
visiting the Whaling City Marina felt less like reaction to a
lack of feeling, sexual or otherwise, than simply an attempt
to reduce a personal wrongness.

It was a wrongness he could not have explained or described except that it seemed heavy and cotton-dense to
him and going to the ICE made him feel less like cotton.

Slocum walked slower as he thought all this, as if slowly
being drained of the ability to move. His decreasing physical energy came in part from the effort it took him to review the details of his old life—and partly because he did
not want to think about the beauty and detail of the
Imperial Palace, and the Byzantine and Viking ships grappling in a blizzard on the Golden Horn.

His survival reflexes still worked at regular speed, however, for when he finally saw the lights of the security gate,
he worried that Teixeira might have already received orders
to hold him.

But all the security cameras pointed toward peril from
the Outside, and the tank traps dropped automatically
when a vehicle left via the authorized exit. Teixeira even
waved when he saw Cakes's Rambler trundling out the
gate; so perhaps Jedd had not made the connection after
all.

Or maybe, Slocum thought as he sat in the warm blast
of Cakes's heater, cruising down the highway between
Bayview and the Mall, Tex had chosen not to stop him out
of some last gesture toward friendly acquaintance. Now
that Jedd's angry words had been spoken, he could recognize what lay behind them: a feeling of loss, that something worthwhile had been broken beyond repair. It was

true that Slocum had not given his friend much chance to understand what he, Slocum, was doing when he left X-Corp. The fact that this was a mechanism of survival on his part did not make it any easier for Jedd. Slocum felt guilty, felt his sadness and depression grow measurably on thinking this; but he took some comfort from the fact that he could feel anything at all. He was not sure he could have been capable of registering such a complex emotion when he quit X-Corp. Maybe his lapse tonight had not set him back as far as he had feared.

————

THE WHARF SEEMED VERY silent and motionless when Slocum pulled the Rambler through MacTavish's gate and over to Cakes's dock. Perhaps this was merely by contrast with the lights and animation at Kumpunen's. Neon burned in the refurbished cement warehouse, though no one moved inside. MacTavish, incredibly, was hunched in the same position over his jambook. A deckhand swung his arms at the guardpost, keeping warm. The gangway was up. Slocum saw the ship but did not examine it. Its shape reminded him of the paper boats in Kumpunen's pool, and thinking of Kumpunen's brought back a hesitation in his stomach, a hint that the reflex behind his gagging was an exception to the desensitization process in that it grew easier, not harder, with use. He got out of Cakes's car, then hesitated; without his UCC card, he realized, he would not be able to top up the gas or do anything else to pay her back.

For some reason, just borrowing Cakes's car and not returning the favor somehow—even though it had been a straightforward offer, she had not mentioned gas—reeked of the kind of convenience, of the path of least resistance, he had taken advantage of in donning that full-sucker.

He got back in the car, drove down the dock to his sloop, retrieved the last full bottle of de Lauzère cognac from behind the bookcase. When he locked up Cakes's car next to her offshore racer, he left the bottle under the front seat.

———

SLOCUM WAS HUNGRY. It was a purely physical sensation, seemingly separate from the mind, like needing food after a joint, or a cigarette after sex. He had been cold and had walked a lot and had been upset and scared and now he was hungry and that was fine, that was good. He peeled potatoes and boiled them with two cloves of garlic. Then he added butter, half a can of hot condensed milk, and crushed garlic as Amy used to do for Bird, and made mashed potatoes.

He opened a can of Sloppy Joe and shook in steak sauce and heated that. Ralfie did not show up when he opened the cans; probably he was on one of his long excursions up and down the wharf, stalking rodents at the processing plant.

Slocum ate fast. Through the porthole above his head he counted six portholes of the great ship, all bright as full moons. He turned on the ECM's radio and listened to commercials in Portuguese, and desultory tugboat traffic on the marine band. The rough-voiced DJ talked soothingly of people who sang *fado* and died of the ensuing pain. He would fill requests, he added seductively, for Anna on Acushnet Steet, Petra on Water Street, Gabriela in the Whaling City Marina.

Slocum poured himself a glass of cognac and got out the Project, but did not open it at once. He finished his plate, scraped both pots clean, and drank more cognac.

Once his stomach was full and the drive to fill it was gone, he found himself thinking of Jedd again. He wondered what he could have done to explain to him why he was leaving Bayview and joining the ICE without making an enemy of him. He found he missed his friend; he also found that this missing once more led to a pool that was fed by deeper springs of loss in him. And now he was back to thinking about Bird's absence. And now it was worse because the camouflage of Flash, and his reaction to it, and his panic over how he'd reacted, were faded and he could address the hard fact of what had just happened: He had played the last card he possessed to bring Bird back into his life. Now the reality was, she was as separate from him as ever, and he had no idea how to get her back.

So he had not slid all the way back into the cotton, Slocum thought. The agony of thinking about Bird was different from the Flash sensation in the way he had come to understand that difference; less jagged but achier, like being shot in the bone versus a flesh wound. He believed the hurt wasn't as clean and strong as before he had grown to depend on the 3-D for emotional response. But he thought—he was almost sure—it hurt harder than when he'd left X-Corp; stronger than when he'd quit the Flash for good.

He opened the Project, first wiping the saloon table so no Sloppy Joe or mashed potato would mar its leather binding. Flipped pages at random, landing on a couple of prints that had worked especially well: a farm scene, with weeding women and a team of Percherons; and a spirit visitation, with a Victorian child cringing away from a bent-over ghoul carrying a swaddled baby in its arms.

That was the part where Claire had to feed a new dragon called Little Blue Dragon who could not make fire and would only eat strawberries in its breakfast cereal. But the owner of the country store, Old Man Ploch, refused to part with his last supplies, because it was morning and Old Man Ploch was mean in the morning. The only other strawberry supplier was Jensen's farm; the only way to the farm was through the old Van Leeren mansion, which was said to be haunted. When Claire and Little Blue Dragon gathered up their courage and entered the mansion, a ghoul dressed in rusted armor pursued them through the molding drapes and spiderwebs. Just before the ghoul chased them onto a piece of flooring so rotten they would certainly have fallen through it to the cellar and unnameable horror, the Countess Lanne appeared, her silver robe shining light into darkness as always. She tripped the ghoul, whose helmet fell off, revealing the bald head and crabby features of Ploch himself.

Slocum turned to the page where Countess Lanne appeared. This image consisted of a tall pre-Raphaelite woman with braided hair and languid wrists swooning over a moonlit pond. He remembered the woman at Kumpunen's who had dressed up as Lanne. She had not been right for the part either, her features had been too sharp, her body too short.

He shut Kumpunen's firmly out of his mind, pouring more cognac to mark that division. He wondered what Bird had truly thought when he turned their bedtime stories into a digital miniseries. He had been certain then that she would be proud to see Claire and Lanne, Little Blue Dragon, and Nidd the dog, all live in headsets, or in stores as dolls, stuffed animals, interactive games. But when it happened, he remembered, she had lost all interest in bedtime stories based on Claire. He had made up others, for a while, but soon after that she grew weary of his stories, no matter whom they featured. She was nine years old at that point and had other interests. Or so he told himself.

Now he looked at the picture of the Countess Lanne and realized, in a cold blue bath of understanding, that Bird at thirteen would have even less interest in this ancient book full of crumbling glued etchings and tales her father had whispered to her at bedtime when she was a kid. This was a girl who surfed affect, after all, no matter what he, Amy, or Dark Denny did to prevent it; hid out on a jagger Chris-Craft, put on a face-sucker, even ate Ex or jisi yomo and then jacked into a 3-D story program that analyzed and fed back your limbic patterns until you were crying or screaming or laughing twice or three times harder than you normally would and your sensations boosted to match.

In that same cool blue light he looked at the book and saw what she would see—an incomprehensible effort to approximate, in black-and-white and painful script, a story that four years ago she could have watched in color and sound so perfect that she might as well have been living it. Worst of all, the gap between what he had put into it as both creation and gift, and what she saw it as, would substantify, more than her mother's words ever could, how the separation between them had grown. If he could not understand how she felt about the stories that had once shaped her life, what could he know of who she was now, or how she felt? And what right did he have to insist that he know the forces she reacted to daily?

Slocum closed the book. He did it with great care. He put it under his arm and climbed the companionway; he could already hear the silence as he flung it straightarmed into the darkness between his sloop and the ship; the insignificant *plounk* as it hit the water. It might float for a while, he should probably weight it with something—the useless injector parts, perhaps, from diesels that had nothing in common with the ailing MarDyne below. Put them all in a sailbag and drop them over the side like the naval codes of a forgotten war. The heavier splash would be more satisfying, the bag would go down at once.

Slocum did not toss the book. He looked at the ship instead. Crewmen moved on a median deck; a knot of them were gathered at the big metal wheels on the forecastle around which hawsers were reeled. One of them threw the weighted end of a thin line across the stretch of water between the ship and Slocum's craft. Three men onshore caught the line, maybe twenty feet ahead of the sloop's bow, and started heaving it in. The line was tied to one of the hawsers, which made a mighty sound as its eye dropped from the giant ship's side. The yellow pools of the port-holes' reflections broke into a thousand liquid sparks.

More hawsers, Slocum thought. A tiny fear, no bigger than those sparked reflections, squirmed inside him. For the first time he wondered seriously if the hurricane might strike here; if all his complacent and cynical comments, about forecasts and marketing and the logic of 3-D rains, might be blown away by a wind powerful as ten thousand locomotives as it roared through the harbor the way an express train tore through fog.

Too many Slocums, Slocum reflected, remembering his earlier musing along those lines. Right now he had to deal with Slocum the inefficient mariner, Slocum the failed ex-ile, and Slocum the recidivist Flash addict, as well as the fact that the last two were not separate, or not all the time, or were fading into and out of each other in ways he no longer seemed to grasp.

It was easier, for all his hurricane worries, to stare at the ship and the men in charge of her protection. It was easier to find refuge—as if all those musings about Countess Lanne, and the perils of Rikka, and the "Lanne" at Kumpunen's, and his wandering around after dark, could end up in only one place—it was definitely easier to find refuge in the idea of the flesh-and-blood woman who lived on that ship beside him.

Easier by far, for all the obstacles she had placed in his way, to find a route back aboard that ship, and maybe to see her again.

Slocum stood for a long time, neck bent, staring at the ship's upper decks, the Project tucked forgotten yet some-how reassuring in its weight and presence under one arm.

By the time his renewed shivering drove him below, he had spent close to an hour trying to figure out a way to board the ship without running the risk of asking for and being refused permission to see Melisande Yonge.

He was unsuccessful.

SEVENTEEN

SLOCUM DID NOT BELIEVE in luck. He had worked long enough in a competitive environment where you had to manage crowds of people of differing talents and energies, in pursuit of goals that others would rip off if they could, to learn that you made your luck by effort and persistence and by setting up as many options as possible and exploiting them to the full once they had presented themselves.

By the same token, though, he knew that in a complex environment you could not predict everything, and often options rearranged themselves in unexpected ways and you had to be ready for that. And sometimes, by the law of averages, an angle you could never have predicted might emerge out of nowhere. Then luck consisted of knowing how to throw out the book of game plans and grab that new chance with both hands.

A form of death wish, the psychiatrist Fernsehen called this type of behavior in his first tome, *Videotherapeutics.*

All this to say that when Slocum got out of his bunk before dawn the next morning to let in Ralfie, who had been scratching at the hatch, and saw the County Diesel truck

and the queue of men in County Diesel jumpsuits filing up
the ship's gangway, he saw the connection at once. He saw
it faster than he could flip emotions on 3-D, or switch from
Flash addiction to allergy: It was a basic sodium-ion neuro-
link, after all, and the speed of it, after what had happened
yesterday in Bayview, reassured him that some of his basic
reactions remained, untainted, from the way they had been
long ago.

He thought also, as he slipped on his own County
Diesel jumpsuit, that the connection might have been
speeded up by the force of his motivation. Because he
had dreamed of the church again, during the night. And
the dream had started out the way it always did, with
Slocum returning from a long journey, and wanting to see
Bird, and turning aside nonetheless to enter the ersatz–
Christopher Wren structure shrouded by pines on the
outskirts of a small village of which he didn't know the
name. There had been snow on the ground, and that was
different.

What was different also was that Melisande Yonge had
been inside the church. He never found her, though he
searched vestry and nave, clerestory and crypt, every pew
and corner chapel. But with each place he checked, with
every minute he spent searching, he saw her clearer and
clearer in his mind's eye: as an embodiment of purity,
something translucent and deep blue as the crystal palace
that dominated the benthic marches of her aquarium. He
could visualize her face even less clearly than before but the
partial memories he did retain of her—the cracked smile,
the break in stance—were keys that unlocked a machinery
of sympathy both physical and mental, that he had somehow built up over the fifteen minutes he spent in her
cabin.

This minute, this morning, he wanted one thing above
all others, and that was to see her again. And it felt good to

surface from the confusion of his unclear motives, his defeats and blocks and the staleness of unrequited desires, to find one clear thirst, and a way to slake it.

At the last minute he turned back into the saloon, took the box of foreign injectors out of the port settee locker, and carried it topside. He made his movements casual, slow and kept the box low as he moved along the side of the processing plant. He need not have worried, for the mist was thick, and the edges of figures blurred enough that the eye tired of definition and moved on to something else. At the corner of the old warehouse, just before the security gate, he slipped off his reefer jacket and laid it behind a disused barrel that once held lime. Then he walked toward the ship, around the County Diesel truck parked at the base of the concrete spur, hoisting the box of parts to his shoulder as he did so.

The box had been a good idea, as many last-minute additions, reacting as they did to late data, often were. The deckhand guarding the gangway's base looked familiar to Slocum, and he might have recognized Slocum's face had he not kept the box between them, features tucked into the cardboard. The gangway seemed to last forever. Finally Slocum ducked through the opening into that alien warmth of ship. A security guard was stationed at the entrance to the purser's lobby, but Slocum shifted the box to hide himself more, and all the guard did was point irritably at the sign reading COUNTY DIESEL with the arrow indicating a corridor leading aft. "You're late," he said. "The others are already in the generator room."

And Slocum was aboard.

He was aboard, and yet, he thought, for all the chances he could see of jumping the tracks laid for his new persona, he might as well have stayed on his sloop. Plastic matting, laid to protect the carpet, led down the corridor. Another guard was stationed halfway down, next to a door

stopped open in the mahogany paneling. The door led to a
staircase, steel and painted white, as solidly utilitarian as the
main staircase in the purser's lobby was decorative. The last
of the County gang was visible ahead of him, manhandling
a wooden box labeled BLOHM & VOSS and "pre-flanged
camshaft/longitudinal-4680BB, generator," with other numbers and bar codes. Slocum kept one turn of stair between
him and the column's tail but he wondered what he would
do when he got to the bottom. There were no doors on
the first three landings; a door on the fourth was locked.
Judging by the sounds of scuffling and advice ahead of
him, the staircase ended two landings down. Slocum tried
the next door, and it opened onto an unadorned corridor
of painted metal panels and handrails. He went through,
and eased the door shut behind him. A sign read J DECK.
He hesitated; then, remembering that Melisande's suite was
on the ship's forward end, he started walking left. And saw,
tucked into the angle between bulkhead and deckhead, the
rounded plastic, the staring black pupil of a video surveillance camera.

He felt a tinge of panic at that point—strangely, for all
that was about to happen, it was as nervous as he got that
day. Turned quickly, too quickly, and, looking well down
the corridor, spotted the camera's twin covering the aft
sector.

Since surveillance was a given, Slocum reasoned, he
might as well go in the direction he needed to go. He
knew from working in a high-security area at X-Corp that
the fact that a surveillance system existed did not necessarily mean it was monitored. He slowed his walk, deliberately. Opened one door—a pantry, and another—a staff
toilet. The third door read STAIRWAY 3 and he went in.

It led downward only. Slocum hesitated, then descended. He would try the next deck down and work forward to the elevator bank he had gone up with the first

officer. As he descended, he realized that this staircase smelled familiar in a way unconnected with ships. It ended at a frosted glass door, which he opened.

Slocum gasped. Before him lay a swimming pool filled with royal-blue water reflecting light from vast fixtures sculpted like the half shells of scallops. The sides of the pool were of rose-gray marble. Doric columns of the same material supported a frescoed ceiling in the depths of which Poseidon spun storms and Ulysses, tied to a mast, gazed at women naked and singing. At the pool's after end, a huge bronze seahorse seemed poised to slide down a marble plinth; it spat a stream of clear water into the pool. Someone moved in a changing room behind the seahorse, a shadow sharply cast against another screen of frosted glass.

Back up the staircase, two decks, hurrying forward, the box masking his features from the cameras' cold stare. He ignored the stairway that led to the generator room. Two-thirds of the way down the corridor and he was sure he was well past where the elevator had been on his first visit. Perhaps it did not go down this far.

This corridor had been mercifully empty and silent since he entered it, except for the mechanical thrumming—deeper and more tactile this low in the ship. Now he passed a cabin door behind which Slappe music played. Someone uttered a comment he could not make out. His heart had settled into an accelerated rhythm. Somehow he retained a sense of the purity of his drive; it was like being in that church again, he thought. That blue crystal palace leading him on.

Finally another staircase. This one led up to the next deck, but a closed watertight door walled off further progress. The corridor on, presumably, I deck, was less utilitarian, paneled in fruitwood, its carpet colorful and deep. The sign opposite the staircase door held one arrow, leading aft, that read SPA, and a second pointing forward that read ELEVATORS. Slocum had taken four steps down its length when the bell began to ring.

It rang loudly, regularly, deep *clang*s at one-second intervals. A door opened thirty feet ahead of Slocum and a man in a white steward's jacket came out and turned left, forward, without noticing Slocum. He disappeared around a bulkhead at the very head of the corridor, where the usual surveillance camera gazed impassively in Slocum's direction. A red light blinked, past the steward's cabin, on the opposite side.

Behind him, from the staircase he had just left, a man shouted an order, another responded. Slocum broke into a trot, trying doors on both sides of the corridor. All were locked; even the steward's door had locked behind him. The flashing light was set in a short wall of glass that included its own glass door. Behind lay a room, one of whose walls was covered with diagrams of the ship's decks, white lines on a black background. Lights of different colors were set into each schematic cabin, saloon, machinery room, galley, and corridor. A pattern of tiny blue lights on decks H, I, and J flashed prettily, like holiday decorations.

Video monitors covered the other wall. There must have been fifty of them, Slocum guessed; as many as in the purser's office. All offered random angles of ship. A third wall held a series of control panels marking watertight bulkheads, pumps, seawater return, ventilation, alarms. Three swivel chairs faced the desk, which was covered with buttons and switches.

Slocum hid his box in one of the back-facing armchairs. Then, resignedly, he slid under the control desk, hunkering into the well so he was out of sight of the glass wall and the men who would soon appear behind it. He figured the one place on the ship there might not be a surveillance camera would be in this glass cage meant to keep tabs on the rest of the ship.

His heart, he noticed, was not beating any faster than it had since he saw the first security camera. Nor was the purity of his reason for being here any less clear than before, and again he was glad of that. In this morning without coffee, without breakfast, it was good to retain the sense of blue. He knew, by dint of harsh experience, how easily it could have faded by now.

Men duly ran up and down the corridor, on the other side of the glass. If he had any chance at all, it would lie in sloppy work caused by a sense of urgency: his pursuers assuming he would not hide in a glass room, giving it a cursory visual check—they might finally quit this deck, leaving him room to move again.

To pass the time while he waited, Slocum watched the various monitors, tracking what the guards were doing. It was not easy; there were a lot of monitors, and most flipped angles or panned across a 360-degree spectrum. One row, obviously hooked to a shuffle program, sampled images from all cameras, five seconds on each. At one point he thought he had spotted a guard, who turned out to be a steward with a tray bearing a silver coffeepot and pastries on china. This drew a rumble of serious lust from Slocum's stomach.

A pass of the foyer from behind the security desk, where the monitors were, showed two guards where you'd expect them to be, both muttering into walkie-talkies. Something about that angle bothered Slocum, but he could not put his finger on it. Another pass of what had to be a large bar or restaurant, quite high on the ship, on its stern, displayed a vista of the upper harbor, or what could be seen of it through the veil dances of mist: the swing bridge, Fish Island, a blur where the ICE lay. A man with lavish white hair sat in an armchair in the middle of the camera's swing, smoking, watching the harbor. Shots of the top deck, full of life rafts, deck chairs, and goosenecked vents that reminded Slocum of old movies and stowaways.... And there, finally, he spotted it: the corridor on J deck, the deck he had just quit. A half-dozen men, and for the love of Mike they all carried automatic assault rifles, probably grabbed out of some armory as soon as the alarm went off. Searching cabin to cabin, two of them standing flat against the sides of a door while a third unlocked each one, and why would they assume he had a key? Then again, they would not know who he was at this point. Slocum's musings trailed off into background because his attention no longer focused on the guards working their way along J deck; because suddenly, and in a fashion more abstract than he'd hoped, he had found Melisande Yonge.

She sat in a black leather reclining chair with levers that adjusted every point of it against back and neck and buttocks. Her dark hair made harsh contrast with the pale V of her face, the white cover on the chair's headrest, the white-paneled room behind. Her mouth, he noticed, made an inverted V against the larger shape; and her arms were stretched in the same pattern, hands crossing over her crotch as if to protect herself from prurient eyes. Under her fingers lay a thin jambook computer, from which a cord led to a pair of earphones buried in the black mass of her hair. She wore the dressing gown she'd had on the last time he saw her, and the Turkish slippers. This time Slocum did not see those details he remembered best about her, mostly because they were details of stance, search, and structure that vanished while she rested; but he recognized her immediately. And he kept staring at her, to make sure, because everything in that 2-D video was so far from what he had expected to find.

For one thing, the collar of her bathrobe was turned down and the scarf she had worn was gone. It was the first time he had seen so much of her neck, which was as pale as her face, long, and had well-defined esophagus, tendons, arteries, and muscles. Yet even now he could not see all of it. The thick intravenous hookup that was taped into the valley of her throat obscured a percentage of the right side.

A bright splashing scarlet, the color of rubies, of cooked wine from Oporto, filled the clear plastic tubing of the IV. Slocum followed the scarlet around an IV pole to a squat, light-blue machine, perhaps two feet by three feet square and three high, that sat on castors between Melisande's seat and an identical but empty chair on the other side. Half of the machine appeared to be a computer terminal with screen and keyboard. The other half included dials, electrical sockets, and a flattened bubble of clear glass, with bright stainless-steel scoops visible at regular intervals around the wheel's periphery. The scoops, too, were filled with arterial blood.

The word BLT/T 14H was clearly visible in chrome script across the top.

She shifted at that point, adjusting her earphones, turning her head to one side. She was not as beautiful as he had thought last time. Someone dressed in white moved in a blur past the video lens, pushing what looked like a plastic collar mounted on another IV stand. Someone offscreen shifted a rack of clamps and surgical tools into a cone of light behind the second chair. Melisande's lips stretched and broke as she said something, but they did not crack into the smile Slocum remembered, and he was absurdly grateful for that, for no reason he could name. Her eyes were open, aimed at a point just to the left of the camera that was directed at her. They were a lighter blue than he remembered.

And that was when Slocum understood that each of these surveillance terminals included a feedback camera with a lens secreted in the upper right-hand portion of the screen.

He knew this because her eyes were directed to the left and down from the camera, so close that she had to be looking right beside its lens.

He knew because he remembered then, with a jolt of pure adrenaline, that the angle of view he'd had of the guards at the purser's desk came from the wall behind, which contained no cameras—but was covered entirely with terminals.

And he knew because Melisande's eyes crumbled into tiny crows'-feet around the outer edges. And her face broke into that smile, half up, half down, her mind forever not made up about whether this was going to turn out funny or depressing. She looked right at him, or right at the lens, and kept on smiling that way, which finally was what he remembered best about her.

———

THE GUARDS FOUND HIM two minutes later. They were young, fit men trained in how the body's joints were supposed to move, or not. They dragged him from the cubbyhole, doubled him over, made his fingers and elbows bend in ways they were not intended to until he yelped in agony. They dumped out all his pathetic engine parts on the carpeting, looking for guns and high explosive.

"What is this shit," one of them said.

"It's for an engine," another replied.

"No shit," a third commented.

"This shit's old. Why would County Diesel—" the first began.

"He's not County Diesel," another interrupted, inspecting Slocum's face. "He's the guy on that little sailboat."

"Fuckin' shit."

"What do you want?" the first one demanded, holding up a Yanmar injector to the neon as he searched for meaning.

"He's just lookin' to rip off shit," the second said. "Just a jerkwater, like everybody in this shithole town."

When no weapons were found immediately, one of the guards took the box away for deeper examination, and from the depths of his physical humiliation and the embarrassment that Melisande Yonge should be watching this from the surveillance cameras' perspective, Slocum was still glad they would be wasting time on a bunch of used and diesel-stinking injectors all chosen for their fancied resemblance to spare parts of the MarDyne Corporation.

Then the guards marched him aft, down a transverse corridor, and up the staircase he had been looking for all this time, a utility staircase running from top deck to bottom. They got off on H deck, in the port corridor, and hustled him quickly past the security-pursers to the gangway. The guard on duty at the doors also held an automatic rifle in a steady grip. He did not get out of the way as the knot of guards plus prisoner approached. Instead, he pointed his chin to the purser's desk, where a man with sunken eyes and a pointy jaw and a thin mustache—a man in a ship's officer's uniform—lounged against the counter, watching Slocum.

"What?" the chief guard said.

"Passenger wants to see him," the officer said. It was Matt Zurbruegge.

"Him?" the guard said incredulously. He looked at Slocum as if to check what he might have missed that would explain why anyone should waste time on Slocum.

"Come on," the first officer said. He glanced once at Slocum. The set of his face was hostile and cold. He led the way to the elevator, and the detail of guards marched Slocum in his wake.

They got off two decks up and turned aft, through a set of twelve-foot bronze doors molded into a classical scene—a boar hunt, a woman with a spear—to enter a lounge that for a few seconds made Slocum forget the complications of where he was and what he was doing.

It was high; the ceiling stood two decks tall, narrowing like a cathedral with perspective. Vast chandeliers of crystal stalactites hung from the highest, narrowest part of the ceiling, while under the overhang of that section smaller sconces shone at intervals. Down the long center aisle, a row of lights that were the twins of the chandeliers, only locked in plinths and pointing up, illuminated burgundy carpets and armchairs clustered around coffeetables of polished walnut. The walls were panels of buffed oak, between which further scenes of classical hunt alternated with church windows affording a narrow view of fog, and lifeboats, and the roofs of warehouses on this, the ship's starboard side.

In alcoves between the columns stood B-Net terminals disguised as Queen Anne secretaries.

At the end of the lounge, twin staircases curved away from each other to meet under a spray of crystal lozenges throwing light in all directions by a doorway one deck up.

A thin, small figure leaned on the railing at the top of those steps. She stood motionless as the guards forced Slocum into an armchair the softness of which made welcome contrast with the hard holds and hands of the men. A silver coffeepot steamed on the table. Pastries oozed on heavy china that carried the seahorse symbol. The mate walked down the carpeting a ways and then stopped, almost uncertainly.

The figure moved. It came down the stairs slowly, deliberately. Slocum knew it was Melisande by her slightness and the darkness of her hair and the color of her dressing gown, but not until she was halfway up the Isfahan runner was he able to make out her features. When she got to Slocum's longitude she did not look at him but said to the mate, who had walked back with her, "Tell them to go away."

"Melisande," Zurbruegge began.

"Tell them. I want to talk to him alone." Slocum now thought it less inconceivable that she should fill an important position in the X-Corp hierarchy; her tone when she spoke to the mate held the capacity to formulate desires simply that went with a habit of command. It also contained the adamantine assumption, of those long used to getting their way, not that her orders were going to be obeyed but rather that they already were obeyed, in the sense that all doubts and contradictions already had been resolved by the fact that she was who she was. The actual commands were follow-through only.

The chief guard protested nonetheless.

"The security document—"

"Screw the security document."

Zurbruegge said, "Melisande, they have to—"

"Then they can wait outside. Stand guard by the windows. Frisk the seagulls, I don't care. I know this man," she continued. "I want you to leave us be."

She sat in an armchair opposite Slocum and closed her eyes. The chief guard, after a moment's hesitation, pointed his men to various exits and they went out and made shadows against the windows; then he retreated as well.

Zurbruegge held out longer. He stood for thirty seconds, watching Slocum, whose earlier sense that the mate felt proprietary toward Melisande was confirmed by the amount of energy he expended looking at Slocum. His eyes lost color. Finally he pointed at Slocum with one finger, then walked out, and the bronze doors hissed shut behind him.

"Are they gone?" Melisande's eyes were still closed. "They didn't hurt you, did they?"

"I'm OK."

"They can be rough. Some of them were commandos."

"They did their job," he said.

"Did you like it?"

"I'm sorry?" For an instant he thought she meant being handled by the goons. One corner of her mouth crept up.

"My entrance."

Slocum smiled. What he liked was how she blindsided him with questions. He remembered it from the first time they had talked. It was a trick of conversation that tended to end-run the circumstances, like the fact that he had been caught sneaking around her ship like a burglar, and was about to be thrown off before she summoned him here.

"It was—spectacular."

"I just love doing that," she said, opening her eyes suddenly. "But you need an audience."

There were two coffee cups. She could not have known he was coming. Slocum wondered who the second cup had been for. The liquid was dark and brown and made ribbons of steam when it hit the cold china. She handed him a cup. "You saw me," she added, almost casually.

He looked at her through the steam as he drank. It felt normal to look at her this way; Slocum supposed that was because, when you lived on Coggeshall Wharf, you got used to seeing everything through a scrim of vapor. The coffee was fine, nutty and deep in taste. It was hot, it was strong, and Slocum put it down and said, "Saw what?"

"Please." She shook her head. Her tone was almost angry. "Don't pretend. You were looking at the monitors, in the fire-control room. I saw you. The monitors are two-way."

"You smiled at me."

"Yes." She was nowhere near smiling now.

"I wondered—" he began.

"I can't talk about it." She poured herself coffee. The spout of the pot chattered slightly against the coffee cup's rim. "Do you know anything about me? About this ship? I don't know what you know. It all gets so—twisted."

"That machine," he began, "I assumed—"

"It's a therapy," she said quickly, and watched her cup being borne to her lips by her hand. "A new process, very good for you, keeps you young and beautiful. We all want that, right? It requires transfusions. You saw all that, right?"

Now she watched him through the coffee mist.

"Are you sick?" he asked curiously.

"Haven't you heard anything I said?"

"I—"

"It's a *therapy*. It's still under development. I'm *fine*. I'd rather talk about you. Who you are, where you come from."

"You know who I am."

"I know." She put down her coffee, looked sideways. The light from the nearest glass sculpture brightened one side of her face. She hadn't smiled since she saw him in the camera, he thought. Not all the way. But he liked looking at her face sideways. His impression of her in the video screen had been that she was not as pretty as he had remembered, though with lots of redeeming qualities. Now, seeing the different slopes of nose, jaw, eyes, lips converging not in a place but toward some mood or word as yet unspoken, he decided he'd been wrong, and her beauty was something that had to be coaxed; it depended on light that turned and flared when she leaned against something, like a doorjamb, or the armrest of a chair, as she was doing now.

"I know your stats," she said, and looked at him and then at the nearest sconce. "I saw the printouts. Dad was a wedding photographer, you almost went to juvenile detention twice. You had a dog named Zep, who died of heartworm. Low-rent college, good grad school. Youngest VP-production ever at X-Corp Multimedia—unusual for a local kid. You were on the shortlist for president of the 3-D division; then you quit, about half a second before you got fired. Right?" She looked at another sconce. "You have a wife and child. You dragged them to live in a sort of marina slum on the other side of this harbor. Since then, separated from your family, moved your sloop to this dock, from which you refuse to budge."

"You know a lot," he said glumly, depressed not so much by what she knew but by the fact that the broad lines of his life could be summed up so quickly and in such dreary fashion by a stranger. This sadness made him feel defensive, and out of this defensiveness he added, "You know way more about me than I do about you."

"That's because this ship belongs to X-Corp; the ship told me."

"Maybe the ship will tell me about you," he said, and glanced at the B-Net terminal in a nearby alcove. "If I ask it."

"This ship won't tell you anything," she said. "The ship protects me. That is its job." She uncurled her legs, rocked to the other armrest. He heard that quiet jingle he had heard the first time he met her. So it wasn't wind chimes. He fought down the notion that her body made music when it moved. "Anyway I told you I don't want to talk about me," she was saying. "I never get off this ship. I never talk about anything other than ship's business, right?" She leaned forward again, placed her elbows on her knees. "I want to talk about something different."

Slocum replaced his cup on the table. There was something in her voice that he recognized, and it took him a while to figure out what it was. He never was to pin it down with words; how he defined it at last was because it resonated with tones that had been in his own voice during the time she mentioned—when he dragged Amy and Bird willy-nilly out of Bayview; when he finally quit the second doughnut.

What had been in his tone then came from the feeling of cotton. Or rather, it came from his inability to live in anesthesia anymore, and a resulting determination to do almost anything to get out of it. He remembered how Amy and Bird had looked at him when he talked about leaving Bayview, quitting and changing everything around them. These were concepts they did not want to accept. He recalled watching bewilderment, contempt, even fear inhabit their features, as they realized he was likely to commit acts that would alter their lives forever.

If Melisande, too, was fighting the cotton-feeling, he thought, she deserved real answers.

She met his gaze, and moved with one finger a ringlet of hair that bounced in front of her eyes.

Outside the windows, and far below the level of this deck, a white ferry moved like a phantom through the rolling ribbons of fog, bound for the Steamship Authority dock at the harbor's head.

"I have this project," he began. "Something I've been making for my daughter."

Her gaze was level and steady. He thought that maybe this was not something she was interested in. He didn't care. The thing about the cotton was, even if the despair it caused was in someone else, it rubbed off on those who recognized it. Now he felt a taste of the ruthlessness that rose inside him when the cotton was more than he could take.

He kept going.

"It's an old hard copy. A blank book, a ledger. I've been writing a story in it. A bedtime story I used to tell Bird. My daughter," he explained.

"I know."

"Of course you know." He did not mean this sarcastically. "Anyways I bought a bunch of other books, ancient ones, with prints they made with copper plates and ink. I cut out the prints that had something to do with my story. I wanted to make something solid, something you did not have to wear a face-sucker for."

He told her the story of Claire and Old Man Ploch and the Van Leeren place. Melisande poured more coffee. She was certainly bored, he thought; but he wasn't talking to her anymore. He was not making an entrance here. He needed no audience. The only audience he required for this was himself. When he finished the story she said, "I saw *Rikka,* of course. It was the top slot of Multimedia's kid programming for almost two years."

He nodded.

"It was interactive. Rikka—or Claire, right?—didn't have to go through the old Van Leeren place. The kids could try different ways. There was a mountebank, I remember, who came to town, and a spaceship that went up or down according to how much you sang, and whether you sang songs that were cheerful or sad. If you sang happy songs, you produced big bubbles, and the ship went up fast."

He nodded again, impatiently. He had not finished the real story. But she seemed interested again. She put her arms around herself and squeezed, and looked off to the side, remembering.

"There were other hazards. I remember Jensen's farm, and that princess—Lane? Lana? Not much of a character, right? But the colors were beautiful, the simulation was Virtix—top of the line." She cocked her head, still looking away, perhaps to spare his feelings. "And you're making a scrapbook?"

He took a sip of coffee.

"Don't understand that part." Glancing back at him. Her eyes had changed color once more, or maybe the fog outside had thinned, allowing more light into this vast lounge.

"No." He sighed. "I realized that last night, when I took it out—of course she won't give a damn about it. She wasn't even much interested in the 3-D, she knew all the stories, she was too old for that level already, I don't know—" He broke off that sentence like snapping a dead branch that had gotten in the way and would not support your weight as you climbed a tree.

"I was doing it myself," he went on, and the sadness swelling in him then was proof enough that he had gotten it right this time. "Because I was so close to her, when I used to tell her those stories. It reminded me of that feeling, it was so peaceful." He leaned forward and picked up the coffeepot. It was something to do. Not much coffee remained. The plated silver was heavy. He held the pot firmly as he poured and its spout did not touch the cup's rim.

"I guess I thought I could buy her back—I could make her care again. Do you see that?" Looking up at her through his eyelashes as he divided the dregs between them.

She shook her head.

"I was going back to how I was. At Arcadia. Manipulating her for what I wanted, buying her with something she might want—"

"That's the part," she interrupted, and she had leaned forward too, the jingle happening once more. "That's the part that doesn't work." She wiggled her nose. The lines in her face were tight with thought. "Not what you want— not even what you tried, the X-Corp thing." Threw one arm out, the sweeping, push-away gesture he remembered. "You didn't even make the effort. To see things as she would. You're not making the effort you made when you invented that story."

She picked up her cup and drained it. Sat straighter in the soft cushions, one arm still hugging herself around the waist. Her nightgown parted slightly when she made that gesture, and he could see the longitudinal shape of one breast, a soft cream among the robe's shadow.

"Those stories," she said, and one side of her mouth lifted a little. "When kids are young it's much easier for adults, I think. They are replicas, one step up from dogs, something to train, right? But later is, well—harder."

She hugged herself with both arms again. She seemed cold. Slocum thought about taking off his jacket and giving it to her, then remembered he wasn't wearing it; only the jumpsuit. He shifted uncomfortably; his crotch was cramped. If he didn't know better he would have thought he was getting an erection. Slocum, looking down, realized—astonished—that he was. Flushing, he looked at Melisande to see if she had noticed. She was not watching him; she watched nothing at all as she chose what she wanted to say from the lockers of her language center.

"My mother told me stories," Melisande continued. Her voice was husky and low again. "She told me one, I remember, about a little girl who lived in a temple full of miniature golden bells. There were many bells, millions and millions of them, so tiny that even walking by you made them ring. All day long that temple was filled with music, and songs, and prayers, because prayers were written on those bells, and every time they made noise the prayer that was written on them went winging up to the gods who lived on the mountain."

Her eyes were on him now. Slocum hoped his flush was gone. His dick was shrinking again, he was pretty sure. His heart pounded.

He thought of the jingle again. She made bell sounds, he thought, she told bell stories; when she moved she prayed: all nonsense.

"My mother is from Kashmir," Melisande said, and this time that one side of her mouth lifted all the way and the other only half lifted so her face seemed perplexed, her smile uncertain, as if the mix of surprise and aperture responsible for this expression was not something she was sure of, or sure if it was a good thing. "A lot of her tales were not happy. This girl, for example. She was deaf, and could hear none of the bells, not a one. When she grew up she went to the mountains to find a holy man who could make her hear again. She had to go to the highest—"

The doors hissed behind Slocum. All at once Melisande's eyes looked like she had put on dark glasses. Her mouth snapped back to the shape it had been before:

curved, but in a way that was straight; ready for trouble, or the lethal padding of cotton. A woman's voice said, "If we put this off another five minutes you're going to have to sign a disclaimer agreement again."

Melisande's eyes flicked back at Slocum.

"I'm sorry, Shanti," she called, "I'm coming. I guess I can't finish the story," she added in her softer voice. "Then again, I know you understand. About unfinished stories, I mean."

"There's a margin for error," the voice complained, "but you can't push it like this."

He stared back at Melisande. He wanted to say that he did not understand at all; that this lack of comprehension was, perhaps, the core of his dilemma. Melisande was talking, though, more urgently than before.

"You have to promise me," she said. "You won't tell anyone, right?" A figure dressed in white steamed into view to stand beside their cluster of armchairs. It was the woman he had seen with her the first time. She did not look at Slocum but alternated her gaze between Melisande and the screen of a jambook hooked to her belt, on which the time in large numerals flicked relentlessly.

"I won't tell anyone what?" he said, almost whispering.

"What you saw," she whispered, and got to her feet. "In the monitor. You know." She was looking behind him. Slocum turned, and saw the mate and two security men walk seriously into the lounge.

Slocum got up. Zurbruegge did not ask for Melisande's opinion this time. He nodded, and the goons each took one of Slocum's arms.

Melisande wrapped her bathrobe tighter around her, and gazed fiercely down at him.

"Not anyone," she insisted, glancing at Zurbruegge. "It would be dangerous for me."

Then she turned and headed back down the long central aisle of the lounge toward the monumental stairs at the

forward end. Zurbruegge nodded again, and while the
women walked gently forward the men, roughly and
quickly, shoved Slocum through the bronze doors, along
the boat deck, and down the stairs toward the purser's
lobby and the gangway to Coggeshall Wharf.

EIGHTEEN

IT WAS LATER IN the morning than the last time he'd
been in the Sunset Tap, but breakfast specials were still being served and Slocum still had an amazing amount of
credit with Obrigado.

Shaneeqwa was in her usual corner—when was she not?
Slocum wondered. It was astonishing to him that Madame
Ling let her girls spend so much time off their backs and in
this place. Luisa and Dinette and Chevette and May were
also there. Then again, morning was a slow time at
Madame Ling's, and she never made breakfast, so perhaps it
made sense after all.

This morning Slocum liked things that made sense. He
had checked the hurricane barrier and it was still open and
that made sense because the storm could not possibly be
within dangerous range, even if it was heading this way. He
had switched on the ECM and found the Whip online,
and that made sense; it also rang true that when he asked
the Whip to meet him this morning, he hemmed and
hawed, on e-mail of course, and made excuses that had
nothing to do with his wife.

And MacTavish had handed Slocum a box from

DownCoast Chandleries that contained new switches for the electronics board and a replacement teardrop zinc to prevent electrolysis, and that made sense, since he had ordered it at least three days ago, when his UCC card worked; three days was average delivery time for Net-ordered goods. MacTavish had also taken another Polaroid of him, which was not going to make sense—but Slocum was shutting away these minor discordant notes, hiding a little, closing his ears.

He had punched Freitas on the way in and Freitas had laughed contemptuously. That made sense.

Cakes was in the Sunset Tap, sitting beside Luisa. She often came here for breakfast. There were more ex-fishermen in here than usual and Slocum would sort out the reason for that in due course. His heart felt like it was still throwing in a few extra beats over a minute's running and he knew the reason for that; it should have been all the rumpus on the ship, but it was really Melisande Yonge. He remembered her face pretty well—he could work his mouth the way she worked her smile, one side rising more than the other, and that made him smile all the way, destroying the mimicry in the process.

Reasons and consequences, cause and effect. He knew how infatuation worked. He did not want to think about it because it felt good and yet it was so new and could go so wrong. But it was a familiar sensation, something he had experienced with Amy and Breena Jakes and even Stacey Quinn, a little, and it was clean of the fuzz and mixed motives of the Flash. (He did not want to think about the fact that Breena Jakes was a Flash construct and all the implications that followed so he simply ignored them.) Anyway, the fact that his system was still jizzed because of the woman on the ship worked to reinforce the idea that the rest of the world also ran on such an easy idea: A happened and it affected B, the way one domino, falling, would knock over the next.

Slocum ordered the special: a beer and a blueberry muffin. He seldom drank beer so early but today it felt like it might help his brain make fine distinctions between what he could usefully address and what he should not waste time on.

His dick, for example. He should not waste time on his dick. There had been a close enough sequence there between when Melisande first smiled, and he caught a glimpse of her breast on one hand, and when he started getting an erection on the other, that he could make a case for cause and effect in that instance. But the last time he'd been able to really get a hard-on had been in the first week of using the haptic suit, when he slept with Breena Jakes on *Wanderbird*. After the first week Breena had become less interesting to him sexually, even with the suit. Sucking and kneading at his crotch as they embraced in the plush couches of the spaceship's cabin, somewhere between the third and fourth systems behind Cygnus X-6—that was the time Breena had become quite concerned about his physical indifference. After two weeks he had found no response at all occurring south of his navel. It was as if he had been frozen down there. Which was fine, he thought then. It made sense, it was simply desensitization, they had workshops for this at X-Corp, and frankly he was becoming a little weary of Breena at that point. It even made sense that his sexual mechanics should remain ungeared with Amy when—it had been their anniversary—they had made the effort to have sex, maybe two months after his last interlude with Breena. They both used face-suckers, and though his crotch was touching Amy's, he was focusing on a half-dozen Samoan women in the hammock with them.

But why, after he had spent eighteen months off the Flash, could he not grow hard when Luisa held him naked and warm in her cocoon of gossip magazines, cheap makeup, and nylon blankets at Madame Ling's?

After ten minutes of waving, Slocum got Obrigado to

fetch him coffee. Beer alone was not enough for the issues of this morning. He did not glance in Luisa's direction now. That issue, too, was something he wished to avoid. The impotence had fit in with everything else he had lost over the last year and a half, and he had chucked it all into the same box with the idea that leaving—abandoning the Town and the proximity of Bayview, leaving his wife, jettisoning all the props and drag of his old life—would destroy everything in the box, including the impotence. Like burning down a house you had lived in a long time and that held all your old and now irrelevant possessions.

Hope was something else, though, Slocum thought, taking alternating sips of coffee and beer. The idea that his dick had responded to something other than reflexes of blocked circulation made his hands tremble. Hope—the possibility of change—was a lot harder to cope with than defeat. Defeat was easy.

Hope required plans.

"Dag," Shaneeqwa yelled suddenly, "ol' bitch come up like a fuckin' ghost or something out of a castle cellar, her necklace clankin' like chains, say, 'Shaneeqwa, where the thirty-eight credits you owe me for personal laundry. *Madre de diosh!*' "

The whores laughed. Slocum searched for Luisa's face, expecting the graze of guilt he would get from her pallor, from the wounded look she might aim were she watching him; from the strain of ignoring him if she was not.

But Luisa was laughing, looking at Cakes as she laughed. Something open and unguarded in how she sat. Now Slocum noticed how close she and Cakes were sitting. His neighbor from the wharf, for only the second time Slocum could remember, had taken off her filthy motocross jacket. She was wearing camo pants and a wifebeater that barely contained her breasts. Her fingers caressed Luisa's neck, the nape of Luisa's neck under her knot of hair, the place he knew she liked.

Slocum took two swallows of beer and one of coffee. That seemed the right ratio for this morning. After two cycles of coffee-beer he took a bite of muffin. He felt stupidly angry—for the usual male reasons, jealousy, loss of sexual territory, whatever that meant in his case. The beer-coffee combo seemed to help. Not quite as fast as vid-flip, he turned smoothly toward the next feeling, which was one of relief, because if Luisa was falling under Cakes's influence she would not be trammeling him with the responsibility her needs imposed. And moored beside that was a lighter feeling, because he liked Luisa a lot, and to see someone he liked smile like that—it had been a good smile, open and full of possibilities of attraction and trust—made him feel less heavy, a little less weighed down, and that much farther away from the cotton.

Oh and of course the moronic male part of him was glad that it was Cakes, who could not show up his failure with a different erection. But he was not going to think about that. He was going back to what he'd thought about last, which had been forward-looking, constructive stuff, the plans. And the Whip came in at that point, along with Freitas, who grabbed him by one elbow at the door.

"Take your best shot," he urged. "Go on."

The Whip said, "I don't do that, Freit."

"Go on, pussywhip," Freitas called after him. The Whip went over to Slocum's table, his face set, and placed his jambook carefully on the zinc.

"I wish Freit would leave me alone."

"It's what he does," Slocum replied.

"Well, he knows I don't like it." The Whip poked at his gut with the fingers of both hands, as if to tuck in love handles. Regulars usually evaded Freitas with a joke jab, a tap at the abdomen that Freitas, disgusted, wouldn't waste a comment on.

"You get away OK?"

The Whip was setting up his computer, bowing the

antenna, switching on the power. "I'm fine," he said. The jambook feeped.

"What'd you tell her?"

The Whip chattered the keys. Finally he said, "Told her I was meeting someone from Arcadia. She knows it's kind of early but she can't question Arcadia, they pay the rent. Anyway," he added defensively, looking at Slocum, "it's true, kind of. You used to be at Arcadia."

Slocum watched him for a second or two. He tried to think of words to use here. All he remembered was Shaneeqwa's: "You so wrapped up in yourself you can't help anyone." Well, here was a case in point, and it showed how facile and maybe inaccurate Shaneeqwa's words had been. The Whip was his friend, and he had no idea how to help him. Finally all he said was, "I appreciate you—you doing this."

"The bank part was easy," the Whip replied. He started rippling at the keys again, hooking in the Nets on Nets, the interlocking waves of ceaseless communication that swaddled the globe like fiberoptic underwear. The rigidity of his features softened, melted, was gone. "You got a bad credit lock."

"Whaddya mean?"

"A credit lock? It's—"

"I know what the fuck a credit lock is," Slocum said. "I mean, that's not possible." He felt as if the tension the Whip had just shed had flowed straight into his own system and multiplied. If the UCC card was the driver's license of financial validity, as well as being your actual driver's license, then the credit lock was its opposite: the Leavenworth of transactional life. A lock could be meted out only by one of the four big companies belonging to the Association of Credit Bureaus, after three months of secret review. Supposedly it could happen only in dire circumstances, for example if you defaulted on two or more online loans and lost the means to make remedial payments. "I haven't done anything, I haven't defaulted—"

The Whip shrugged. "Did you leave some UCC bills in Bayview? They don't like UCC bills."

"I cleaned everything up. Everything. Anyway, that's not enough, they're not supposed to—"

"Slocum." The Whip took his eyes off the computer screen for an instant. He shook his head. "Grow up. You *know* how you left X-Corp. You *know* they own X-Credit Services. I mean," he added, cutely quoting the slogan of X-Credit, "how much data do you need today?"

"But they can't—"

"Grow up," the Whip repeated. "Happens all the time. Blackball comes down one part of the system, the next circuit along lets it pass, doesn't wanna deal with it. Nothing personal, nothing planned—it's just how it works. An Org has no percentage in dealing with fuckups, they got plenty of people with good credit to sell to. And the people who work for the Org are scared to get involved. Failure is catching, you know?" He tweaked the joystick controls. Music played from the tiny computer's speakers. "What did you want to ask me, anyway? Not the bank thing, you said."

Slocum took two sips of beer, two of coffee, a bite of muffin. He watched the Whip. As he chewed and swallowed, Slocum thought, *All those months.* All those months in the ICE developing pity for his former colleagues who accepted the domination of what Hawkleyites called the Orgs, and liked it. People who got diarrhea at the pale thought of anything interfering with their dependence. Like getting fired, or quitting, or falling behind on UCC bills.

And now here he was, eighteen months later, shattered because of a credit lock. His heart beat twice as fast as when he was being hunted by guards carrying automatic rifles on that ship. He had almost forgotten about the ship, he suddenly had no interest in the strange hope that had come to him when he last saw Melisande Yonge. He had almost no interest left in her compared to the castrating fear that his UCC card had not been the victim of a cybernetic slipup, a few 0s and 1s rearranged by chance or magnetic interference; that this might have been done to him on purpose, and with no hope of recall. Credit locks were notorious for being almost impossible to reverse. It took five years or seven, it might even take ten to get a hearing—

"So," the Whip asked, and pulled a half-sucker from his satchel, repeating unkindly, "how much data do you need today?"

Slocum forced himself to remember why had he contacted the Whip. He called up in his mind's eye the scene he had witnessed in the ship's security terminals. He told the Whip about the white-paneled room, the articulated chair, the squat light-blue machine; half terminal, half control panel, its clear wheel shining with blood. A box with the name *BLT/T 14H* in chrome script across the top.

He told the Whip and the Whip simply nodded. Slocum felt a little insulted. He wondered—and it was not the first time he had asked himself this—why exactly the Whip came to the Sunset Tap. Everyone knew it was to get away from Dolores and the way she chained him down, but Slocum had thought he recognized something he himself felt: that he was tired of the security of his life, that he found some different mode of living in the Tap, as Slocum had found in the ICE. That here was a place where things might happen that were not scripted, or insured with down payments and automatic monthly withdrawals factored in. Well, here Slocum had done something completely unscripted and somewhat pushy even, and all the Whip did was zip on the tight black helmet with the smoky half-goggles that were a feature of Indian viewers and hit a couple of keys and mumble to the voice pickup, changing search engines by audio.

Slocum averted his eyes. He watched an ex-fisherman, leaving in the kind of beery and half-suppressed rage that seemed to characterize ex-fishermen, plant a punch into Freitas's abdomen that would have knocked over anybody else. He saw another ex-fisherman, a man with startling blue eyes, peel off from the group of draggermen and slump alone and depressed over beer next to his own table. He watched Obrigado flip through his *fado* collection. He listened to Carlos do Carmo sing *Fado do Campo Grande,* which was a song he knew well and could even sing along with. "My old house takes me by the body, past my sorrows, back to my old loves." He listened to Shaneeqwa and tried not to look at Luisa but all of a sudden he felt fingers on his shoulders and a hot wet tongue snaking into his right ear. He twisted around, to see Cakes's freckled cheeks at close range, her compromised grin, her not-so-great teeth.

"Thanks for the bottle, y'old wanker," she grunted. "Whyn't you come over and talk to us?"

Slocum gestured at the Whip. "It's all right, Cakes," he said, and he meant more than abandoning the Whip. Cakes said, "He's in another world, man. Shitgoddamn, I seen him do this for hours." She flipped a pack of cigarettes out of her pants, flicked a lighter. Smoke poured from her nose and mouth in practiced streams. She coughed and coughed again, and Slocum realized from this that she was nervous. Then she doubled over. Slocum slapped her back ineffectually. He could deduce Luisa's dark attention to what was happening here from her rigid stance on the edges of his vision. Cakes pulled over a chair and sat, the back between her legs, quite close to Slocum's chair. She regained control of her breathing. Her eyes were wet from tears, and Slocum, looking at her, got the weird idea that the tears, though released by coughing, had actually been there all along, waiting to come forth into the fields of her face to give expression to a sadness that might never go away.

Or maybe that was the *fado* talking. *"Quem compre o teu chao sagrado, mas a tua vida nao."*

"Should give it up," Cakes wheezed. As soon as she could breathe easily she took a drag only slightly less abandoned than the last. This time the smoke went in without a hitch. "Wanted to talk to you about something."

"Luisa," Slocum said.

Cakes wiped what remained of the tears from her cheeks.

"Yeah."

"None of my business."

"You say that." Cakes shook her head. "I know you guys were—"

"We were nothing." Slocum sipped coffee. Out of nowhere he saw Melisande Yonge doing that sweeping gesture with her hands, washing things away to her right. Always to the right, he thought, whatever that might signify. "I like Luisa," Slocum added. "I like to see her smile."

Cakes glanced back at Luisa and smiled, as if the mention of one smile would elicit another. Luisa did not smile back. Cakes leaned her chin on the top of the chair's back. Her eyes were hazel and tired-looking.

"You really sneak on that ship?"

"Yeah. Who told you?"

"Leaky Louie was in here. He said the ship's captain called the cops on you—then he changed his mind. How'd you do it, anyway? They got guards up the ass."

He told her about the County Diesel jumpsuit. He added, "One thing I'm learning is, ships got these things in common. They have engines, and engines have their own logic, and when that logic breaks down they just have needs. They're like sick people with needs, and harbors are full of them. There's a point there, a fulcrum, where all ships and boats and harbors are the same, and if you know where the fulcrum is you can maybe change things, make things happen—"

He was waffling, he knew, trying to express a concept that he might handle emotionally but not intellectually. He was not surprised when Cakes hissed, "Bullshit." The way the hazel in her eyes darkened, however, took him aback. She straightened in her chair and repeated, "Bullshit, Slocum. Engines are engines and mechanics are mechanics and outboards are outboards. The only thing they all have to teach you is about yourself, and how you react to 'em. I react one way, you react another."

She caught her breath, threw away her cigarette, automatically took out the pack again. She did not remove a cigarette but just looked at the pack as if the design on it held the key to her own systems of thought.

"Wanna know something?" she asked the pack, more softly. "You're not goin' anywhere. You don't *want* that engine to be fixed. You're scared to move, Slocum—what you really want is, you wanna stay in this harbor forever."

Slocum stared at her. His rates of breathing and heartbeat were up again; he was going through a workout this morning. He looked at Luisa, who looked away. He looked at Obrigado, polishing glasses; at the ex-fishermen, glowering together as they made unforgivable comments about a man who had just left. Noticed Freitas, who now lay on the linoleum, clutching his stomach. It had only just happened; now Obrigado noticed too, and began to move from behind the bar. The fishermen fell silent, their nasty words hanging like invisible black clouds in the air. Slocum's own surprise almost changed the subject in his head. Freitas never got knocked down. No one knew how to hurt Freit that way. But the chair where the solitary ex-fisherman had sat next to Obrigado was vacant, and Freitas was lying on the ground, and Slocum knew there was truth in what Cakes said and he also thought it was deeply untrue and he said, "What do you think I'm doing, Cakes?

You think I'm hanging around by choice? You think if I had a mechanic who—"

"It's not the Mechanic."

"No?"

"It's how you handle him. Shitgoddamn, Slocum." Cakes rested on her arms again, watching Obrigado and another ex-fisherman haul Freitas back onto his stool. Her voice had lost intensity. "You were an exec at X-Corp, you know you don't just hang around for a guy like that. He doesn't come, you go where he is."

"I tried that. He wasn't there."

"Then you camp out. You go there early early." Now Cakes slipped out a butt and held it in her mouth, while her hand jacked off the Zippo, clinking its top up and down. "You catch him when he comes in, you don't let him go till he gets you the parts you need."

"And if that doesn't work?"

Cakes shrugged.

"You fuck him?" Slocum said.

She looked at Slocum. Just looked at him, without letting the hazel waver a bit. Now she lit the cigarette. The flame burned blue, yellow, then blue-gray as the paper caught.

"That don't work," she said evenly; and taking a drag not quite as deep as the others, licked tobacco off her lips. "Tell you what. I'll drive you there tonight. Just on account of that crack.

"I'll come get you around oh-three-hundred and we'll see just how much you really want to get that bullgine fixed."

She stood up, glanced at Luisa. "And you'll see I'm right.

"Or if I'm wrong—if you get your engine fixed and git the fuck out—then I get your slip once the ship goes.

"Either way I win."

She walked back to the hookers' table and sat next to

Luisa and talked to her while the girl just sat not looking at her or at Slocum. Freitas was back on his stool, white faced, shrugging off the concerns of patrons. Three of the ex-fishermen decided they would go find their colleague who had done this thing and make him regret the action. No one could remember what his name was. Slocum took alternating sips of beer and coffee and found they no longer helped; nor did altering the pattern or frequency of the sips change things. Although in the course of figuring this out he found he had decided to take Cakes's advice.

He decided also he would not think about what might happen if the Mechanic finally fixed his engine. He was still considering which things to address when the Whip looked into the air for ten seconds, the way practiced Flash pilots did when preparing to peel out of the Net. Slowly, he unzipped the helmet. He blinked several times, looking at the dark bar. "Coffee," he said, and waited while Slocum went to refill his cup. He did not speak as he finished the joe; his eyes were slightly unfocused.

Finally he jabbed at his midriff, leaned over the table, and unscrolled spills of flimsy paper from the printer port.

"BLT/ 14," he began without preamble, pronouncing it like the sandwich. "It's commercially classified, but not really; it's just beta tested at this stage and the FDA hasn't approved it, so they're being coy."

Slocum said nothing. The Whip passed over the hard copy. Fine color thumbnails, set-up publicity shots. The thumbnails were smaller than usual and Slocum had to squint to make out the squat blue machine sitting amid paraphernalia not unlike what he had seen on the ship's monitors. "BETA-2H: Binary Lymphocyte Triage/Transfusion," the caption read, and listed eight columns of specs that, with the exception of a few terms like voltage, resistance, and unit of temperature, Slocum failed utterly to comprehend.

"Is that the one?" the Whip asked.

"Looks pretty close."

"Then this will tell you more about it."

The Whip printed out another hard copy. It was a feature from a medical trade journal called *Dialysis Outlook Online*.

> *Sources at Merck LaRoche say that clinical trials of the BLT/T, the company's revolutionary in-vivo mobile triage/transfusion system, are proceeding successfully. The computer-based system treats the patient's immune system as a logical program that has been infected by a virus that rearranges the system's memory, much as a computer virus breaks into and distorts a server's memory circuits. This treatment, therefore, debugs the patient's immune system by contouring the ones and zeros of his blood-borne enzymes according to patterns detected by realtime computer screening of the donor's hematological system. Simultaneous blood-exchange with the donor raises the therapeutic impact to levels necessary to combat the virus. The treatment has proven 88.4 percent effective in preliminary clinical trials on Kundura River Swine Flu victims; however, trade applications for this therapy alone are unlikely to justify its development, a source at Merck LaRoche said. The Kundura epidemic, largely contained by vaccination in the developed world, continues to ravage less-developed regions. The cost of BLT/T therapy averages $26,000 per trimester per person, making it difficult to use in such situations; the need for occasional input of untainted blood to compensate for donor losses further complicates the problem.*

Slocum took a sip of his beer, as if booze might irrigate the dry prose. The bottle was empty.

> *The other principal application was in therapy for victims of Lee Shan Syndrome, an extremely rare viral condition whose exact pathology is not well researched. It*

*appears to originate among frequent air travelers and spe-
cifically men and women who traveled by air to all three of
the following regions: the coast of Sindh in Pakistan, the
southern suburbs of Urumxi in Xinkiang, and a stretch of
saltmarsh and coastland south of Quonset, Rhode Island.
Other loci are probable, though unconfirmed; what seems
likely is that the binary Asian-American vector will continue to hold through further statistical screens. The disease, like AIDS, is transmittable only through mingling of
bodily fluids such as occurs in unprotected intercourse or
tainted transfusions and the number of confirmed cases of
LSS is not high, says Merck LaRoche. The uniformly
lethal nature of the virus's course, and the fact that these
wide-traveling patients tend to come from a prosperous
socio-economic background, make this avenue an exciting
one for the BLT/T software team. One aspect of the de-
bugging that particularly excites researchers is that it appears to be effective at any point along the different virus's
vector, from first symptoms to coma. After coma sets in,
however, the Merck spokesman says, it has proved impossible to halt the onset of the virus, which massively attacks
white blood cells so that the patient typically dies of opportunistic infection within 24 hours. Initial research also
shows that because of structural inelasticity in the immune
system itself, the life span of Lee Shan patients cannot be
extended past the five-year mark, even with BLT/T
therapy.*

*Eight LSS patients so far have been selected for clinical
trials on this application.*

Slocum looked up. The Whip was grinning. "Not bad,
eh? The insurance companies will have records on that,
and they're easy to crack through the credit bureaus. Bet
you anything I can dig out exactly who signed up for
Kundura trials."

"That second one," Slocum said, watching his friend. "Lee Shan?"

"There's almost no documentation on it I can find, and I've been using the marsh circuits," the Whip replied. "A thousand terabytes of data per second and nothing comes up; you know it's new, you know it's rare." The sullen aura the Whip had carried into the Sunset Tap with him had vanished. Now his eyes shone with the thrill of the hunt. He looked around the bar as if every woman in there were a princess needing rescue and he had just assumed the mantle of Galahad. "I bet I can get every bill for therapy and blood delivery, the way Merck LaRoche works."

"There are blood deliveries," Slocum agreed. He was thinking, She is sick. She is one of the rare people who, out of choice or criminal carelessness, did not get vaccinated for Kundura, in which case her chances, according to the brochure, look pretty good. Or else she is among the world travelers who apparently are most vulnerable to the Lee Shan virus, whatever that is, and she is certain to die before her time.

Slocum looked into his empty cup, expecting to feel a corresponding void inside. After all, this was the first woman in years for whom he had felt such high-voltage attraction, and to have it turn out that she was possibly suffering from a terminal illness seemed impossibly cruel, to him as well as to her.

He did not feel empty, though. He felt sad, but in a way not so different from how he usually felt. It seemed to him that he spent his days facing a spectrum of amorphous losses that he did nothing to palliate. The imminent loss of Melisande Yonge at least was something concrete, and if it was concrete that meant it was a thing he could approach and touch, if only by finding out how it happened. In this it felt very different from the loss of his family; it felt different from the loss of Bird.

The Whip was rattling at his jambook again and at the

same time exchanging mild insults with Shaneeqwa, who told him that he and Slocum had to be queer for each other because neither did business at Madame Ling's. The Whip laughed and prodded his gut with one hand and with the other piloted his cursor over the lightspeed connections of whatever Netline he was following. Slocum watched Luisa, who talked quietly to Cakes, her left arm hooked over the chrome back of the chair, her eyes never wavering from Cakes's.

Slocum wrote a note for the Whip: "Tomorrow, Madame Ling's, 6 P.M.?" He showed it to the Whip, who hesitated, then nodded.

He signed Obrigado's credit chit and left.

NINETEEN

Slocum was back at Coggeshall Wharf before he remembered that he had not asked anyone what the hurricane was doing. The TV had shown only entertainment news while he was there, and though the ex-fishermen might have discussed it before Freitas was knocked down, he had heard nothing.

Now, back on the sloop, he woke up the ECM-pak from its standby state, and it was odd, but he felt absolutely no qualms about that, no fear of the lust that might be suggested here. Probably the backslide into full VR at Kumpunen's had burned away his angst about the Nets, the way someone who shot heroin no longer worried about his pot habit.

Or maybe he was so fully readdicted, Slocum thought, that he had lost all power to oppose it.

In any event he flicked the pak's controls to VHF and NOAA weather radio. There were a lot of station reports, and then the warning loop came on:

This is a NOAA weather radio special bulletin for the area extending from Cape Henlopen to Nantucket Shoals. At 1300 Zulu a hurricane was centered at 37 degrees 51 minutes north,

*72 degrees 35 minutes west, proceeding north-northeast at 25
knots. Pressure at the eye was 0898 millibars; winds of 130 knots
gusting to 150 have been reported. A severe hurricane warning is
in effect for all coastal waters extending fifty miles offshore from
Cape Henlopen to Nantucket Shoals. A hurricane watch is in effect from the Hague Line to Monhegan Island. If the storm stays
on its present course it is expected to transit the area or pass close-
by at approximately 2200 local time tomorrow. This is a category-
four storm and is rated extremely dangerous. Mariners are advised
to proceed immediately to safe harbor and—*

Slocum switched off the VHF application. Automatically he clicked to his father's portal to see if the old man
was online. He was; the little icon that read IMAGEMAN. was
talking to someone named Hattie.

IMAGEMAN—PROBABLY THE BEST ROUTE IS UP THE HIGH MESA
TO SEE THE SPANISH CHURCHES
HATTIEZAZ—I DON'T LIKE DRIVING SO HIGH, SNOW ICE ETC.
IMAGEMAÑ—I'LL DRIVE YOU. I HAVE 4X4

Switching to Wild, Slocum grinned. If his father was
chatting up the ladies on the Net it meant everything was
OK in that direction, and it felt good to have an area of his
life where everything was OK and predictable. Although
Slocum knew that his father, for all he liked to flirt with
women in the virtual retiree "communities" they set up on
the Flash, never got beyond tearoom chat. He did not talk
much about his wife, Slocum's mother, even to Slocum;
their last exchange had been the exception, not the rule.

Still, the way he brought her up when he did, and the
space between those mentions, were such that Slocum
knew he thought about her constantly, and deliberately
prevented himself from wiping off the hemorrhage of
those memories on others.

Sometimes Slocum wished that he himself had the kind
of memory of his mother that, he thought, might keep

people warm through the cold and dark of such a loss. But when he thought of Zelda Slocum he remembered mostly early thoughts: an amorphous though comforting presence; someone there to stick on Band-Aids and comfort a crying child; who had a sense of fun and could make odd faces or comments or poopoo jokes and kick up her heels to make a kid laugh. Later on she had seemed to shut herself up in her room more and more. The sense of fun had frittered away and then she got sick and not necessarily in that order.

None of this explained the reluctance he felt to approach her memory, or the fact that he did not approach it much at all anymore.

Slocum did not send his father a message. He shut down the ECM and took out a general sailing chart of the northeast coast that he had ordered early on, when he still thought the diesel would be fixed in a couple of weeks. The latitude and longitude showed the storm was 382 miles south, off a promontory notorious for attracting circular storms.

If the hurricane was due here tomorrow night, he needed to make sure the sloop was ready, or as ready as he could make it.

He was already in his jumpsuit, and he got right to work. He unfastened the dodger and collected all the loose gear that had accumulated in the cockpit and stowed it all below. He took the running sheets and topping lifts off the boom, unslotted it from the mast, and stowed it fore and aft on the cabin sole. He doubled up all the mooring lines and ran them around the fairleads and cleats to spread the strain, reciting "Ye cataracts and huricanoes spout, till ye have cracked the steeples" from some half-forgotten English course in school; saying it over and over to keep down nervousness in him, cushion the images of what a 140-knot wind would do to the harbor, to the ship, to his boat. He wrapped mooring lines in chafing gear, put out every bumper he owned. He checked that his water tanks were full, the battery charged, the kerosene lamps topped up and in good working order. He got out the storm jib, just in case the ship sank and the wharf disappeared and he had to sail the sloop out of here somehow. He looked at the sail sadly, shook his head, and put it back in the sail locker.

When he was finished the day was drawing to a close, but he still had hours before Cakes picked him up. He painted the teak trim around the hatch with linseed oil. He put the red gel in the chart-table lamp and changed the switches that needed replacing. While caulking around a couple of midships stanchions that had started to leak, he heard a roar overhead and looked to see the ship's helicopter swinging up and over the harbor, navigation lights blinking as it disappeared to the north.

It was full night at this point. He fixed himself a dinner of sardines and beans and coffee. He wondered where Ralfie was; he had not been around last night either. He usually came back by dinnertime. If he were within thirty yards the smell of sardines should have brought him, limping and yowling to be fed.

Ordinarily after making dinner he might have worked on the Project, but not now. The words he had spoken to Melisande Yonge about that still rang in his head, and the way they echoed told him they were the truth, or at least they held truth for him, enough that he could not continue the Project. He poured a cognac and thought of Melisande and that ballroom he had seen her in. Everything about her was so full of movement and tension and retension and burgeoning and the opposite of death and stopping, he thought. The way her smile cracked, and how her shoulders were not even, as if the load she bore was constantly in flux. How she made an entrance down that ornate staircase for him, for him alone. He still did not feel sad or fearful on her behalf, if what she was being treated for was in fact a fatal disease. Part of it, he supposed once more, was the way in which the idea of something dying seemed to fit in with this moribund harbor and his own life, so full of deep, if less final, losses. Also—so he reminded himself, opening his last bottle of de Lauzère—he had a talent for ignoring the solidity of loss. The way he had ignored the growing distance between Amy and himself. Not that the distance wasn't his fault. In many ways, given how, toward the end, he had split his time between Arcadia and the ICE, he was profoundly culpable. Often, when the ICE council debates were long, he would sleep on the sloop and go straight to the doughnut from the marina. Even then Bird was hanging out with affect surfers at the ICE and she had little interest in a sleepover with her father—still, he never invited her. And it came to pass that at the end he paid attention to his family only to the extent that he dragged them to big ICE events like Halloween or James Brown's birthday, and tried to make them see the pretty structures and finials of the political and social constructs he was also trying to build there.

So he should not have been surprised, that day he came home for lunch—he never came home for lunch, it only happened then because of his biannual physical (it had been simpler for some insurance reason to have blood drawn by a phlebotomist at the Bayview Professional Center)—he should not have been surprised at Amy's ill-concealed shock when he walked in and saw her and Dark Denny doing nothing at all suspicious at the great butcherblock island of the kitchen-den. The sugary smell of baking from the oven. *Wanderbird* playing on the half-suckers, on repeat-monitors above the microwaves; he'd had that weakness—frowned on in the ICE—in common with Denny. Lieutenant Commander Nortt guiding the starship, all photon sails set, around the event-horizon of yet another black hole that would not, must not, lead them home. Amy disappeared and Denny said he was just making coffee and did Slocum want some and Slocum said, "Sure," feeling ill-at-ease for no reason he could define, watching the monitors, wishing as always he could dive in full-metal-jacket and join Breena and Nortt in that dangerous tack-by around the red dwarf. Denny measured out the Kenyan Highlands organic espresso roast and then neatly and without thinking added exactly half a teaspoon of organic cinnamon from the spice freezer, just as Amy used to, and Slocum knew they were fucking. The thought came to him like a complete house of suspicion already wallpapered, peopled, and furnished by little details he had noticed before but had never placed in context or hooked together.

How she had started to hug him again, out of the blue.

How Denny watched her move.

"You're sleeping together," he told Dark Denny in surprise.

Denny did not reply. He busied himself with the coffeemaker, leaving options open.

Slocum repeated the question that was not a question.

"I'm sorry," Denny said. You had to give him that, he was always polite and rational, considering. "That sounds like something you and Amy should discuss together."

Slocum left. He powered the Raptor down the Bayview roads at close to 100 mph, which was stupid and selfish because school buses used those routes. His hands were trembling when he parked the car in the garage under Arcadia. He picked up the bag containing the sealed vial of blood and automatically slotted in to the routine he was already engaged in. Elevator up six flights to the health-resources doughnut—then kept right on going, punching top doughnut, all the way to Kumpunen's suite. It had been beautiful up there, he remembered; the top doughnut was high enough often to be clear of fogbanks and this was one of those days. The third-growth forest seemed to stretch for miles inland, and off to the east he thought he caught a glimpse of blue, of sea. Kumpunen was videoconferencing with Bangalore, fingering a pile of peripherals from *Pain*, toy-software packages for Mahal Schrenk and Vincenzo Stronzo game environments lined up across his vast desk. Slocum marched over to the desk, took the vial out of his bag, removed the stopper, and showered Kumpunen and the peripherals with his still-warm blood. He remembered how it had looked; it seemed like there was so much more than could be contained in that little test tube splattered crimson the color of holly berries over Kumpunen's shirt and the brushed steel of his desk.

"I guess I quit," Slocum told Kumpunen.

Kumpunen stared at his shirt.

"I guess you're fired," he said, and then added, clearing his throat, "Has that blood been screened?"

"No." It was a lie; Slocum's blood had been screened twice a year since he'd been at X-Corp. But it kept Kumpunen busy, cleaning himself, while Slocum went down to the next doughnut, grabbed the stuff he wanted out of his office, and left. There were all sorts of laws Kumpunen could have used to hold Slocum then had that blood really been unsafe. Possession of a deadly weapon, attempted grievous bodily harm, attempted second-degree murder even. Kumpunen's lawyers later started all those procedures but quietly dropped them, for reasons of P.R., when tests showed the blood to be clean and Slocum's own. By the time Kumpunen called the guards that day, Slocum was on the highway. Forty-five minutes later he was on his sloop, letting go the docklines, the diesel putting regularly under the cockpit deck as he made ready for sea.

Slocum did not know then how useless his diesel was. It had quit on him twice but each time he'd been able to restart, and he put it down to condensation in the fuel tank, something enough running would sort out. And he had never taken the boat for a long ride; only changed berths or gone to the dock for ice blocks or kerosene or groceries or just to get a taste of what it would be like to sail. Anyway in one sense, and in one sense only, it did not matter how bad that engine was or how short the trip would be, because he would never forget how it felt to do something like what he had just done and then go to his boat, cast off all his lines, put the engine in forward gear, stand at the helm of his own oceangoing sloop and head out of the cove that had sheltered him. He had felt like a god at that point. He had felt like a mighty hero who had survived perils that would have killed lesser men and was still capable of wresting back his own life and forging out into unknown terrain and starting over. He had felt, despite what Amy had done and what he had done to her—despite the violence they had committed together on their innocent lives and on their daughter—he had felt brave and moral and worthy of respect.

The diesel drove the sloop at a steady six knots. He steered it through the hurricane barrier and maybe four hundred feet down the sea channel. The bends and S-curves of the marsh and its particularly dense fog were beginning to encroach on his horizon when the engine cut out.

Almost no warning, either. A reduction in revs, a speed-up to the previous rate. Then, inexorably, the rhythm of the cylinders slowed and stopped.

The quiet then would have been something beautiful had it not been so terrible also. The wavelets of the marsh gossiped at the fiberglass hull as it lost way against the wind. The wind whispered in the shrouds. A fishhawk cried, a crow responded.

He drifted into eelgrass beside the main channel. An hour and a half later the *Valkyrie* came surging up-channel and found him and towed him to Coggeshall Wharf.

He had stayed on the wharf for eighteen days, never leaving the sloop except to arrange things with MacTavish and buy essentials. During all that time he never contacted

Amy. Far more seriously, he never tried to get in touch with Bird.

Slocum poured himself more cognac. He always needed booze when he got to this point in the memory. He needed cognac more for something to do than for assistance in absorbing the shock, because the liquor did not help and it did not erase the fact that waiting eighteen days to tell his daughter seemed to have smashed for good the trust she had placed in him since she was a baby. He did not know how that had happened or why it should be so; he supposed the delay had demonstrated to her satisfaction a lack of interest, a lack of respect, that he figured must exist and that he must have demonstrated to her before in smaller, less traceable ways. Only he could know that it was balanced by a strength of love and a long-term loyalty—however diluted by the desensitization the Flash wrought—that he had been doing his best to sketch for her, in the Project.

Or perhaps the love was not relevant, he thought as he slid into his bunk now, making sure the bottle stood within easy reach. Perhaps it was too easy to love someone and even live with them the way he had done; with the business and preoccupation of work and competition defining the rivers and tributaries of his days; with the deadness of a thousand VR loves and ties making the process spongy and ill-defined; and only what was left, in runnels and trickles, for his daughter to drink of and dam if she could.

Maybe the only element that really counted was the effort of imagination it took to do it decently: to engineer the emotional waterworks according to what he believed was most important.

He woke to what sounded like the flugelhorns of hell blasting simultaneously against the fiberglass skin of his boat.

A three-tone blast, repeated over and over, lower A and E and G, a car horn.

Cakes. He switched on the saloon light. The honking stopped. High overhead, someone yelled from the ship; then that too stopped. He dressed quickly and got in the Rambler and Cakes took off fast, slowing down only in the vicinity of the Middle Street doughnut shop, where the two Town cruisers on duty were sixty-nined, cops talking to each other over the steam of coffee.

"What time is it?" Slocum asked her.

"Three-forty."

"Early."

"I wanna get back. That hurricane—"

"You gonna haul your boat?"

"How'm I gonna get it to the lift?"

"Get it towed."

"Shit," Cakes said. "There's no guarantee, you haul the boat, wind like that could just lift it off the ground."

Slocum looked at her. In the glow of the dashboard Cakes appeared as grim and determined as usual but something else was visible. Slocum could not put it into words but he got a sense of changed speeds in Cakes, as if she had found a slower, easier drive she had not known she had. He wondered if Luisa was waiting back in the giant bunk filled with pink stuffed bunnies in Cakes's offshore racer. He felt vague envy at the thought of her, Luisa's, softness; the clove and coffee scent of her skin.

They reached the Zone in less than five minutes. The razor-wire fence was bright with spotlights and the outskirts of the guardhouse were defined in the dead-dog glow of neon. Behind the Zone, the X-Corp billboard advertised, in bold Futura and a blur of video, a new series called *Byzantium: The Fall*. "Treachery, Lust, Assassination," the accompanying copy read. "Just another boring day in Constantinople."

Slocum got out. Cakes did a U-turn and laid rubber going the other way and the gate cameras followed her car as it peeled down the access road. Slocum, remembering the proximity sensors and recognition patterns, slipped into the shadows while the cameras tracked Cakes. He settled down to wait for the Mechanic between two of the massive sewer pipes he had noticed on his earlier visit.

THERE WAS NO TRAFFIC at all for two hours except for a security car that trundled through the gates and then out again ten minutes later. Slocum dozed and woke, dozed and woke. He felt curiously optimistic knowing that no truck or car could get by without his noticing. After all, the Mechanic eventually had to get to his shop. That meant Slocum would see the Mechanic this morning; it gave him a form of control over events, he realized, albeit a tenuous one. He would look the man in the eye and refuse to let him go until he found out once and for all how to get the sloop's diesel fixed. And then he would pick up the trip he had started the day he left X-Corp Multimedia. Pick it up not in the desperate fury and total lack of preparation with which he had started, but deliberately and with water and fuel tanks replenished and spares for everything and all his equipment fixed and lubed. He would leave clean and calm and having paid his dues and he would tell Bird his plans this time, for all that was worth now, when it was too late. He would inform Melisande—not that it would mean much to her. And the Whip. And Luisa and Cakes. Watching light sprinkle over the mist like confectioner's sugar on a doughnut over the ragged skyline of the Town and the round slope of his sewer pipes, Slocum suddenly felt as if he really did not want to leave at all. Or at least not right now, or in the near future.

This was a strange feeling, Slocum thought. It came out of uncharted portions of his personality, because his entire existence since he left his job and his family and his house and even his second community, if you could call the ICE that, had been based on the fact that he was on his way.

Coggeshall Wharf had always been a halfway house, a place that held value only insofar as it allowed him to regroup and plan his move out and beyond. The mere idea that it might have illegally stolen the accoutrements and potency of home both pissed him off and caused doubt to creep in among his intentions. If the place he was leaving became a place he wanted to stay in, what did that mean for the places he had already left? And what did that imply for the voyage that had become the focus of his life here?

The doubt was too big, Slocum thought desperately. It felt almost on the order of the feelings and regrets about Bird that he could never properly clean up and sort out, it was all far too big to try to measure let alone deal with as the dawn crept up on the Zone.

Slocum shut his eyes hard, concentrating to the exclusion of all else on what he would say to the Mechanic, or on ancillary thoughts that would not leave tentacles clinging to this other stuff that had crept up on him in the fustiness of predawn. He focused on tracing in the visual centers of his brain the brass abdomen and the copper arteries of the fuel injectors, which had become the equivalent of some magic key in a fairy tale: the freighted object that could unlock a different world. He concentrated so hard that he almost missed the Mechanic. He was conscious of the articulated eighteen-wheeler rumbling slowly around the loop of access road. But because he was still thinking about details in which the Mechanic had traded—rates of flow in cubic millimeters per second and more mystical elements, like degree of oxygen-differential corrosion around the flange, ideas Slocum only vaguely understood and which he believed even the Mechanic had to gauge by feel and experience—he missed for a while the secondary shine of lights belonging to a pickup truck in the eighteen-wheeler's wake. Only when the eighteen-wheeler was level with him did he process the shape of the pickup behind: jacked-up hydraulics, a row of foglamps on the roof, a changing sequence of neon mounted under the chassis so the truck looked like it was riding a bubble of tinted light. The king cab, the rows of tool lockers dimly visible in the row of purple sidelights. The words TWO DOG MARINE ENGINEERING, and the head of a live hound thrusting, barking, out of a vent from the backseat of the cab.

Slocum scrambled to his feet so fast he felt as if he had left his ass behind. He ran into the road, heading for the gap between eighteen-wheeler and pickup. The pickup lurched as the driver stood on his brakes. The dog was thrown forward and its head disappeared from the window. The barking stopped, adding value to the roar of airbrakes as the lorry slowed for the security gate; to the declining roar of the pickup's diesel; to the blast as the driver, invisible against his lights and the darkened windscreen, leaned on the airhorn, coming to a stop with shiny bumpers three feet from Slocum's crotch.

Both dogs' heads were out the window now. Their incisors gleamed in the backwash of light and their barking was something infernal but it could not compete with the volume of the pickup's loudspeaker.

"You nuts, pal? Get out of my way."

"It's me." Slocum was catching his breath from the speed of his intervention and the possibility of being run over that had become very real there for a second. Three words were all he could manage. "Slocum," he added. "I want—"

"Get outta the fuckin' road!"

"I can't." Slocum held his hands up. "I need. Talk to you."

"You're the guy," the loudspeaker declared, no less aggressively. "At the wharf. The sailboat."

"Slocum," said Slocum.

"Slocum," the Mechanic repeated. "That's nice. I don't have time right now. I'll call you."

A warning horn sounded. The other truck rumbled up

the gears as the gate opened. Slocum shook his head, squinting away from the pickup's lights.

"I just need. An update," he said. "I have to know what to do with the diesel."

"You an' everybody else," the loudspeaker began angrily, and then another voice, even louder, more mechanical, joined in from behind.

"Normally twenty seconds is the average budgeted time to transit security access A."

Slocum glanced behind him, rather desperately.

"What about the spares?"

"Of course you are only three times over that average, at the beep. Beep. But don't let that worry you," the security gate said.

"What spares?" the Mechanic's speaker asked.

"The fuel injector you were trying to order." Slocum waited, expecting the gate to chime in but it did not; it was as if the gate were listening, the cameras checking with an expert system for further instructions.

"You were looking for a YQM20 injector," Slocum finished.

The pickup's engine revved. The dogs howled and trembled now in their lust to close black jaws around Slocum's calves. There was a yelp. One of them disappeared from the vent once more.

"You have a YQM20?"

Slocum nodded. The gate cleared its throat. "Stand by," it said. "Two Dogs Engineering! You have been cleared to enter! Notify at once of out-gate interference, I mean out of gate, outside of inner sector of gate."

"Oh, shut the fuck up," the pickup's loudspeaker grumbled unexpectedly and added, "You ain' goin' nowhere with that."

"I am stating perimeter!" the gate responded peevishly. "I am stating perimeter. Inside perimeter is *cleared;* outside perimeter is considered a hot zone, repeat, a hot zone."

"MarDyne doesn't just not stock those parts—they don't *make* them anymore. That engine's seven years old, man, not s'posed to last so long as yours did. They gone on—"

"It is possible on Zone Board review," the gate interrupted, "to reschedule portions of the perimeter based on subscriber ownership or needs that appertain to discrete sectors of the security perimeter."

"They gone on to turbo now. Computerized injection with injection on the injection. The YQM20 is like the ark."

Slocum felt the Mechanic's words come at him. They did not seem to go very deep into his gut, though he knew in his head what they meant. Maybe his gut was still focused on the unexpected reluctance he'd just felt about leaving.

Well, what the Mechanic was saying now was, He would not be leaving. If his old engine was unrepairable it meant he would have to install a new one. New engines cost enormous sums of money and without an UCC card or a serious job it would take five years to—

"None of this applies to this case, which we are coding o-five-hundred slash o-one as it fulfills four out of six characteristics of a potential urgency situation."

"You could go to So Savage," the Mechanic added doubtfully when the gate had fallen silent again. "Down to—" his words were lost as the second dog resumed where he'd left off.

"What's so savage—"

"The question arises as to emergencies arising inside the security perimeter and their effect on the definition of inside and outside the Zone. Stand by—"

"The yard of dead engines." The Mechanic's voice had never gone soft or friendly though it had grown more conversational in tone as he dealt with the nuts and bolts of Slocum's case. Now it regained all the Teflon it had displayed when Slocum first ran into the pickup's high beams. "You take 25 north to Old Mill Road—but you don't have a car, do you?"

Slocum said nothing.

A pause.

"Otherwise," the Mechanic continued, "you go to the railroad spur, by the Mall, follow that north—maybe five miles, it's right on the tracks."

The truck's loudspeaker grizzled. Slocum stayed silent. Even the dogs reduced their output to a slathery whimper. Everyone waited for the security gate, which duly announced:

"We are *still* on standby."

From the Mechanic's pickup came a slightly pissed-off sigh.

"There's a big ol' rusty sign, how you can tell you've gotten there. Used to read 'DONALDSON SALVAGE.' Now the letters fell off so it just says, 'SO SA VAGE.' That's what it's called now—'So Savage.' Meant to go there—didn't have the time. Should have your engine. They might have a fuel injector. Might even work."

"That's a lot of mights."

"It's all—"

"Emergencies in the Zone are to be treated similarly to emergencies outside the Zone, but the question here is still: Is the Zone really a Zone if it has emergencies inside it?"

The gate's searchlights began flashing on and off. Slocum wondered if the response program, or the guard, or the expert-system it referred to, or whoever was in charge, was actually working up to some code red that called in the Bayview cops and X-Corp security. The gate's P.A. fell silent again. The truck's loudspeaker clicked.

"It's all you got. There's nothing else I can do for you." The Mechanic paused. "You gonna let me go to work now?"

Slocum stared at the windshield. He could see nothing through the reflection of security lights. He turned, and walked to the side of the access road. The pickup's diesel roared, and it was past him in an instant, as if the driver was so unsure of Slocum's sanity that he was expecting the kind of split-second change of mind that might characterize a madman, or a teedee. As the pickup passed, the dogs stretched their necks out, and they drooled and howled for Slocum's flesh. He thought he saw a glint of the Mechanic's dark glasses through the driver's window, turning to observe him, catching a glint of the lightening fog to the east, but he could not be sure.

The truck was replaced by dust. Slocum watched the pickup pause briefly at the gate, then drive through the opened tank traps, which shut fast and without feeling or mercy or regard for the different kinds of emergency status outside.

————

AN HOUR LATER SLOCUM was walking north along the old railroad spur that connected the Bayview Mall to a secondary branch line well inland of Town.

He was not sure why he was doing this. The Mechanic's description of So Savage was such that he had only marginal hope of finding there what he needed. And the idea of walking ten miles over and back when a level 4 hurricane was due later that night put the whole project on a shelf labeled foolhardy, excessively fraught with risk.

He kept walking. The only rational part of his decision lay in the fact that the sloop was as ready as he could make it and there was nothing more he could do except wait for the storm.

He hated waiting for things to happen. He had lost whole slices of his life that were vitally important to him, and he had been waiting now for a year and a half either to get them back or create a new life to compensate; but so far all he had done was wait and wait some more and he was sick of hanging around—sick of waiting to leave; sick of waiting to stay, if that was his destiny.

What he really wanted was for something to happen and for him to have a hand in it, no, not even a whole hand, just a fingernail or two, on the order of a cricket putting its shoulder to the wheel of a train to get it going; just some tiny role in the cause-and-effect of the core dynamics of his life.

A detail that he could affect by what he did.

The air had grown still and warm and increasingly humid as the morning advanced. The tracks were still used by shunts rolling containers full of consumer electronics to the Mall and they were shiny with traffic, but all around them—because the railroad was constantly in financial trouble as big trucks continued the century-old process, interrupted here and there by fuel shortages but always allowed to continue, of poaching cargo from train lines—all around them were the signs of neglect: tall weeds, rusted signal boxes, broken-down boxcars, discarded tires, jungles of kudzu and poison ivy moving toward the last defensive positions of the line. Many of the ties were rotted, which accounted for the slow speed of the one freight Slocum saw all morning, a black and orange diesel thrusting its load of six container cars in the opposite direction.

It was hard work in the heavy air to slog against the weeds or hop from tie to tie up the track and Slocum sweated freely as he walked. At the same time he enjoyed the trek because he had not sweated and worked in such a free and arm-swinging manner for longer than he could remember. Maybe it was at X-Corp, in the gym; the boat work he had done since was hard and sweaty and kept you fit but it was also cramped and neurotic work, up and down the companionway for tools, screwing yourself into impossible positions to turn a bolt that had been put there before the deck was laid, opening a valve that you had to twist yourself around the exhaust system to get at, meanwhile reaching beyond your left ankle to change socket wrenches. Working like this—legs pushing hard, wiping the back of your hand against your forehead to clear sweat—it was a good feeling. Moving through thick woods on a broken-down track was also good because every turn brought a different sight: an abandoned water tank, a kid's treehouse; and he was thirsting for different sights. That at least had not changed. All of this was a feeling that got in the way of thinking about much else, which was the state he craved most of all.

Thus he was both elated and disappointed when after what felt like three hours of walking but was probably two, he caught sight of a tall gridwork, rising over a patch of cattails and scrub oak, that bore among its rusted struts the letters

SO
SA VAGE

like a commentary on the lack of care that had brought the sign, and the environment around it, to a situation of such decrepitude.

A spur ran off this line into the junkyard and Slocum followed it. Immediately the rails turned brown and bushes sprang up to bar the way. He noticed a path worn on one side, by deer, rabbits, and humans, too, to judge by the litter. It followed the spur on an opportunistic tangent that circumvented downed trees and an abandoned Dodge and he went down it, down the easy going, and walked into a camp of men.

There were three of them visible around a concealed campfire. A fourth moved behind the open windows of a car door that was part of a larger cabin made of corrugated tin and plywood. At first Slocum assumed they were teedees, but, though the men had the worn-out clothes and unkempt look of the teledysfunctional, they carried no dead electronics. And no self-respecting teedee would live so far from a power main.

Also the four were alert, even wary—not like teedees, who fixated only on the buzz of receivers. These men looked sharply at Slocum, assessing him. A couple nodded. On the car door Slocum noticed symbols that looked vaguely familiar: a three-quarter square with a stem on top, a semicircle cradling a dot.

They were boiling coffee. Slocum wished they would offer him some. But he could see the junkyard from here, opening before him through a gap in what once had been a barbed-wire fence and now was an irregular mesh woven through and through with kudzu.

Slocum nodded back at the men and, moving slowly, in deference to whatever boundaries he was crossing here, moved into So Savage.

It was a vast field, obviously cleared on an occasional basis by graders to keep the trumpet vines and poison ivy at bay. And it was filled with engines.

An order in the field was immediately clear. The row to Slocum's right was all Caterpillar diesels, mammoth truck engines, most rusted and infiltrated by honeysuckle. They dwindled in size and horsepower before him.

The row to his left was Ford V-8s and V-6s.

Past the Fords and Cats lay further rows of car motors, like a forlorn mechanical harvest staked out on a mulch of fallen-off gear rings, flaked rust, and leaked transmission fluid, rolling off toward the woods on either side.

To the east, where most of the field lay, the vista of engines continued to the top of a slope beyond which, presumably, they kept right on going.

Here and there, between the rows, men moved. Thin, almost sticklike figures in the gray light, they walked slowly, stooped, looked, and walked on, like migrant workers poorly paid to pick an alien and worthless fruit.

"Jesus," Slocum muttered. He glanced behind him, toward the camp, which was invisible in the darkness of the grove and behind the screen of kudzu. Even the campfire smoke was hard to spot; it stuck to the leaf canopy and trailed off only in reluctant wisps, as if unwilling to rise at all in such humidity.

He stepped forward and began his search.

———

SLOCUM FOUND THE YQM20S about twenty minutes after it began to rain.

The rain had started with slow violence. Only a few drops here and there, but they were large, the size of grapes; they exploded on the ground like minigrenades, raising little spurts of dust.

Then a minute or so later it was as if some distant ocean had found its range and decided to bomb this dry field into a subsidiary loch. The sky fell in, and water poured in a barrage whose solidity recalled thrown battlements. It was the second time in three days Slocum had gotten caught in a heavy rain and he still did not mind the wetness. What bothered him was the visibility. He had found his way to the marine engines by this time, worked his way down the Atomic 4s, the Listers, Graymarines, Westerbekes, Volvo Pentas, to the first row of MarDynes. But the rain fell so hard that it raised a secondary mist, and the dead MarDynes here were as numerous as a fallen legion; it took him another ten minutes to find the low end of their horsepower, and finally isolate the sixteen YQM20s, all on their own at the frontier of kudzu and corroded fence, at risk and already tangled, some of them, in vine. Another five minutes, hand over his eyes as a visor, to sort out that thirteen of the engines were useless, injectors dissolved by corrosion; and even the three that were relatively new were hardly perfect and most of their injectors were green with verdigris and one was crushed and another had couplings missing.

He realized then what he should have thought of before—that he had no tools with which to remove the injectors. And he had no credits to buy them if he took them off. He had been moving in the tow of a reluctance to cope with pressing issues other than putting one foot in front of the other, and tools and credits were part of the world he'd been avoiding.

A handful of the other men moving around this cemetery of engines had not been driven off by the weather. Slocum tracked them down through the rain. Two refused to talk to him at all; a third was one of the men who'd been brewing coffee in the camp by the tracks. He agreed to lend him the two three-quarter-inch wrenches he needed for the five minutes he needed—provided, like a porn surfer, he could stand beside Slocum and watch.

The tools worked poorly in the rain. They slipped off the oily and well-dinged brass. Slocum skinned two knuckles as they betrayed his trust. He stripped nuts, applied the full thrust of torque to a corner of cooling jacket or fuel line. Slamming the wrench against the engine in rage at the second wound, he cracked the pipe on one of the good units. But finally he stood triumphant and streaming rainwater with two injectors that were full of crud and dead spiders. One of them had a bent flange, and on the other, Slocum was pretty sure, the fuel lines were for some reason of different sizes. But otherwise they didn't look too bad and he held them toward the rain in praise, toward the invisible sky like a trophy, willing in that place and at that moment to celebrate even the smallest, most temporary of victories.

"You got cashchip?" the man whose tools he had borrowed asked, torpedoing Slocum's tiny exaltation. When Slocum shook his head, the man said nothing but reclaimed his tools and walked off diagonally across the field, toward the railroad line and the camp. Slocum, not knowing what else to do, or where to go to find someone who could advise him how to buy these things when he had nothing of exchange value, followed him through the gap in the fence and into the kudzu jungle.

The three campers were all inside the shack, which was lit by kerosene lights with red bull's-eye lenses; railroad lanterns, Slocum thought, as he entered and crouched uncertainly by the car door. They were eating bacon and eggs. More food warmed on a truck hubcap perched over another fire, to which a hood of bent sheetmetal and a truck's diesel exhaust formed a chimney. Even through the flavor of wet, unwashed bodies the smell of frying bacon was strong and good. Slocum had not eaten since yesterday and the smell shot immediately through his nose and down the spinal column to his stomach, making his guts contract. An old fellow with yellow-white hair was reeling off what sounded like a list of names in an East European accent. "Appalachicola and Southern," he said. "They are among the dead. Though you can still ride on the Shoreline, and the Norfolk and Western up to Savannah." His companion slopped two fried eggs, a strip of bacon, and a slice of bread on a hubcap and handed it to the man who had led Slocum here. Then he did the same for Slocum and, giving him a plastic fork, motioned him to sit on a rolled-up sleeping bag.

Slocum squatted and ate with the efficiency and single-mindedness of the truly hungry.

"Tuskegee and Birmingham, Burlington Northern," the old man said, and belched.

"I rode the Santa Fe from Tombstone to Springfield," the man to the left of him said, "and only had to use cars once to make the line."

Slocum looked at the two injectors he had taken off the MarDynes. They lay in the mud, looking misshapen and ugly and dead. He tapped the shoulder of the man he had come in with, intending to ask how he should pay for these things; but when the man put down the bread with which he had been wiping his hubcap, Slocum pointed instead at the inside of the Dodge door. The symbols daubed on that surface resembled those gracing its outer panel. Touching one, a three-quarter square with a stem that held a square holding, in turn, a dot; he recognized it from Coggeshall Wharf.

"What is that?" he said.

"Stay away—cops," the man said.

Slocum stared at him.

"I'm sorry," he said. "I just came because I was looking for—"

"No." The man swallowed the last of his bread, shook his head impatiently. "That's what it *means.*" He pointed to another symbol, the semicircle cradling a dot. "This one," he said, "means the opposite: 'Friendly for track people.' People like us," he continued, looking at Slocum with more curiosity than he had shown so far. "People, I guess, like you."

"I'm not track people," Slocum said uncertainly, and picked up his injectors, as if this link with diesel gave him identity, a country he belonged to, a nation of the mind that would define him against what made these men different.

The older man stopped reciting and noticed Slocum specifically for the first time.

"You are not driving," he said. "You walk in the rain, on the tracks. One day, perhaps, a freight will come. Not many are left, but one always comes, in the end. And you will climb on a flatcar, or a tank car, and ride it."

The other men nodded, and one of them grunted, "You got that right, Marak." Slocum stood up. The old man said, "You need coffee—Seth, give him coffee." Slocum in fact did need coffee. He felt he would kill for a mug of steaming hot coffee to counter the chill of the rain, which was finding every crack and rotted piece in the cover of this makeshift shelter and pooling and dripping on them, not as much as outside, but often enough. He needed coffee too to counter the damp, and the smell of defeat and doom of this tawdry camp.

He wanted to get out of here even more than he wanted coffee.

"Look," he said, "I just don't know how to pay. For these," he added, thrusting the injectors into the glow of the fire, where they added their own drip to the other runoff, and hissed against orange embers. The man nearest the fire shook his head, another laughed.

The man he had come in with stuck his hand through a hole in the wall and snapped a twig off a sapling outside. He stripped off pine needles and started to clean his teeth.

"Look," he said, "I was just kidding." He took the twig out of his mouth and pointed it at the valves that Slocum now cradled like doves, like precious objects.

"No one wants those," he said. "No one uses engines that old. If no one wants them, they have no value. If they have no value, how can you pay for them?"

"No one pays for what they take out of So Savage," another man said. "Shit, it's more like, they pay you to take stuff out. 'Cept they don't."

"But *I* want these things," Slocum said, looking at the four men one after another; "*I* want them—" knowing he was making a point, not sure exactly what the point was.

One of the trackmen nodded, uncertainly, as if to mollify him. The man he had come in with lay back and picked at his molars. The old man said, "Where was I? The Burlington Northern, I think."

Slocum looked around the little structure; the bloody glow of railroad lamps, the mud of the floor, the odd symbols that in some fashion he could not understand drew a line connecting this place and Coggeshall Wharf and a sign warning people away from the Zone. As if a nation existed, far below X-Corp, below the ICE, below the teedees even, that he had never imagined before.

More rain was coming into the cabin. It was driven by a small breeze that blew through the car door, and subsided, and wafted gently again. After a moment Slocum turned and went out the flap and started down the rabbit trail that led to the railroad spur.

TWENTY

THE DINGHY MOVED DOWN a path of beaten gold.

It was still raining—if anything it was raining harder than when Slocum had left So Savage, a good five hours ago. Behind and above the deluge the sky seemed to swell and tighten like a bruise. The rain had slackened and resumed, and every time it resumed it had come a little stronger. The wind was still weak, uncertain, but somehow in the last few minutes it had cut a path through the injured sky, allowing a jailbreak of sun: refined light, rays purified in the star's furnaces, only partially twisted by passage through the atmosphere; to stream through that fault in an otherwise omnipotent cloud cover, and turn the stretch of harbor Slocum navigated into precious plate, like a conquistador's booty.

He was on the fringes of the ICE, looking for a narrow channel separating the massed boats from the wedge of marsh and the overarching freeway to the north.

The hurricane was not far off now. Even if he had not stopped by the sloop and surfed the NOAA Website he would have known; by the rain, by the third set of extra hawsers the ship's deckhands were rigging up- and down-harbor of his own fragile rigging; above all, by the hurricane barrier, which had closed in his absence, a maneuver that the selectmen allowed only if the threat was pretty serious. It cost a great deal, in power and overtime and maintenance, to slide the seven hundred tons of gate back and forth across the harbor mouth.

Slocum kept his eyes averted from the slab blocking the only clear view of horizon one could get in this harbor. It made him feel trapped; worse, it made him feel locked in with elements of his life that could drag him backward into a situation he had tried to flee—though god only knew his present circumstances were not much better.

Still, if he had to make a mistake, he would prefer it were his: a path he sought, a direction he intended. Not a lockdown; not a continuation of harm. The barrier made them all victims linked by the specificity of their destroyer: the sloop and Slocum, the ship and Matt and Melisande, Cakes and Lopes, every man woman and child in the floating village of the ICE.

Even Larsen, who spent nine days out of ten at sea, had sought shelter. The black outline of the *Valkyrie* was limned by the escaping sun at the end of a row of pilings behind which lurked another fifteen draggers, all condemned.

The break in clouds helped Slocum spot hard-to-see buoys and mooring cables; he made out the channel, a shadow against the crosshatching of hawsers, rigging, and rafted hulls, a few seconds before the clouds rolled over on the chink that had allowed light to penetrate this threatened world. Slocum reduced power on the outboard and turned cautiously to starboard. It was possible to make out different boats, even in the combination of spreading dusk and darkness of rainclouds, because the occupants were awake and busy with preparations for the wind. Spreader lights and cockpit lamps burned bright. Extra lamps hung in shrouds, men and women and even kids were busy as ants, wrapping cloth around mooring lines to reduce chafing. They rigged extra bumpers and topped up fuel tanks and broke down power windmills. Oilskins glistened. Music rippled from hatchways protected by Bimini tops and makeshift canopies. Different kinds of music, Slappe and reggae, *fado* and streetfight, Mozart, Casseco, and ballad; all seemed the same, woven into one wet tune by the relentless and fractal tympani of rain. Slocum listened and watched, feeling a vague pleasure at what he saw and heard, which he realized with some surprise came from a vestigial sense of belonging to this place.

He was proud of these people, he reflected; proud of how they had sewn these mismatched craft and motivations into an agreement for living. He admired the energy and even the semblance of maritime efficiency in the measures they took to prepare for the storm.

Then the skeg of his outboard hit a submerged hawser, snapping Slocum out of his reverie. He could not afford to get a line wrapped around his prop at this stage. Squinting, wiping tepid rain from his eyes with the back of one hand, like a clichéd whalefishing character from the virtual voyage of the *Pequod,* he proceeded slower down the channel.

The metal artist, De Vere, lived on a retired Bureau of Nationalizations patrol vessel that stuck out from the Morgans, Cape Dorys, Hatteras, and other production pleasure boats. Slocum made it out through the rain and gloom because of the blue flare and spark of welding tools. He moored the dinghy, picked up the canvas bag that held both his scavenged fuel injectors and the VR navigation module from his ECM-pak. He scrambled up a ladder welded to the starboard side. The percussion from a two-stroke generator made the hull tremble. A man stood on the foredeck. It was not De Vere. He was making a line fast from a piling farther south. "He hasn't got this thing secure enough," he complained to Slocum, "tell him he's got to rig more warps to the south."

Slocum found De Vere in a saloon built of the ship's mess and officers' cabins with the bulkheads taken down to form one big workspace. He wore a welding mask and was binding a scrap of metal that had once been a rack-and-pinion system to a chunk of iron from a lawn mower. Around him stood pieces he called finished: rusty beings erected from fragments of machines, conjured into a form of tortured life by the arc of torch, resuscitated from inanimate metal but to what end? To scream and strain against the gravity of earth and the indifference of men all eaten to the bone by debt and job concerns?

Slocum shook his head; he was prone to fantasy this evening, he thought. Perhaps he was affected by the drop in atmospheric weight, that would only deepen further as the hurricane, a low-pressure system, approached. He felt odd anyway, spaced out by all the walking. He felt chemically altered by the amount of water that had washed over him. It dripped from his clothes as if he were melting, forming almost immediately a puddle at his feet.

He was anxious, because he was in the ICE, because the storm threatened, because Bird was so near. Because he now knew he could not come to the ICE for whatever reason without trying to see her again.

De Vere noticed him and lifted his mask. "Slocum," he said, "haven't seen you for, like, years."

"Haven't been around," Slocum told him.

"I'm calling this Vector 29," De Vere said, pointing at the lawnmower/rack-and-pinion woman he was welding. He put down his torch, looked at the water pooling around Slocum's feet, and switched off the generator. In the sudden, relative silence, the hard rain sounded gentle.

Slocum took the injectors out of the shopping bag. De Vere put on a pair of drugstore reading glasses and looked them over carefully. He clamped one of them to his workbench and poked at it with wires, grunting as he did so. "That other one," he called over his shoulder, "is, like, fucked. And this one has oxygen-differential corrosion on both flanges. But there might be enough metal left. If I, like, built it up with zinc—"

"Would it work?" Slocum asked. His voice trembled as he spoke. He was starting to feel cold. "Will it do what it's supposed to do, will it run?"

De Vere shrugged. "I have to, like, do it. Then we'll see."

"But it could do it?" Slocum insisted. "Could it keep it running if you, uh, built up the flange?"

De Vere shook his head.

"Shit, Slocum," he said. "I'm not a magician. There aren't, like, philosophers' stones, you know? All we can do is, like, fix it, try it, test it. Maybe it'll do the job. Maybe it won't. My guess is," he added, "if you want me, like, killing the chicken, reading the, like, guts—I could do it."

"But not—" Slocum stopped. He was staring at De Vere with a killer's intensity. If De Vere could do it now; if the injector worked; if the storm by some miracle snapped the ship's hawsers without slicing his boat in two and blew his neighbor out of Coggeshall Wharf—he could be mobile. He could move his boat tonight. At dawn he might be circling the harbor, waiting for the barrier to reopen.

"Not now," De Vere said, as if talking to a child. "Not this week either. Like, early the week after."

Slocum wanted to smile. He couldn't bring himself to. The power of hope that surged in him when De Vere said he could probably fix the injector was too much, and never mind the delay, a week or ten days didn't matter and he couldn't realistically leave now anyway. Hope that carried all before it was too much to craft smiles from, it was too much for what triggered it. "Inappropriate" was what people in Bayview, people at X-Corp, would have termed it. By "inappropriate" they usually meant it offended their sense of safety, of emotion neatly cut to fit situations previously defined by rules governing such scenarios at X-Corp.

He should not have so much emotion connected to his diesel. He wondered if, far from being a sign that he was shedding the anesthesia of Bayview, it might not be a symptom of the wounding of affect, in that emotion repressed might become, in some circumstances, emotion displaced. He should not feel that his life depended on leaving the harbor. He fumbled in the canvas bag, brought out the navigation hard drive, and placed it on the workbench. De Vere squinted at it.

"That a Mark Four?" he asked.

"I think so," Slocum said. "It's two gigabaud. Full VR. Whole damn world," he added, "with online updates."

"I'm not gonna charge you that much," De Vere said. "I wouldn't charge you a tenth what that's worth."

"You can give me change in barterchips," Slocum suggested. "Or I can sell it to Bleeker, on the Friendship sloop in channel P. He wants it."

De Vere was still looking at the virtual-reality navigator.

"Why don't you just hang on to it for now?" Slocum urged. "We can figure out what I owe you, or what you owe me, later."

"You wanna deposit?" De Vere asked. He was eyeing the hard drive the way Slocum had been looking at the injector earlier. He's dying to own the thing, Slocum thought, with a twinge of distaste. He wants to feel the 3-D it will bring him, all the cheap-video sensation of being able to touch the shoals and channels his boat will navigate, virtually if not in fact.

De Vere dragged his eyes away, walked out a door to port, and came back with a handful of ICE barterchips—spindles that gave you credit with other ICE merchants.

"Two hundred," he said, "as a deposit. There's twelve hundred here."

"All right," Slocum said. "The repairs can come out of that."

"Whatever," De Vere said. He picked up the hard drive

and placed it carefully in a locker. Touching the instrument seemed to have broken its spell. He picked up his welding mask. Slocum turned to leave, and paused.

"Guy on the forward hatch. He said you need to put out more warps to the south."

De Vere did not answer. He fitted the welding mask over his whiskers and turned to the generator. As Slocum putted down the channel, heading for the Nexus, the heart of the web of channels defining the ICE, shadows seemed to leap out of the rain behind him, forged by blue flashes of welding fire that sprang from the portholes of De Vere's boat.

HE GOT TO DARK Denny's cat five minutes later. Only five minutes later but it was raining much harder and the wind blew more fitfully, and also with greater strength. He could distinguish three shapes around a kerosene lamp in the cockpit and, as if the rhythms of the approaching storm had imposed their timing on all actions, the rhythm of events immediately began to spiral out of control with all the fatal impulse, the lust for destruction of a stalling jet. He tied the painter and climbed aboard, disguised by the rain and dark so that they were not sure who he was until he had seated himself between a winch and a cleat on the gunwale and thrust his streaming features under the canopy, into the circle of light.

"Slocum," Dark Denny said, and the worry he usually locked out of his tone was sprung by surprise.

"What are you doing here?" Amy asked, not surprised or pleased. She wiped her hair off her face with the back of one hand.

"Bird," Slocum said.

She was leaning against the aft end of the coach cabin, knees drawn up to her chest, a half-sucker flipped up over her forehead. At least she was not surfing, Slocum thought. She surfed affect way more than was good for her—always had, since she came to the ICE. It had been a bone of contention between himself and Amy, and he suppressed the fiddle of anger that stirred in him at the thought. His daughter's long nose, so like his own, gleamed blue in the glare of the Coleman lamp. Her eyes reflected light only partially, dark creatures hiding in a darker cavern, looking out in apprehension and unhappiness—almost, he thought, in fear. He was uncomfortable on the hard gunwale, against the winch, but he felt incapable of movement.

"Slocum," Amy repeated. "What are you doing here? Tonight of all nights."

"I have a right to be here," Slocum said, still watching Bird's face. "I have a right to visit my daughter."

His gaze clearly made Bird uncomfortable. She turned aside as if he had touched her. Then she lifted off the half-sucker, put it down beside her jambook, and retreated backward down the hatchway and disappeared into the forward cabin, still without looking at him directly.

Dark Denny and Amy stared at her jambook. Dark Denny mumbled something and followed.

There was nothing left in the cockpit now but Slocum and the drumroll of rain on the glass deck and the *slish* of rain hitting the harbor and Amy, who hunched forward, deeper into the circle of light, and said, "Let's get this over with.

"You have no right to come here like this," she continued. "Not after what you did."

"What do you mean, what I did. What I did—"

"You left," Amy said. "Don't try to weasel out of that one."

Slocum stared at her. He was doing too much staring this evening, he thought. His eyes were reacting to an excess of force in him, or worse—a maelstrom of different forces, each of which occasionally got the upper hand and drove his emotions like stampeding cattle in one direction, which obliged him to look that way.

"I left because of you," he said. "Because you were sleeping with Dark Denny. Because—"

"That's bullshit," Amy interrupted, and wiped her hair from her face again. "The fucking was not the point. You'd been fucking Stacey Quinn for months—"

"I slept with her three times," Slocum said hotly. "It was wrong, it was idiotic, it was part of who I was in Bayview. Anyways it was a year and a half before you and Dark—"

"And you changed?" Amy asked. She twisted her shoulders left, then right, as if trying to unknot a muscle in her back. It was an old habit. As far as Slocum knew, she had no problems with her back; he had never been sure if the stress of arguing strained her muscles temporarily, or if it simply reminded her of constriction, which she sought to relieve as she wished to relieve her stress. "You've become someone different, which is why you're here—is that what you're trying to tell me?"

Slocum looked across the cockpit, into the rain, which was like looking at nothing, or at a mirror of himself. "I'm not sure it's possible to change," he said slowly. "But sometimes you can see more clearly, like, who you are. Like—"

"You been seeing De Vere or something?" Amy asked sharply. "You always hated when people said 'like.' "

Slocum ignored her.

"See who you are more clearly," he continued, "and see how you might have separated yourself from that. Sometimes if you simplify things down you can figure it out. Do you understand? It's what I've been trying to do—"

"So you've simplified things. And?"

"And I'm trying to get down to what I really want," Slocum said quickly, to forestall another interruption, "and what I really want—who I really am—is to see my family. To be a dad, to be a—"

"You didn't think about that when you left, did you?" Amy pointed out. "Oh, and you're right," she added unexpectedly, "when you left Bayview it was not that important, because you'd already left in your mind—when you started driving around, when you first started working at the credit office."

"I couldn't breathe," Slocum said. "I didn't know what was wrong, but I couldn't breathe. It was not because of Bird, it wasn't even you and me—"

"And now you want to get back together?"

"Can you ever stop interrupting?"

"It's just that I always know where you're going."

"And where's that?"

"You want us to get back together."

"No," Slocum said. "I want to go sailing. I haven't worked that out yet. I want to get out of this harbor, which is still under the shadow of Arcadia, of my old life. I want to get out somewhere I can just sail," he continued, and his voice thrummed like a mainsail on a hard reach, "just sail and sail with nothing but horizon around me. Pushed by the wind, which goes on and on forever.

"But I also want to come back," he went on. "And then I can be with Bird, and see her. She wants that, I know she needs that—"

"What unbelievable arrogance," Amy said, and pulled the mainsheet tighter through its snatchblock. "You know she doesn't want to see you anymore."

"She never sees me; how could she know?"

Amy let go of the mainsheet. She leaned over, almost impulsively, and touched Slocum's knee.

"You're soaked."

He shook his head, unwilling to change the subject

"I'm trying to protect you too," she said in a lower voice. "I told you that last time. Let things slide for a while. There's too much force, too much anger bottled up in you. In all of us. You have to give it time, you have to ease off the pressure. You *should* go sailing, John—let things settle, let it all ease out."

Slocum heard her words as if they were part of the downpour, sliding and dripping over him, eroding him a little. She had always been good with words; when she worked in sales she had one of the top closing records at X-Corp, and because of that she had ridden a fast track in marketing. They were thinking about making her a VP when she got pregnant.

And she had resented her pregnancy for a while because of that missed opportunity. She had resented his promotions, his ability to conduct a life outside the house. He wondered if she was working for the ICE now. He hoped she was, for her sake, for the sake of the small and vulnerable marine village she and her daughter lived in. They could use fast talkers, in the ICE.

But for all the strength and saturation of her words, they did less to him than the single touch of her finger on the soaked twill of his pants. It was the first time she had touched him in eight months. He reached out and removed her hand, very gently.

"I've given it time," he said. "It's not time Bird needs, it's contact with me. I'm making her a present—" He stopped, wondering where that sentence had come from. He already knew how useless the Project was; why bring it up now? In that gap of confusion Amy said, "I was with her, Slocum. Don't you understand? That whole time, when you left without telling her, I was with her. You never told her what you were doing."

"I know that."

"Do you know what that does to trust?"

Slocum stood up. "I want to see her."

Amy's face, tilted up toward him, was drained of color in the sheen of kerosene light.

"I keep telling you—"

Slocum turned toward the hatchway. "Bird?" He heard

Dark Denny talking below. He poked his head into the saloon. The discarded jambook mumbled and hissed familiar sounds of VR drama from stereo speakers. In the wedge of light spilling from the forward cabin he saw his daughter's face in profile. The sight was warm and cool in his perception; warm because it was the same avian shape of lips he had known ever since she was an infant at her mother's breast; cool, because it had changed somehow. The bones had grown stronger, her chin was more defined, she had put meat on her cheeks. Or maybe it was something else, a strength in the way she held her head. In the chin he saw elements of her mother that he had never noticed before; he saw a lot of Amy in her forehead somehow. A power of concentration lay there that was a stranger to childhood. The duality of her struck him now, stopped the plea he had been about to make.

He watched her for a few seconds more. She wiped her nose with her knuckles, a young gesture, and smeared the snot on her eyelids as she wiped them too. She knew he was there, she refused to look at him. He blocked his ears to the music shimmering from the jambook.

He turned abruptly, banging his knee on the binnacle.

He did not talk to Amy again. He went back into the rain, over the side, performing all the mechanics of seamanship. The spatial mechanisms he was really addressing were more abstract, however. They had to do with the area inside his frontal lobes, in the storytelling sector, where had lived until now the fantasy he had built of seeing Bird again; a fantasy of spending Thursday afternoons with her, taking her to the Sunset Tap, or for walks by the hurricane barrier.

That room in his mind had collapsed suddenly. Like one of those tall buildings deliberately demolished by explosives, all the pinions and girders were sheared by the blast of this last refusal to see him. And the explosions of raindrops, the stir of sound from the VR deck, the ribald splutter of his outboard, the crash of waves newly sprouted from the strengthening wind, all seemed to fit with that impulsion. All fit with the dying of what he now knew—partly from Amy's words, more from the conviction behind them, and the fact of what that conviction must have shown Bird by example—knew to have been an illusion he had clung to all this time, a fossil of his old life he had foolishly believed he could revive, when all around him the bones and tendons of that life were loosening, rotting, and falling away forever.

———

HE BARELY MADE IT across the harbor. There were no ferries, they were all at storm moorings, and thus no high wakes to come out of nowhere. But the wind, though variable, came strongly enough out of the southeast to kick up a two-foot slop. And the rain had filled the dinghy to the floorboards and sunk it five inches deeper into the water, so that it took much more slop over the bow than usual. The combination was dangerous, and he had to bail continuously with one hand as he steered with the other, peering into the sting of driven rain, setting his course for one-third of the run by the lights of the ICE over his stern, and then by the blink of aircraft lights on the radio antennas on Fish Island, and finally the lights of the theme park to the west.

The dinghy almost capsized twice. He felt nothing but mild excitement, even a weird form of pleasure that came from entering a room inside him that he could only know naked, stripped of the cares and fears of his habitual life; a room for complete ecstasy, or utter despair. He baled obsessively. His shoulders ached and his face hurt from the lashing of rain. He was convinced now that the hurricane would hit the Town dead-center and destroy everything and everybody and then all the external landscape would look the way he felt inside that room: that third space in his head, where nothing existed but Slocum, naked with the truth of what he had done to his daughter; first by raising her in a place where ease of affect was the only rule; then by ripping her up by the roots and transplanting her to a place where very little was easy. And then, when he had committed such violence to the young and flowering plant that was Evangeline Bird Slocum, he had left her, without care or explanation, for the pathetic reason that his wife had fucked another man. "Stupid," Slocum muttered in rhythm to the outboard, to the hiss of wake and the scrape of his bailing. "Stupid. Stupid." He shivered harder, and baled like a robot-guided piston machine, and felt the new pain of his shoulders join forces with the ache of his over-walked thighs as well as other aches less easy to pin down.

When he got to the sloop it was moving back and forth in the gusts, but it was still well tethered and cushioned. The wind whistled in the rigging and the bumpers squeaked as it tugged at its lines. He dropped the outboard into the lazarette and dragged the dinghy onto a raft down-wharf. There he flipped the dinghy to spill out the water and lifted it onto the wharf and tied it down between a dis-used container and the ship's offices.

Back on the sloop, Slocum took off all his clothes and heated up coffee. He drank the dark java, wrapped in a blanket. If the wind was mostly southeast, he thought—if his meteorology was right—that meant the hurricane must be roughly southwest of here; which meant, in turn, it was following the trend of coast.

Slocum warmed his hands on the mug. He would boot up the ECM-pak when he had warmed the rest of him. He would download the latest satellite pictures that showed where the storm was exactly; he would scan realtime video of massive breakers pounding beaches and harbors to the southwest, the piers swinging like loose teeth in a boxer's mouth amid the raging fists of foam; the flying roofs, the flooded cars, the gyrating traffic lights. Pleasure craft crushed, washed up in potato fields. He hummed the tune that had whispered out of Bird's jambook in the catamaran's cockpit. He could e-mail his dad, he thought suddenly. He felt a need to see the old man, to see his corny shots of mesas and chili peppers, and all the leathery retired ladies who baked him meatloaf. He wanted to ask him about his mother, and why she never left her room—not when she was sick, because that was understandable, but *before*. Before, when he was eight and ten and other crucial years of his growing up. Stayed inside, with the family scrapbooks laid out on the bedspread around her, pasting photos, or flowers that his father brought in from the garden and that she dried between the pages of school sketchpads. Moored to her bed, secured in her room as he was in this boat, in this harbor.

"She's tired," his father used to say, or use the code words for menopause: "change of life"; "hormonal stuff." "Your mother gets scared sometimes" was what he said when it got to him, pushing closer to what Slocum suspected might be the truth.

Slocum flicked on the ECM-pak with a hand movement so violent he could feel the switch's hinge bend slightly. The time icon showed 18:14. He was almost twenty minutes late to meet the Whip, assuming the Whip had braved the storm to go to Madame Ling's. Normally nothing Dolores could dream up would keep the Whip from an evening at Madame Ling's. It was after work hours, so she could not use forgone salaries as an argument.

Slocum wondered if the nickname everybody used for the Whip was not somewhat of a misnomer, if Dolores did not, sometimes, have a point in wanting him to stay home. A hurricane would definitely fit in the box of good reasons not to go out. The background tune from Bird's jambook was so familiar he paradoxically could not find a name for it; like a word that you had used all your life, whose spelling all at once seemed odd, and you had to open the dictionary to check how to write "ahead" or "nighttime."

Then memory synapses shifted slightly, and it was there, where it had been always: the voyaging theme from *Wanderbird,* the tune that accompanied those long shots of the great-sailed spaceship moving past planets striated in pink and yellow and red atmospheres and into the indigo of space.

Slocum clicked off the ECM-pak. He took out his *Smuggler's Bible* to see if there was a hurricane checklist he should follow, or some of the philosophical smuggling bullshit that sometimes contained a big enough kernel of truth to shift his ideas in a useful way. He found only a passage about storms being helpful to smugglers:

> The smuggler should always jive on the boundary layer between earth, air, water, and space. Interface like a beach, a storm front, a dewpoint; this is the space where different kinds of waves meet, flirt—and zoom-zoom into craziness, because it is the nature of a wave to believe it is unique.

That, and his checklist of maintenance chores. The stern tasks were pretty much finished, except for replacing the sacrificial anode. The midships chores—like checking through-hull fittings and keelbolts, replacing the cable that lifted the centerboard—those he had barely started. And then the bow chores: cleaning out the anchor locker, reattaching the little chain that kept the stainless-steel cover to the spurling pipe from falling overboard. . . .

Slocum sighed. He put on dry clothes: jeans and a T-shirt and dry socks. He covered those with his damp jacket, his workboots darkened by water. He shut down all accommodation electrics. Now the only light in his cabin came from the ship's portholes.

Changing his mind, he flicked on the steaming light, a single white light on the top of his mast that was supposed to denote a small craft under power. If the storm got bad, it was unlikely he would see that light in the rain and blowing wrack. But it made him feel better to know his boat had a light burning, to show where it lay in case someone should see; to prove someone cared for this vessel.

Then he left. The light was just visible at the top of his mast, dimming and strengthening as the rain increased and slackened. Flashlights winked high on the ship as inspection teams tightened covers on lifeboats.

MacTavish's office was dark. It was the first time Slocum had seen the trailer shut like that. He supposed it had something to do with the storm.

The streets were empty, except for a police cruiser floating silently around a corner five blocks down-harbor, near the Moby Dick.

Slocum did not feel like he was being followed.

———

MADAME LING'S E-Z KREDIT Laundorama was closed, and though the Lisboa was open, for the first time Slocum could remember it was almost entirely empty. Only a couple of diehards hung from their drinks at the side of the bar like alpinists from a piton.

The purple neon of the fortune-telling sign was switched off. Slocum had been walking steadily, insulated by his dry clothes, feeling neither warm nor cold—feeling almost, in the absence of serious exposure, as if living in that third space he had entered after seeing Bird, or not seeing her, was protecting him from reaction to mundane acts of weather, and even from weather that was not so mundane.

He pressed the bell, half expecting no answer. But the light above the entrance came on, and then Shaneeqwa stood there, cursing the flecks of rain and wind that spat on her as Slocum walked in.

"Blew your chance," Shaneeqwa told him as they walked through the garlic–smelling darkness. "Luisa been all over Cakes for two days, like a pilotfish on a shark."

"Cakes isn't a shark," Slocum said.

"It's just an expression," Shaneeqwa said.

Maybe it was an effect of the weather outside, maybe it was only the thermostat reacting to loss of heat from wind blowing across the chinks of this ancient boardinghouse. Or perhaps it was the psychological effect of knowing a storm crouched feral nearby, ready to spring and tear open your shelters and feast on the warmth and safety inside. At any rate Madame Ling's kitchen felt twice as warm and bright as it normally did.

It was not crowded. The ex-fishermen were absent, unless you counted Lopes, who stood where the fishermen normally stood, under the television, watching the circle of spun-off moisture repeat itself from the viewpoint of a satellite. Luisa sprawled in an armchair by the stove. The Whip was there as well, leaning over one arm of her chair as Luisa tapped his wrist to the rhythm of WFDO. Madame Ling castled the stove, stirring the usual pot. When she spotted Slocum she yelled "No fuhget it. You can't come in cadgin' meals no more, anyway Cakesh she just left to go to her boat."

"I got barterchips," Slocum said. He had not been interested in dinner until ten seconds earlier when he smelled the garlic in the parlor.

"You got ICE chips?" Madame Ling asked, her eyes narrowing.

"Yeah but we can use those," Danielle piped up. "They sell boxes of cheap condoms, in one of those boats."

Madame Ling stood, swaying a little in the small hurricane of her own stew-steam and the storm of her always-conflicted angers. "Ah, Shlocum," she said finally. "I warn you I warn you, *Madre de diosh,* nevah you listen. Trouble written all ovah you." She turned back to the stove and, with a twist of her fat hand, dumped into the stew a smaller pot full of salt cod mixed with garlic, tomatoes, and thyme. "You give me da blood-presh," she added, almost happily.

The Whip made room for him on the other side, away from Luisa. Slocum crabbed around the table, in the center of which stood a kerosene lamp with a cream-colored glass mushroom for a chimney. The mushroom gave off a golden glow that made the girls look younger and the men almost handsome. A salad bowl of orange cheese-flavored snacks stood beside it. Luisa's head lolled sideways on a filthy antimacassar. "*Quanto canto nao penso,*" she recited, and fell silent as she listened to another stanza of the *fado* playing on the radio. Then she sang, "*No que a vida e de ma.*" She looked at Slocum and smiled slightly. The tears in her eyes, he knew, were from the *fado.* The Whip had his jambook cradled between sneakered feet. He glanced down at it, a little anxiously; touched it with one finger for reassurance.

Slocum put a ten-unit barterchip next to the cheese snacks and watched the hurricane spin and the weather-men flap their jaws, almost inaudible against the calm chatter of the prostitutes and the clink of Madame Ling's spoon and the Portuguese guitars fretting about a love that was fated to end badly and somehow wound up even worse than expected. Luisa's eyes were streaming now, but she was still smiling and marking the beat with her fingers. Behind all the kitchen noise lay something else; for the storm outside was strong enough for its idiot mumble to intrude through the windows, and once in a while a slap of rain rattled the panes; and occasionally the wind sat up outside to box the house's east and west sides so that the whole structure shook slightly, and everyone looked around, not making eye contact, then seeking it, and smiling nervously.

Between commercials, the TV visuals showed the hurricane eighty miles to the south, maybe a little east of south now but pretty much on course to hit the Town with the full force of its Wankel drive.

"Nem sequer ne perienco," Luisa sang. *"Nem o mal se me da."*

The song was replaced by an ad for cut-rate charter flights to Lisbon. The TV switched to international news: A massive server crash had disabled the Frankfurt bourse. Army helicopters, caught in a video clip, rocketed a hilltop convent in a South American town where terrorists had taken refuge; smoke poured from a clerestory. Renewed tension in Kashmir. Slocum, in this kitchen, felt in no time, in no place—suspended in a limbo that was mostly emotional but also to some extent geographical and cultural, and all of it was fine with him, limbo was fine with him; in limbo he didn't have to think about what emotions spinning elsewhere in his brain were doing, where they were heading, what destruction they might wreak once they got there.

The Whip picked up his jambook and placed it carefully on the oilcloth. He did not open it. Instead he put all his fingers on the closed lid and his thumbs on the compartment in which you stored the half-sucker, like a concert pianist touching the keys before beginning his recital.

"Found it," he said. "Easy, like I told you.

"The pharmaceuticals are harder to get into than the Air Force Space Command," he continued, "if you're looking for tests of drugs in development, or some kind of proprietary research. But when they're trying to bill insurance companies for treatment, or get funds from the feds—well, let's just say that they get a lot less anal about some of this data."

He hit a button on the jambook's side, and hardware chattered, and the curl of flimsy paper spat out of the instaprinter port. He ripped it off and handed it to Slocum.

MERCK LAROCHE—AETNA BLUECROSS
DIVISIONAL MULTITASKING UNIT/BILLING
BLT/T
Beta Test account 34110-45090-B
12/17. 08-32. 16:18

A list of names followed. Each name was preceded by
one of two numbers: 111 or 1672.

Slocum glanced at the Whip, but his eyes were on his
jambook screen again. Slocum went down the list, reading
the names, a classic compendium of names for early third-
millennium America, a hodge-podge of races and histories
getting closer to the cultural temperature where the individual molecules of difference began to break down and
fold together.

> *Pierce Asekrem*
> *Anne Gart*
> *Fulgencio Vajpatay*
> *Derek O'C. Brixton-Bulawayo*

Someone handed Slocum a glass of wine. He took it
and sipped without looking up.

> *Latreya Finestein*
> *Jean-Francois Krupskayevitch*
> *Felony Jones*
> *Victoria Chaves-Jones*
> *Melisande Sloane*

"Not Yonge?" he said.

"No." Now the Whip looked up from his computer.
His fingers were bent as if almost at the point of springing
into cybernetic concerto.

"My god." Slocum felt his lungs slow as he drew breath.
"His *daughter?*"

"Who else?"

"Wycliffe Sloane." Slocum thought of the man he had seen in the armchair in the after restaurant or saloon or whatever it was. "He's on the ship?"

"Where else?" the Whip replied. "Most of the Lee Shan ones are hooked up to a parent for the live transfusion. 'Cause what wasn't in that publicity thing is this: The treatment only lasts four or five years, then the logic corrupts for some reason."

"That was in there," Slocum said, pointing at the jambook. "In the article."

"Sure. But what they *didn't* say was that both people, the one who's sick, the one who's healthy—they *both* need another donor, or they'll die."

Slocum found he was holding the flimsy printout tight enough to rip it.

"How do you know she's Lee Shan, she could be Kundura. And the Kundura was a cure, it was over eighty percent—"

"The number." The Whip pointed to Melisande's name. "See—1672. That's from Merck LaRoche's pathology index. I looked it up: Lee Shan."

Slocum nodded. He found the news did not surprise him; in fact, what would have surprised him was if she were not a Lee Shan victim, if early death were not in the cards for her. He was not sure if it was how she acted, how she moved and talked and smiled, or whether he had picked up subtler clues nestled in her environment; perhaps his first sight of that bizarre hookup, with the great urgency and expense implied, had engendered an accurate, if not justified, assumption that the stakes being played for here were as high as they got.

Still, now that he knew for sure, he also knew that the substance of his understanding was unchanged. He could slot this certainty into spaces that before contained only likelihood, and proceed as he had before.

"Thanks," Slocum said. "I owe you one—again."

The Whip's hands moved, dug at the fat rolls under his shirt. Madame Ling yelled loudly for thyme and wine. Shaneeqwa fetched a bottle of *vinho verde,* opened it, and filled Slocum's glass, looking him boldly in the eyes as she did so, continuing a conversation she was having with a group of whores in the corner.

"Amy Duggan really broke up with Mahal because he's gonna switch over to *Thunder Beach,*" she said. Luisa shook her head. May said, "He's like in love with Lara Love, like, he won't do that," and Shaneeqwa said, "You poor bitch, that's just on the show." She flipped her hair back in a way that reminded Slocum a little of Amy and a little of his mother, and mostly of women in general, how they shared acts and gestures of conceit. Shaneeqwa had big eyes, and makeup that made them look even larger. Her mouth was bloodred. Crumbs from the cheese snacks were stuck to the lipstick. She looked about fourteen, though she was, Slocum knew, in her mid-twenties. He felt absurdly grateful to Shaneeqwa, all of a sudden; grateful because in the killer hug of a hurricane and the ominous stink of mortality that surrounded what the Whip had said, she could focus on *Pain in the Afternoon* and *Thunder Beach,* and nothing but *Pain* and *Thunder Beach,* and all without a VR headset or much of a monitor to multiply her drive toward such trivia.

He wondered, for a moment, if he might not be far off-base in his feelings—if his addict's revulsion for VR and what was shown through that medium was not missing some core relaxation, some safety valve that allowed people to not care so much, and thus enjoy more what they did pay attention to. The people at X-Corp claimed they only gave people what they wanted—what they cried for, in fact. Slocum could testify that this used to be true for him as well.

He turned toward the Whip.

"I got an idea. Really cool idea."

"I'm listening, babe," the Whip said. His hands were on the laptop's keyboard, typing trial commands.

"I'm gonna get that diesel running," Slocum continued.

"I know," the Whip answered softly. "After you win the lottery," and his eyes wrinkled, and the estuary color of them seemed as gritty and hopeless as ever. Slocum leaned toward him.

"How 'bout you come with me?"

"Where?"

"Wherever. When I get the diesel going. Outta here—"

"Slocum," the Whip said. "You been working on that thing since you've been here."

There was a lull in the ambient sound. The wind had softened, and quiet graphics showed on the TV. Shaneeqwa leafed through *Shine*. Danielle said, "Yeah, but if you soak *bacalhao* in white wine you can eat *and* drink." Madame Ling seemed to be listening to the Whip.

"No, I got a feeling this time," Slocum said. "Look, I got these injectors off an old MarDyne, I gave it to a guy at the ICE, and he thinks he might be able to fix one up."

"Injectors," the Whip repeated. His crow's-feet were smooth; now his forehead crinkled a bit.

"They shut down the Whale!" someone shouted, watching the newscast. "They shut down the Moby Dick." Those still talking fell silent. No one had ever shut down the theme park since it opened. No one had ever shut down the Spouting Whale.

"It's coming," Madame Ling said. "Lock da doors."

"I'm gonna get that engine running," Slocum insisted with more fierceness than he meant to convey. "I'm gonna go down the channel and out to sea.

"I'm gonna buy provisions, fill up on fuel and water," he added. "Two weeks at the outside." Slocum's heart was speeding up a bit; he was almost beginning to believe what he said.

The Whip looked at him calmly. His fingers had not left his jambook.

"You could come with me, Howard," Slocum continued softly. "Come sailing. I got four bunks on that boat. Out the hurricane barrier. Down the channel, then down the coast. We'll go south of the channel, to the islands, wherever."

"You would take me?"

"Sure. I mean, I'd really like you to go."

The Whip looked at his jambook again. He hit a key, and the small screen grew a map of flowers, with bees flying between, and sentences appearing on the course of their flight.

"Down the channel," the Whip told the bees. "South down the coast."

"With a sailboat, we could go forever. We don't need the engine, once we're out of the harbor. Except for emergencies."

The Whip's lips curved almost imperceptibly, then straightened.

"Nice of you, Slocum," he said, and looked at Madame Ling. "I gotta go," he announced. "I want to get back to the house, make sure everything's tied down before the wind really hits."

He did not look at Slocum again, though he did repeat "nice of you," once.

He packed up the jambook and hooked it to his belt. He dug deeply at his waist, tucking in the love handles. He stood up, edged around the table, picked his coat out of a pile near the door, and left.

The sound of wind grew much louder when the parlor door opened, and for a few seconds it pulled air out of the kitchen as if a giant vacuum cleaner spun outside, its hose fastened to the whorehouse door.

Slocum watched the door. So did Luisa and Shaneeqwa and Madame Ling. It was Madame Ling who finally broke their gaze and silence.

"Whatsa matter with you, Slocum," she called, because the wind was beating loudly again. "You don't call a man's bluff like that. Not if he's your friend.

"All dat man's got is, leaving his wife. *Madre de diosh,* what's he gonna have left if he really does it?"

The *fado* was still lisping from the radio. *Chego a querer a verdade, e a sonder.* Luisa shook her head, maybe at Madame Ling, maybe at the Whip, or Slocum. Her eyes were fixed on the radio. Slocum thought about what he had said, but the only part that seemed to hold mass or weight—the only part that pulled at him—was the MarDyne injector.

He found he wanted the hurricane to be over so he could go back to De Vere and find out how the repair was going. He drained his glass of wine, and stood up. He felt Shaneeqwa and Madame Ling refocusing on him.

"I should go too," he said. "Check on the boat."

"So go," Shaneeqwa said.

Slocum looked at her. She stood by the stove, by Madame Ling, blocking his path toward the door. Her dark eyes were calm and steadfast as they usually were, and the rule of their gaze somehow broke open a passage to all the missing of Bird that he had kept at bay for so long because he never actually saw her. Now that he had seen her again the missing stood poised, ready to fall on him the next time he thought of his daughter's face.

He bulled past the stove, then stopped next to Shaneeqwa. He put his arms around her and hugged her hard.

He bent his head down and kissed her on the lips, long enough to taste the dust of cheese snacks on his tongue.

"Dag," Shaneeqwa said, and laughed hoarsely. "I didn't know you liked me so much."

"You take care of yourself, Shaneeqwa," Slocum said. "Keep making those pretty metaphors."

"Met-a-what?" Shaneeqwa asked suspiciously. "I never met nothing I didn't scope out first."

Slocum put on his jacket.

TWENTY·ONE

THE POWER CUT OUT when Slocum was halfway between Madame Ling's and Coggeshall, but that didn't seem
to change things much because people, thanks to the endless "Hurricane Special Broadcasts" and other Flash bul-
letins, had ample notice. Bright lights in frame houses
disappeared and then, after only a few minutes, were replaced by soft glows and circles of citron light against the
blur of massive humidity, magically transforming shabby
tenements into storm-tossed galleons.

The carnival neon of the Moby Dick vanished. This
was strange, for a while, and then quickly it felt normal.
Traffic lights went dark. Those that hung over crossroads
swung crazily—as scripted, Slocum thought; as traffic lights
always did in hurricane newscasts.

There were almost no cars out. Down Purchase Street a
fire blazed in a package store. Black shapes, probably
Sagres, resembled dancers as they fire-ganged booze into
the street. Then came the red flashing lights of the fire
trucks, the blue lights of cops. Against the backdrop of
flames the combat of gangbangers and police became another dance, less fluid than before but not without grace.

Except for the emergency vehicles and the looters'
sedans, the only traffic consisted of Action News vans, cutting the wind and dark with headlights and the booms of
satellite feeds.

Walking was OK on the north–south streets, parallel to
the harbor, but going down the east–west streets, toward the
water, meant leaning heavily eastward to counter the blows
of wind, then staggering to recover if the wind slowed for
an instant, all the while peering through one's fingers into
the storm to watch for flying debris. Once, a hunk of corrugated iron twenty feet square cartwheeled only a car's
length ahead of his bent form. By the time he reached
MacTavish's trailer, Slocum felt physically beaten up.

No sign of the security guard. The windows of his
trailer were still dark. Slocum was about to try the door, or
at least shelter in the lee of the doorframe to accumulate
strength for the haul down-wharf in the full ravage of
wind, when he saw that someone had gotten there ahead
of him.

It was not MacTavish. This person was too small and
unobtrusive.

Slocum pressed himself against the booth. A green
emergency light cast its gleam through the inspection window. Slocum was twice as soaked as when he had made
that trip last time. His ears smarted from the great orchestra
of the storm. He flexed his shoulder muscles, which had
cramped from the effort of walking bent over.

The man pressing into the closed door ahead of
Slocum, peering through the storm toward the harbor,
should have been incapable of hearing Slocum's movements, but he turned suddenly and looked straight at him.

It was a County Diesel mechanic. Slocum did not have
to read the name to recognize the jumpsuit. The man
looked at Slocum with mild surprise and complete indifference. Slocum did not recognize his face, though
MacTavish's emergency light reflected in the man's eyes,

revealing a startling color of blue. Slocum was suddenly sure he had seen him before. Probably on the wharf, he thought. After all, County Diesel mechanics had been present every day since the ship arrived.

Slocum opened his mouth to say something, for the great peculiarity of this weather seemed to require comment. The storm was so strong and the Town so empty that he felt need for a friendly comment, if only to reinforce the possibility of human cooperation against an outside danger.

But the man immediately stepped out into the rain and wind. He went through the gates, into Coggeshall Street. The wind and dark seemed to take him, and he was gone.

Slocum gawped after him till he had to shut his mouth to keep from breathing water.

Then he took his place. He noticed a line of MacTavish's Polaroids, taped just inside the window, waving in the inside draft. They were all of the ship, distorted and stained by his magnetic "scrying," till its great bulk looked like brash wreckage, or an abandoned space station left to wander under alien stars.

Slocum peered into the storm again. The doorway afforded him somewhat more shelter from the wind.

He saw the ship first, for of course the ship used its own generators—or rather, he saw a kind of pastiche canvas of the ship, a wall of lights shining from portholes, decklights, cargo-work areas; and one County Diesel truck parked near the guardpost—or that was what they all had been before the mad action-painter of hurricane took their colors and smeared them in a million furious gestures to the southwest, every yellow porthole streaked into a dozen portholes beyond, the mast lights become swirling banners, the cargo lights long rectangles of white flapping toward the invisible, motionless whale of the theme park, the rain tearing horizontal scratches across the entire painting.

A square of light—the hatch in the ship's hull that gave

access from the gangway—appeared and disappeared, appeared and disappeared, as the wind slapped the heavy steel door back and forth.

Slocum shut his eyes. His sloop was not visible from MacTavish's because of the short wall of warehouse to the south, on which the trailer was tacked. And he had not really meant to look at the ship. Though a quadrant of his psyche was still taken with Melisande Yonge, or Sloane. Or rather, was still taken with the flare of infatuation Melisande had catalyzed, and perhaps even more with the mix of infatuation and despair that she exuded for him like cheap perfume.

But other things were happening here and he needed to pay attention to them. The hurricane, for one, and the safety of his sloop.

Bigger than that was Bird, the memory of her face, her long nose turned from him in Dark Denny's cockpit; her eyes never once meeting his.

He knew that buried in the core of this image lay a new arrangement of his life, because he suspected now that she was truly gone from him. He did not know if she was gone forever or for a slightly shorter time: a year or two; the end of adolescence? He knew only that he could think of nothing that might break down the depths of her rejection. And this knowledge—even at the stage he was at now, where like Bird he dared not look it square in the face, but rather see it from the corner of one eye—this knowledge seemed to gust in a circle of potential misery; just like the wind, like this hurricane spinning left-handed up the coast toward the Town; until it devalued other poles that might attract his interest.

It made him distrust, for example, his crush on Melisande, and the cocktail of emotional and physical needs fueling it. Because such a spark had lit up the situations between him and Stacey Quinn, between Amy and

Dark Denny, between him and Breena Jakes even, till it set off the explosion that blew up his family like a pocket of sewer gas.

He dived back into the hurricane. Thoughts like this had one good effect: They made flying debris, and rain that felt like razors against his skin, and wind that must be seventy knots or more, feel inconsequential or almost. He rounded the southeast corner of the warehouse. He would use the County Diesel truck as temporary shelter. The wind, which was much stronger by the harbor, picked him up, like a giant Labrador scooping up a Frisbee, and dashed him on the cobbles, rolled him against the truck's windward tires. Slocum used a tire to lever himself against the wind as he got, shakily, to his feet.

The vehicle's hazard lights flashed. Under ordinary circumstances Slocum might have wondered what the truck was doing here after quitting time, and with a hurricane scheduled at that. But he was a little dazed from the fall. And concern for his sloop occupied the front of his brain. He pushed himself off the truck and staggered crosswind, using the sloop's range light, just visible now above the wrack, to guide him, like some shepherd in a Judeo-Christian myth; feeling a surge of tenderness for that beacon shining bravely, the boat struggling to stay alive in the wild harbor. The dolphins and pilings of the wharf, not to mention the bulk of ship, must be protecting his sloop somewhat, he thought. By implication he understood that he had been right to stick to his guns about the berth, which was sheltering his craft against this storm, as he told Vera it would. It felt good to see his position proven to make sense, if only in the limited context of the waterfront.

He was almost across the concrete spur, wading in puddled water six inches deep, water surging as waves crashed white and hungry over the back of the spur; the tide had to be two feet over its normal high mark for the waves to do that. He would have to tighten up the mooring lines to compensate.

He wasn't sure why he stopped at that point. Nominally, it was the square of light blinking as the door in the ship's side opened and closed that got to him.

More likely his cache-memory finally overflowed with impressions of strangeness that had accumulated without his being aware: the absence of MacTavish; the lack of movement of any kind, either aboard the ship or in the guard booth at the gangway's base; the gangway itself, which was in the down position.

That huge iron door slamming back and forth, unse-cured, in the wind.

So they evacuated, he thought—though that seemed unlikely. Matt Zurbruegge, at least, was a professional. Surely he would not abandon a ship already well secured in safe harbor against a storm? And why would he leave the door open like that, with the gangway down?

Slocum stopped—which was a matter of leaning left and forward a bit, letting the wind support him at a fifty-degree angle against its force. Something raw and hard thwacked into his chest, and was pinned there by the wind. He reached for it with one hand, the slimy streamlined shape, the sharp-gummed hole, the stink of rot—a fishhead—snapped it away into the night with a cry of disgust.

Would Melisande have gone too? Wiping his eyes as he looked eastward at the ship. Surely she could not leave for any length of time the equipment that kept her alive, or the ship that supported her treatment?

He should go to his sloop. His boat needed him. He could rely on his sloop, as he could not on the outside world, with its complexities and backflows of emotion.

He would board the ship, find Melisande, and then re-turn to his sloop.

Slocum had a weakness for the idea of having your cake

and eating it too, though he knew it seldom worked in practice, in that having and eating both were full-time jobs.

He had thought, for a while, when he worked at X-Corp, lived in Arcadia, moonlighted at the ICE, and used his sloop as an office, that he had managed the trick, only to be taught in his own kitchen how wrong he was.

This was a lesser compromise, though; a stab at twin goals that should not be hard to achieve in practice. Anyway the insanity of wind and the effort of fighting it made thought useless beyond a certain level. "Hell with it," he shouted into the storm, and drove eastward, like ramming himself into the soft, wet belly of a huge animal, down the spur where waves rolling from the fetch of harbor plucked at his boots as he walked.

The booth at the base of the gangway was empty. He started up the ramp, gripping the aluminum rail with both hands; the wind, funneled by the ship's side, twisted into small tornadoes that attacked him now from the front, now from the back, making his progress slow and uncertain. And his stomach turned, for the gangway itself was moving back and forth, up and down, pulled between the solid quay and the wall of ship that at this range he now saw was moving also—shifting just this side of perception—sliding forward, pushed by the approaching hurricane, till its forty hawsers tightened, stretched, and relentlessly pulled it back. Moving up and down also, in the confusion of short-cycle waves being churned up inside the harbor. Slocum shut his ears to the thrash of waves and the groan of solid things—hawsers, buffer rafts, quay pilings—that rose around him on the gangway. He refused to think about forces that could do this to a ship that in the gut of him he had believed was immune to weather. He fought his way up the rest of the incline and jumped heedlessly through the gaping, slamming square of yellow light that was the entry to the purser's lobby. Behind him two tons of steel door crashed shut as the ship rolled slightly to port, then reopened as the wind levered itself through the gap and shouldered it outward again.

Slocum stood on the soaked carpet. When the door closed, shutting out the wind, the silence around him became so great that it seemed louder than the storm. The next time the door slammed, he dogged the hatch shut. Then turned back to face the relative quiet of the ship.

It was not entirely silent, of course. The carpet beneath his feet shivered with the rhythm of generators. As his ears lowered their threshold he heard the clock over the purser's desk ticking loudly. And the storm was playing the ship too, playing it like the largest and most complicated of percussion instruments, moving it so it creaked and stretched and popped in its thousands of welds and joins of paneling.

But no sound of people could be heard. The desk was empty. He moved to the cherrywood counter, watching the rows of monitors: the stolen angles of corridors restaurants conference-areas lounges libraries staff-rooms promenade gym hospital. The hospital, he noted, was empty as well, the BLT/T unit shiny and alone between its mechanical chairs.

Many of the monitors contained a flashing icon in the top right-hand corner that read CODE: OCTOBER. It was an emergency icon, but Slocum had no idea what Code October meant. He stood there for a minute, dripping water on polished fruitwood, somewhat awed by the loneliness that came out of these emptied screens like a forgotten opera. It seemed of a scale with the immensity of this vessel.

Then he turned, and set off to find Melisande.

He walked forward, following the path he remembered from the first time he had visited. The elevator worked, and whisked him up—six decks, he didn't remember how far to go so he chose six, and the corridors at that height seemed right, running fore and aft with teak rails and mahogany-louvered doors on either side.

But many of the corridors resembled one another. He walked for fifty yards and did not spot the library or the entrance doors to the boat deck; in fact the corridor ended at an office door with a brass plaque reading FIRST OFFICER'S DAY CABIN, and a set of steep stairs over which a sign read BRIDGE—OFFICERS ONLY. NO ADMITTANCE.

Slocum took the stairs. He was breathing hard, from walking fast, from the stress of the storm, from the tension that seemed to inhabit this great ship built to contain dozens of humans, and that now seemed to hold no one at all, but went right on running anyway.

He thought the first mate might well turn to face him when he opened the door to the bridge but all he saw was a spare expanse of deck, interspersed with pedestals holding computer screens, radar viewers, a joystick and binnacle, and radios. Chart lights tinted everything red.

Right across the width of bridge and ship ran a series of square windows whose shape Slocum recognized from wharfside.

He walked to the windows. It took an appreciable amount of time. He saw nothing except water and streaks of salt and spume smashed against the glass by the pressure of wind. The storm howled and tore at the glass from every side and whistled and shook this compartment set so high and forward, and the roar it made seemed to inhabit the otherwise empty space, and Slocum had the feeling that if the wind ever found an easy way in, parts of the ship, like the bridge, might start to separate from the rest.

He walked to starboard, looking over what would be the wharf and warehouses and the Town far below if he could see any of it, which he couldn't; he was looking for his masthead light, but the berth where his sloop lay was hidden by the boat deck two levels below. He noticed, when the rain lightened marginally, that two lifeboats lying just under a deck light had had their canopies torn off, despite the earlier precautions of the deckhands. He felt for the first time a glimmer of sympathy for this ship, which despite its scale was still a seagoing craft, still vulnerable to the fury of elements. He almost felt responsible, because this vessel was empty, and he was, by default, all it had left for skipper, mate, and crew.

If the boat deck was two levels below, he had gone one deck too high, and Melisande's suite was one flight down.

Walking back toward the door, he passed a computer terminal set to a live NOAA weather alert, with the familiar satellite loop showing an infrared map superimposed on readings of moisture content. This, Slocum knew from the *Smuggler's Bible,* was a perfectly accurate way to track hurricanes, which were vast rotary engines fueled by the heat of seawater and the rising and cooling of vapor.

In this case the image showed nothing new: the usual furious spin jerking up and down in time-lapse along the coast, coming as far northeast as fifty miles away on the same track as the last image he had seen. An icon on this screen, too, blinked green. CODE: OCTOBER flashed as it had in the purser's office.

For the hell of it, Slocum clicked on the "home" icon. A giant X appeared, glowing in black light. It was the X-Corp logo, with a scroll of options attached.

Somewhere on the bridge a radio crackled.

Slocum headed for the door.

HE FOUND MELISANDE'S SUITE easily, once he got the decks straight. Found her door and knocked hard against the increasing creak of ship and yowl of wind and got no reply. The window of her dressing room spilled cracks of light around the blinds and into the streaking rain. He knocked again and tried the handle.

It turned. He went inside.

The cabin, incredibly, was messier than before. Every

piece of clothing in her closet had been dumped on the rug. The nightgown he had seen her in last bunched around his feet as he walked in. The telescope lay on its side, the mattress had been pulled off the bed. Every light was on. Books lay splayed on the floor. In the aquarium the fish darted and turned hysterically; maybe the ship's discomfort unsettled them, too. The aquamarine crystal castle glowed. He called, "Melisande?" and checked the other door, which led to a little office, like a reduced version of the library, with the same green-shaded lamps and a writing desk covered with magazines, and what appeared to be insurance forms.

Shine; Atlantis; Marine Biology Monthly.

The book on her nightstand was titled *Hard Bottom—A Novel of the Northeast Coast.*

Leaving the cabin, he saw a ship-safety diagram on the back of the door, all rooms and lifeboat stations clearly marked. He studied it, but since he wasn't sure where he was going, it did him little good.

He returned to the corridor. Forward, the passage ended at another suite. So he headed aft.

He was halfway down the corridor when he got the feeling that he was being followed.

The feeling, though he had not had it in several days, was like an old friend; familiar enough from the times he'd experienced it that it did not scare him. He turned slowly. The corridor was empty, except for a security camera that stared at him, its "active" light bloodred.

The corridor met a passage perpendicular to it that communicated with the ship's other side between elevators and a conference lounge. The second such corridor provided access to a lobby full of bronze statuary and the deeply polished expanse of the grand staircase. He was about to take a right, down the staircase, when movement caught his eye in a doorway he had just passed.

Slocum walked quietly back. Through the doorway lay a small pantry. A coffeemaker steamed. A tray was set with toast, butter, jam, and a plate of smoked herring.

A face appeared. A whiskered, beaten face, with one eye open and glaring and the other gouged out, poked from the lower portion of the doorjamb. The mouth bulged with purloined kipper. It growled at Slocum.

"Ralfie!" Slocum gasped.

He kneeled down to pet the cat. Ralfie jerked away, swallowed mightily, and jumped back to tray level.

Slocum watched him for a few seconds. He was relieved that Ralfie was not missing. He was also pissed off, a little, that the cat had ditched Slocum and his sloop as soon as he got an opportunity to board the bigger, fancier vessel.

The flip side of that, Slocum found, was that he admired Ralfie, for his feline opportunism, his willingness to take a risk on the main chance.

"Well, good for you, shipmate," he said finally to the cat, who growled, but did not look at him again.

Slocum continued aft. The third transverse corridor marked the end of this hallway. It provided access to a set of frosted-glass doors covered with stylized seahorses, mermaids, the wrecks of galleons, and other underwater motifs. A brass sign read OCEANUS LOUNGE. He pushed open one of the doors—not an easy task—and stepped inside.

He stood at the apex of a wedge-shaped lounge that took up the whole width of ship on this deck, and fell away in two levels, each slightly lower than the previous, toward a curve of floor-to-ceiling windows opening onto the stern. The walls on each side were of gray marble cut into triangular alcoves with art-nouveau couches lurking behind potted palms. Before him was a bar carved out of one giant block of the same marble. A grand piano stood on a marble plinth to the side. As the room opened out and descended, art-nouveau armchairs, arranged to face the curving windows, had been spaced among glass tables on which were set linen napkins and heavy ashtrays. Fluted sconces, in the same motif as those Slocum remembered from the swimming pool, cast fans of light. These were reflected in fluted crystal vases in the center of every table. Each vase held one fresh, white lily. Slocum, eyeing the backs of the chairs, realized he had seen this lounge before. From the perspective of a security camera mounted above the bar, while he had crouched under the desk in the fire-control room, he had noticed a white-haired man sitting in an armchair, looking north toward the head of the harbor and Arcadia.

No such head was visible now. Slocum called "Melisande?" without hope of a reply. A sound system played music. A woman sang low: "... nor sleep at night, for thinking ..."

He walked around the bar, trailing his hand over the polished marble. Wind sucked lasciviously at the windows. Blue lights inset behind the bar illuminated the usual set of shakers, spoons, icepicks, and other paraphernalia of mixology. On impulse Slocum ducked through the service hatch and opened the refrigerator. He took out a foreign ale, chilled just this side of freezing. He sipped. It cooled his throat. He leaned on the counter as a bartender might do, looking out the dark windows at hell, or its maritime equivalent: flailing rain like a thousand Medusas thrash-dancing in a carwash; the rope from a life ring come undone and whipping frenziedly back and forth under a spotlight; a deck chair splintered against a rail, bits of debris or trash batted about the baffles of deck; and behind, the indistinguishable wrestle of wind that raised its voice into a shriek and lowered it to a curse and evoked from the ship as it moved against the dolphins a sympathetic if quieter music.

Slocum took another sip. The beer tasted good and yet

it didn't really taste like anything he wanted. What he wanted was the same as when he first got here, to find Melisande and return to his sloop, in either order.

When the wind dropped, he made out whole phrases of what the woman was singing. "And on another night, I'll choose another bar," she crooned in a voice as smoky as MacTavish's whiskey. "Where you will not be drinking . . ."

Torch songs.

He put the beer in a trash slot and lingered an instant longer, marveling at how pristine this seagoing lounge remained in the depths of such a storm; not a single lily had fallen out of its vase or wilted even, though one antimacassar had slipped from a backrest and curled on the armrest of a chair.

Only these armchairs carried no antimacassars.

It was a finger, or a couple of fingers. As white as linen, folded like cloth.

"Melisande?" Slocum asked. His breath came loose. He ducked out of the bar and moved around the piano and down the aisle till he could see the front of the armchair.

A man dressed in evening clothes, with a white silk scarf knotted around his neck, slept in the chair. He had craggy features and a wave of pure white hair. He had fallen asleep reading—the book lay in his lap—and in doing so had slumped till his head fell below the level of the chair's back, which was why Slocum had not spotted him earlier. A martini glass and shaker stood on his table. The drink was half finished, the olive intact, an icepick inside the shaker, which still held a slurry of ice.

Slocum recognized him. He had seen Wycliffe Sloane in the flesh only twice, but he had watched him on many hundreds of occasions in videoconference and promotional VR. His features were easily as recognizable to an X-Corp Multimedia vice president as those of Lara Love or Mahal Schrenk or any of the stars who also worked for the firm.

He stood on the deep carpet for a moment, considering. Twelve years of X-Corp engineered a semiautomatic deference that he had to remind himself he was no longer obliged to maintain. Curiously, the fact that this was Melisande's father lessened the deference, probably because it excised the hugeness of X-Corp from the lines that connected them, making the remaining ties personal, by definition.

Finally he stepped over to the sleeping man and shook him gently by the shoulder.

Wycliffe Sloane did not stir. The hand Slocum had seen from the bar wiggled, and his head fell slightly sideways, but that was because of the shaking. His neck was revealed a bit more and Slocum saw, under the winding of scarf, a metallic-looking lump identical to Melisande's. The BLT hookup, he thought, and shook Sloane again.

The man did not move and his chest did not rise or fall even microscopically. Above the scarf, at the base of his skull, a single drop of blood rolled from a hole in the skin exactly the size of an icepick shaft, and was sopped up by the silk.

Slocum stretched out an arm. He felt Sloane's throat. The *Smuggler's Bible* first-aid section said the only place worth feeling for a pulse was in the valley between the windpipe and the larynx. Sloane's throat was warm and soft, but though he kept his finger in that valley for a couple of minutes, and moved it around in case he had missed the artery the first time, nothing pulsed there that Slocum could feel, and finally he removed his hand.

TWENTY·TWO

SLOCUM STOOD BESIDE WYCLIFFE Sloane for several minutes after he withdrew his hand.

He felt detached, in a way that was as familiar to him as the features of the man he was looking at, and partly for similar reasons; because he had seen Wycliffe Sloane on 3-D video, hundreds of times, and he had seen men killed in the same medium tens of thousands of times, as true to life (or death) as if he'd seen them in fact; and such video familiarity bred that same cotton feeling, of contempt, and disassociation, that had ended up metastasizing throughout the rest of Slocum's life.

The good side of it was that he could watch this man— a goodlooking, fit man in his late sixties or early seventies sprawled dead on an armchair—and not panic or feel so sick he could no longer function.

The bad side was that this was the first dead man he had ever seen at such close range without a separating medium, and if this tangible expression of his own mortality did not make him nervous, he had, as usual, to wonder what the hell else was being screened out that he might really need to know.

Except that something else had happened, beyond detachment. And maybe Slocum had not recognized it earlier because he did not want to see it. For a curious and fierce joy was spreading in him.

Here he is! Slocum wanted to shout. Here is the chief of X-Corp lying dead as a slab of corned beef. Here is the high priest in the cult of winners, the fast-living, high-flying executive who (via Otto Kumpunen) cut out "losers" and "nonperformers" and "non-team-players" and those who had "lost their edge" as ruthlessly as a butcher discarded gristle. In the space of one missing heartbeat, Wycliffe Sloane had become as lost and nonperforming, as little of a team player, as any of the men Kumpunen had fired. Just look at that son of a bitch now, Slocum crowed internally. He did not appear high-flying or brilliant; he looked pathetic and tired. He seemed abstract, as if focused on a problem he knew he could never solve. He looked, frankly, a little bit sad.

Slocum shook his head. He supposed *Schadenfreude* was better than nothing; better than cotton, the lack of affect. Presumably, too, such a mean emotion—along with evidence of the revulsion that had hit him after Kumpunen's—was further proof that despite the last jolt of VR, he had not fallen so deeply back into disassociation as he had feared at Kumpunen's. Still he was ashamed that he could feel this way about a man he had never known. A man—so Slocum reminded himself—who had put himself under a slow sentence of death in order to keep his daughter alive for five more years.

The name "Melisande" resonated with "alive" and the connections the adjective made. Slocum's brain squiggled to avoid the deductive chain but there was no getting around the logic.

If her father was dead he could no longer be a donor. If she no longer had a donor then she was about to die from Lee Shan Syndrome.

And Slocum realized that, despite his earlier distaste for small infatuations, he wanted to find her. He did not want to see her like this, abstract and sad and gone. He wanted to see her angry and impatient and half smiling the way she was with him.

His eye fell on the book Sloane had been reading when he died. It was a cheap, print-on-demand hardcover, open to a page near the beginning. Sloane's finger still curled over a paragraph. Slocum took it from him.

He read the sentence Sloane had last touched, for no reason except that he still felt bad about what he had thought earlier. He wanted, in some kind of compensation, to mark this; to acknowledge what Sloane might have been thinking when he died.

They were careless people, Tom and Daisy—they smashed up things and creatures and then retreated back into their money or their vast carelessness, or whatever it was that kept them together, and let other people clean up the mess. . . .

He turned the book over.
The Great Gatsby.
Slocum glanced at the icepick. You did not, as far as he remembered, use an icepick with a martini shaker.

Something moved behind him, to one side. He swiveled, a clutch of panic constricting his throat, and took a reflexive step backward.

From behind a couch, on the other side of the aisle that divided the lounge in two, a head came into view, lolling a little on a neck that seemed to have very little energy with which to support its weight. The gelled hair was rumpled, strands of it sticking straight out. The uniform-style dress hung slightly off-angle under a vicuña coat. The eyebrows twitched.

Vera Consalves dragged herself off the floor and sat

heavily on the couch. She picked up a glass and checked that it really was empty. Her makeup was smudged. With her strong nose and popping eyes she resembled more than ever a bird of prey. She glanced at Slocum.

"Get me a drink?"

He put down *The Great Gatsby* but did not otherwise move.

"Coursh not," she mumbled. "Had too much to drink, Vera. Shudd-off." She tried to get the olive out of her glass, and failed.

"You were here?" Slocum asked finally. "Did you see what happened?"

She laughed. It was not a pretty laugh. It was like a cormorant with laryngitis. The laugh became a cough. She held her head with one hand to dim the pain coughing caused.

"Dead," she said eventually. "Mister Wycliffe fugging Sloane. Mister *God* Wycliffe fugging Sloane. Dead as a fugging doornail."

"Did you see it?" Slocum insisted.

Vera shaded her eyes as she looked at him.

"Said he was gonna take a lil' nap," she said. "I went to look for him." Her eyes drifted down and settled on Sloane once more.

"Oh, he was gonna back me," she added, "when Gerry resigned. *Sure* he was. Congresspersh—Congress*person*—Consalves." She hiccoughed. "Thank you very much, Mister Wycliffe-God-fugging-Sloane."

Her fingers were long, and finally they grasped the olive. She popped it into her mouth and chewed it for a second. Her eyes grew distant. She doubled over and threw up on the carpet.

Slocum went to look for Melisande.

———

HE FOUND HER ALMOST at once, and mostly by luck, if you could call luck the memory that surfaced amid the turmoil of angst and questions and possible plans. The re-call was a thumbnail image, her small form leaned over the rail, scarf whipping downwind—where he had seen her, the very first time. Despite his conviction that no sane person would go outside in such a storm, he poked his head out the exit door midships, on the starboard side. It was like sticking your head inside a washing machine in rinse cycle and his hair was drenched immediately and his breath was sucked out of his lungs. But he saw something that shouldn't be there, a shape curled in the lee of a stack of life rafts. Here on this otherwise unprotected section of deck the wind was twice the strength it was on the wharf. It was a giant, alien monster, terrifying and beyond his experience and the only way he could cope with it was by not thinking about it. Instead he dropped to his knees and pulled himself hand over hand along the rail until he got to the life rafts. "Melisande!" he yelled.

She jumped—she had been facing shelter. The three-quarter moon of her face turned toward him, alternating between light and shadow as a torn canopy flapped around a nearby deck light. Her hand emerged from the whipping fabric of her dress, and gripped his arm, as if to make sure he was real.

"Come inside!"

"What?"

"Come inside?" He was screaming at her now.

"No!" she screamed back.

He wanted to touch her. She had withdrawn her hand.

"Why not?"

"Did you kill him?"

"Your father?"

"My father—"

"No!"

"No?"

"Of course not!"

She watched him for a few seconds. She grabbed the

rope handle hanging off one of the rafts, and pulled herself halfway to her feet. Or tried to, but the wind wound its own hands in the folds of her nightgown and twisted her sideways, overbalancing her small frame. He reached with his left arm—his other grasped the rail—and pulled her into the arc of his shoulder and chest. She felt both light and solid to him. She was shivering, also, with cold. He walked her backward, sliding along the rail, holding them both against the wind, to the doorway. He lifted her over the coaming, and shut the door behind.

The relative silence of the ship packaged them.

"Shitgoddamn," he said.

She leaned against a bulkhead, head thrown back.

"It feels," she said, "like it will go on forever."

"I didn't kill him," he repeated.

"Oh, I know," she said, and swallowed. "You're not him. That Gatsby guy, right? The killer they're always talking about, in *Shine*." She shook her head. "Fitzgerald. How utterly ridiculous."

"I think I saw him. On the wharf."

Her eyes had a dazed look to them. She did not respond immediately. When she did, she said only, "He was miserable. My father. All his life, he was only happy when he was working. I think he decided to help me—he decided to help with my therapy because; oh, because it fit with the image he wanted of himself. The responsible guy, the mensch. Or do I mean *übermensch*?" She swallowed again, opened her eyes, stared at the paneling.

"I don't think he even minded that it would—the treatment—it would put him where I was, four years from now. And I let him—I let him." Her gaze did not waver. Slocum resisted the urge to look at the paneling, to see what she saw.

"But being on this ship; ah, that drove him crazy. He couldn't fly around to meetings at a moment's notice, in that goddamn jet, that X-Corp jet. So he spent all his time in videoconference instead. I'd had in mind more of a father-daughter cruise...." One side of her mouth lifted. She shrugged. Her eyes filled with liquid. She blinked and glanced at him, and looked away.

"I never told you. The treatment. The truth is—"

"I know what it is."

Looked back.

"Then you know—without a donor—what's going to happen to me?"

He nodded.

"Twenty-four hours, maybe," she said, in a matter-of-fact tone. "But I'll start to feel the effects after only seven or eight. The fever will come back first, and then I will grow weaker and weaker.

"But it's the other stuff that will get me—the flu, stupid little illnesses that lie dormant as long as the immune system works.... After fourteen, fifteen hours, I'll go into a coma. After that, another ten hours. Doesn't really sound so bad, right?"

He did not wish to look at her. He knew he was feeling different things on different levels and it was all too complicated to track at short notice; far too complicated to keep tabs on and reply as well.

"I want to live well," she was saying, "those seven or eight hours." Melisande dropped her head and shut her eyes. "I don't have time for fancy arguments, or games," and she opened her eyes again and looked at him, and her gaze was as steady as a rifle barrel.

"I want to go to bed with you," she said.

"You don't have to fuck me, right?" she continued, in a tone that was almost angry, and threw her right hand out, away, in that airscooping gesture he remembered. "Though I have protection. But that's not the point....

"To hold me. Kiss me. Lee Shan does not spread by kissing. To hold me, Slocum, most of all. I know you want to. Say you want to."

Slocum met her gaze. He could hold a stare—his X-Corp training again—while processing other data.

The other input surprised him, because his first reaction was reluctance. His sloop still needed care. In the first hurricane to hit the Town dead-on since he'd owned the boat, he had to see if its moorings and bumpers were all right, he had to tighten its spring lines if the storm surge continued. He had stronger loyalties, deeper commitments; he did not have time to take care of Melisande Sloane tonight.

And then came the guilt from such a thought. It hooked up to doubts that had started with that perverse glee he'd felt when he saw her father dead. He could not withhold comfort from a woman who had only seven hours to live.

After that, colors. No, that couldn't be right—but the way different shades of mahogany in her eyes seemed to separate and remix in his vision the way they had done the first time he talked to her.

And he remembered the deep desire to be with her he'd had after seeing her the second time. It was something whole and alive as a tame leopard, an animal of memory, full of jizz and the joy of junglebounding. It filled his stomach with a tingling that moved both up into his chest and down into his groin and shifted his loyalties around, just a little, until all options seemed open, at least while this storm endured.

"I want to," he said. "Of course I do."

———

BY THE TIME THEY reached her cabin she was trembling again. "Is it the fever?" he asked, but she said, "No, not yet," and pressed his hand to her forehead, which was cool.

He removed his boots and oilskins and tossed them on a heap of dresses that seemed to be evacuating her closet. "God," she said, "someone's been in here," and threw around items that were lacy and that floated casually for a while before alighting. She opened the bar cabinet and took out a bottle of champagne whose glass was thick with frost. "At least he didn't take that," she said, then put down the bottle and stared, frowning, at the aquarium.

Slocum's inner layer of clothes was now fully as soaked as his reefer jacket. Wood, kindling, and newspaper had been pulled out of the Dutch-oven arrangement that normally held them beside the hearth so he set to building a fire: knotted paper, kindling crossed like Lincoln Logs, three birch logs in a pyramid. It caught fast—he supposed the wind blowing across the flue on deck was pumping air out of the fireplace. The kindling cracked and smoked, loud even against the thump and shriek of storm. The flames felt good on his skin. He looked around to see if she had seen or approved, and his mouth shut, conserving his air supply for future use. She had taken off her soaked nightgown and was stripping off her scarf and an undershirt. She wore nothing else.

She stood there naked, her back to him, like a song of call and response, curve this way matching curve that way—all this came to him out of the blue and without great relevance—still frowning at the aquarium.

She pulled a chair over and climbed on it; bent over the tank till her hair dipped in the bubbling water and he could see, in the triangle where her thighs did not quite meet, an upside-down barrow of ground cover. Her hands, groping in the depths, were magnified by the water into pale green flippers.

The fish panicked. She straightened, dripping, and stepped carefully off the chair, holding the turquoise castle in both hands. Turned toward him, and half smiled when she saw his face. Around her neck and against her breasts hung something he had not noticed before: a thin chain with a tiny golden bell suspended from it. Her breasts were small, with large, dark areolas. In the valley of her neck nestled the canula he had noticed in the monitor at the fire-control station.

A couple of minnows flipped out of the castle and wriggled against the carpet. She scooped them up, dropped them back in the tank one-handed. Then she kneeled in front of him, the bell swinging, jingling just a little.

He watched her thighs, like the opposite cords of a golden moon. Her shoulders rose to hold the castle against the angle of collarbone, against the angle of her cheeks and eyefolds.

He was happy with the forms she made.

She poked two fingers into the castle, beside the dungeon, deep into the siege well, and twisted. Her eyes narrowed. Something popped. She pulled her fingers out slowly. The tips grasped, just barely, an aqua cylinder.

She grasped the cylinder, unscrewed a watertight plug, and eased out a data spindle.

She held it up and looked at it, then looked at him. Her smile had gone.

"This is why they killed him," she said. "This is what they were looking for."

He shifted leftward. His crotch was tight. His dick was not hard but it was not entirely soft either. He did not want to think about it.

"My father had a tech assistant," Melisande continued, as softly as it was possible to speak and still be heard over the storm. "Rick Santos. Weird little guy, but strangely attractive, in a way. Always doing regression analyses of X-Corp Webmail traffic, that kind of stuff."

She put the spindle down beside her, moved sideways, still on her knees. One hand stroked the slope of her upper arm, to spread the fire's warmth. She continued staring at the spindle.

"He found something," she continued. "The parallel-server system, they used expert programs, for handling interactive VR? Billions of different images and stochastics all processed at once—but you, of all people, know what kind of processing they were capable of.

"Anyway, Santos found they had started talking to each other. The servers, right? *Changing the stories,* in ways Arcadia had not planned. And that wasn't all."

He was thirsty. He wanted that champagne. He did not want to interrupt, though he found he was, in many ways, uninterested. The twists of X-Corp politics seemed so irrelevant to life as it was meant to be lived—to people who breathed and felt pleased or bad, thirsty or at peace; to a body both so doomed and so bursting with life as that of this woman in front of him—that they fulfilled every definition of obscene, anathema, worthy of burning and forgetting.

She could tell he did not care. She frowned, but continued anyway.

"Apparently the servers hooked up to that marsh, south and west of here—you've heard of it? The one that was contaminated with organic circuitry. X-Corp biochips, from what I heard ... Anyway, it gave the processing programs this kick in complexity. And no one knows exactly how, but last spring they began changing policy traffic—altering directives, cutting accountants in San Jose, promoting someone in Arcadia—boosting our investment in other Syndicate companies. They were talking to processors in the Syndicate intranet."

Her eyes were distant, focused on old events.

"White papers from 'Policy Planning'—Dad paid attention to those—from people who always seemed to be unavailable. 'Policy Planning' was the servers, Santos found."

She sighed.

"Someone—the processors themselves, maybe, or the people they promoted, who were all for Policy Planning, which had made them top-doughnut—someone took out a contract on Santos. And when they found out he had this data, on my dad too. He was going to pull the plug on the servers, right? Instead, they pulled the plug on him." She reached out, rolled the spindle toward Slocum. "I want you to have it."

"Gee," Slocum said. "Thanks."

She looked up at him.

"No," she said. "You can do what you want with it. Destroy it—that would be safest for you, I think. But there's nothing I can do anymore.

"My dad would have wanted me to pass it on."

She glanced at the spindle again. Picked it up and pressed it into his hands.

"So there," she said. "I've passed it on."

The ship creaked more loudly at that point, and rocked to starboard, and stayed there, with six or eight degrees of list. Slocum got up, walked to the porthole. He stood on tiptoe, looking down. He saw absolutely nothing through the smash of weather.

"They sent a message," she said behind him. " 'Urgent—evacuate.' They said I had already been taken off. That's why Shanti left. I was swimming at the time."

He kept looking for his sloop. He wondered if it had been torn from its moorings, flung against the wharf, sunk.

"But Matt would never have left the ship."

He turned, reluctantly.

"Did you see Matt?"

He shook his head. Her left hand fingered her chain. The little bell jingled again. He could just hear it against the wind, which now subsided, enough for the ship to roll back to the vertical.

When everything was level again Melisande stood, picked up the champagne, and opened a panel that Slocum had not noticed before, next to the bathroom door. He looked at the spindle in his hand. Then, not knowing what to do with it, put it back in its container and stashed it in his pants pocket. He looked at the fire, which burned merrily. It seemed a waste to leave a strong warm flame in favor of such deep uncertainty. After a few seconds, though, he followed Melisande through the door.

He was in a sleeping cabin, paneled in cherrywood, with two bunks, one on top of the other; a small folding washbasin under a mirror at one end; reading lamps and miniature hammocks for gear at the head of each bunk. The bunks were neatly made up. The blankets were blue and carried the seahorse motif. She had already climbed to the top berth. She was sitting up, knees mounded under the bedclothes. The champagne made its hieratic pop as she manipulated the cork. She cursed as foam flowed freely.

He took off his clothes. His dick was not hard. That wouldn't matter, not with this woman, not tonight. He climbed the ladder. She shifted toward the bulkhead. The bunk held just enough room for two. When he slid in next to her, her skin was cold against his, and he felt concern for her; though the coolness after all remained a reassuring sign, given her disease. She took a swig of champagne from the bottle, and handed it to him.

The wine was old, the bottle of a type of heavy glass that had not been made in years. It did not taste like wine at all, but like liquid wind from a high mountain country perfumed by blue flowers and a race of irritable, dedicated bees who made honey that was half sweet and half savory and endowed one with the ability to tell the future.

He took another gulp, and felt warmer. She found a pack of peanut butter crackers in the gear hammock, which was otherwise filled with books and cosmetics and medicine boxes. She opened it, and offered him one. He ate a cracker. It tasted good with the champagne. She drank from the bottle again and put it aside and lay back against the pillows. Something jumped on their feet and she sat straight upright, knocking her head against the ceiling, and screamed "Ohmigod what's *that*!" And for a second Slocum was scared too. Then he felt the kneading of claws on his ankles and the familiar, dirty-old-man purr.

"Shit," he said. "Ralfie."

"What?" She had pulled the blankets to her chin. Her eyes were white in the reading-lamp light. Her cabin had been searched by a killer, her father had been icepicked to death, they were in the middle of a category four hurricane and she was about to die anyway and he had never seen her so terrified as when Ralfie jumped on her feet. "What in god's name is a *Ralfie*?"

"My cat."

"You brought your *cat*?"

"He snuck aboard—I saw him, earlier."

She peered over the blanket, rubbing her bruised head. "My god, he looks rough."

"He is rough," Slocum said. "He's a professional harbor cat." He rolled sideways and curved his right arm around her. He dug his nose in the corner between her collarbone and her hair. She smelled of apricots, pea soup, driftwood warmed in the sun. His chin touched the stainless steel of her IV fitting. Maybe to spare him this she rolled toward him till their foreheads met. Her bell tinkled a warning.

The paneling creaked as the ship surged slowly against its moorings, whether forward or astern he could not tell, and was pulled back. His hands moved down her skin, which seemed both smooth and rough to him, and held something of all the textures in between—thousands of textures, too many for his fingers to cope with.

She shivered and he held her closer, touching her in six or eight places, up and down the front of her body. Her toes moved against his foot, the nails scratching a little. She breathed softly, quickly, against him. Her breath smelled of peanuts and champagne and a deeper odor, a sort of hollowness that he could not identify. Though the cabin had no porthole the wind was easily audible from their bunk; it was a high note, two or three octaves higher than her breathing. He wondered if it was still coming from the east, or southeast. If he remembered the navigation tomes he had studied, that would mean they were still in the path of the storm, more or less.

If it was from the north and east, however, it meant the storm was veering off seaward.

He was trying to read the storm, he thought, the way he tried to read the weather of her body—the feet of her, the textures and smells, the pause between her movements, the rapidity of her breaths. Trying to gauge from all this where she was headed and how that might affect the complex systems of his own body, both in how they worked and how they broke down. In the darkness and warmth of the bunk, in the nest of sounds they made and the ship made and that the storm outside created, he felt all of a sudden that he had found a place of calm for himself: a pivot point. A refuge warm and dark, with Melisande in the heart of it.

And he knew that it was not so much the geographic position as what he found there that was crucial. It was the ability to have only one feeling at a time; it was the nature of this feeling also, which was a unitary, powerful drive, as absolute in what it wanted as was the impossibility of attaining that which it desired.

What it wanted was not to leave her; not to give her up to the complexity of Outside, whatever "outside" meant here. It was to keep her in the arc of his affection, in the circle of his need, in the twist of his protection. It was to keep her as he had not been able to keep Bird—to make up, in part, for the mistake that had cut Bird away from him.

It was to hold another human, as once he had held Amy, as closely as possible, to blend as perfectly as it was possible to blend. To cock a snook, in so doing, at all the barriers to feeling that had accreted from the hundred facile dramas he had crafted on the Flash. There was no way he could do all this now—to enter Melisande, with the tension of his living registering accurately between his legs, as the heat between her thighs measured out in degrees the hours she had left. He separated her legs with his knee and the liquid from inside her was as hot as her skin was chilly, and his dick was hard, certainly not as hard as it ever had been but far more than it had been in eighteen months and hard enough, he thought with a spasm of elation; by god, hard enough. .

He rolled up over her, his crotch touching hers, and almost went into her then, drawn by the strength of his need. Of course fear held him back—less a fear of doing this than fear of poor process, of having made the wrong decision, an irremediable mistake.

And her fear was active also because she fought him off and hissed, "Don't be mad," and, "Wait." She rolled left and picked a plastic box out of the hammock. Flicked a switch on the box, that turned on a red light. When the red light went orange she rolled out a sheet of warmed-up plastic skin. It felt hot on his crotch as it molded and sealed to his form. "Wait," she repeated. "Wait thirty seconds."

The wind kept howling, the ship kept creaking. Ralfie kept on purring and her heart kept pounding, pounding, as did his and Ralfie's. The orange light was a timing device; after thirty seconds it turned green. "Now," she said. And entering her, letting his dick slide down the wet, warm isoceles of her sex and open the lips of her, go into the endlessly soft, endlessly warm, endlessly deep center of her, was like, no it *was* falling into the hole that had opened up inside himself at the center of the circles of which he and Melisande and her ship and the harbor and the storm and his life and her death were all made.

Pulling himself into his own circle like a trapdoor spider, he became not what he fled but the need in him that sought to need; that which, in its circularity, allowed him to become part of her, who was part of him by the nature of the bootstrapping that allowed any of this.

It felt way bigger than the sharp joy at being able to do this again, though that was part of it also.

Finally the only forms of expression left were the grip of her hands on his back, and the rhythmic ring of the tiny bell as they moved together, and the liquid that came generously from between her legs and the fluid that came with equal abandon from between his, and the insanity of rain and wind and the groans of the hull as it shifted against the twist of hurricane; that, and the unexpected sobs all this pulled out of him as he came; sobs deeper and more regular than the gusts of storm or the surge of water or the gentling movements of Melisande beneath him.

HE GOT UP ONCE, to look out the porthole in the next cabin. He saw nothing, as usual. The wind seemed as powerful as ever. He had a feeling all clocks had stopped; that this night, this storm, would go on forever.

It was fine with him. To stay with Melisande in that bunk while time stood still—it was fine with him.

The plastic skin bothered him. He reached down, removed it, dropped it onto the orange embers of the fire, where it smoldered and stank. He went back to the sleeping cabin. Melisande's eyes were open. She handed him the champagne bottle. Only a gulp or two was left. He drained it. He felt like crying once more. Crying, suddenly, seemed to him a luxury finer than champagne, better than the feelings that engendered it.

He dropped the bottle and got under the covers. She put her arms around him. He was conscious of not being hard anymore.

He said, "You never told me the end of the story."

"What story?"

"The one about the deaf girl. And the temple of golden bells. You know, when I told you the Claire stories?" He moved his hand up her body and touched the chain around her neck. She breathed deeply.

"How far did I get?"

"When she went to find the holy man."

Melisande put her own hand on the necklace. After a while she said, "Well, she went up the mountain. She walked for three days and saw no one. Finally she found a goatherd. And she asked him if he was a holy man. He told her holy men were rare, and he was not one of them—but she could not hear his explanation, right? She asked if she could stay in his cabin. He was of a mountain tribe and hospitality came naturally to him. He fed her and made her up a bed to sleep on. She stayed with him for a year, watching the mountains change with the seasons, going red with sunset and white with snow and gold when the leaves died and violet when spring came.

"After a year the girl went back to the temple. She still could not hear the little bells. She started to pray, so she would not feel anger at the goatherd who, she thought, had lied to her. But every time she prayed, she saw in her mind the mountains going red with sunset and white with snow and gold when the leaves died and violet when the spring came. After that, she was never angry at the goatherd again."

The textures of Melisande's skin had warmed and softened further, if that was possible, against Slocum's. He wanted more than ever to go inside her without plastic or anything else separating them. This was the same feeling he'd had when they first went to bed, and it made his chest freeze in terror with the power of it, *because he knew he could do this*—he wanted so much not to abandon her, not let her slip into unconsciousness, that he could commit this act that would bring Lee Shan into his body and so change his life forever, not to mention shorten it by a considerable amount.

The side-fears held him back: a continued distrust of that unbalanced ratio between fast decision and such weighty consequence. As he lay against Melisande, though, Slocum realized that a greater phobia had grown in him in

the eighteen months or so since he'd been thinking about
these issues, in one way or another. It was the disgust for
always thinking about consequences, for preparing endlessly, waiting for everything to fall into place, for systemati-
cally cutting out every risk until what was left was sterile
and predictable and not worth doing anyway. That had
been his living: a producer's life; a life of cotton and safety,
a virtual life. A perfect score of timidity, with only one exception, one event he was proud of: when he splashed his
blood all over Otto Kumpunen and left X-Corp forever.

No wonder, Slocum thought, he preferred living on
Wanderbird.

Everything about what he wished to do now was irre-
sponsible and ill-considered and the utter antithesis of how
he used to live, yet worth it, he was sure; a thousand times
worth it.

He held her tighter. Her arms tightened in response.
But he had come only an hour or so ago and had been
fearing too much and his dick still was not hard.

After all this worry and dialectic, he thought wryly, his
damned genitals had let him down again.

Slocum smiled to himself in the dark.

He lay more closely against Melisande, smelling her
neck, listening to her breathe against his skin.

———

WHEN HE WOKE, a wedge of gray light barred the cabin
bulkhead. Ralfie was gone. Melisande was asleep beside
him. Her skin was hot against his.

He lay there, senses on full alert.

Everything was quiet. The wind had died. No noise of
rain or weather penetrated here. The ship did not surge. Its
paneling and joints did not crack or complain. The generators trembled, deep in the engine room.

Her skin was hot against his.

He rolled onto one elbow, looking at her. She stirred,

and said one word: "island." Her cheeks were flushed. He put a hand against her forehead. Something snapped under his sternum.

"Melisande," he whispered.

The sheets were damp against his knees.

He kneeled, looking down at her. Her mouth was curved, relaxed. At peace, he thought.

His dick was hard. How completely irrelevant, was his first reaction. The impulse he had felt last night, to fuck her without protection, had stayed with him in the back of his mind; he had thought about it when he got up to look out the porthole and it had stayed active in his synapses, like a switch left on that kept his counters ticking, wires live, a circuitry whole and doing its job.

No doubts at all, this morning.

"Melisande," he whispered again. She opened her eyes. The half smile.

"I'm not," she whispered.

"What?"

"Dead. Yet." She reached down, touched his crotch. She kicked off the covers, and closed her eyes.

A moment later she was asleep again.

Slocum got up and left the sleeping cabin and walked over to the porthole. He took a deep breath.

Then he stood on tiptoe, pressed his cheek against the glass, and peered down.

It was not there. He craned his neck.

It was where he did not expect it, farther aft than he re-membered—the aluminum block of his masthead, the blink of sun against the cover of his steaming light.

The VHF's whip antenna was gone. But his sloop was still afloat.

The warehouses of Coggeshall Wharf had lost tiles. A telephone pole leaned at a crooked angle. Behind a haze of cirrus, blue sky shone as if nothing happened ever. Slocum wondered if they might be in the eye of the storm, but there was no wall of clouds on the horizon; there was nothing on the horizon at all.

"It veered off," he muttered to himself.

He brought both hands up and massaged the muscles of his face.

Then he walked out of Melisande's suite to the ship's other side. The sun was strong here. This was the port side, and faced east, and it was morning. He had to practically close his eyes against the sun as he stepped out onto boat deck.

The harbor was mad with light. Gulls wheeled and dipped for the fun of it. Just below him, Lopes's condemned dragger had wrapped itself around the dolphins that secured the ship from the east. It was sinking, its mast at a fifty-degree angle from the vertical. A pot of geraniums hung askew off a bridge windowbox. Lopes had been at Madame Ling's, Slocum remembered; Lopes, who despised Slocum because he did not believe in anything, had let his boat be taken by the wind.

He looked north, toward the end of Coggeshall. One of the barges had sunk, taking a half-dozen condemned draggers with it. But the black fiberglass of Cakes's circuit boat lay, gleaming and apparently intact, right where it should be.

A ferry hooted, maneuvering toward the ferry dock. Slocum shaded his eyes and looked across the harbor. His breathing slowed. His heart hurt.

Nothing was different.

The tracery of masts, rigging, laundry and mooring lines seemed exactly the same as before.

When he looked a little more carefully, he saw a pair of hulls slung onto the marsh nearby; a couple of ICE families whose precautions had not been good enough. Yet overall they had done well, and he experienced a resurgence of the pride he'd felt last night, when he watched the inhabitants of the marina making ready. Pride, and a stronger contentment, because no final cut-off from Bird would affect her safety: She was protected by the network that he had, when all was said and done, chosen for her.

He looked at the ICE again, imagining Bird waking and seeing these skies, and feeling the clean air, and rejoicing in something as simple and good as sunshine.

Then he went back to Melisande's suite, where he examined the safety diagram on the back of her door. He counted the different decks. This time he knew where he wanted to go. He put his finger on it, and traced the various ways he could get there.

He went back to the sleeping cabin. He climbed most of the way up the ladder, wrapped the sheet around Melisande; then, grunting with effort, he slung one arm under her knees and the other around her neck and half dragged, half carried her down the ladder.

"Slocum," she whispered. Her eyes were open. She squirmed a little, but her strength seemed to have drained out overnight. Presumably the virus had already disrupted her immune circuitry and other germs were attacking her blood cells, a dozen latent illnesses taking her down. Her lack of resistance made his job both easier—because he could do what he wanted without interference—and harder, because the fear seemed to weaken him. He was terrified that he was too late, everything was always too late.

"Intervention before the onset of coma is almost always effective," the literature had said.

He remembered his tears last night. He felt capable of sobbing again. This was a shock. He did not remember himself crying, let alone sobbing, at any time over the last ten years. He had cried, a little, when his mother died; he remembered crying when Zep was put to sleep. But not in the last ten years.

Even when he confronted Amy about Dark Denny his eyes had stayed dry.

He did not have the luxury of tears now. She was not a big woman but by the time he carried her down the deck to the elevator he was almost as warm as she was and trembling with the effort. Inside the elevator, he wedged her body between the wall and his own naked abdomen, to hold her, to shift his grip on her body.

The doors opened on F deck. The chart had placed his destination close to the doors of this lift, just forward and on the left. He saw them immediately, the swinging doors padded for gurney traffic, and felt a fierce, navigational joy that the chart was right. It was good to find your way on a chart and watch what you had sought crop up as scheduled. The noise of generators was much louder here. He was gasping with exertion and fatigue.

She opened her eyes, coughed, and said something that sounded like his name. Her arms flailed. Not the coma, he thought, with an equal joy; not yet.

He used her ass to push the doors open, and jammed through them with his shoulders. Her right foot caught in the swinging door, painfully, and she did not react.

"Stay awake!" he gasped. "Please stay awake."

The setup was shiny, recognizable: The video had not lied, either. He thought there might be a lesson in that for him, something to modify his revulsion: The video had not lied. The stainless-steel scoops behind the BLT's round window turned slowly, frothing their cargo of scarlet like the paddles of a soda machine. He staggered over and stood for a moment trying to remember: left or right? She had sat in a black leather chair, with levers and wheels molded to her form; the left-hand chair, he was almost sure, and oh what if he was wrong? But a big red arrow on the BLT's left side, pointing outward, seemed to confirm his memory. And most likely the thing could work in either direction.

It was all computerized, anyway. The program would tell him, when the time came. He dumped her without ceremony into the left-hand chair. The sheet fell off, leaving her naked except for the canula, and the small golden bell, which sounded in its miniature way. Her head fell to the side. She straightened her neck, slowly. It hurt to watch how much that cost her. Her eyes opened, and looked around, and grew wide.

Her lips formed the single word, "No."

Then her eyes closed again.

He fit the tubing into the valve on her neck, holding the golden chain clear. The machine beeped. From speakers he had not noticed, set in the base of the machine, a voice, a woman's voice, said, "IV connection completed, output side. Confirm yes/no."

Slocum stared at the machine.

"Yes," he said finally.

"Affirmative?"

"Affirmative," Slocum said.

The machine was silent.

He checked the terminal screen. The opening menus were complicated, and he was glad of that, because he was charged and full in his drive but he sensed that if things went too easily, if slack time intruded, his conviction might dilute, or even waver.

And he loved this feeling, he loved the near-totality of it. Had he fully analyzed the affect, he would have found it was why he was doing this: to feel totally, with no holdback.

Because he had not felt like this for what seemed like the last half of his life.

Because five years of living, when you felt as much as this, seemed far more desirable than thirty years of cotton.

Melisande muttered something. Her eyes were still closed. Her hand waved ineffectually. He stooped and put his ear close to her mouth.

". . . godsakes," she whispered. "Computer—ship's computer." And then what sounded like "ex."

The BLT terminal was set to the ship's homepage, which was a subfile of an internal X-Corp homepage. He clicked on "menu." The options list included something called "independent operation." He had no idea if operating the BLT depended on the massive servers X-Corp could provide, for which the ship's computers must act as linkage. On *Wanderbird,* for example, the starship computers—which ran everything on board—should have been permanently hooked up to Planetary Command, in the databanks of which enormous quantities of information about every planetary system the ship might visit were stored. The absence of these data formed part of the mystery, part of the danger, that shadowed *Wanderbird*'s crew after she was pulled into the Cygnus black hole.

But this ship was X-Corp, its computers were X-Corp. And if what Melisande had said was true, then X-Corp's corporate consciousness was being expressed through, and embodied in, its computers. This was far-fetched, on the face of it; but if you accepted that premise, you were bound to admit that X-Corp's computers were quite capable of subverting the BLT if they wanted to. The fact that they had chosen not to kill Wycliffe Sloane that way was irrelevant: They might yet decide to kill his daughter through a trickery of blood. He was familiar enough with X-Corp's corporate consciousness to know how inconsistent it could be, even in pursuit of its own self-interest.

He touched the icon for "independent operation." The voice said, "You have chosen 'independent operation.' "

"That's right," Slocum answered.

"Yes or no," the voice prompted.

"Yes," he said.

"Are you sure you wish to disconnect from the network?"

"I'm sure," Slocum said.

"Affirmative?"

"Affirmative," he said, through tightened jaws.

"Please confirm disclaimer," the voice continued. "While enzyme-triage is possible in local mode, Rio Sur S.A. and X-Corp Holdings and Merck LaRoche Incorporated cannot jointly or singly be held responsible for any and all health-maintenance operations performed on Rio Sur or X-Corp or Merck LaRoche equipment when 'independent operation' has been selected and the network has been de-accessed."

"Sure," Slocum agreed.

"Do you confirm?" the voice insisted.

"Yes," Slocum said.

"Please say 'confirm.' "

"Confirm, damn you!" Slocum yelled.

The stainless-steel paddles circled faster. Slocum waited for the voice to start up again, but it did not, and after a few seconds he turned his attention back to the hardware.

The part he had dreaded, thinking about this, was doing his own canula, but it turned out to be both easier and more painful than he had expected. The IV system was listed on the computer's sequence of operations, with a schematic of the collar. The collar stood on its own mobile stand to one side of the BLT. When he fitted the device around his neck, a series of questions appeared on the screen for him to check off. He already knew, from the frequent corporate blood tests, that his blood was O-positive and compatible, at least, with the blood they used to top up Wycliffe Sloane. This must mean his blood was compatible with Melisande's—a factor he had failed to consider before.

After he had answered the questions he pulled the collar's Velcro tight. The BLT hummed, and its sensors palpated his throat with electronic and infrared fingers—and inserted, automatically, what felt at first like a steak knife. An anesthetic went along with it, however, and soon it hurt no more than a normal hypodermic and finally was reduced to a tingle only.

The BLT beeped. Slocum pulled the collar assemblage

so he could lean away from the chair and check the instructions again.

Green lights worked up and down the panel. An icon labeled "setup complete" blinked cheerfully. The screen read, DO YOU WISH TO INITIATE IN VIVO TRANSFUSION—[Y]ES/[N]O.

He looked over at Melisande. He knew that if she were dead he would not want to live; he also knew this was a feeling that would not last. However, while her eyes were closed, she was breathing regularly.

He freed a leg and kicked her hard on the shin. Her eyes flickered. She opened them. It took her a while to focus, but she managed it, and looked straight at him, and one corner of her mouth lifted, a millimeter maybe.

The article, he reminded himself, said this would work. Anytime short of a coma—and she was not in a coma.

He would have to have faith, in the research, in the rightness of what he felt.

He thought of Bird, and how the ICE had survived the hurricane. Five years: Maybe five years would be time enough for her to finally understand. Slocum tried to see Bird's face in his mind's eye—as a totem, for this moment, it seemed right—but he could not.

For some reason he saw Zep instead. Zep, the perpetually filthy half-Briard whose escapes had shot his childhood with drama. The image made him smile.

He could hear *fado* in his head. *Un braseo tristesa, o otro s saudade, saum sem liberdade.*

He wondered if Melisande would like the Sunset Tap, when he brought her there.

He wondered also when the ship's crew would come back; wondered if someone would walk into the sick bay during the next hour, and what he would say about these two buck-naked people become a single system, of blood and wrong information and information, also, that worked.

The thought made him smile. And then he was sick of thinking.

In one fast movement he dragged the cursor to "yes," and clicked twice.

The machine went to work.

ABOUT THE AUTHOR

George Foy is the author of ten novels. He lives with his family on a sloop somewhere on the East Coast.